MATTHEW REILLY

PAN
Pan Macmillan Australia

This is a work of fiction. Characters, institutions and organisations mentioned in this novel are either the product of the author's imagination or, if real, used fictiously without any intent to describe actual conduct.

First published 1996 by Karanadon Entertainment
Published in Macmillan in 2000 by Pan Macmillan Australia Pty Limited
This Pan edition published 2001 by Pan Macmillan Australia Pty Limited
St Martins Tower, 31 Market Street, Sydney

National Library of Australia
cataloguing-in-publication data:

Reilly, Matthew, 1974– .
Contest.

ISBN 0 330 36271 2.

1. Suspense fiction. I. Title.

A823.3

Typeset in 10/11.5 pt Palatino by Post Pre-press Group
Printed in Australia by McPherson's Printing Group

For Mum and Dad

Acknowledgements

Special thanks to Stephen Reilly, my brother—marketing genius, tortured writer (aren't we all?) and loyal friend. To Natalie Freer—the first person to read my work, and the most patient and giving person on this earth. To my parents for letting me watch too much television as a kid and for their unwavering support. And to Peter Kozlina for his monumental show of faith in this book before he had even read a word.

And of course, thanks once again to everyone at Pan Macmillan—Cate Paterson, for being a brilliant publisher; Jane Novak, for being a fantastic publicist (and for being the only person I know who could read *Voss* and then pick up *Ice Station* and enjoy them both!); Julie Nekich, for being an understanding editor (you have to be to work with me); and lastly, once again, all the sales reps at Pan for the countless hours they spend on the road between bookshops. Thank you.

To anyone out there who knows a writer, never underestimate the power of your encouragement.

A note from the author about *Contest*

Hello there. Matthew Reilly here.

Now before we get on with the show, I'd like, if I may, to share with you a few secrets about *Contest*.

First of all, as some of you may already know, *Contest* was my first novel. The story of how I self-published it after every major publisher in Sydney rejected it has been pretty well documented elsewhere, so I won't go into that here. Suffice it to say that only 1000 copies of *Contest* were ever released, all paid for by yours truly.

And then came *Ice Station*.

Now, many people have taken the time to tell me what a ride they found *Ice Station* to be. Such comments please me immensely because that is what it was *supposed* to be—a non-stop rollercoaster ride on paper.

What few people know, however, is that when I wrote *Ice Station*, I had one all-consuming goal: to top *Contest*.

Contest is the book that made *Ice Station* (and later *Temple*) what it was. If it doesn't seem as large in scale as its two successors, it is because it was the first. It was the prototype upon which they were built; a prototype for a different *style* of book—a superfast-paced, absolutely *non-stop* thriller. Everybody has to start somewhere. I started with *Contest*.

That said, I think the story in *Contest* is easily the fastest of all my books. It is like a sports car stripped down to its raw components—wheels, frame, engine. No fancy paintwork. No fancy upholstery. Just raw non-stop *energy*.

As any author will tell you, you only get one first book. And that first one always occupies a special place in your heart. *Contest* is like that for me. It was the first one, and now as I look back on it, I can see without a doubt that it set the tone for everything to come.

I truly hope you have as much fun reading it as I did writing it.

Matthew Reilly
November 2000

THE NEW YORK STATE LIBRARY

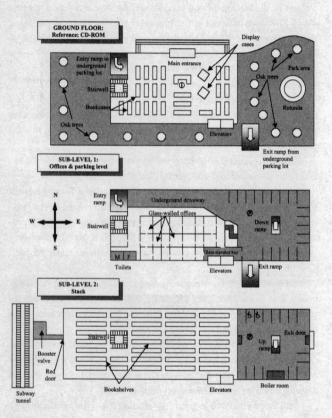

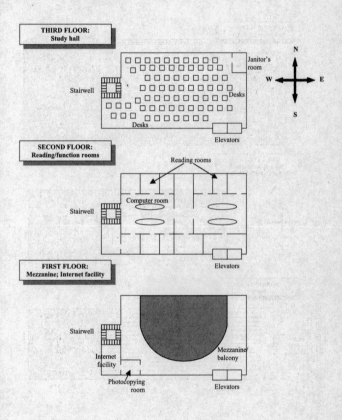

THIRD FLOOR:
Study hall

Janitor's room

Stairwell

Desks

Desks

Elevators

N
W ←→ E
S

SECOND FLOOR:
Reading/function rooms

Reading rooms

Computer room

Stairwell

Elevators

FIRST FLOOR:
Mezzanine; Internet facility

Stairwell

Internet facility

Mezzanine/balcony

Photocopying room

Elevators

Do I dare
Disturb the universe?
              – T. S. Eliot

INTRODUCTION

From: Hoare, Shane
        Suetonius: The Picture of Rome
        (New York, Advantage Press, 1979)

'CHAPTER VII: THE FIRST CENTURY A.D.

. . . ultimately, however, it is Suetonius' classic work, *Lives of the Emperors,* that provides us with the best picture of court life in Imperial Rome. Here Suetonius might well be writing a modern day soap opera, as he outlines the lust, the cruelty, the intrigues and the numerous *insidiae*—or plots—that dominated life in the Emperor's presence . . .' [p. 98]

'. . . not least of whom was Domitian, who, although well-known for his *ex-tempore* executions of scheming courtesans, provides perhaps the most brutal of all examples of Roman intrigue—that of Quintus Aurelius.

A distinguished former captain in the Roman army

who rose to prominence in the Senate under Domitian, Aurelius apparently fell out of favour with the Emperor in 87 A.D. Initially recruited by Domitian to aid him in military matters, Aurelius was also a prolific writer, who not only instructed Domitian on military strategy, but who also committed those instructions to his own personal record. Much of this writing has survived to the present day, dated and intact.

However, Quintus Aurelius' writing ceased abruptly in the year 87 A.D.

All correspondence between senator and Emperor was severed. Aurelius' personal record cited no further entries. There was no mention of Aurelius in Senate documents from that year onward.

Quintus Aurelius had disappeared.

Some historians have speculated that Aurelius—who, it was said, would appear in the Senate in full military attire—simply fell out of favour with Domitian, while others have proposed that Aurelius was discovered plotting . . .' [p. 103]

From: Freer, Donald
       From Medieval to Modern: Europe 1010–1810
       (London, W. M. Lawry & Co., 1963)

'. . . by comparison, the wheat riots in Cornwall were but a trifle when compared with the confusion that overwhelmed a small farming community in West Hampshire in the spring of 1092.

Historians have long pondered over the fate of Sir Alfred Hayes, the Lord of Palmerston Estate, whose disappearance in 1092 upset the entire feudal balance of his small agrarian community in West Hampshire . . .' [p. 45]

'. . . However, the most startling aspect of the whole affair is that if Hayes did, in fact, die suddenly (of cholera or anything else for that matter), why was his death not listed in the local church register as had always been the custom? A man so renowned for his past glory on the battlefield, and of such stature in the community, would not be overlooked by the death registrar. The sad fact is that since no body was ever found, no death was ever recorded.

Writing after his lord's disappearance, the local abbot of West Hampshire observed that, apart from necessary military excursions, Sir Alfred had never left West Hampshire before, and that during the days immediately prior to his disappearance, he had been seen about the village carrying out his business as usual. It was odd, the abbot wrote, that here was a man who could be 'certified as born', but who had, officially, never died.

Putting aside all medieval myths of witchery and demonic intervention, the facts are quite straightforward: in the spring of 1092, Sir Alfred Hayes, Lord of Palmerston Estate, West Hampshire, simply vanished from the face of the earth.' [p. 46]

CONTEST

PROLOGUE

New York City
30 November, 2:01 a.m.

Mike Fraser pressed himself flat against the black wall of the tunnel. He squeezed his eyes shut as he tried to block out the roar of the subway train flashing by in front of him. The dirt and dust kicked up by the speeding train hit his face like a thousand pin-pricks. It hurt, but he didn't care. He was almost there.

And then, just as soon as it had come, the train was gone, its thunderous rumble slowly fading into the blackness of the tunnel. Fraser opened his eyes. Against the black backdrop of the wall, the whites of his eyes were all that could be seen. He peeled himself away from the wall and brushed off the dirt that had clung to his clothes. Black clothes.

It was two o'clock in the morning, and while the rest of New York slept, Mike Fraser was going about his work. Silently and swiftly, he made his way up the subway tunnel until he found what he was looking for.

An old wooden door, set into the tunnel wall, held shut by a solitary padlock. Pasted across the door was a sign.

NO ENTRY—BOOSTER VALVE
HIGH VOLTAGE AREA
CONSOLIDATED EDISON PERSONNEL ONLY

Fraser examined the padlock. Stainless steel, combination lock, pretty new. He checked the hinges of the old wooden door. Yes, much easier.

His crowbar fitted snugly behind the hinges.

Crack!

> *Status Check: Initialise program systems.*
> *Officials in charge of third element*
> *please confirm delivery.*

The door fell from its frame, and dangling from the padlock, swung silently into Fraser's waiting hand.

He peered inside the doorway, slipped the crowbar back into his belt and stepped inside.

Large box-shaped electricity meters lined the walls of the booster valve room. Thick black cables snaked their way across the ceiling. There was a door on the far side. Fraser headed straight for it.

Once through the booster valve room, he made his way down a narrow, dimly lit passageway until he came to a small red door. It opened easily and as Fraser looked out from the doorway, he smiled at the view.

Endless rows of bookshelves—each one rising from floor to ceiling—stretched away from him as far as the eye could see. Old and faded fluorescent lights lined each aisle, but at night only every third one was on. The lights themselves were so old that the whiteness of their fluorescent tubes had gone a mouldy ivory colour and a powder of oxidised fluorine had settled inside them. Their sickly state gave the lowest floor of the New York State Library a haunting yellowish glow.

The New York State Library. One hundred years old, a silent sanctuary of history and knowledge—and also the owner of twelve brand-new Pentium III computers whose hard drives would soon be in the back room of Mike Fraser's apartment.

Fraser checked the lock on the door.

Safety lock.

From the booster room you didn't need a key, but from the library side you did. One of those automatically closing doors designed to keep the curious out, but not to accidentally lock the electricity workers in.

Fraser thought for a moment. If he had to make a hasty escape, he wouldn't have time to pick the lock. He searched around for an answer.

That'll work, he thought, spying the nearest bookshelf. He grabbed the first book he could reach and wedged it on the floor between the red door and its frame.

The door now safely ajar, Fraser hustled down the nearest aisle. Soon the small red door marked BOOSTER VALVE—NO STAFF ACCESS PERMITTED was but a tiny square in the distance behind him. Mike Fraser didn't even notice, he knew exactly where he was going now.

Terry Ryan looked at his watch—again.

It was 2:15 a.m. Four minutes after he'd last looked. Ryan sighed. Jesus, the time crawled on this job.

> *Status Check: Officials in charge of third element confirm delivery complete.*

Idly, Ryan peered out through the massive floor-to-ceiling windows of the atrium of the New York State Library. Nothing stirred on the streets outside.

He touched the gun by his side and grunted a laugh. Security guards in a library—a *library*, for God's sake. The pay was the same, he guessed, and so long as that kept coming, Terry Ryan didn't care what they asked him to guard.

He continued to stroll around the atrium, whistling quietly to himself—

Clink-clink.

He froze.

A noise.

There it was again: *clink-clink.*

Ryan held his breath. It had come from the left. He drew his gun.

Behind the Information Desk, Mike Fraser swore as he picked his screwdriver up from the floor. He peered out over the counter.

No one to the left. Nor to the right. He let out a deep breath. No one had—

'*Freeze!*'

Fraser snapped around. He took in the scene quickly. Security guard. Gun. Maybe fifteen metres, twenty at the most. As if there was a choice.

'I said, freeze!' Terry Ryan yelled. But the thief had already made a break for it. Ryan broke into a run.

Books on shelves became streaking blurs of colour as Fraser bolted down a narrow aisle. His heart pounded loudly inside his head. And then suddenly he saw the door. And the sign: STAIRS.

Fraser hit the stairs running, grabbing the banister, sliding down the first flight. The security guard, Ryan, flew in two seconds later, taking the stairs three at a time.

Down and down, round and round, Fraser went, clinging to the banister, hauling himself around at every turn. He saw the door at the bottom. He flew down the last flight of stairs and hit the door at full speed. It burst open easily—too easily—and Fraser went sprawling face-first onto the hard wood floor.

He could hear heavy footsteps bounding down the stairs behind him.

Fraser reached for the nearest bookshelf to hoist himself up and immediately felt a searing pain rip through his right arm. It was then that he saw his wrist. It had taken the full weight of the fall, and now, bent grotesquely backwards, it was undoubtedly broken.

Teeth clenched, Fraser hauled himself up with his good arm and had just made it to his feet when—

'You stay right where you are.'

The voice was soft and sure.

Fraser turned around slowly.

In the doorway behind him stood the security guard, with his gun levelled at Mike Fraser's head.

Ryan pulled out his handcuffs and threw them to the injured thief.

'Put 'em on.'

Fraser closed his eyes in disgust. 'Why don't you,' he began, 'kiss . . . my . . . *ass*!' Then suddenly, like a wounded animal, he lunged at the guard.

Without a blink, Ryan raised his gun and fired it into the air above the fallen thief's head.

The booming shot rang out in the silence of the library.

Fraser dropped back to the floor as small white flakes of plaster began to flutter down around his head.

Ryan stepped forward into the aisle, tightened his grip on his pistol, reasserted his aim at Fraser's head.

'I said, *put 'em on*. So put—' Ryan's eyes darted left. 'What was that?'

Fraser heard it, too.

And then—ominously—it came again.

A long, slow growl. Like the snort of a pig. Only louder. Much louder.

'What the hell was that?' Fraser said quickly.

Boom. A loud, dull thud.

The floor shook.

'There's something down here . . .' Fraser whispered.

Boom. Again.

The two men stood there frozen.

Ryan looked down the aisle beyond Fraser. It stretched endlessly away from them, disappearing into darkness.

Silence.

Dead silence.

The wooden floor was still again.

'Let's get the fuck outta here,' Fraser hissed.

'Shh!'

'There's somethin' down here, man!' Fraser raised his voice.

Boom.

A tremor shook the floor again.

A book teetering on the edge of a shelf fell to the floor.

'Let's go!' Fraser cried.

Boom. Boom. Boom.

Books began to fall off the shelves in bundles.

Ryan leaned forward, grabbed Fraser by the collar. He pulled the thief's face up to his own.

'For God's sake, shut up,' he whispered. 'Whatever it is, it's hearing your voice. And if you keep talking—'

Ryan stopped abruptly, and frowned at Fraser. The young thief's eyes were wide with fear, his lower lip quivering madly, his whole expression one of total and utter disbelief.

Ryan felt his blood run cold.

Fraser was looking over his shoulder.

Whatever 'it' was, it snorted again, and as it did so Ryan felt a wave of hot air rush across the back of his neck.

It was behind him.

It was right behind him!

The gun went off as Ryan was yanked bodily off the floor. Fraser dropped to the ground, staring at the hulking mass of blackness before him.

Ryan screamed as he struggled uselessly in the powerful arms of the dark shape. And then suddenly, the creature bellowed loudly and hurled him through the nearest bookshelf. Books cascaded everywhere as Ryan's body doubled over and crashed *right through* the old wooden casing.

The massive black shape lumbered around the bookshelf, looking for the body on the other side. In the dull yellow light, Fraser could see long black bristles flowing over a high, arched back, saw demonic pointed ears and powerful muscular limbs, caught glimpses of matted black hair and gigantic scythe-like claws.

Whatever it was, it picked up Ryan's body like a rag doll and dragged it back around to the aisle where Fraser sat.

The flight through the bookshelf must have broken Ryan's back, Fraser guessed, but the security guard wasn't dead yet. Fraser could hear him moaning softly as the creature lifted him to the ceiling.

It was then that Ryan screamed.

A shrill, ear-piercing, inhuman scream.

To his absolute horror, Fraser saw what was going to happen next and he put his hand up over his face just as he heard the sickening *crack* and an instant later, he felt a torrent of warmth wash all over the front of his body.

Ryan's scream cut off abruptly and Fraser heard the beast roar a final time, followed by the thunderous crunching of wooden shelves.

And then there was nothing.

Silence.

Total and utter silence.

Slowly, Fraser removed his hand from his face.

The beast was gone. The guard's body lay there in front of him, twisted and mangled, motionless. One of the bookshelves to his right lay horribly askew, wrenched free from its ceiling mountings. Blood was everywhere.

Fraser didn't move, couldn't move.

And so he just sat there, alone, in the cold emptiness of the New York State Library, and waited for the dawn.

FIRST MOVEMENT

30 November, 1:27 p.m.

The sun shone brightly over Norwood Elementary School. It was lunchtime and groups of schoolchildren were out playing on the school's enormous grassy playing field.

Status Check: Initialise electrification systems.

Norwood was one of the leading private elementary schools in Connecticut. An impressive academic record—and one of the biggest building funds in America—had made it one of *the* sought-after schools for the well-to-do.

At the bottom corner of the grassy playing area, a cluster of children had gathered. And in the middle of this cluster stood Holly Swain, nose-to-nose with Thomas Jacobs.

'He is not, Tommy.'

'Is too. He's a *murderer!*'

The crowd of children gathered around the two combatants gasped at the word.

Holly tried to compose herself. The white lace collar of her uniform was beginning to feel very tight now and she was determined not to let it show. She shook her head sadly, raised her nose a little higher.

'You're so childish, Tommy. Such a *boy*.'

The girls behind her chirped similar comments in support.

'How can you call me childish when *you're* only in the third grade?' Tommy retorted. The group assembled behind him echoed their agreement.

'Don't be so *immature*,' Holly said. *Good word*, she thought.

Tommy hesitated. 'Yeah, well, he's still a murderer.'

'He is not.'

'He killed a man, didn't he?'

'Well, yes, but . . .'

'Then he's a murderer.' Tommy looked around himself for support. 'Murderer! Murderer! Murderer!' The group behind him joined in.

'Murderer! Murderer! Murderer!'

Holly felt her fists clench by her side, felt her collar tighten around her neck. She remembered her father. *Be a lady. Got to be a lady.*

She spun around, her blonde ponytail flinging around her shoulders. The girls around her were shaking their heads at the taunts of the boys. Holly took a deep breath. She smiled to her friends. *Got to be a lady.*

Behind her, the boys' chant continued.

'Murderer! Murderer! Murderer!'

Finally, Tommy called out above the chant, 'If her father's a murderer, then Holly Swain will probably grow up to be a murderer, too!'

'Yeah! Yeah, she will!' his group urged.

Holly's smile went flat.

Slowly—ever so slowly—she turned back around to face Tommy. A hush fell over the crowd.

Holly stepped closer. Tommy chuckled, glancing

around at his friends. Only now his supporters were silent.

'Now I'm upset,' Holly said flatly. 'I think you'd better take back those things you've been saying. Would you, please?'

Tommy smirked and then he leaned forward. 'Nope.'

'Okay, then,' Holly said, smiling politely. She looked down at her uniform, straightened her skirt.

Then she hit him.

Hard.

The clinic had become a battlefield.

Glass exploded everywhere as test tubes exploded against the walls. The nurses leapt clear of the melee, hurriedly moving the multi-million-dollar equipment out of the line of fire.

Dr Stephen Swain burst out of the adjoining observation room and immediately set about calming the source of the storm—a 57-year-old, 240-pound, big-busted woman named Rosemary Pederman, a guest of St Luke's Hospital, New York City, on account of a small abnormality in her brain known as a cerebral aneurism.

'Mrs Pederman! Mrs Pederman!' Swain called. 'It's okay. It's okay. Just calm down,' he said gently. 'What seems to be the problem?'

'The problem?' Rose Pederman spat. 'The problem, *young man*, is that I will not put my head in that . . . that *thing* . . . until someone tells me exactly what it does!'

As she spoke, she jerked her chin at the enormous Magnetic Resonance Imaging—or MRI—machine which occupied the centre of the room.

'Come on, Mrs Pederman,' Swain said sternly. 'We've been through this before.'

Rose Pederman pouted, child-like.

'The MRI will not harm you in any way—'

'Young man. *How does it work?*'

Swain pursed his lips tightly.

At 39, he was the youngest ever partner in Borman & White, the radiologist collective, and for a very simple reason—Swain was *good*. He could see things in an X-ray or a CAT-scan that no-one else could, and on more than one occasion, had saved lives by doing so.

This fact, however, was difficult to impress upon older patients since Swain—sandy-haired and clean-shaven, with a lean physique and sky-blue eyes—*looked* about ten years younger than his actual age. Except for the fresh red vertical scar that cut down across his lower lip, a feature which seemed to age him, he could have passed for a third-year resident.

'You want to know how it works?' Swain said seriously. He resisted the urge to look at his watch. He had somewhere to be. But then, Rose Pederman had gone through six radiologists already and this had to stop.

'Yes, I do,' she said stubbornly.

'Okay. Mrs Pederman, the process you are about to undertake is called Magnetic Resonance Imaging. It's not unlike a CAT-scan, in that it generates a cross-sectional scan of your skull. Only instead of using photovoltaic methods, we use controlled magnetic energy to re-align the ambient electrostatic conductivity in your head in order to create a three-dimensional composite cross-section of your cranium.'

'What?'

'The magnet in the MRI machine affects the natural

electricity in your body, Mrs Pederman, giving us a perfect picture of the inside of your head.'

'Oh, well . . .' Mrs Pederman's lethal frown instantly transformed itself into a beaming, maternal smile. 'That's quite all right then. That was all you had to tell me, lovey.'

An hour later, Swain burst through the doors of the surgeon's locker room.

'Am I too late?' he said.

Dr James Wilson—a red-haired paediatrician who, ten years previously, had been the best man at Swain's wedding—was already moving quickly toward him. He hurled Swain's briefcase to Swain. 'It's 14–13 to the Giants. If we hurry, we can catch the last two quarters at McCafferty's. Come on, this way. We'll go through the ER.'

'Thanks for waiting,' Swain hurried to keep up with his friend's rapid strides.

'Hey, it's your game,' Wilson said as he walked.

The Giants were playing the Redskins and Wilson knew that Swain had been waiting a long time for this game. It had something to do with Swain living in New York and his father who lived back in D.C.

'Say,' Wilson said, 'how's that lip healing up?'

'It's okay.' Swain touched the vertical scar on his lower lip. 'Still a bit tender. Got the stitches out last week.'

Wilson turned as he walked, grinning. 'Makes you look even uglier than you already are.'

'Thanks.'

Wilson arrived at the door to the emergency room, opened it—

—and was immediately met by the pretty face of Emma Johnson, one of the floating nurses at St Luke's.

The two men stopped instantly.

'Hey, Steve, how are you?' Emma looked only at Swain.

'Gettin' there,' he replied. 'How about you?'

A coy cock of the head. 'I'm good.'

'I'm fine, too,' Jim Wilson chimed in. 'Not that anyone seems to care . . .'

Emma said to Swain: 'You wanted me to remind you about your meeting with Detective Dickson, about the . . . *incident*. Don't forget you have to see him at five.'

'Right,' Swain nodded, absently stroking the cut on his lower lip. 'No problem. I can do that after the game.'

'Oh, I almost forgot,' Emma added. 'You got another message. Norwood Elementary called about ten minutes ago. They want to know if you can come down there right away. Holly's been fighting again.'

Swain sighed. 'Not again. Right away?'

'Right away.'

Swain turned to Wilson. 'Why today?'

'Why not?' Wilson said wryly.

'Is there a delayed telecast of the game later tonight?'

'I think so, yeah,' Wilson said.

Swain sighed again. 'I'll call you.'

Stephen Swain leaned on the steering wheel of his Range Rover as he pulled it to a stop at the traffic lights. He glanced across at the passenger seat beside him. Holly was sitting with her hands in her lap and her head bowed, her feet jutting out horizontally from the seat, unable to reach the floor. They weren't swinging wildly about as they usually did.

The car was quiet.

'You okay?' Swain asked softly.

'Hmmm.'

Swain leaned over to look at her.

'Oh, don't do that,' he said gently, reaching for a tissue. 'Here.' He dabbed at the tears that had run down her cheeks.

Swain had arrived at the school just as Holly was leaving the vice-principal's office. Her ears were red and she'd been crying. It was harsh, he thought, that an eight-year-old should get such a dressing down.

'Hey,' he said. 'It's all right.'

Holly lifted her head. Her eyes were watery and red.

She swallowed. 'I'm sorry, Daddy. I tried.'

'You tried?'

'To be a lady. I really did. I really tried hard.'

Swain smiled. 'You did, huh?' He grabbed another tissue. 'Mrs Tickner didn't tell me what made you do it. All she said was that the lunchtime teacher found you straddled on top of some boy, beating the hell out of him.'

'Mrs Tickner wouldn't listen to me. She just kept saying that it didn't matter what made me do it, only that it was wrong for a lady to fight.'

The lights went green. Swain put the Range Rover into gear and moved off.

'So what did happen, then?'

Holly hesitated, then said, 'Tommy Jacobs was calling you a murderer.'

Swain closed his eyes momentarily. 'He was, was he?'

'Yes.'

'And you tackled him and punched him for that?'

'No, I punched him first.'

'But for that. For calling me a murderer?'

'Uh-huh.'

Swain turned to face Holly and nodded. 'Thanks,' he said seriously.

Holly smiled weakly. Swain turned his eyes back to the road. 'How many lines did you get?'

'One hundred times: "I must not fight because it is not ladylike".'

'Well, since this was partly my fault, what do you say you do fifty, and I'll do the other fifty in your handwriting.'

Holly smiled. 'That would be good, Daddy.' Her eyes began to brighten.

'Good,' Swain nodded. 'Just next time, try not to fight. If you can, try to *think* your way out of it. You'd be surprised, you can do a lot more damage with your brains than with your fists. And you can still be a lady at the same time.' Swain slowed the car and looked at his daughter. 'Fighting is never the answer. Only fight when it's the last option you've got.'

'Like you did, Daddy?'

'Yeah,' Swain said. 'Like I did.'

Holly lifted her head and began to peer out the window. She didn't recognise this area.

'Where are we going?' she said.

'I've got to go to the police station.'

'Daddy, are you in trouble again?'

'No, honey, I'm not in trouble.'

'Can I help you!' the harried-looking receptionist yelled above the din.

Swain and Holly were standing in the lobby of the 14th Precinct of the New York Police Department. There was activity everywhere. Beat cops hauling drug dealers away; phones ringing; people shouting. A prostitute in the corner winked sexily at Swain as he stood at the check-in desk.

'Uh, yes, my name is Stephen Swain. I'm here to see Detective Dickson. I was supposed to see him at five, but I had some time, so I—'

'That's fine, you're on the list. He's up in his office now. You can go right up. Office 209.'

Status Check: Electrification systems ready.

Swain headed for the stairwell at the rear of the bull-pen. As he did so, Holly bounded to his side and grabbed his hand. Swain looked down at the blonde ponytail bobbing madly up and down beside him.

Wide-eyed and interested, Holly was taking in the pandemonium of the police station with the curiosity of a scientist. She certainly was resilient, that was for sure, and with her natural blonde hair, blue eyes, button nose and sharp-eyed gaze, she was looking more and more like her mother every day . . .

Stop it, Swain thought. *Don't go there. Not now . . .*

He shook his thoughts away as they ascended the stairs.

On the second floor, they came to a door marked: **209: HOMICIDE.** Swain heard a familiar voice shouting from within.

'I don't care what your problem is! I want that building shut down, okay!'

'But sir—'

'Don't give me that, John. Just listen for a moment, will you. Good. Now look at what we have here. A security guard found lying on the floor—*in two pieces*—and a two-bit thief who's found sitting there next to him. Yeah, that's right, he's just sitting there when we arrive.

'And this thief, he's got blood all over his face and all down the front of his body. But it's not his blood, it's the guard's. Now I don't know what's going on. You tell me. Do you think this thief is from one of those crazy sects, who goes out, chops up a security guard, rubs the blood all over himself, and then manages to overturn a couple of ten-foot-tall bookcases?'

The voice paused for a moment, listening while the other man mumbled something.

'John, we don't know shit. And until we find out more, I'm shutting down that library. Okay?'

'Okay, Sarge,' the other voice relented.

'Good,' the first voice was calm again. 'Now get

down there, set up the tape around all entrances and exits, and put a couple of our guys inside for the night.'

The door opened. Swain stepped aside as a short officer came out of the office, smiled quickly at him, and then headed down the corridor and into the stairwell.

Status Check: Electrification to commence in two hours.
Earth time: sixth hour post meridian.

Swain knocked softly on the door and peered inside the office.

The wide room was empty, save for one desk over by the window. There Swain saw a large barrel-chested man seated in a swivel chair, his back to the door. He was gazing out the window, sipping from a coffee mug, savouring, it seemed, a rare moment's silence.

Swain knocked again.

'Yeah, come in,' the man didn't look up.

Swain hesitated, 'Ah, Detective—'

Captain Henry Dickson swung around in the swivel chair. 'Oh, I'm sorry, I was expecting someone else.' He got up quickly, crossed the room and shook Swain's hand. 'How are you today, Dr Swain?'

'Gettin' there,' Swain nodded. 'I had some time so I thought I'd come in and get this thing out of the way, if that's all right.'

Dickson led them to his desk where he reached into an open drawer and pulled out a file.

'Sure, no problem,' Dickson fished through the file. 'It shouldn't take more than a few minutes anyway. Just give me a minute here.'

Swain and Holly waited.

'All right,' Dickson said at last, holding up a sheet.

'This is the statement you gave on the night of the incident. What we'd like to do is include it in the departmental report, but by law we can't do it without your written consent. Is that okay with you?'

'That's fine.'

'Good, then I'll just read it to you to make sure it's okay, and then you can sign the report and we can all be out of here.'

> *Status Check: Officials from each system report that teleports are ready. Awaiting transmission of grid co-ordinates of labyrinth.*

Dickson straightened himself in his chair.

'All right, then,' he began to read from the statement, 'at approximately 8.30 p.m. on the night of October 2, 2000, I was working in the emergency room of St Luke's Hospital, New York City. I had been called in to do a radiology consult on a gunshot wound to a police officer. X-rays, C-spines and a CAT-scan had been taken and I had just returned to the emergency ward with the films when five young Latin American men wearing gang colours burst in through the main doors of the emergency ward with automatic weapons firing.

'Everyone in the ward dived for the floor as the wave of bullets smashed into everything in sight—computer screens, whiteboards, everything.

'The gang members fanned out immediately, shouting to each other, "*Find him and kill him!*" Two of them brandished automatic rifles while the other three held semi-automatic pistols.'

Swain listened in silence as Dickson recounted the events of that night. He remembered being told later that the wounded cop had been with the Vice Squad. Apparently, he'd been working undercover in Queens with a crack-dealing gang when his cover had been blown during a botched raid. He'd been winged during the shoot-out, and now the gang-bangers—incensed at his role in the bust—were here to finish him off.

Dickson kept reading: 'I was standing just outside the wounded policeman's room when the five men stormed the hospital. There was noise everywhere—people were screaming, the men's guns were booming—and I ducked behind the nearest corner.

'Then suddenly I saw one of the pistol-bearing gang-bangers rush toward the wounded cop's room. I don't know what made me do it, but when I saw him reach the doorway to the room and see the cop inside—and smile—I leapt at him from behind, tackled him hard.

'We slammed into the doorframe together, but he elbowed me sharply in the mouth—cutting my lip—and we fell apart and then suddenly before I knew what was happening, he was swinging his pistol around toward me.

'I caught his wrist in mid-flight—held the gun clear of my body—just as one of the *other* gang members arrived right in front of us.

'This second youth saw our struggle and instantly raised his own pistol at me but—still holding onto the first gang member's wrist—I whirled around and, with my free hand, punched the second youth square on the wrist of his gun-hand, causing his fingers to reflexively spring open and drop the gun. On the return journey, I used that same fist to backhand the youth across the jaw, knocking him out cold.

'It was at that moment that the first gang member started pulling indiscriminately on the trigger on his gun—even though I was still gripping his wrist. Gunshots boomed, bullets shredded the walls.

'I had to do something, so, pushing my feet off the doorframe, I hurled us both to the floor. We tumbled to the ground together—a clumsy rolling heap, so clumsy in fact that the youth's gun was pushed awkwardly up against his own head and then—'

And then abruptly—*shockingly*—the gun had gone off and the youth's head had simply exploded.

Swain didn't need to listen to Dickson any more. He could see it all in his mind's eye as if he was still there. He could remember the star of blood that had sprayed all over the door. He could still *feel* the youth's body go limp against his own.

Dickson was still reading the statement.

'—as soon as the other gang members saw their dead comrade, they fled. I believe it was about then that I passed out. This statement is dated 3/10/00, 1:55 a.m., signed Stephen Swain, M.D.'

Dickson looked up from the sheet of paper.

Swain sighed. 'That's it. That's my statement.'

'Good,' Dickson handed the typewritten statement to Swain. 'If you just sign there where it says "Consent granted", that'll just about do it, Dr Swain. Oh, and may I say once again, on behalf of the New York Police Department, thank you.'

> *Status Check: Grid co-ordinates of labyrinth to be transmitted to all systems upon electrification.*

'We'll see you in the morning then,' Officer Paul Hawkins said as he stood inside the enormous translucent glass doors of the New York State Library.

'See you then,' the lieutenant said, closing the doors on Hawkins' face.

Hawkins stepped away from the doors and nodded to his partner, Parker, who stepped forward with a large ring of keys. As Parker began to bolt the first of four locks on the huge translucent doors, Hawkins could see the blurred outline of the lieutenant affixing bright yellow police tape across the entrance. The tape pressed up against the other side of the glass and Hawkins could make out the familiar words: POLICE LINE—DO NOT CROSS.

He checked his watch.

5:15 p.m.

Not bad, he thought. It had only taken them twenty minutes to skirt the building and seal off all the entrances and exits.

Parker finished off the last lock and turned around. 'All done,' she said.

Hawkins thought about what the other cops had said about Christine Parker. Three years his senior, she was hardly pretty—for that matter, hardly petite. Big hands, dark heavy-set features, good with a gun. Unfortunately, her image hadn't been helped along by reports of insensitivity—she was known in the department for her rather icy demeanour. Hawkins shrugged it off. If she could hold her own, that was all that mattered to him.

'Good,' he turned to face the enormous atrium of the library. 'Do you know what happened? I was only called in this afternoon.'

'Somebody broke in and slashed up a security guard. Pretty messy,' Parker replied casually.

'Broke in?' Hawkins frowned. 'I didn't see any forced entry on any of the doors we sealed.'

Status Check: 0:44:16 to Electrification.

Parker put her keys in her pocket and shrugged. 'Don't ask me. All I know is that they haven't determined point of entry yet. SID's coming in tomorrow morning to do that. Guy probably picked the lock on one of the storage doors. Those things have got to be at least forty years old.'

She cocked her head indifferently. 'Larry at Dispatch told me they spent most of the day just trying to clean it all up.'

Parker walked over to the Information Desk and sat down. 'Anyhow,' she put her feet up on the counter, 'this isn't so bad. Doesn't bother me if I get double time for sitting in a library all night.'

'Come *on*, Daddy!' Holly said impatiently. 'I'm missing Pokémon!'

'Okay, okay,' Swain pushed open the front door. Holly burst past him, dashed into the house.

Swain pulled his key from the door and called after her, 'Don't slide on the carpet!'

He stepped inside as Holly charged out of the kitchen, biscuit tin in one hand, a can of Coke in the other. Swain stopped in his tracks as Holly cut across his path, making a beeline for the TV.

Watching her, Swain put his suitcase down, folded his arms and leaned against the bench that separated the kitchen from the living room. He watched as, unsurprisingly, in mid-stride Holly dropped to the floor and slid gracefully across the carpet, coming to a halt inches away from the television set.

'Hey!'

Holly gave him a throwaway smile. 'Sorreee.' She flicked on the TV.

Swain shook his head as he went into the kitchen. He always said not to slide on the carpet and Holly always did it anyway. It was kind of a ritual. Besides, he thought, Helen had always said it, and Holly had always ignored her, too. It was a good way for both of them to remember her.

It had been two years now since Swain's wife had been killed by a drunk driver who had tried to run a red light at fifty miles an hour. It had happened late one August evening, around eleven-thirty. They had run out of milk, so Helen had decided to walk to the 7-Eleven a few blocks away.

She never came back.

Later that night, Swain would see her body at the morgue. The mere sight of it, bloodied and broken, had knocked the wind out of him. All the life, the essence, the personality—everything that had made her

Helen—had been sucked from it. Her eyes had been wide open, staring blankly into space, lifeless.

Death had struck—brutally, swiftly, unexpectedly. She had gone out for milk and then all of a sudden she was gone. Just gone.

And now it was just him and Holly, somehow continuing life without her. Even now, two years on, Swain occasionally found himself staring out the window, thinking about her, tears forming in his eyes.

Swain opened the fridge, pulled out a Coke for himself. As he did so, the phone rang. It was Jim Wilson.

'You missed a *great* game.'

Swain sighed. 'Oh, yes . . .'

'Man, you should've seen it. It went into—'

'No! Stop! Don't tell me!'

Wilson laughed loudly on the other end of the line. 'Now would I do that?'

'Not if you wanted to live. Want to come over and watch it all over again?'

'Sure, why not? I'll be there in ten,' Wilson said and hung up.

Status Check: 0:14:38 to Electrification.

Swain glanced at the microwave. The green LED clock read 5:45 p.m.

He looked over at Holly, camped less than a foot away from the television screen. On the screen, multi-coloured creatures danced about.

Swain grabbed his drink and went into the living room. 'What are you watching?'

Holly didn't move her eyes from the screen.

'Pokémon,' she said, feeling for the biscuit tin beside her and grabbing a biscuit from it.

'Any good?'

She turned quickly, scrunched up her nose. 'Nah. Mew isn't there today. I'll see what's on the other channels.'

'No, wait!' Swain leaned forward, grabbing for the remote. 'The sport will be—'

The station changed, and a newsreader appeared on the screen.

'—while in football, fans in the national capital were not to be disappointed as the Redskins scalped the Giants twenty-four to twenty-one in an overtime thriller. At the same time, in Dallas . . .'

Swain closed his eyes as he sank back into his chair. 'Aw, man.'

'Did you hear that Daddy? Washington won. Grandpa will like that. He lives in Washington.'

Swain laughed softly. 'Yes, honey, I heard. I heard.'

> *Status Check: Officials attending to*
> *Earth Contestant await special*
> *instructions regarding teleportation.*

Paul Hawkins strolled idly around the foyer of the library.

His every footfall echoed hauntingly in the open space of the atrium.

He stopped to survey the atrium around him. It was, quite simply, a massive interior space. When one took into account the rail-lined balcony that ran in a horseshoe above the lower floor, its ceiling was actually two storeys high. In the early evening darkness, the atrium looked almost cavernous.

Ten-foot-high bookcases loomed in the brooding semi-darkness. Indeed, with the onset of night, apart from the harsh white glow coming from the Information Desk where Parker sat reading, the only light that penetrated the gigantic room was the slanting blue light from the streetlights outside.

Status Check: 0:03:04 to Electrification.
Teleport Officials standby.

Hawkins looked over at Parker. She was still sitting behind the Information Desk, her feet up, reading some Latin book she said she'd read back in school.
Jesus, it's quiet here, he thought.

Status Check: 0:01:41 to Electrification.

Status Check: Officials on Earth confirm
receipt of special instructions.
Standby.

The phone rang again. Holly leapt up from the floor and grabbed the receiver.

'Hello, Holly Swain speaking,' she said. 'Yes, he's here.' She put the receiver to her chest and yelled at the top of her lungs, 'Dadd*eee*! Phone!'

Swain emerged from his bedroom down the hall, doing up the buttons on a clean shirt. The belt around his jeans dangled from his waist and his hair was still dripping from the shower.

He gave Holly a crooked smile as he took the phone from her. 'Do you think the whole neighbourhood now knows I've got a phone call?'

Holly shrugged as she danced away toward the refrigerator.

'Hello,' Swain said into the phone.

'It's me again.' It was Wilson.

Swain glanced at the microwave clock. 'Hey, what are you doing? It's almost six. Where are you?'

'I'm still at home.'

Status Check: 0:00:46 to Electrification.

'Home?'
'The car won't start. Again.' Wilson said, deadpan.
Swain just laughed.

Hawkins was bored.

Idly, he poked his head inside the library's central stairwell, flicked on his heavy police flashlight. White marble stairs flanked by solid oak banisters rose in a wide spiral up into the darkness.

Hawkins nodded. Had to hand it to these old buildings, they were built to last.

Status Check: 0:00:15 to Electrification.

Parker stood up from her seat behind the Information Desk. She gazed lazily around the atrium, squinting in the darkness.

'What're you doing?' she called.
'Just looking around.'

Status Check: 0:00:09 to Electrification.
Standby.

Parker walked over to Hawkins. He was standing at the doorway to the stairwell, his flashlight on, peering up into the darkness.

:06

She stopped next to him.

'Nice old place,' Hawkins said.

'Yeah,' Parker nodded. 'Nice.'

:04

:03

:02

:01

Standby . . .

—Electrification initialised.

At that moment, while Hawkins and Parker stood in the stairwell, bright blue sparks flashed out from the main entrance to the library. An electric blue current shot up between the large glass doors while sizzling claws of electricity lashed out around the edges of the door frame.

Every single window of the library shook as tiny forks of blue lightning shot out from their panes. At the small side entrances to the library, yellow police tape bubbled slowly, boiling under the intense heat of the electricity now flowing through the doors.

And then, in an instant, it stopped.

All the windows and doors giving access to the library were suddenly still.

Suddenly silent again.

The State Library, old and dark, stood sombrely in the darkness of New York City, its magnificent glass doors grey in the moonlight. To the casual observer a few feet away they looked regal and austere, just as they had looked the day before.

It was only when one came close that one would see the intermittent flash of tiny blue lightning that licked out from between the two huge doors every few seconds.

Just as it did at every other entrance to the library.

Status Check: Electrification complete.
Dispatch grid co-ordinates
of the labyrinth.

Commence teleportation.

Holly grabbed onto Swain's leg. Swain shook it play-fully as he spoke into the phone.

'It won't be much of a surprise anyway. I already heard who won.'

'You did?'

Swain frowned down at Holly as she reached into his jeans pocket. 'Yes. Unfortunately I did.'

Holly pulled her hand out of his pocket and frowned at the object in her hand.

'Daddy, what's this?'

Swain glanced down at her and cocked his head in surprise. 'May I?' he said.

Holly gave him the small silver object.

'What's going on?' Wilson asked.

Swain turned it over in his hand. 'Well . . . *Doctor* Wilson, maybe you can tell me. Maybe you can tell me why my daughter has just pulled a Zippo out of my jeans. *My* jeans that *you* borrowed for your little cow-boy thing on the weekend.'

Wilson hesitated. 'I have absolutely no idea how that got there.'

'Why don't I believe you?'

'All right, all right, don't start.' Wilson said. 'What are my chances of getting my lighter back?'

Swain put the cigarette lighter back into his pocket. 'I don't know. Sixty–forty.'

Status Check: Teleportation sequence initialised.

'Sixty–forty!'

Holly grabbed another drink from the refrigerator. Swain shifted the telephone to his shoulder and bent down to pick her up. He grunted under the weight.

'God, you're heavy.'

Initialise teleport: Earth.

'*Dad* . . . Come on, I'm eight now . . .'

'Too old to be picked up, huh? All ri—'

At that moment the room around Swain began to brighten. A mysterious white glow filled the kitchen.

'Daddy . . .' Holly gripped his shoulders tightly.

Swain turned around slowly, staring, mesmerised, at the soft white light glowing around him—glowing around him—*growing* around him.

Growing.

The kitchen was getting brighter. The light was gathering intensity.

Swain spun. All around him, the soft white glow had become a dazzling white light. Wherever he turned, his eyes reeled at the brilliant light. It seemed to come from every direction.

He lifted his forearm to shield his eyes.

'Daddy! What's happening!'

Swain held her closer, pushed her head into his chest, guarding her from the light. He squinted as his eyes tried to penetrate the blinding wall of white light surrounding them, searching for a source.

Recoiling from the light, he abruptly looked down at his feet—and saw a perfect circle of white light ringing his sneakers.

And then Swain realised.

He was at the centre of the light.

He was the source!

Gusts of wind shot through the kitchen. Dust and paper swirled around Swain's head as he held Holly close to his chest. He shut his eyes, bracing himself against the screaming wind.

Then, strangely, above the howling of the wind, he heard a voice. A soft, faint, insistent voice saying, 'Steve? Stephen Swain, are you still with us?'

It took him a second to realise that it was the phone. Wilson was still on the line. Swain had forgotten that he was still holding onto the phone.

'Stephen, what's going on. Ste—'

The phone went dead.

A deafening thunderclap boomed and Swain was instantly plunged into complete darkness.

SECOND MOVEMENT

30 November, 6:04 p.m.

A lot of people would say that fear of the dark is nothing but a phenomenon of childhood.

A child fears the dark simply because he or she does not have the experience to know that in fact nothing is there. But as Stephen Swain knew, fear of the dark was common in many adults. Indeed, for some, the human need for sight was often as basic as the need for food.

Standing in pitch darkness, without a clue where he was, Swain felt it strange that he should be thinking of his college studies in human behaviour. He remembered his lecturer saying, 'Human fears are very often irrational constructs of the mind. How else would you explain a six-foot-tall woman being petrified by the mere sight of a single white mouse—a creature barely four inches long?'

But no fear was seen as more irrational—or more innate in man—than a fear of the dark. Academic theorists and weary parents had been saying for centuries that there was nothing in the dark that was not already there in the light . . .

But I'll bet something like this never happened to them, Swain thought as he stared into the sea of blackness around him.

Where the hell are we . . . ?

His heart pumped loudly inside his head. He could feel a wave of panic spreading slowly through his body. No. He had to stay calm—rational—had to look after Holly.

He felt for her at his shoulder. She held him tightly, frightened.

'Daddy . . .'

If he could just see *something*, he thought, trying to contain his own ever-increasing fear. A break in the darkness. A splinter of light. Anything.

He looked left, then right. Nothing.

Only black. Endless, seamless black.

A fear of the dark didn't seem quite so irrational now.

'Daddy. What's *happening*?'

He could feel Holly's head pushed close against his shoulder.

'I don't know, honey,' Swain pursed his lips in thought. And then he remembered.

'Wait a minute,' he said, stretching his hand awkwardly underneath Holly to reach into his jeans pocket. He breathed a sigh of relief as he felt the cold slippery metal of the lighter.

The Zippo flipped open with a metallic *calink!* and Swain flipped down on the cartwheel. The flint sparked for an instant, but the lighter didn't catch. Swain tried again. Another spark but no flame.

'Christ,' he said aloud. 'Some smoker.'

'Daddy . . .'

'Just hold on, honey,' Swain put the lighter back in his pocket and turned to face the darkness again. 'Let's see if we can find a door or something.'

He lifted his foot and took a hesitant step forward.

As he lowered it, however, he began to understand why some people feared the dark so much. The sheer helplessness of not knowing what was right in front of you was terrifying.

His shoe hit the floor. It was hard. Cold. Like slate, or marble.

He took another step forward. Only this time, as his foot came down, it didn't find any floor. Just empty space.

'Uh-oh.'

His sense of panic began to rise again. Where the hell was he? Was he standing on the rim of a ledge? If he was, how far down did it go? Was it on every side of him?

Shit.

Swain slowly lowered his foot further over the edge.

Nothing.

Slowly. Further. Still nothing.

Then his foot hit something. More floor, not far below where he was standing.

Swain pushed down and forward again. Another piece of floor. He smiled in the darkness, relieved.

Steps.

Holding Holly close to his chest, Swain cautiously descended the stairs.

'Where are we, Daddy?'

In the darkness, Swain stopped. He glanced at Holly. Although everything was still dark, he could just make out the outline of her face. The hollows of her eye sockets, the shadow of her nose across her cheek.

'I don't know,' he said.

He was about to take another step forward when he

snapped up to look at Holly again. The hollows of her eye sockets, the shadow across her cheek—

A shadow.

There must be a light.

Somewhere.

Swain looked closely at her face and, scanning the shadow of her nose, he suddenly saw it—a soft green glow, so dim that it barely revealed her other features. Swain leaned closer and—abruptly—the gentle glow vanished.

'Damn it.'

He slowly moved his head back and, equally slowly, the glow returned, half covering Holly's face.

Swain's eyes widened. It was his *own* shadow covering his daughter's face.

The light source was somewhere behind him.

Swain spun around.

And there, in the sheet of blackness in front of him, he saw it. It was hovering in the darkness, level with his eyes and yet completely still—a tiny green light.

It couldn't have been more than six feet away, and it shone like a small pilot light on a VCR. Swain stared intently at the tiny green light.

And then he heard a voice.

'Hello, Contestant.'

It came from the green light.

It sounded prim, proper, refined. And yet at the same time high-pitched, as if spoken by a midget.

It came again.

'Hello, Contestant. Welcome to the labyrinth.'

Swain squeezed Holly close. 'Who is that? Where are you?'

'I am here. Can you not see me?' The voice was not threatening. It was almost, Swain thought, helpful.

'No. It's too dark.'

'Oh, yes. Hmm,' the voice sounded disheartened. 'Just a moment.'

The tiny green light bounced away to Swain's left, bobbing up and down. Then it stopped.

'Ah. Here we are.'

Something clicked and some overhead fluorescent lights immediately came to life.

In this new-found light, Swain saw that he was standing halfway down a flight of wide marble stairs with banisters made of dark polished wood. The stairs seemed to spiral down several floors before disappearing into darkness.

Swain guessed he was at the top of the stairwell,

since no stairs ascended from the landing above him. Only a heavy-looking wooden door led out from the landing.

His gaze moved left from the door, and suddenly he saw the owner of the voice.

There, standing next to a light switch, stood a man no more than four feet tall, dressed completely in white.

White shoes, white coveralls, white gloves.

The little man was holding something in one white-gloved hand. It looked like a grey wristwatch. Swain noticed that the small green light he had seen before was attached to the face of the wristwatch.

In addition to his completely white outfit, Swain saw that the little man wore an odd white skull cap that covered every part of his head, except for his face.

'Daddy, it looks like an eggshell,' Holly whispered.

'Shh.'

The little man in white stepped forward, so that he stood on the edge of the landing, his head a little higher than Swain's. He spoke perfect English, without trace of an accent.

'Hello. Welcome to the labyrinth. My name is Selexin and I am your guide.' He extended his little white hand. 'How do you do?'

Swain was still staring in disbelief at the little white man. He absently offered his own hand in return. The little man cocked his head.

'You have an interesting weapon,' he said, looking down at the telephone receiver in Swain's hand.

Swain glanced at the receiver. The spiral cord leading out from the phone had been cut several inches from where it met the hand-piece. He hadn't realised that he was still holding it. He quickly handed it to Holly, and shook hands awkwardly with the man in white.

'How do you do?' Selexin bowed solemnly.

'I'm gettin' there,' Swain said, warily. 'How about you?'

The man in white smiled earnestly and nodded politely. 'Oh, yes. Thank you. I am getting there, too.'

Swain hesitated. 'Listen, I don't know who or what you are, but . . .'

Holly wasn't listening. She was staring at the hand-piece of the telephone. Without a spiral cord snaking back to a base unit, it looked like a cellular.

She examined the shortened phone cord. The cut at the end of it looked as if someone had snipped it with a pair of extremely sharp scissors. It was a clean cut. A *perfectly* clean cut. The wires inside the cord were not even frayed.

Holly shrugged and put the phone in her uniform pocket. Her own cellular phone, even if it didn't work. She looked back at the little man in white. He was talking to her father.

'*I* have no intention of harming you,' he was saying.

'You don't?'

'No,' Selexin paused. 'Well, not *me*.'

'Then if you don't mind, do you think you could tell us where we are and how the hell we can get out of here?' Swain said, taking a step up the stairs towards the landing.

The little man seemed shocked.

'*Get out?*' he said blankly. 'No one gets out. Not yet.'

'What do you mean no one gets out? Where are we?'

'You are in the labyrinth.'

Swain looked at the stairs around him. 'And where is this labyrinth?'

'Why, Contestant, this is Earth, of course.'

Swain sighed. 'Listen, ah . . .'

'Selexin.'

'Yes. Selexin,' Swain offered a weak smile. 'Selexin, if it's okay with you, I think my daughter and I would like to leave your labyrinth. I don't know what it is you're doing here, but I don't think we're going to be a part of it.'

Swain climbed the stairs and walked over to the door leading out from the landing. He was reaching for the door handle when Selexin snatched his hand away.

'*Don't!*'

He held Swain's hand away from the heavy wooden door. 'Like I said, no one gets out, *yet*. The labyrinth has been sealed. Look.'

He pointed to the gap between the door and its solid wooden frame. 'You see?'

Swain looked at the gap and saw nothing. '*No,*' he said, unimpressed.

'Look *closely*.'

Swain leaned closer and peered at the inside of the door frame.

And then he saw it.

A tiny blue fork of electricity licked out from the gap between the door and the frame.

He only just saw it, but the sudden electric blue flash of light was unmistakable. Swain's eyes followed the door frame up its vertical edge. Every few inches there was a distinct flicker of the bright blue charge between the frame and the door.

It was the same on all four sides of the door.

Slowly, Swain stepped back onto the landing. He spoke as he turned, his voice soft and flat.

'What the hell are you doing here?'

In the atrium of the library, Officer Paul Hawkins was pacing back and forth in front of the Information Desk.

'I'm telling you, I saw it,' he said.

Parker was sitting with her feet up on the desk, chewing on a candy bar, now happily reading a back issue of *Cosmopolitan*.

'Sure you did.' She didn't even look up as she spoke.

Hawkins was angry. 'I said, *I saw it*.'

'Then go and check it out for yourself,' Parker offered him a dismissive wave. As far as she was concerned, Hawkins was green. Too young, too fresh and far too eager. And like every other rookie, always suspicious that the crime of the century was happening right under his nose.

Hawkins walked off toward the bookcases near the stairwell, mumbling to himself.

'What'd you say?' Parker called lazily from behind her magazine.

'Nothing,' Hawkins muttered as he stalked off. 'I'm going to see if it happens again.'

Parker looked up from her magazine to see

Hawkins disappear through the stairwell doors. She shook her head.

'Rookie.'

Slowly, Hawkins climbed the wide marble stairs, peering around every turn, hoping to see it happen again. He leaned out over the banister and looked up into the shaft.

With the stairwell lights out, he knew he would barely be able to see beyond the first landing—

There was a light!

Up at the top.

One of the fluorescent lights up at the very top of the stairwell was on—and it hadn't been on before.

Hawkins felt his adrenalin surge.

Someone was in here.

What should he do now? Get Parker? Yes, backup—backup was good. No, wait. She wouldn't believe him. She hadn't before.

Hawkins peered back up into the shaft and saw the light. He took a hesitant step up the stairs.

And then it happened.

Hawkins immediately leapt back from the banister as a blinding stream of white light burst up through the central shaft of the stairwell, instantly illuminating everything around it.

Flecks of dust swirling around the hollow core of the stairwell suddenly came to life as the rising light struck them, creating a dazzling column of vertical white light.

Hawkins stared at it in awe. It was exactly what he had seen before—a brilliant stream of white light pouring through the shaft of the stairwell.

And yet, somehow, this time it was different.

The *source* was different. This time, it wasn't coming from somewhere high up in the stairwell.

No, this time it was coming from below.

Slowly, Hawkins peered out over the edge of the banister, looking down into the shaft.

The light seemed to be coming from underneath one of the landings below him. All he could make out was the edge of what looked like a large glowing sphere of pure white—

It went out.

It didn't fade. It didn't flicker. It just disappeared to black. Just as it had done before.

Hawkins suddenly found himself standing in the empty stairwell again, the hollow shaft in the centre now no more than a silent, gaping hole of blackness.

He looked back over his shoulder toward the atrium. Beyond the bookcases, he could see Parker's feet resting lazily on the counter of the Information Desk. He thought about calling to her, but decided against it.

He turned back to face the darkened stairwell.

He swallowed, and suddenly forgot all about the fluorescent light that had been turned on upstairs.

Hawkins pulled his heavy police-issue flashlight from his belt and switched it on.

Then he began his descent into the darkness.

Selexin was still holding the grey wristband. It was heavy in his hand, mainly because of the thick metal straps used to clasp it to its wearer's wrist.

He glanced at the face. It was rectangular—like an elongated digital watch—broad in width, short in height. At the top of the face, the little green pilot light burned brightly. Next to it was another light, slightly larger than the green one, dull red in colour. At the moment it was lifeless.

Good, Selexin thought.

Beneath the two lights there was a narrow oblong display that read:

INCOMPLETE—1

Selexin looked up from the watchface. He saw Swain and Holly standing at a window, gazing out, both careful to stay a safe distance from the electrified window panes.

Selexin grunted, shook his head sadly, and looked back down at the wristband. The display flickered.

INCOMPLETE—1

The words disappeared for an instant. When they returned, they had changed. The display now read:

INCOMPLETE—2

And it was stable again.

Selexin walked over to Swain at the window and stopped beside him.

'Now do you understand?'

Swain continued to stare out the window.

After he had seen the electrified door at the top of the stairwell, he had immediately come down the first flight of stairs and opened the nearest door. It was a large fireproof door marked with a red '3'.

It had opened onto an extremely broad, low-ceilinged room, perhaps fifty yards wide. Swain had gone straight across it—winding his way through a forest of odd-looking steel-framed desks—heading directly for the nearest window.

The room was completely filled with the peculiarly shaped desks. Each had a vertical partition attached to the rear edge, so that it formed an L-shape with the horizontal writing surface. Hundreds of these desks, bunched together in tight clusters of four, covered the vast floorspace of the room.

Now, as he looked out the window and saw the familiar inner city park, surrounded by the darkened streets of New York City, Swain began to understand.

'Where are we, Daddy?'

Swain's eyes took in the multitude of partitioned desks in the room around them. In the near corner of the room was a heavy-looking maintenance door, next to which was a sign:

QUIET PLEASE.
THIS ROOM IS FOR PRIVATE STUDY ONLY.
NO CARRY BAGS PERMITTED.

A study hall.

Swain turned to face Selexin. 'We're in the library, honey. The State Library.'

Selexin nodded. Correct.

'This,' he said, 'is the labyrinth.'

'This, is a *library*.'

'That it may well be,' Selexin shrugged, 'but that is of little concern for you now.'

Swain said, 'I think it's of a lot of concern for me now. What are you doing here and what do you want with us?'

'Well, first of all,' the smaller man began, 'we do not

61

exactly want both of you.' He looked at Swain. 'We actually only want *you*.'

'So why did you bring my daughter too?'

'It was unintentional, I can assure you. Contestants are strictly forbidden to have assistance of any kind. She must have entered the field just before you were teleported.'

'Teleported?'

'Yes, Contestant,' Selexin sighed sadly. 'Teleported. And you can count yourself extremely fortunate that she was fully inside the field at the time. If she had been only partially inside the field, she might have been—'

There was a loud rumble of thunder outside the window. Swain looked out through the glass and saw dark storm clouds rolling across the face of the moon. It was well and truly dark outside now. Streaks of rain began to appear on the window.

He turned back. 'The white light.'

'Yes,' Selexin said, 'the field. Everything inside the field at the time the systems are initialised is teleported.'

'Like the phone,' Swain said.

'Yes.'

'But only half the phone came with us.'

'Because only half the phone was inside the field,' Selexin said. 'In its simplest form, the field is merely a spherical hole in the air. Anything inside that sphere is, at the time of teleportation, lifted up and placed elsewhere, whether it is attached to something else or not.'

'And you determine where we go. Is that right?' Swain said.

'Yes. Now, Contestant—'

Swain held up his hand. 'Wait a minute. Why do you keep calling me that?'

'Calling you what?'

'"Contestant". Why do you keep calling me "Contestant"?'

'Because that is what you are, that is why you have been brought here,' Selexin said, as if it was the most obvious thing in the world. 'To compete. To compete in the Seventh Presidian.'

'Presidian?'

Now it was Selexin who frowned.

'Yes,' his voice tightened. 'Hmmm, I suspected this might happen.' He gave a long sigh and looked impatiently at the metal wristband in his hand. Its green light was still burning and its display still read:

INCOMPLETE—2

Selexin looked up and spoke to no-one in particular: 'Well, since there is still time, I will tell you.'

Holly stepped forward, pointed to the grey wristwatch. 'What is that?'

Selexin gave her a sharp look. '*Please*, I will come to that. Just listen for a moment.'

Holly backed away immediately, reaching for Swain's hand.

Selexin was taking short, quick breaths, showing his irritation. As Swain watched him, it seemed increasingly obvious that the little man in white simply did not want to be here.

'The Presidian,' Selexin began, 'has been held on six previous occasions. And this,' he said, looking at the study hall around him, 'is the seventh. It is held approximately once every thousand Earth years, each time on a different world, and in every system, except Earth, it is held in only the highest esteem.'

'Systems?' Swain asked.

'Yes, Contestant, *systems*.' Selexin's tone was now that of a weary adult addressing a five-year-old. '*Other* worlds. *Other* intelligent life. There are seven in total.'

Selexin paused for a moment, lifted a hand to massage his brow. He looked as if he was trying very hard to keep himself calm.

Finally, he looked up at Swain. 'You didn't know that, did you?'

'The part about other worlds and other intelligent life? Ah, no.'

'I am dead,' Selexin whispered, presumably to himself. Swain heard him clearly.

'Why?' he asked innocently. 'Why are you dead? What is this Presidian?'

Selexin sighed in exasperation. He held his hands out, palms up.

'What do you *think* it is?' he said sharply, barely concealing the condescension in his voice. 'It is a *competition*. A *battle*. A *contest*. Seven contestants enter the labyrinth and only one leaves. It is a fight to the death.'

He could see the disbelief spread across Swain's face. Selexin threw up his hands. 'By the Gods, you do not even understand what you are here for! Do you not see?'

Selexin slowed down for a moment, lowering his voice, trying desperately to control himself.

'Let me begin again. You have been chosen to represent your species in the ultimate contest in the universe. A contest that dates back over six millennia, that bases itself on a principle that goes light years beyond any notion of "sport" that you could possibly imagine. *That* is the Presidian.

'It is a battle. A battle between hunters, athletes, warriors; creatures coming from every corner of the

64

universe, possessed of skill, courage and intelligence, prepared to stake their very lives on their extraordinary talents—talents at hunting, stalking and killing.'

Selexin shook his head.

'There is no coming back from defeat in the Presidian. There is no return match. Defeat in the Presidian is no loss of pride, it is *loss of life*. Every contestant who enters the labyrinth accepts that in this contest the only alternative to ultimate victory is certain death.

'It is quite simple. Seven will enter. The best will win, the lesser will die. Until only one remains.' The little man paused. 'If, of course, one *does* remain.

'There is no place for the ordinary man in the Presidian. It is a contest for the extraordinary—for those prepared to risk the ultimate to attain the ultimate. On Earth you play games where you lose nothing in defeat. "Winning isn't everything," you say. "It doesn't matter if you win or lose, but how you played the game."' Selexin grunted disdainfully. 'If that is the case, why should anyone even *try* to win?

'Winning is devalued where defeat involves no loss, and humans are quite simply unable to comprehend that idea. Just as they are unable to comprehend a contest like the Presidian, where defeat means exactly that—losing *everything*.'

The little man looked Swain squarely in the eye. 'Winning *is* everything when you have everything to lose.'

The little man laughed weakly. 'But your kind will never understand that . . .'

Selexin paused, dropping his head, withdrawing into himself. Swain just stood there, entranced, staring in amazement at the little man before him.

'And that is why I am dead,' Selexin looked up. 'Because *my* survival depends on *your* survival. It is a highly prized honour to guide a contestant through the Presidian—an honour bestowed upon my people since we are prevented by our size from competing in the contest—but when one accepts that honour, one also accepts the fate of his contestant.

'So when you die, I die. And as I see it now,' he raised his voice, 'since you appear to know *absolutely nothing* about the Presidian or anything it entails, I would say quite confidently that at the moment our collective chances of survival are approximately zero!'

Selexin looked Swain up and down. Sneakers, jeans, a loose-fitting shirt with the sleeves rolled up, hair still slightly wet. He shook his head.

'Look at you, you haven't even come *prepared* to fight!'

He began to pace, gesturing with his arms, despairing for his situation, until finally he was totally indifferent to Swain and Holly's presence: 'Why me? Why this? Why the *human*? Keeping in mind the distinguished history human participation has had in the Presidian . . .'

Swain watched the little man pace back and forth in front of him. Holly just stared at him.

'Hey,' Swain said, stepping forward. Selexin continued to mutter to himself.

'*Hey!*'

Selexin stopped. He turned and stared at Swain.

'What?' he said angrily. In his anger, the little man possessed a ferocity that belied his size.

Swain cocked his head. 'Are you saying that humans have been in this thing before? In this contest?'

Selexin sighed. 'Yes. Twice. In the last two Presidia, humans have participated.'

'And what happened to them?'

Selexin laughed sadly. 'Both were the first to be eliminated. Neither one ever stood a chance.' He cocked an eyebrow. 'Now I know why.'

He looked down at the wristwatch. It now read:

INCOMPLETE—3

Swain said, 'And how exactly were they selected for this thing?'

As Selexin explained, but for one crucial modification, the process for human selection for the Seventh Presidian was largely unchanged from that which had operated for the two Presidia before it. Beings unable to accept the fact that other lifeforms existed in the universe could hardly be expected to choose a contestant of their own accord, let alone appreciate the concept of the Presidian.

After all, humans had not even been considered for inclusion in any Presidian until two thousand years ago—human development having been disappointingly slow.

All six of the other systems chose their own representatives for the millennial Presidian either by holding a competition of their own or by choosing their greatest sportsman, huntsman or warrior. Earth, on the other hand, would be surveyed for some time, and from that surveillance, a worthy contestant would be chosen.

'Well, they didn't look too hard this time,' Swain said. 'I've never picked a fight in my life.'

'Oh, but—'

'I'm a *doctor*,' Swain said. 'Do you know what a doctor is? I don't kill people. I—'

'I know what a doctor is, and I know precisely what they do,' Selexin shot back. 'But you have forgotten what I said earlier—*one crucial modification* was made to the selection criteria this time.

'You see, for the last two Presidia the choice of the human contestant was based largely on combat skills, and combat skills alone. This was obviously a mistake. After the dismal performance of those two human contestants, it was decided that other, less obvious skills should be taken into account in the selection process for this Presidian.

'Of course, fighting skills would be necessary, but this time they would *not* be conclusive. Now, from our observations of your planet, we could see that human warriors were adept at using artificially propelled weapons—firearms, missiles and the like. But such weapons are forbidden in the Presidian. Only *self*-propelled weapons are allowed—throwing knives, bladed weapons. So, first of all, we needed a human proven in hand-to-hand combat. Naturally, several warriors of your race fulfilled this requirement.

'But other skills were also deemed necessary, skills which are not often found in your warrior types. High mental aptitude levels were a primary consideration— in particular, the ability to respond to a crisis, objective rational thinking in the face of the potentially bizarre, and most importantly, adaptive intelligence.'

'Adaptive intelligence?'

'Yes. The ability to evaluate a scenario in an instant, take in all the immediately available solutions, and then *act*. We often call this reactive thinking—the ability to think clearly under pressure and use *any* available means to solve one's problem. Based on our prior experience with humans, it was anticipated that the human contestant would probably not be an *offensive*, proactive contestant. Rather, he or she would be more defensive, *reactive* to a situation of someone else's making. So a quick-thinking, adaptive personality was required. You.'

Swain shook his head. He hardly thought of himself as a quick-thinking, adaptive personality. He saw himself as a good doctor, but not brilliant. He knew of countless other surgeons and physicians who were miles ahead of him in both knowledge *and* ability. He was just good at what he did, but quick-thinking or adaptive?

'Make no mistake, Contestant, your skills as a physician have been under scrutiny for some time now. Clear, *reactive* thought, under intense pressure— have you ever experienced that before?'

'Well, yes, lots of times, but still . . . I mean, God, I've never been in combat—'

'Oh, but you have,' Selexin said. 'Your selection was based on your response to a life-threatening combat situation not so long ago, a situation that involved multiple enemies.'

Swain thought about it. A life-threatening combat situation involving multiple enemies. He wondered if college football counted as life-threatening. Christ, it sounded like something that would be better suited to somebody in the army or the police force.

The police force . . .

That night . . .

Swain thought about that night one month ago in October, when the five heavily armed gang members had stormed the ER at St Luke's. He remembered his fight with the two pistol-toting youths—remembered tackling the first one, then punching the second one in his wrist, dislodging his gun—and then struggling with the first one again—and falling to the floor in a heap—and then hearing the gun discharge that final fatal shot.

Life-threatening? Definitely.

Swain suddenly realised that he was rubbing the cut on his lower lip.

'There is another thing,' Selexin said, interrupting his thoughts. The little man lifted his small white hand, offering the grey wristband to Swain.

'Take it, put it on. You will need it. Especially if we are separated.'

Swain took the wristband but did not put it on. 'Now, wait just a minute. I haven't agreed to be a part of this little show of yours yet—'

Selexin shook his head. 'You have not understood what I have been telling you. Your selection for the Presidian has been finalised. You no longer have any choice in the matter.'

'It doesn't seem like I ever did.'

'Please, just look at your wristband.'

Swain looked at the watch, at the display beneath the glowing green light. It read:

INCOMPLETE—3

Selexin said, 'See that number—three. Soon that number will reach seven. When it does, we will know that all seven contestants have been teleported into the labyrinth. Then the Presidian will begin.' He looked seriously at Swain. 'You are here now, and whether you like it or not, you have become an integral part of this contest.'

Selexin pointed at the wristband. 'And when that number hits "7" you will become fair game for six other contestants who all have the same goal that you have. To get out.'

'What's that supposed to mean?'

'Remember what I told you,' Selexin said. 'Seven enter, but only one leaves. The labyrinth is completely electrified. There is absolutely no way out. Except by teleport. And that is initialised *only* when one contestant remains in the labyrinth. *That* is the exit from the labyrinth—and only the winner leaves. If, of course, there is a winner.'

Selexin slowed down. 'Mr Swain, the other contestants, they don't care whether or not you decide to accept your status as a contestant. They will kill you anyway. Because they are all well aware that unless every contestant bar one is dead, *no-one* leaves the labyrinth. The ultimate contest, Mr Swain.'

Swain looked at the little man in disbelief. He let out a slow breath through his nose. 'So you're telling me that not only are we stuck in here, but that soon there will be six other guys in here too, whose only way out is to make sure that I'm dead.'

'Yes. That is right.'

'Holy shit.'

Swain stood in the stairwell, by the fire door leading to the study hall. Holly stood behind him, holding onto his shirt tail.

He looked at the thick grey wristband now clasped firmly around his left wrist. It looked like a manacle from the arm of an electric chair—thick and solid, and heavy too. The little green light glowed while the display still read:

INCOMPLETE—3

Swain turned to Selexin, 'So there are only three of us in here now. Is that right?'

'Yes. That is right.'

'Does that mean that we can walk around safely now?'

'I do not understand.'

'Well, not everyone is in the labyrinth yet,' Swain said. 'So say I want to wander around and have a look at this place—what happens if I bump into another contestant? He can't kill me, can he? Not yet.'

Selexin said, 'No, he cannot. Combat of any kind between contestants is strictly prohibited until *all seven* have entered the labyrinth. In any case, I would advise you against "wandering about".'

'Why not, if they can't hurt us, we can safely have a look around the library.'

'That is true, but if you decide to wander, you do hazard the risk of being sequenced.'

'Sequenced?'

'Yes. If you do happen to meet another contestant before all seven have been teleported into the labyrinth, you can be assured that he—or she—cannot hurt you in any way. You may converse with other contestants if you want to, or you may ignore them completely.' Selexin spread his palms. 'Very simple.'

Then he held up a finger.

'However. If you do meet another contestant, there is nothing to stop that contestant *following* you until the remaining contestants *have* been teleported into the labyrinth, and the Presidian has commenced. That is sequencing, and it has proved to be a common tactic in previous Presidia.

'Another contestant can quite rightfully walk two feet behind you for the whole time until the Presidian commences and you cannot touch him—for just as he cannot hurt you, you cannot hurt him either. And once the last contestant has been teleported into the labyrinth and your wristband reads "7", well . . .' Selexin shrugged. 'You had better be ready to fight.'

'Great,' Swain said, frowning at the thick grey wristband clamped to his wrist.

At that moment, the display flickered.

Swain was momentarily startled. 'What's this?'

Selexin looked at the wristband. The display read:

Then it vanished and the screen came up again, reading:

'What's that mean?' Swain asked.

'It means,' Selexin said, 'that another contestant has arrived in the labyrinth.'

In the atrium of the library, Officer Christine Parker sat behind the Information Desk with her mouth agape and her eyes wide.

She was staring at the hulking seven-foot figure standing before her, in front of the massive glass doors of the library.

Parker remembered how Hawkins had wandered off twenty minutes ago, looking for some damned white light that he thought he had seen. She also remembered laughing loudly when he'd told her about it.

Now she didn't feel like laughing.

Moments ago, she had seen a perfect sphere of brilliant white light appear in front of her. It was fully ten feet in diameter and it lit up the whole cavernous space of the atrium like an enormous light bulb.

And then it had vanished.

Extinguished in an instant.

Gone.

And now in its place stood a figure that looked something like a man. A seven-foot-tall, perfectly proportioned man—with broad muscular shoulders narrowing to an equally muscular waist.

A man clad entirely in black.

Parker stared at him in awe.

The streams of soft blue light that filtered in through the great glass doors of the library surrounded the tall black figure before her, creating a spectacular silhouette, while at the same time highlighting one particularly distinguishing feature of the man.

The 'man' had horns.

Two long beautifully tapered horns that protruded from both sides of his head, and then stretched upwards so that they almost touched two feet above his head.

He stood absolutely still.

Parker thought he might have been a statue, but for the slow, rhythmic rise and fall of his powerfully built chest. Parker's eyes searched the head for a face, but with the light source behind him, all she could see beneath the two sharp rising horns was an empty space of ominous black.

But there was something wrong with the silhouette.

Something on the man's shoulder that was not black, something that broke the perfect symmetry of his body. It was a lump. A small white lump that seemed to slump over his left shoulder.

Parker squinted in the darkness, tried to determine what the small lump was.

She leaned back in her seat, her eyes wide.

It looked like another man . . .

A very small man. Dressed completely in white—

And then, suddenly, there was light again.

Sharp, sudden, *brilliant* white light filled the atrium of the State Library. Blinding spheres of light, four feet in diameter—half the size of the one she had seen before—illuminated everything around Parker.

Parker saw two small spheres of light before her . . . then three . . . then four. Loose sheets of paper began to blow about all around her, just as they had done before.

She looked beyond the swirling sheets of paper, trying to catch a glimpse of the tall man in black. But amid the billowing pages and the blinding light, the horned man remained completely still, impervious to distraction.

And then, in a flare of white, Parker saw the man's face.

He was staring at her.

Straight at her.

It was terrifying. Their eyes locked and a flood of adrenalin instantly rushed through Parker's body. All she could see were deep blue eyes set against a harsh black face. Eyes devoid of emotion. Eyes that simply stared.

Stared right at her.

Sheets of paper fluttered wildly around his unmoving frame and then—

And then abruptly, darkness again.

The four white spheres of light had vanished instantly. The wind stopped abruptly, and all over the atrium, sheets of paper glided softly to the floor.

Parker spun to face the spot where one of the spheres had been—

—only to see something small scuttle away behind a nearby bookcase, its long black tail lashing against the bottom shelf of the bookcase as it disappeared from view.

An eerie silence filled the atrium.

The enormous room was once again bathed in the soft blue light of the street lamps outside.

Parker looked back from the bookshelf, saw the carpet of loose paper spread out on the floor before her. In the silence, she could hear herself breathing heavily.

'*Salve, moriturum es!*'

A voice—a deep, baritone voice.

Echoing loudly in the atrium.

Parker's head snapped up. It had come from the silhouetted man.

'*Salve, moriturum es!*' he repeated, loudly. His face was again masked by blackness, shadowed by the blue light behind him. Parker couldn't even see his lips move.

She heard the words. *Salve moriturum es.* They sounded vaguely familiar, like something she had learned at school, something that she had long since forgotten . . .

The big man took a step toward her. A glint of gold flashed off his dark shadowed chest.

Now she could see the small white lump on his shoulder quite clearly. It was a man all right, a small man, held in a fireman's carry over the horned man's shoulder. The little man groaned as the tall horned man moved toward the Information Desk.

Behind the counter of the desk, Parker leaned back, and slowly—silently—eased her Glock 20 semi-automatic pistol from its holster.

The tall man spoke.

'Greetings, fellow competitor. Before you stands Bellos. Great-grandson of Trome, the winner of the Fifth Presidian. And like his great-grandfather and two Malonians before him, Bellos shall emerge from this battle alone, conquered by none and not undone by the Karanadon. Who be'st thou, my worthy and yet unfortunate opponent?'

There was silence as the man waited for an answer.

Parker heard a soft, insistent scraping sound from the bookshelves to her left. It sounded like long fingernails moving quickly back and forth on a blackboard. She turned back to face him.

The man—Bellos—was looking at her, examining her, up and down, right and left.

Parker swallowed. 'I don't—'

'Where is your guide?' the deep baritone voice suddenly interjected. A demand, not a question.

'My guide?' Parker's face displayed her incomprehension.

'Yes,' Bellos said. 'Your guide. How will you confirm any conquest without a guide?'

Beneath the counter, Parker's hand gripped her gun tightly. 'I have no guide,' she said coolly.

The big man cocked his head, his sharp horns tilting to the side. Parker watched him carefully as he pondered over her comment for a moment. He glanced down at the large metal band attached to his wrist. It had a green light on it . . .

The scraping sound behind the bookshelf got faster, more intense.

Impatient.

Bellos looked up from his wristband and levelled his eyes at Parker.

'You are not a contestant in the Presidian, are you?'

He looked at the wide atrium around him, at the bookshelves to his left and right. Then he looked back at Parker, a glint of menace in his eyes.

'Good,' Bellos said, smiling. '*Kataya!*'

The attack came from Parker's left. From the bookshelves.

The creature sprang forward, leaping at the counter

of the Information Desk with frightening speed. It hit the counter hard, grabbing the edge with two vicious-looking foreclaws, baring twin rows of long, razor-sharp teeth, squealing a loud reptilian squeal.

Parker reeled back in horror, staring in shocked disbelief at the creature before her.

It was the size of a large dog, about four feet tall, with hard scaly skin that was gunmetal black in colour. It had four bony-but-muscular limbs and a long, black scaled tail that slithered madly behind its body.

Stunned, Parker just stared at the creature as it struggled to climb over the counter.

Supported by a thin black neck, its head was totally bizarre. Two lifeless black eyes sat on either side of a round black skull, whose sole purpose it seemed was to accommodate the creature's enormous jaws.

The creature lashed out at Parker, clamping its pointed teeth down in front of her.

Parker pulled back from the counter, away from the creature, raised her gun—

—and then in a strange, flashing instant she saw the creature's limbs on the counter.

It was not struggling to climb over the counter anymore—*it was already there.*

It lashed out at her again. Missed again.

Parker was momentarily startled.

It wasn't even *trying* to get her. It was as if this creature were merely trying to keep her attention . . .

It was then that a second creature hit her from the side. Knocking the wind out of her, jolting the pistol from her hand.

Parker stumbled from the impact, catching a split-second glimpse of what had hit her—another creature, identical to the first.

A third creature charged her from behind, pitching her forward, face-first onto the ground. Parker rolled quickly onto her back and suddenly felt a heavy weight slam down onto her chest.

A loud reptilian squeal pierced her ears as two rows of long jagged teeth opened wide in front of her eyes.

It was standing on top of her!

Parker screamed as the creature slashed its long foreclaw across her stomach and ducked its head.

And as she lay on the floor, helpless to resist the slicing of the creatures' sharp teeth as all four of them began to feed on her belly, Officer Christine Parker suddenly remembered—quite irrationally—what the words '*Salve moriturum es*' meant.

They were Latin words—words similar to those spoken by Roman gladiators when they were presented to the cheering crowd before combat—'We who are about to die, salute you'.

However, as Parker sank to the floor, her strength fading, and the weight of the four creatures now pressing down heavily on her body, she realised that Bellos had changed the words slightly, changing the meaning.

'*Salve moriturum es*' meant: 'I salute you, *you* who are about to die.'

'I am not sure this is such a good idea,' Selexin said as he followed Swain and Holly through the fire door into the stairwell.

Swain peered down into the shaft, ignoring Selexin. Holly, however, turned to face the little man.

'If you're from another planet,' she said, 'how come you speak English so well?'

Selexin said, 'My native tongue is based of an alphabet comprised of seven hundred and sixty-two distinct symbols. With only twenty-six base letters to choose from, your language is exceedingly simple to learn apart from the dreadful idioms.'

'Oh.'

Swain continued to stare down the shaft.

'I was saying,' Selexin repeated for him, 'that I am not sure this is a very good idea. The chances of sequencing increase as more contestants enter the labyrinth.'

Swain was silent for a long moment.

'You're probably right,' he said, looking down into the dark shaft. Then he turned to face Selexin. 'But then again, if I'm going to be running for my life in this place, I don't want to be doing it in rooms and corridors that I don't know. At least if we look around, we might get to know where we can and can't run if we are followed. I sure as hell don't want to run into a dead end with some half-cocked killer behind me. And besides,' he shrugged, 'we might even find somewhere to hole up if we have to.'

'Hole up?'

'Yes, hole up. Hide,' Swain said. 'You know, escape. Maybe even just stay in the one place until everybody else has killed each other.'

'That is improbable,' Selexin said.

'Why is it improbable? Surely it must be the best way to survive this whole damn thing. We just hide away somewhere, let the others do the fighting and maybe they'll . . .'

Selexin wasn't listening. He was just standing there, staring at Swain, waiting for him to stop talking.

Swain said, 'What? What is it?'

Selexin cocked his head to one side. 'If you remember what I told you before, you will understand.'

'What? What did you tell me before?'

'As I have said from the beginning, only one contestant leaves the labyrinth. And if not one, none.'

Swain nodded. 'I remember. But how can that happen? If only one contestant is left in the maze, he's safe to find the exit and leave, because there's nothing left to kill him . . .'

Selexin did not answer.

Swain sighed, '. . . unless there's something else in here.'

Selexin nodded. 'That is right,' he said. 'The third element of the Presidian.'

'The *third* element?'

Selexin stepped back into the study hall and sat

down at one of the L-shaped desks. Swain and Holly followed.

'Yes, an outside agent. A variable. Something that is capable of altering the conditions of combat instantly. Something that can turn victory into defeat, life into death. In the Presidian, the third element is a beast, a beast known throughout the galaxy as the Karanadon.'

Swain was silent.

'It is a most powerful beast, like no other,' Selexin said. 'As tall as the ceiling, as broad as three men, and as strong as twenty—and its considerable strength is only matched by its unbridled aggression—'

'Okay, okay,' Swain said, 'I think I get the picture. This thing, it's in here too, right? Trapped inside, like the rest of us?'

'Yes.'

'So what does it do? Does it just wander around killing whoever it pleases?'

Selexin said, 'Well, for one thing, it does not just wander around . . .'

Swain let out a breath in relief.

'. . . all of the time.'

Swain groaned.

'But if you will just look at your wristband for a moment,' Selexin said, 'I will explain everything.'

Swain looked down at the heavy grey band on his wrist. The display still read:

INCOMPLETE—4

'You will remember,' Selexin said, 'that when I gave you your wristband, I told you it would be of vital importance to you, yes? Well, it is more than that. Without it, you will not survive the Presidian.

'Your wristband serves many purposes, one of which is to identify you as a contestant in the Presidian. For example, you cannot win the Presidian unless you are wearing your wristband—you will simply be denied entry into the exit-teleport when it is opened. In the same way, other contestants will know that you are competing in the Presidian because they will see your wristband. This will protect you in the time before the Presidian commences—but it will also tell others that you are still a competitor who must be eliminated.

'However, in addition to this, your wristband provides several other, more important functions. First of all, as you have no doubt already noticed, there is a glowing green light on it. That light answers your previous question: no—the Karanadon does not just "wander" around. The green light you see indicates that the beast is at present dormant, nesting somewhere within the labyrinth. Or more simply, asleep. Wherefore, movement throughout the labyrinth is, at least for the moment, uninhibited by the Karanadon. Hence the green light.'

'The band can tell when it's asleep?' Swain said doubtfully.

'It is done through a device, surgically implanted in the beast's larynx, that electronically measures its rate of respiration. Respiration below a certain rate indicates sleep, respiration above—animation. That device, however, also provides some degree of control over the beast. It can, at official command, either secrete a sedative that will put the beast to sleep or inject a hormone that will rouse it immediately.'

'When would that happen?' Swain asked. 'When would you *want* it to wake up?'

'Why, when there is only one contestant left, of course,' Selexin said. 'Perhaps I can explain this another way. There have been six previous Presidia. Three have been won by Malonians, one by a Konda, and one by a Crisean.'

'Okay.'

Selexin stared at Swain. 'Well, that's it. That's the point.'

'What's the point?'

'There have been six Presidia, while there have been only five winners,' Selexin said.

The little man sighed. 'That is what I am trying to tell you. There may be *no* winner in the Presidian—unless one is worthy, none are worthy. There was no winner in the last Presidian, because the Karanadon killed all of the final three contestants when they happened upon its nest during combat. In the space of two minutes, the Presidian was over, due solely to the beast.'

'Oh.'

Selexin went on: 'And, as has always been the case, when only one contestant remains, and the exit-teleport to the labyrinth has been opened, the Karanadon is roused. One may choose to avoid it and search the labyrinth for the exit. Or one might attempt to kill it if he dares.'

Swain said, 'And has anybody ever done that before? Killed one?'

Selexin looked at Swain as though he had asked the most stupid question in the world.

'In a Presidian? No. Never. Not ever.' There was a short pause. Selexin moved on. 'But, anyway, as you will hopefully live to see later, when the beast is awake, the red light on your wristband will ignite.'

'Uh-huh. And this beast, this Karanadon, it was teleported into the library at the same time I was?'

'No,' Selexin said, 'the Karanadon is traditionally teleported into the labyrinth at least a day before the Presidian is to commence. But that does not really matter, because it would have been asleep all that time. Unless, of course, it was aroused. But that is unlikely.'

'I have one more question,' Swain said.

'Yes?'

'What if someone got out of this maze of yours? Now I know you think it can't happen, but what if it did? What happens then?'

'You credit me with a faith I do not possess. No, I accept your question quite easily, because it can happen. In fact, it *has* happened. Contestants have been known to be ejected from the labyrinth, either by design or by simple accident.'

'So what happens?'

'Again, it is your wristband that governs this situation,' Selexin said. 'As you know, an electric field covers this labyrinth. Your wristband operates in accordance with that field. If for some reason your wristband detects that it is no longer surrounded by the electric field, it automatically sets a timer for self-detonation.'

'A timer for self-detonation,' Swain said. 'You mean it explodes?'

'Not instantly. There is a time limit. You are allowed fifteen min—'

'Jesus Christ! You put a goddamn bomb on my wrist! Why didn't you tell me that before!' Swain couldn't believe it. It was incredible. He began to fiddle hurriedly with the wristband, trying to get it off.

'It won't come off,' Selexin said calmly. 'It *can't* come off, you waste your time even trying.'

'Shit,' Swain muttered, still grabbing at the solid metal band.

'Language,' Holly said, waving an admonishing finger at Swain.

'As I was saying,' Selexin said, 'if by some chance you are expelled from the labyrinth, you will have fifteen minutes to re-enter it. Otherwise, detonation will occur.'

He looked sadly at Swain, still fiddling with the wristband. Finally Swain gave up.

'You needn't worry,' Selexin said. 'Detonation will only occur upon expulsion from the labyrinth, and as I admit that it has happened before, I also add that it has not happened often. No-one gets out. Mr Swain, you must see now that whichever way you go there remains but one answer. Unless you leave this contest as the victor, you do not leave at all.'

Hawkins stood at the base of the stairwell, the beam of his flashlight the only light. There were no more stairs going down from here. Nothing but concrete walls and a large fire door that read: SUB-LEVEL 2.

Must be the bottom.

Hawkins moved cautiously over to the fire door. The handle turned easily and he slid the door open. He peered around the doorframe and instantly felt a rush of bile rise up the back of his throat. He turned back into the stairwell and vomited.

Several moments later, wiping his mouth and coughing to clear his throat, Hawkins looked back out through the doorway.

Aisles of bookcases stretched endlessly away from him, disappearing into darkness, beyond the reach of the mouldy overhead lights. But it was the aisle directly in front of him that seized his immediate attention.

The bookshelf to his left—twelve feet high and twenty feet long—had been wrenched free from its ceiling mounts and was now leaning backwards against the bookcase in the aisle behind it. Like two enormous dominoes: one upright, holding up its fallen neighbour.

The opposite bookshelf—to Hawkins' right—

remained upright. It simply had a gaping hole of splintered wood bored through its core. For some reason, books littered the aisle behind it, as though, Hawkins thought, something had—well—something had been hurled right *through* this bookshelf . . .

And then there was the aisle in between.

The flat pool of blood that filled the aisle had dried somewhat in the past twenty-four hours, but the stench still remained.

Of course, the body had been removed, but as Hawkins noticed, the sheer amount of blood was staggering. It lay everywhere—on the floor, on the ceiling, spattered all over the stairwell door. Those books that had remained on the shelves had been sprayed with flying blood. Those that had fallen to the floor had simply changed colour. They were maroon.

Hawkins swallowed as he saw the trail of smeared blood that stained the floor around the shelf with the hole in it. It looked as if someone had been dragged *around* the shelf, back into the original aisle.

By New York Police Department standards, Paul Hawkins was young. Twenty-four. And his youth, combined with his relative inexperience, had made him the obvious choice for baby-sit assignments like this one. Domestic violence protection, post-trauma custody, that sort of thing. He'd seen battered wives and beaten-up teenagers, but in sixteen months of duty, Paul Hawkins had never seen a murder scene.

He felt it odd that the first thing that struck him about the scene was how the movies got it all wrong. Even the most violent film could never successfully achieve the sheer *ugliness* of a murder scene. This was it, he thought, as he stared at the wide pool of dried blood before him.

It was ugly. Dirty and crude and brutal. Hawkins wanted to be sick again.

He looked up at the endless rows of bookshelves that lined Sub-Level Two.

Someone—something—is down here.

He lifted his flashlight. And then slowly, cautiously, he ventured out into the aisles.

'Daddy,' Holly said, following her father into the stairwell.

'In a second, honey,' Swain turned to Selexin. 'Are you sure there isn't anything else you should tell me about before we go any further? No more exploding devices?'

'Daddy.'

Selexin said, 'Well, there is one thing—'

'Dadd*ee*!'

Swain stopped. 'What is it, honey?'

Holly held up the telephone receiver, giving her most winning smile. 'It's for you.'

Swain bent down and took the dead phone. He spoke into it while looking at Holly. 'Hello? Oh hi, how are you?—Yeah?—Is that so?—Well, I'm kinda busy at the moment. Can I call you back? Great. Bye.' He gave the phone back to Holly. Satisfied, she grabbed Swain's hand and fell back into step with him and the egg man.

Selexin spoke quietly, 'Your daughter is really quite charming.'

'Thanks,' Swain said.

'But she provides far more risks to your safety than you should be willing to accommodate.'

'What?'

'I am merely suggesting that you might be better off

without her,' Selexin said. 'It might be wise for her to "hole up", as you say. Hide for the duration of the Presidian. If you survive, you will be able to come back for her. If, of course, you care for her that much.'

'Which I do.'

'And likewise,' Selexin went on, 'if you are defeated, she will not also be killed. In any case, to what efficiency can you aspire if you are defending her life as well as your own? An act to prevent her from injury might—'

'Might jeopardise my own life,' Swain said, 'and therefore jeopardise yours. This is my daughter. Where I go, she goes. *Not* negotiable.'

Selexin took a gentle step back.

'And another thing,' Swain said, 'if something does happen and we are separated, I expect *you* to look after her. Not to hole her up and hope nobody stumbles onto her, but to make sure that nothing—*nothing*—happens to her. Do you understand?'

Selexin bowed. 'I have been at error and I apologise with all my heart. I was unaware of your attachment to your child. In as much as I can, I will do my utmost to serve your wishes should such an eventuality occur.'

'Thank you. I appreciate that,' Swain said, nodding. 'Now, you were saying there was something else. Something I should know about.'

'Yes,' Selexin regathered himself. 'It pertains to combat, or rather, the end of any fighting. Whenever any contestant defeats another—either in combat or ambush or otherwise—the conquest must be confirmed.'

'Okay.'

'And that is my purpose,' Selexin said.

'You confirm a kill? Like a witness?' Swain asked.

'Not exactly. I am not the witness. But I do provide the window *for* the witness.'

'Window?'

Selexin stopped on the steps. He turned to Swain. 'Yes. And only at your command can the window be initialised. If you would be so kind, would you please say the word "Initialise".'

Swain cocked his head. 'Initialise? Why—'

And then it happened. A small sphere of brilliant white light—perhaps a foot in diameter—burst to life above Selexin's white skull cap, illuminating the entire stairwell around them.

'What is it?' Swain asked.

'It's coming from the egg—' Holly marvelled.

Selexin looked at Holly, somewhat surprised. 'Yes. You are correct. My rather odd-looking hat is the source of this teleport, small as it is. If you will, Mr Swain, please say "Cancel" lest my superiors believe you actually have killed somebody.'

'Oh, okay. Ah . . . cancel.'

The light disappeared instantly.

'You say it's a teleport. Like before?' Swain asked.

'Yes,' Selexin said, 'exactly the same as before— simply a hole in the air. Only much, much smaller, of course. There is merely another official like myself who is watching at the other end of this teleport. He is your witness.'

Swain looked at the white skull cap on Selexin's head. 'And it comes from that?'

'Yes.'

'Uh-huh,' Swain said, continuing down the stairs.

Selexin followed in silence. Finally he said, 'If I may be so bold as to inquire, where are we going?'

'Down,' Holly said, shaking her head. '*Derrr.*'

Selexin frowned, puzzled.

Swain shrugged. 'Like the lady said, down.'

He gave Holly a quick wink—masking his own very real fear—and she grinned back at him, reassured by the almost conspiratorial nature of the gesture.

They continued down the stairs.

The switchboard operator stared at the panel before her in stunned disbelief.

When is this going to stop? she thought.

On the switch in front of her, two rows of incessant flashing lights indicated that there were a hell of a lot of phone calls waiting to be answered.

She took a deep breath and pressed the flashing square that read '9', and began:

'Good evening, Con Edison Customer Service Line, my name is Sandy. How may I help you?'

Her headset rattled with the tinny voice of yet another disgruntled New Yorker. When finally it stopped, she punched the code—401—into her computer console.

That made fourteen in the last hour, on her panel alone. All coming from inside grid two-twelve— central Manhattan.

A 401—power out due to a probable short in the electrical main. The switchboard operator looked at the words on her computer screen: 'Probable short in the electrical main'. Electronically, she didn't know what a short in the main meant nor how it was caused. She simply knew all the symptoms of power cuts and failures and, in much the same way as a doctor identifies an illness, all she did was add up the symptoms and identify the problem. To know how it was caused was someone else's job.

She shrugged, leaned forward and pressed the next flashing square, ready to face the next complaint.

The lowest floor of the New York State Library is called the 'Stack'. It contains no toilets, no offices, no desks, and no computers. In fact, the Stack holds nothing but books, lots and lots of books.

Like other large libraries, the State Library of New York is less a borrowing library than it is an information library—chiefly computers, Internet, microfilm and CD-ROMs.

As far as actual books are concerned, only the more recent and popular are on display on the Ground Floor. If patrons seek other books, then they are to be found—by staff only—in the Stack, Sub-Level Two.

Wherefore, the Stack acts as little more than a holding pen for several million books.

Lots of books. In *lots* of bookshelves. And these bookshelves are arranged in a vast rectangular grid formation.

Twenty-two long rows of bookshelves stretch the length of the floor, while horizontal passageways cut across these longer rows at intervals of twenty feet—creating an enormous maze of right-angled twists and turns, blind corners, and long straight aisles that stretch away into infinity.

An enormous maze, thought NYPD Officer Paul Hawkins as he wandered through the Stack. *Wonderful*.

Hawkins had been wandering through the dusty aisles for several minutes now and had so far found nothing.

Damn it, he thought, as he turned back for the stairwe—

A soft noise.

From off to the right.

Hawkins' hand whipped to the automatic by his side. He listened intently.

There it was again.

A low, rasping sound.

Not breathing, he thought. No. More like . . . *sliding*. Like a broom sweeping slowly over a rough wooden floor. Like something *sliding* along the dusty floor of Sub-Level Two.

Hawkins drew his gun and listened again. It was definitely coming from the right, from somewhere within the maze of bookshelves around him. He swallowed.

There's someone in here.

He grabbed the radio on his belt.

'Parker!' he hissed. 'Parker! Do you copy?'

No answer.

Jesus.

'Parker, where are you?'

Hawkins switched off the radio and turned to look back at the receding rows of bookshelves before him. He pursed his lips for a moment.

Then he lifted his gun and ventured out into the maze.

Gun in hand, Hawkins quietly zig-zagged his way between the bookshelves, moving quickly and easily, searching for the source of the sound.

He came to a halt at the base of a bookcase full of dusty hardcovers. Held his breath for a moment. Waited . . .

There.

His eyes snapped left.

There it was again. The sweeping sound.

It was getting louder—he must be getting closer.

Hawkins darted left, then right, then left again—moving smoothly in and out of the aisles, stopping every few metres at the flat end of a bookcase. It was disorienting, he thought. Every aisle looked the same as the one before it.

He stopped again.

Listened.

Again, he heard the soft brushing sound. Like a broom on a dusty wooden floor.

Only louder now.

Close.

Very, very close.

Hawkins hurried on along a passageway that cut across the long vertical aisles of the Stack until suddenly he was confronted by a wall of bookshelves—a solid wall of bookshelves that seemed to stretch away into darkness in both directions.

A wall? Hawkins thought. He must be at the edge of the floor—at one of the long sides of the enormous rectangle.

The sound came again.

Only this time, it came from . . . behind him.

Hawkins spun, raised his gun.

What the hell—? Had it turned?

Cautiously, he edged his way down the alleyway of books.

The aisle closed in around him. The nearest cross-passageway branched away to his right—there was nothing but the unbroken wall of bookshelves to his left—about twenty feet away. It was cloaked in shadow.

Hawkins stepped forward slowly. The passageway came fully into view.

It was different.

It wasn't a T-junction, like the last one. More like an L-shape.

Hawkins frowned, and then he realised. It was a corner—the very corner of the floor. He hadn't realised that he'd come this far from the stairwell at the centre.

Listening.

Nothing.

He came to the L-junction and listened again. There was no sound.

Whatever it was, it was gone now.

And then Hawkins began to think. He'd followed the sound, the source of which had presumably been unaware of his presence. But its last few movements had been odd.

It was as though whoever it was had lost direction and had started circling . . .

Circling, Hawkins thought.

No-one would consciously go in a circle, would they, unless they were lost or . . . *or unless they knew someone was following them.*

Hawkins' blood went completely cold. Whoever it was, it wasn't just circling.

It was doubling back.

It knew he was here.

Hawkins spun to face the long aisle behind him, jamming his back into the corner shelving.

Nothing.

'Damn it!' he could feel the beads of cold sweat forming on his forehead. 'Damn it, shit!'

He couldn't believe it. He'd walked right into a corner. A goddamn corner! Two options—straight or left.

Shit, he thought, at least among the bookshelves he'd have had four. Now he was trapped.

And then suddenly he saw it.

Off to the left, moving slowly and carefully, out into the passageway.

Hawkins' eyes widened.

'*Holy* shit.'

It looked like nothing he had ever seen before.

Big and long, but low to the ground like an alligator, the creature looked almost dinosaurian—with black-green pebbled skin, four powerful stubby limbs and a long, thick counterbalancing tail.

Its head was truly odd. No eyes, and—seemingly— no mouth. The only distinguishing feature: a pair of long spindly antennae that jutted up from its forehead and clocked rhythmically from side to side.

It was twenty feet away from Hawkins when the tip of its tail finally came into view. The tail itself must have been eight feet long, and it slid across the floor in long, slow arcs, creating the soft sweeping sound. Hawkins saw that the tail tapered sharply to a point at its tip. The whole animal must have been at least fourteen feet long.

Hawkins blinked. For an instant there, behind the tail, he thought he caught a glimpse of a man, a small man, dressed completely in white—

And then the creature's head eased slowly upward—the folds of its skin peeling back to reveal a hideous four-sided jaw that opened with a soft, lethal hiss. Four rows of hideously jagged, saliva-covered teeth appeared.

'Jesus *Christ*,' Hawkins stared at the creature.

It moved forward.

Toward him.

One of the animal's forelegs caught his attention. A green light glowed from a thick grey band strapped to the creature's left forelimb.

It was close now—its jaws wide, salivating wildly, dripping goo all over the floor. Hawkins' eyes were locked on the swaying antennae on its head, clocking from side to side like a pair of metronomes.

It was three feet away . . .

Two feet . . .

Hawkins tensed to run, but for some terrifying reason, his legs wouldn't move. He tried to raise his gun, but couldn't—it was as if every muscle in his body had gone completely, instantly limp. He watched helplessly as, to his horror, his gun slipped from his unresponsive hand and dropped loudly to the floor.

The antennae kept swaying.

One foot . . .

Hawkins was sweating profusely, breathing in short, rapid breaths. He just couldn't take his eyes off them. The antennae. They seemed to move in perfect rhythm, swaying in smooth hypnotic circles . . .

He watched—completely defenceless—as the creature's sinister-looking head came slowly up to his knee.

Ohshit.Ohshit.Ohshit.

And then, suddenly, unexpectedly, like a cobra coiling up off the ground, the creature's long, pointed, eight-foot tail lifted off the floor and swung forward—over its low reptilian body—so that now it was pointing *forward*, arcing over its frame like a scorpion's stinger, the tip of the tail *pointing right at the bridge of Paul Hawkins' nose.*

Hawkins saw it happen and his terror hit fever pitch. He desperately wanted to shut his eyes, so he wouldn't see it happen, but he couldn't even do that—

'*Hey!*'

The creature's head snapped left.

And in an instant, the trance was broken and Hawkins could move again. He looked up and saw . . .

. . . *a man.*

A man, standing a short way down the aisle. Hawkins hadn't even seen him approach. Hadn't even heard him. Hawkins took in the man's appearance. He had wet hair, and was wearing jeans and sneakers and a white shirt that hung out at the waist.

The man spoke to Hawkins.

'Come over here. Now.'

Hawkins looked down warily at the big alligator-like creature at his feet. It ignored him completely, simply faced the man in jeans, its body dead still.

If it had eyes, Hawkins thought, it was definitely *glaring* at him. A low rumbling noise rose threateningly from the back of its throat.

Hawkins glanced back questioningly at the man. The man just kept his eyes levelled at him.

'Come on,' the man said calmly, eyes unmoving. 'Just leave the gun there and walk very slowly over to me.'

Tentatively, Hawkins took a step forward.

The creature at his knee didn't move. It remained steadfastly focused on the man in jeans.

The man pushed Hawkins behind him and slowly stepped backwards, away from the creature.

Hawkins looked down the aisle behind them and saw two figures standing maybe forty feet away—a small one in white, and another, equally small, who looked like . . . he squinted . . . like a little girl.

'Move,' Swain said, pushing Hawkins down the aisle, his back to him.

Swain kept his eyes up, focused on the book-shelves, *away* from the creature's swaying antennae, watching it only out of his peripheral vision.

The two men stepped slowly down the aisle, away from the frozen creature.

And then suddenly it began to follow them, moving around the corner in a darting crab-like manner that belied its size. Then it stopped.

Swain pushed Hawkins further down the aisle. 'Keep moving. Just keep moving.'

'What the—'

'Just *move*.'

Swain was walking backwards, still facing the creature. Again it made a darting, scuttling movement ten feet forward, and then stopped again, well short of Hawkins and himself

It's being cautious, he thought.

And then it charged.

'Oh, *shit!*'

The large animal bounded down the narrow confines of the aisle.

Swain looked frantically for somewhere to run. But he was still ten feet away from the nearest passageway into the maze of bookshelves.

There was nowhere to go!

Swain braced himself, the ground beneath him vibrating under the thumping weight of the fast-approaching creature. *Christ, it must weigh nearly four hundred pounds*.

Hawkins turned. He saw it over Swain's shoulder. '*Holy* Christ . . .'

Swain just stood there, feet spread wide, taking up the whole aisle.

The creature kept coming. It wasn't stopping.

'It's not stopping!' Hawkins yelled.

'*It has to!*' Swain called. '*It has to stop!*'

The creature bounded forward, bearing down on Swain like a runaway freight train, until abruptly, three feet short of him, it reared on its hind legs and clasped the bookcases on either side of it with its clawed forelimbs, bringing it to a sudden, lunging stop.

The four-sided jaw stopped just inches away from Swain's unmoving face.

The creature hissed fiercely, challenging him. Its saliva dripped down onto the floor in front of his shoes.

Swain averted his gaze, stared at a nearby bookshelf, keeping his eyes off the animal's oscillating antennae. The horrifying alligator-like creature, now standing up on its hind legs, towered over him, *looming* above him like an evil apparition.

Swain wagged an admonishing finger at the infuriated animal: 'Ah-ah-ah. No touching.'

And he began to walk backwards again, pushing Hawkins.

Hawkins stumbled down the aisle, looking back over his shoulder every few seconds. This time the creature didn't follow them, at least not immediately.

They reached the little white man and the girl, and were a good thirty feet from the creature when it began moving toward them again.

The little man spoke: 'Sequencing! She's sequencing!'

The man in the loose-fitting shirt and jeans looked at Hawkins, standing there in his well-pressed police uniform.

'We don't have time to talk right now, but my name is Stephen Swain, and at the moment we're all in big trouble. You ready to run?'

Hawkins answered without thinking. 'Yuh-huh.'

Swain looked back down the aisle at the large dinosaur-like creature. Twenty feet. He picked up Holly.

'You know the way back to the stairwell?' he asked Hawkins.

The young cop nodded.

'Then you lead the way. Just keep zig-zagging. We'll be right behind you.' He turned to the others. 'You two ready?' They nodded. 'Okay then, let's move.'

Hawkins broke into a run, the others close behind him.

With a great lunge, the creature leapt forward in pursuit.

Swain brought up the rear, carrying Holly on his hip. He could hear the pounding of the great weight on the floor behind him.

The stairs. The stairs. Got to reach the stairs.

Left, right, left, right.

He could see the cop weaving up ahead, and then finally, beyond the policeman, he saw the central stairwell block. But he couldn't see the doorway.

They were coming from the wrong side.

'Daddy! It's *catching up*!' Holly yelled from his shoulder.

He looked behind him.

The creature was indeed closing in on them—a giant black-green monster galloping down the narrow aisle with its salivating jaws bared wide.

Swain wasn't worried for himself. Selexin had been right about that. Whatever it was, it was another contestant, and it couldn't touch him. Not yet. Not until that number on his watch read '7'.

But if it got Holly . . .

He saw the cop round the central stairwell block up ahead, then Selexin. Swain rounded the concrete block last of all, panting hard.

The door!

He saw Selexin duck inside it, and then the policeman appeared in the doorway, his hand outstretched.

'Come on!' he was yelling.

Swain heard the creature slide around the corner behind him.

He kept running, kept holding Holly to his chest. He was breathing very heavily now. He was sure he was running too slowly. He could hear the creature's snorting grunts close behind him. Any second now it would be all over him, ready to pluck his daughter—the only family he had left—right from his very arms . . .

'*Come on!*' Hawkins called again.

Behind him, Swain heard the creature's tail slam against a bookcase, heard the sound of books crashing to the floor. Then suddenly, he was at the door and he reached for Hawkins' outstretched arms and Hawkins grabbed his hand and hurled him and Holly inside the stairwell just as Selexin slammed the door shut behind them.

Selexin turned, breathless, exhilarated. 'We made it—'

Bang!

The door behind him shuddered violently.

Swain lifted himself up from the floor, gasping for air. 'Come on.'

They were a whole floor up the stairwell when they heard the door to Sub-Level Two bang open with a loud bone-jarring *crack!*

Swain frowned at the wristband. He'd missed the arrival of the last two contestants. Now there was no knowing when the next—and last—contestant would enter the library.

No knowing when the Presidian would begin.

The group had left the stairwell and were now hiding in an office on Sub-Level One. Like all the others around it, this office was partitioned by waist-high wood panelling with glass reaching the rest of the way up to the ceiling. Everyone was careful to stay low, out of sight, below the glass.

Swain had found a directory of the library attached to the wall of the stairwell and wrenched it free. He was looking at it now while Selexin sat behind the desk, quietly explaining their situation to Hawkins. Holly was sitting on the floor nestled up to Swain, holding him tightly, sucking her thumb. She was still a little shell-shocked by their close encounter with the big creature downstairs.

The directory showed a cross-section of the library. Six floors—four above ground, two below—each a

106

different colour. The two sub-levels below the Ground Floor were both shaded grey and stamped with the label NO PUBLIC ACCESS. The others were brightly coloured:

THIRD FLOOR — STUDY HALL
SECOND FLOOR — READING ROOMS,
FUNCTION ROOMS,
COMPUTER SERVICES
FIRST FLOOR — ON-LINE SERVICES,
CD-ROMS, COPIERS,
MICROFILM
GROUND FLOOR — CATALOGUES,
CD-ROMS, REFERENCE

Swain remembered the study hall on the top floor with its odd-looking desks. He tried to memorise the rest. Small blue squares picturing a stick-man and woman indicated toilets on every other floor. Another blue square, with a car pictured in it, was tacked to the edge of Sub-Level One. The parking lot.

He checked his wristband again.

INCOMPLETE—6

Still '6'. Good.

He looked over at Selexin and the policeman, and shook his head in wonder.

That young cop was lucky to be alive. It had been only blind luck that had led Swain to his rescue—the instant when he, Holly and Selexin had been descending the stairs and seen a long shadow stretch out onto the landing below them.

They had watched from the shadows above as the

creature—Selexin said its name was Reese—stepped slowly into view, accompanied by its guide. It stopped on the landing, seemed to examine the floor with its snub dinosaur-like snout, and then peered down the stairwell.

Then it had slithered quickly down the stairs.

Something had caught its attention.

Curious, they had then followed it down into the Stack and seen it weave purposefully in and out of the bookshelves for several minutes—stalking something, leading it on. It was only at the last moment that Swain had ventured out into the furthermost aisle to actually see Reese's quarry—a lone policeman, trapped in the corner.

He'd moved instantly—stopping only for a piece of last-minute advice from Selexin: avoid all eye contact with Reese's antennae.

And so they had met Hawkins.

Swain turned to Selexin. 'Tell me more about Reese.'

'Reese?' Selexin said. 'Well, for one thing, Reese is, in human terms, female. Her tail tapers sharply to a point, like a spear. Males of her species possess only blunted tails. This is because in their clans, the female is the hunter, and her chief weapon is her sharp pointed tail.

'Didn't you see, when Reese was moving in on your new friend here,' Selexin nodded to Hawkins, 'that her tail was poised high over her body, in a large arc, pointing *forward*? And *he* couldn't move an inch.

'That is why I told you not to make prolonged eye contact with her antennae. Any extended visual contact with them will cause instant paralysis. Just like it did with him.' Selexin gave Hawkins a look. 'That is how Reese hunts. You look at her antennae for too long and you suffer hypnotic paralysis, and—*bang!*—before you know it, she's got you with that tail. Right between the eyes.'

The little man smiled. 'I would say she bears a rather strong resemblance to the female of your own species, aggressive *and* instinctive. Wouldn't you say?'

'*Hey*,' Holly said.

Swain ignored the remark. 'Tell me more about her hunting methods. Her stalking methods.'

Selexin took a breath. 'Well, as you no doubt noticed, Reese has no eyes. For the simple reason that she does not need them. She comes from a planet surrounded by opaque, inert gases. Light cannot enter their atmosphere, and the inert gases are impervious to any chemical change. Her race has simply adapted over time to utilise and enhance their other senses: increased auditory acuity, sensitive ampullae for detecting the distressed heartbeat of frightened or wounded prey, and, most of all, a highly evolved scent detection mechanism. In fact, I would say that her sense of smell is her most well-developed hunting tool.'

'Wait a second,' Swain said, alarmed, 'she can *smell* us?'

'Not now. Reese's sense of smell has a very limited range. No farther than, say, a couple of feet.'

Swain breathed in relief. Hawkins did, too.

'But *within* that range,' Selexin went on, 'her sense of smell is incredibly astute.'

'What do you mean?'

'I mean,' Selexin said, 'that the manner by which she detected *him*,'—Selexin pointed roughly to Hawkins—'was by his scent.'

'But I thought you said her range wasn't that good. How could—'

Swain cut himself off. Selexin was waiting for him again, giving him an expectant 'are-you-finished?' look.

'That is correct,' Selexin said, 'in a way. You see, Reese didn't smell *him*. What she smelled was the *scent* he left behind. Do you remember when Reese first came into our view in the stairwell? She bent low and sniffed the floor?'

Swain frowned. 'Yeah . . .'

'Footprints,' Selexin said. 'A trail not long cold. With any fresh trail like that, Reese doesn't *need* to smell anything beyond two feet, because she just follows the scent of the trail itself.'

'Oh,' Swain said.

And then it hit him.

'Oh, *shit!*'

He shot up to look out through the glass partition above him—

And found himself staring at Reese's menacing four-pronged jaws—wide open, foully salivating— pressed up against the other side of the glass, only inches away.

Swain fell backwards, stumbled away from the glass.

Hawkins leapt to his feet, mouth agape.

Reese slammed against the partition, smearing saliva everywhere.

'Eyes down!' Swain yelled, snatching Holly up in his arms. Reese rammed the partition again—hard— and the whole office shook. 'Keep your eyes away from the antennae! Go for the door!'

There were three glass doors to this square-shaped

office—one west, one south and one east. Reese was banging on the western wall of the room.

Swain ran for the eastern door, threw it open and charged into the next office, Selexin and Hawkins close behind him.

With Holly in the crook of his arm, he slid smoothly over a desk in the centre of the office, opened the next door.

'Close the doors behind you!' he yelled back.

'Already doing it!' Hawkins called forward.

And then, from behind them, there came a loud crashing sound—the sound of breaking glass.

Up ahead, Swain continued to run. Over desks, through doorways, dodging filing cabinets, sending paper flying everywhere. Then he came out of the last office and was suddenly faced with something different.

A heavy blue door set into a solid concrete wall.

Hawkins was yelling, 'She's *coming*! And she seems really *pissed off*!'

Swain looked at the heavy blue door. It looked strong, with a hydraulic opening mechanism. At the end of the short corridor to his right, he saw another option—a glassed-in elevator bay. He glanced back at Hawkins racing through the offices behind him.

Better do something . . .

With Holly still in his arms, Swain turned the knob on the hydraulic door. It opened.

Three concrete stairs. Going down.

He stepped through the doorway, pulled Selexin with him and waited for Hawkins. Hawkins was running hard, through the last glass-walled office.

Beyond Hawkins, Swain could see nothing but offices divided by glass partitions.

And then he saw it. Saw the long pointed tail flashing up above the waist-high wood panelling. It was barging through anything that lay in its path—like a great white shark's fin slicing through water—launching desks and filing cabinets and swivel chairs high into the air.

Two offices away and heading directly toward them.

Moving fast.

Closing in.

Hawkins ran past Swain, through the doorway, and Swain shut the big hydraulic door behind him. It closed with a dull thud.

Strong door. Good. It would give them some time.

Holding Holly, Swain took the lead again, heading down the three concrete stairs. White fluorescent lights lit a modern grey-painted corridor. Black piping snaked its way along the ceiling.

The four of them followed the winding corridor for about twenty yards before, suddenly, they burst into open space.

Swain stopped and took in the scene before him.

An underground parking lot.

It looked new—almost brand new, in fact. Glistening newly paved concrete, white-painted floor markings, shiny yellow wheel clamps on the ground, pristine white fluorescent lights. It was quite a contrast to the old dusty library they had seen so far.

Swain scanned the parking lot.

No cars.

Damn.

There was a Down ramp in the centre of the lot, about twenty yards in front of them. Swain figured that the Exit ramp going up to the street must be on the other side of the Down ramp.

There came a sudden, loud bang from somewhere behind them.

Swain spun.

Reese was through the door.

He quickly led the others to the Down ramp. It was wide—wide enough for two cars to pass each other side-by-side. They had just reached the top of the ramp when he heard a hissing sound from behind them.

Swain turned around slowly.

Reese was standing at the entrance to the parking lot, her guide positioned silently behind her.

Swain swallowed—

—and then, suddenly, he heard another sound.

Clop . . .

Clop . . .

Clop . . .

Footsteps. Slow footsteps. Echoing loudly in the deserted parking lot.

Swain, Holly, Selexin and Hawkins all spun at the same time and they saw him instantly.

Coming up the Down ramp.

Walking slowly, purposefully.

A six-foot bearded man, dressed in a broad-shouldered animal-skin jacket, dark pants and knee-high black boots that clip-clopped loudly on the concrete ramp.

And behind him, yet another guide, dressed completely in white.

As the big bearded man stepped onto level ground and stopped, Swain instinctively pushed Holly behind him.

At the sight of the new contestant, Reese became visibly agitated. She hissed even louder.

They all stood in silence—the three groups forming a precarious, unspeaking triangle.

It was then that Swain looked down at his wristband. It now read:

INITIALISED—7

Seven.
Swain looked up slowly.

The Presidian had begun.

THIRD MOVEMENT

30 November, 6:39 p.m.

The parking lot was silent.

Somewhere off to his left Swain could hear the drone of New York traffic, the honking of car horns. The sounds of the outside world—the ordinary world.

Selexin drew up beside him.

'Just keep looking forward,' Selexin was staring intently at the tall bearded man before them.

'He is Balthazar. The Crisean. Small-blade handler: knives, stilettos, that sort of thing. Technologically, the Criseans are not well-developed, but with their hunting skills, they don't need tech—'

Selexin cut himself off.

The bearded man was staring right at them. Looking directly at Swain.

Swain kept his eyes locked on Balthazar.

Just then the big man turned slightly, revealing something hanging from his waist. Something that glinted under the harsh electric light of the parking lot.

A blade.

A sweeping, curving, vicious-looking blade. An extra-terrestrial cutlass.

Swain lifted his gaze. A thick leather-like baldric hung over Balthazar's shoulder, attaching itself to the belt at his waist. Fastened to the leather strap were various sheaths and scabbards—and in them, a whole assortment of lethal throwing knives.

'You see them?' Selexin whispered.

'I see them.'

'Criseans,' Selexin said respectfully. 'Very impressive bladesmen. Very quick, too. Fast. Take your eyes off him for a second and before you know it, you'll have a knife lodged in your heart.'

Swain didn't answer. Selexin turned to him.

'Sorry,' he whispered. 'I shouldn't have said that.'

'Daddy . . .' Holly said. 'What's happening?'

'We're just waiting, honey.'

With one eye on Balthazar, Swain scanned the parking lot. Looking for something . . . looking for a way out . . .

There.

In the south-west corner of the lot, maybe twenty yards away from them—a pair of elevators, encased inside a brightly lit glass-walled foyer. It was the same elevator bay he had seen earlier, only here it opened out onto the parking lot.

Swain handed Holly to Hawkins, at the same time as he pulled Hawkins' heavy police flashlight from his gunbelt.

'Whatever happens here,' Swain said, 'I want you to run as fast as you can to those elevators over there, okay?'

'Okay.'

'Once you're inside and the doors are shut, let it go halfway up a floor and press the Emergency Stop button. Okay?'

Hawkins nodded.

'You should be safe there,' Swain said, rolling the

big flashlight over in his hand. 'I don't think they'll have figured out how to use elevators yet.'

Beside them, Selexin was watching the other two contestants warily. 'What happens now?' Swain asked him.

At first there was no reply. The little man just stared intently at the empty carpark. And then, without turning his head, Selexin said, 'Anything.'

Reese moved first. Darting towards Swain. Heavy, bounding steps.

Swain felt adrenalin surge through his body. He swallowed, gripped the flashlight tightly.

Reese kept coming.

Christ, Swain thought, *how the hell do you fight a thing like that?*

He tensed to run, but suddenly Selexin grabbed his arm. '*Don't*,' he whispered. 'Not yet.'

'Wha—?' Swain watched Reese charge toward them.

'Trust me,' Selexin's voice was like ice.

Reese was *bounding* toward them now. Swain wanted desperately to run. Out of the corner of his eye he saw Balthazar slowly unsheath a pair of throwing knives—

And then Reese turned.

Sharply and unexpectedly. *Away* from Swain and the group.

Toward Balthazar.

'Ha! She had to,' Selexin whispered proudly. 'Had to. Classic huntsman behaviour . . .'

Then suddenly, in a blur of motion, Swain saw Balthazar's right arm move in a rapid throwing action—and abruptly two flashes of silver fanned out from his hand, whistling through the air.

Thud!

A glinting steel throwing knife embedded itself in the *concrete* pillar between Swain and Hawkins, missing them both by inches!

The second futuristic-looking knife was intended for Reese, but unlike Swain, she was ready for it. Running low and fast, she rolled right when she detected the flying blade coming toward her and—*crack!*—the throwing knife, flying downward, lodged in the floor of the parking lot underneath her, cracking the shiny new concrete, standing almost upright.

Selexin was still praising his tactical decision. 'I tell you, classic huntsman behaviour. You take out the more dangerous prey first, catch it off-guard—'

'Tell me about it later,' Swain said as he glanced over his shoulder to see Reese—shrieking wildly—slam into Balthazar, toppling him over backwards.

Swain pushed Hawkins toward the elevator bay. 'Go!'

Hawkins took off, holding Holly close to his chest, running straight for the elevators.

Swain was about to follow them when he turned for a final look at the battle behind him.

Reese had Balthazar pinned to the ground beneath her, jamming his hands down beneath her powerful stubby forelimbs. Balthazar was struggling desperately, reaching for his cutlass on the floor, inches out of his reach.

But the weight was too much.

Reese's jaws were salivating wildly above his head, the saliva gushing in heavy torrents all over Balthazar's face. And then Reese began to slash at him with her foreclaws—vicious sweeping slashes that drew whole chunks of flesh from Balthazar's chest.

It was disgusting, Swain thought. Disgusting, violent and brutal.

He watched in horror as Balthazar shook his head rapidly from side to side, screaming in pain trying to avoid eye contact with Reese's swaying antennae, trying to get his head clear of the blinding saliva, while at the same time feebly attempting to fend off her savage blows. It was *desperation*. The total and utter desperation of a man fighting for his very life.

And Stephen Swain felt angry. Indignant and furious at the whole scene in front of him.

He spun quickly to see Hawkins and Holly reach the glassed-in elevator bay and enter it. Hawkins quickly pressed the UP button on the wall. Neither of the two elevators opened immediately. The lifts were on the way.

They'd be safe.

Swain turned back to face the battle, the anger welling up inside him. Balthazar was still struggling, swishing his head from side to side, his cries of pain drowned out by the saliva gushing down into his screaming mouth. Reese was still firmly on top of him, violently slashing, squealing maniacally.

And then Swain saw Reese's tail rise. Slowly and silently behind her, like an enormous scorpion, out of Balthazar's view.

And with that, Swain knew what he had to do.

He ran.

Straight at them.

Reese's tail was poised now, arcing high over her head . . . ready to strike . . . and then Balthazar saw it too and he began to scream . . .

With Hawkins' heavy police flashlight in front of him, Swain slammed into Reese, knocking her off Balthazar, sending all three of them sprawling onto the concrete floor.

Reese fell onto her back and Swain tumbled on top of her. She let out an ear-piercing shriek as her body writhed about on the concrete, bucking and kicking, trying desperately to throw Swain clear.

Swain's grip on her slipped and suddenly he was in mid-air and all he could see was a kaleidoscope of grey walls, white fluorescent light and concrete pavement. He hit the floor hard, chest-first, and rolled onto his back—

—only to see Reese's sharp tail rushing toward his face!

Swain swerved his head left and the tail hit the concrete with a loud thud.

Swain glanced quickly at the spot where his head had been. Broken chunks of cement surrounded a small crater the size of a tennis ball in the concrete floor.

Jesus Christ.

Swain was still on the floor, rolling fast. Reese was crab-walking next to him, moving equally fast, banging her tail down like a piledriver.

The tail came crashing down again, *right next to Swain's head*.

In the nanoseconds of time in which the mind operates, Swain tried to weigh up his options. He couldn't run. There was no way he could get up and clear in time. And he couldn't *fight* Reese. Christ, if a warrior like Balthazar couldn't beat her, how the hell could he?

No, somehow he had to get out of here. But to do that, he had to do something that would buy him enough time to get clear.

And so Swain did the only thing he could think to do.

With all his strength he swung Hawkins' heavy police flashlight—baseball-style—at Reese's tail, planted in the concrete.

He aimed for the tip of the tail, the thinnest part, from the side.

The flashlight hit its mark—hard—impacting against the tapered tip of the tail. There was a loud, blood-curdling *snap!* of breaking bone as the tail bent instantly and Reese roared in agony, instantly pulling away from Swain.

Swain seized the chance.

He leapt to his feet and looked over at the two elevators inside the glass-walled foyer. The doors to the left-hand elevator were opening and Hawkins, carrying Holly, was getting inside, looking back questioningly at Swain with every step.

'Go! *Go!*' Swain yelled. 'I'll catch up!'

Hawkins ducked inside the elevator and hit a button and the elevator doors closed. Swain swung back to the fight.

Reese had backed off several steps, consumed with her broken tail. Balthazar was now rising unsteadily to his feet, his head bent as he tried to clear the saliva from his eyes.

Swain stumbled over to Balthazar. The big man's eyes were still covered in gooey saliva, the exposed skin on his chest horribly shredded and caked in thick blood, his face locked in a grimace of extreme pain.

Swain grabbed his arm and simply said, 'Come with me.'

Balthazar said nothing, merely allowed Swain to

take his arm and pull him away. Swain looped the big man's arm over his shoulder and helped him towards the elevators.

Selexin just stood there, gaping at Swain in utter amazement.

'You coming?' Swain said as he dragged Balthazar past the little man.

Stunned, Selexin looked from Swain to Balthazar's guide—who just shrugged uncomprehendingly—then to Reese, and then finally to the elevators. Then he hurried after Swain.

Swain burst into the glass-walled elevator bay, hit the UP button. Balthazar was still draped over his shoulder, his guide right behind him. Swain spun to see Reese banging her tail on the concrete floor. Two loud bangs were followed by a third that emitted a sickening cracking sound.

Reese roared savagely and Swain knew at once what that meant. She had straightened the fracture. Once she was over the instant pain she would be moving again—

Reese was moving again. Toward the elevator.

Swain jammed his finger down on the UP button. 'Come on! Come on!'

Reese was darting left and right, scuttling in a crablike manner across the wide parking lot floor, coming closer . . .

She stopped. Fifteen yards away from the elevator bay.

Swain noticed that this time her tail didn't swish menacingly back and forth behind her. It just sat there, limp on the floor, motionless.

Reese hissed softly in the silence of the parking lot, her antennae swaying hypnotically above her head.

Swain watched her through the glass walls of the elevator bay, entranced.

Selexin shoved him hard, jolting him sideways. '*Don't* look at the antennae!'

Swain blinked back to his senses. He couldn't even *remember* looking at the antennae . . .

There was a loud *bing* from behind him and he spun to see the second elevator's doors grinding open.

'Everybody inside,' he said, suddenly back to life, hurling Balthazar into the lift. Once inside, he hurriedly pressed '1' and then DOOR CLOSE.

Nothing happened.

Swain looked out and saw Reese bounding toward the glass elevator bay.

He pressed DOOR CLOSE repeatedly.

The doors remained open.

Reese was getting closer, charging.

Suddenly there was a click and the elevator doors slowly began to close.

Smash!

Glass exploded everywhere as Reese burst through the clear glass door of the elevator bay. She landed clumsily inside the small foyer, sliding across the floor on a carpet of tiny glass fragments, sprawled out on all four legs.

The doors were inching closer.

And then, to Swain's horror, Reese slid to a halt *right in front of the elevator* and started getting to her feet.

The doors kept closing. Reese was on her feet again. The doors were almost joined. Reese tensed herself to leap—

And the doors joined.

And the lift began to move upward.

Swain exhaled with relief.

And then with all her weight Reese hit the exterior doors.

Hard and loud. Denting the doors inward, tearing them apart at the centre, shaking the whole elevator and *stopping* it with a loud scraping lurch.

Two feet above the ground.

The lift rocked. Selexin clutched at Swain's leg for balance. Balthazar sat in the rear corner, head bent, body limp, swaying with the elevator's movement.

Swain regained his balance and saw the doors, pushed inward, creating a gap one foot wide at the centre.

Too narrow, he thought. *She can't get in.*

Reese rammed the doors again.

The elevator shook. The gap widened.

Swain pressed the UP button on the panel, but the elevator still didn't move. The large inward dent in the doors was keeping them from closing, and the lift wouldn't move again until they were shut.

Reese now had her snout and antennae inside the elevator doors. She was snapping her jaws ferociously from side to side, flinging saliva everywhere, desperately trying to force the doors open—her antennae slicing through the air like twin whips.

Swain tightened his grip on Hawkins' flashlight and stepped toward her.

Suddenly Reese surged forward, rocking the elevator. Swain fell, slipping on the wet floor, falling backwards, the flashlight flying from his hand into the corner of the lift. He looked up to see Reese lunging ferociously at his feet, snapping wildly, held back by the doors—saw the frenzied, salivating jaws, the four sets of bared, jagged teeth only inches away from his feet. About to—

Swain turned his eyes clear, took a deep breath and in a flashing instant thought, *I can't believe I am going to do this*. Then he kicked hard, landing the sole of his shoe squarely on Reese's front teeth, breaking three instantly.

Reese recoiled, shrieking fiercely as she fell backwards onto the floor below.

Swain kicked again, this time at the doors, in a vain attempt to straighten the large inward dents. He gave them three hammering blows, but barely made an impression. The doors were double-strength, too strong.

And then suddenly—*whack!*—a giant leather boot came crashing down on the battered doors, and the dents straightened markedly.

It was Balthazar!

He had slid over to where Swain was lying and, despite his injuries, had unleashed a powerful kick of his own at the doors.

Whack! Whack!

Two more thunderous blows and the dents straightened fully and the doors eased shut and Balthazar fell to the floor in exhaustion and the elevator lifted and at last, there was silence.

'Grid two-twelve,' the assistant said, reading from his clipboard. 'The area bounded by 14th Street and Delancey on the north–south axis. Medium rise zone: standard commercial–residential area, couple of buildings on the National Register, a few parks. Nothing special.'

Robert K. Charlton sat back in his chair.

'Nothing special,' he said. 'Nothing special, except that in the last couple of hours, we've had over *a hundred and eighty* complaints from an area that hardly ever says boo.'

He handed a sheet of paper over his desk to his assistant.

'Take a look at that. It's from the switch. One girl down there has had—what is it now?—fifty-one, no, fifty-two probable 401s on her own. All from two-twelve.'

Slightly overweight, 54 years old, and a man who had spent *way* too much time in the same job, Bob Charlton was the evening watch supervisor for Consolidated Edison, the city's main electricity supplier. His office was situated one floor above Con Ed's switchboard and it was hardly ostentatious. It comprised a wraparound Ikea desk—with a computer on it—surrounded by that beige-coloured shelving common to middle-management offices the world over.

'And do you know what that means?' Charlton asked.

'What?' his assistant said. His name was Rudy.

'It means that somebody has got to the main,' Charlton said. 'Cut it off. Shut it down. Or maybe even overloaded it. Shit. Run down to Dispatch and see if any of our guys were down in that grid today. I'll give the cops a call, see if they've found any punks cutting cables.'

'Yes, sir.'

Rudy left the room.

Charlton swung around in his swivel chair to face a map of Manhattan Island he had pinned to the wall behind his desk.

To Charlton, Manhattan looked like a warped diamond—three perfectly straight sides, with one side, the north-eastern, jagged and twisted. Electrical grids stretched across the island's breadth like lines on a football field.

He found the horizontal rectangle that displayed grid two-twelve. It was down near the southern end of the island, a few miles north of the World Trade Centre.

He thought about the report.

Medium rise zone. Standard commercial–residential area, couple of buildings on the National Register. A few parks.

The National Register.

The National Register of Historic Places.

He thought about that. Lately Con Ed had been bullied by the Mayor's Office into linking up some of the older buildings of the city to the new mains. Not surprisingly, there had been a truckload of problems. Some of the older buildings had circuitry dating back before the First World War, others didn't even have circuitry. Linking them up had been unusually difficult and it wasn't uncommon for one building's overload to screw up the networking for an entire city grid.

Charlton flicked on his computer and called up the file on the National Register. It wouldn't have *all* the historically protected buildings in the city, only the ones that Con Ed had worked on. That would be good enough.

He called up grid two-twelve. There were five hits. He pressed DISPLAY.

The screen scrolled out a more detailed list of names and Charlton was leaning forward to read them when the phone rang.

'Charlton.'

'Sir, it's me.' It was Rudy.

'Yes?'

'I'm down in Dispatch, and they say that none of their guys has been in two-twelve for nearly three weeks.'

Charlton frowned. 'You sure?'

'They've got records on disk if you want them.'

'No, that will be fine. Well done, Rudy.'

'Thank you, si—'

Charlton hung up.

'Damn.'

He was hoping it had been someone from Dispatch. At least then it would have been traceable. There would be a record of where the break—or shutdown, or overload—in the main was. A record of where the work had been done.

Now there was no knowing where the break was. Other shorts could be detected with Con Ed's computers, tracing every line. But for that you needed the main to be on-line.

But with the main down in a particular grid, that grid became a black hole as far as computer tracing was concerned. And the break lay somewhere within that black hole.

Now it was guesswork.

Charlton swore. The first thing to do was call the police. See if they had pulled in someone in the last twenty-four hours hacking at the cables somewhere. Anything like that.

He sighed. It was going to be a long night. He picked up the phone and dialled.

'Good evening, this is Bob Charlton, I'm the evening watch supervisor down here at Consolidated Edison. I'd like to speak with Lieutenant Peters, please. Yes, I'll hold.'

As he waited on hold, Charlton looked idly back at the map of Manhattan Island. Soon his call was put through and he turned away from the map altogether.

All the while the computer screen on his desk remained on.

And for the whole time he was on the phone, Bob Charlton never noticed the last line of the list of historic buildings on the screen. The line read:

GRID 212: LISTING No. 5
NEW YORK STATE LIBRARY (1897)
CONNECTED TO NETWORK: 17 FEBRUARY 1995

After a few moments, Charlton said excitedly, 'You *did*—when? I'll be down there in twenty minutes.'

Then he hung up, grabbed his coat and quickly left his office.

A few seconds later, he returned and leaned across his desk.

And switched off his computer.

Swain pressed the red EMERGENCY STOP button and the elevator creaked loudly to a halt. He reached up for the hatch in the ceiling.

Balthazar, his energy now completely spent after repairing the elevator doors, sat propped up against the corner of the lift, his head bowed, groaning. His guide stood unsympathetically beside him, glaring at Selexin.

Swain was opening the hatch in the ceiling of the elevator when the other guide spoke. 'Come on, Selexin, get on with it.' He nodded at Balthazar. 'Finish it.'

Swain stopped what he was doing and turned to face the others.

Selexin said, 'That is not for me to decide. You of all people know that.'

The other guide spun to face Swain. '*Well?* Look at him'—a jerk toward Balthazar in the corner—'he cannot fight anymore. He cannot even defend himself. Finish it. Finish it now. Our fight is over.'

Swain swallowed. The little guide possessed an unusual strength in his defiance—the strength of a man who knows he is about to die.

'Yes,' Swain said slowly to himself. 'Yes.'

He looked again at Balthazar. It was only then that he noticed just how big the bearded man was. Not six foot. More like six-eight. But that didn't seem to matter now.

Balthazar lifted his head and stared up at Swain. His eyes were severely bloodshot, red-rimmed; his chest ripped to shreds.

Swain took a slow step forward and stood over him.

Selexin must have noticed his hesitation. 'You must,' he said, softly. 'You have to.'

Balthazar never took his eyes off Swain. The big bearded man took a deep breath as Swain reached down and slowly—very slowly—unsheathed one of the long daggers from the baldric draped across his chest. The dagger hissed against the sheath as Swain pulled it out.

Balthazar shut his eyes, resigned to his fate, unable to offer any defence.

Knife in hand, Swain shot a final questioning glance at Selexin. The little man nodded solemnly.

Swain turned back to Balthazar, lowered the knife, pointed it at the big man's heart. And then he did it.

He slid the blade gently back into its sheath.

And then he stepped away, back toward the hatch in the ceiling of the elevator, back to what he'd been doing.

Balthazar's eyes opened, puzzled.

Selexin rolled his eyes.

The other guide was simply thunderstruck. He said to Selexin, 'He can't do that.' Then to Swain, who was back at the ceiling, tossing open the hatch, 'You can't do that.'

'I just did,' Swain said. The hatch banged open.

He turned, not looking at the other guide, but rather, straight at Selexin. 'Because that's not what I do.'

With that, Swain grabbed Hawkins' police flashlight and poked his head up through the open hatch. He had something else on his mind.

He peered up into the dark elevator shaft, flicking on the flashlight. He was hoping that Hawkins had done what he had told him to do.

He had.

The other elevator lay right there, only a few feet away, right alongside Swain's elevator, halted halfway between this floor and the one above. Swain aimed the beam of the flashlight up into the shaft. Greasy cables stretched up into the darkness. The doors to the next floor were about eight feet above him. On them were written the black-painted words: GROUND FLOOR.

The shaft was silent.

The other elevator sat still, perhaps a foot above Swain's, a small slit of yellow light betraying a crack in its side panelling.

'Holly? Hawkins?' Swain whispered.

He heard Holly's voice—'Daddy!'—and he felt a wave of relief wash over him.

'We're here, sir,' Hawkins' voice said. 'Are you all right?'

'We're fine here. How about you two?'

'We're okay. Want us to come over?'

'No. You stay where you are,' Swain said. 'Our elevator has taken a beating, the doors are busted. They probably won't open again, so we'll come over there. See if you can open the hatch in the roof.'

'Okay.'

Swain dropped back into his elevator and surveyed the group around him—Balthazar and the two guides. Hmmm.

'All right, everyone, listen up. We're all going over to the other elevator. I want you two little guys to go first. I'll handle the big fella. Got it?'

Selexin nodded. The other guide just stood there, his arms folded defiantly.

Swain scooped up Selexin and held him up to the hatch. The little man disappeared into the darkness.

Swain poked his head up through the hatch after him and saw Selexin step up onto the roof of the other elevator. A weak haze of yellow light appeared above the other lift. Hawkins must have opened the hatch.

Swain motioned to the other guide. 'Your turn.'

The guide looked cautiously at Balthazar, then said something in a grunting guttural language.

Balthazar responded with a dismissive wave and grunt.

As a result, the guide reluctantly offered his arms to Swain, who duly lifted him up through the hatch. The guide disappeared into the shaft.

Swain turned back to face Balthazar.

The big man was still sitting slumped in the corner. Slowly, he looked up at Swain.

Whatever he was, Swain thought, he was badly injured. His eyes were red, his hands bloodied and scratched. Some of Reese's saliva still bubbled on his beard.

Swain spoke gently, 'I don't want to kill you. I want to help you.'

Balthazar cocked his head, not understanding.

'Help,' Swain held out his hands, palms up—a gesture of aid, not attack.

Balthazar spoke—softly—in his strange guttural tongue.

Swain didn't understand. He offered his hands again.

'Help,' he repeated.

Balthazar frowned at the communication breakdown. He reached down for the long dagger Swain had held before, now back in its sheath across his chest.

He pulled it out.

Swain stood dead still—unflinching—staring Balthazar squarely in the eye.

He can't do that. He can't.

The bearded man reversed the knife in his hand, and placed the handle in Swain's palm. Swain felt the warmth of Balthazar's hand as they both gripped the knife—pointed at Balthazar's chest.

Balthazar then pulled their hands toward his chest. Swain didn't know what to do, except allow Balthazar to pull the glistening blade closer, and closer, and closer to his body . . .

And then Balthazar guided their hands sideways, sliding the knife back into its sheath.

As Swain had done before.

He looked up at Swain, his eyes bulging red, and nodded.

And then Balthazar spoke again—slowly, deep-throated—trying to get his mouth around the word Swain had just used.

'Help.'

The elevator doors rumbled open and Stephen Swain peered out to see the First Floor of the State Library.

Dark and quiet.

Empty.

The first thing Swain noticed about the First Floor was the peculiar way it had been arranged: it was an enormous U-shape, with a wide gaping hole in the centre, so that one could look down onto the Ground Floor atrium.

Clearly, the floorspace of this floor had been sacrificed to provide for a grander, higher ceilinged Ground Floor—in the process, making the First Floor of the State Library little more than a glorified balcony. A mezzanine.

The elevators themselves stood at the south-east corner of the floor, to the right of the curved base of the U-shape. Opposite them—at the open-end of the U—stood the enormous glass doors of the library's main entrance.

Off to his left, Swain saw a room filled with photocopiers. A door at the far end of the room had INTERNET FACILITY stamped on it. The rest of the floor was deserted and dark, save for the blue streams of reflected city light that penetrated the enormous glass doors and windows way over at the other end.

Swain pulled Balthazar out of the lift and dragged him over to the hand-railing overlooking the Ground Floor. He was propping the big man up against the railing when the others joined them.

'What do we do about that?' Hawkins said, indicating the open elevator behind them. He spoke softly in the darkness.

'Turn the light off,' Swain whispered. 'If you can't find the switch, just unscrew the fluorescent tube. Apart from that,' he shrugged, 'I don't know, leave it there. As long as it's here, nobody else can use it.'

As Hawkins headed back toward the elevator, Swain saw Selexin draw up alongside him. The little man was peering cautiously up at the ceiling all around them.

'What are you doing?' Swain asked.

Selexin sighed dramatically: 'Not all the creatures in this universe walk on *floors*, Mister Swain.'

'Oh.'

'I am looking for a contestant known as the Rachnid. It is a trap-laying species—large and spindly, but not particularly athletic—known for lying in wait in elevated caves and hollows for long periods of time, waiting for its prey to step underneath it. It then lowers itself silently to the floor behind its victim, clutches it within its eight limbs, and constricts it to death.'

'Constricts it to death,' Swain said, glancing nervously up at the uneven shadow-covered ceiling above him. 'Nice. Very nice.'

'Daddy?' Holly whispered.

'Yes, honey.'

'I'm scared.'

'Me too,' Swain said softly.

Holly touched his left cheek. 'Are you all right, Daddy?'

Swain looked at her finger. It had blood on it.

He dabbed at his cheek. It felt like a cut, a big one, running down the length of his cheekbone. He looked down at his collar and saw a large red stain on it—a lot of blood had been running down his face.

When had that happened? He hadn't felt it. And he certainly didn't remember feeling the sting of being cut. Maybe it was when he was thrown on top of Reese, after bowling her over. Or when Reese was bucking and kicking like a mad horse. Swain frowned. It was a blur. He couldn't remember.

'Yeah, I'm okay,' he said.

Holly nodded at Balthazar, up against the steel railing. 'What about him?'

'Actually, I was just about to check,' Swain said, getting up onto his knees, hovering over Balthazar. 'Could you hold this for me?' he offered Holly the heavy police flashlight.

Holly flicked on the torch and held it over Swain's shoulder, pointed at Balthazar's face.

The big man winced at the light. Swain leaned forward, 'No, no, don't shut your eyes,' he said gently. He held Balthazar's left eye open. It was heavily bloodshot, reacting badly to Reese's saliva.

'Could you bring the light in a bit closer . . .'

Holly stepped forward and as the light came nearer, Swain saw Balthazar's pupil dilate.

Swain leaned back. That wasn't right . . .

His eyes swept over Balthazar's body. Everything about him suggested that he was human—limbs, fingers, facial features. He even had brown eyes.

The eyes, Swain thought.

It was the eyes that were wrong. Their reaction to the light.

Human pupils *contract* when hit by direct light. They dilate—or widen—in darkness or poor light, so as to allow as much light as possible onto the retina. These eyes, however, dilated in the face of brighter light.

They were not human eyes.

Swain turned to Selexin. 'He looks human, and he acts human. But he's not human at all, is he?'

Selexin nodded, impressed. 'No, he is not. Almost, though—in fact, as close as he can be. But no, Balthazar is definitely not human.'

'Then what is he?'

'I told you before, Balthazar is a Crisean. An excellent blade-handler.'

'But why does he look human?' Swain asked. 'The chances of some alien from another world evolving to look exactly like man would have to be a million to one.'

'A billion to one,' Selexin corrected him. 'And please, try not to use the term "alien" *too* liberally. Such a harsh word. And besides, in your current situation, aliens do form the standing majority.'

'Sorry.'

'Nevertheless,' Selexin went on, 'you are correct. Balthazar is not human, nor is his form. Balthazar, and for that matter one other contestant named Bellos, is amorphic. Able to alter his form.'

'Alter his form?'

'Yes. Alter his exterior shape. Just as your chameleon can change its skin colour to blend in with its surroundings, so too can Balthazar and Bellos do the same, only they do not alter their colour: they alter their entire external shape. And it makes sense. One makes one's self human when competing in a human labyrinth, because any doors or handles or potential weapons will all be made for the human form.'

'Uh-huh,' Swain said, turning back to attend to Balthazar.

Hawkins came back from the elevator.

'It took a bit of doing,' he said, 'but I finally got the tube out of its—'

Swain held Balthazar's other eye open, peering at it under the light of the flashlight.

'Out of its . . . what?' he said, not turning around.

Hawkins didn't reply.

Swain looked up. 'What is it—' he cut himself off.

Hawkins was staring out over the railing, at the Ground Floor atrium down below. Swain swivelled around, following Hawkins' gaze down into the atrium.

'*Oh my God*,' he said slowly. And then quickly he turned to Holly, reaching for the flashlight. 'Quick, turn it off.'

The flashlight went out. Blue moonlight covered them again and Stephen Swain peered out over the railing.

The man was just standing there. Tall and black. Two tapering horns rising high above his head. The soft moonlight glinted off the lustrous gold metal attached to his chest.

He was standing next to a glass display case down in the atrium. Just standing there, staring intently into one of the aisles in front of him, at something out of Swain's view.

Swain felt a chill.

He's not staring, he thought. *He's stalking*.

Selexin came up beside him.

'Bellos,' he whispered, not taking his eyes off the horned man in the atrium below. There was a sense of awe in his voice, a reverence that was unmistakable. 'The Malonian contestant. Malonians are the most lethal huntsmen in the galaxy. Trophy collectors. They have won more Presidia than any other species. Why, they even conduct a six-way internal hunt to determine who among them will compete in the Presidian.'

Swain watched as he listened. The horned man— Bellos—was a magnificent specimen of a man. Tall and broad-shouldered, built like a house, and, except for his golden chest, completely dressed in black. An imposing figure.

'Remember. Amorphic,' Selexin said. 'It makes sense to adopt the human form. Makes better sense to adopt a *highly developed* human form.'

Swain was about to reply when he heard Hawkins whisper behind him, '*Oh Christ*, where's Parker?'

Swain frowned. Hawkins had said something about that before. Parker was his partner. Stationed in here for the night with him. Maybe she was still here, somewhere inside . . .

'*Salve, moriturum es!*'

The voice boomed throughout the atrium. Swain jumped, a wave of ice-cold blood shooting through his veins.

He's seen us!

'Greetings, fellow competitor. Before you stands Bellos . . .'

Swain's mind was racing. Where could they go?

They'd have a good head start. They were still one whole floor above him.

'. . . Great-grandson of Trome, the winner of the Fifth Presidian. And like his great-grandfather and two Malonians before him, Bellos shall emerge from this battle alone, conquered by none and not undone by the Karanadon. Who be'st thou, my worthy and yet unfortunate opponent?'

Swain swallowed. He took a deep breath and was about to stand up and reply when he heard another noise—a strange clicking–hissing noise.

Coming from below.

From somewhere else in the atrium.

Swain dropped like a stone, out of sight. Bellos hadn't seen them.

He was challenging someone else.

And then, slowly, another contestant came into view. From the left. A dark, skeletal shadow creeping slowly among the bookcases.

It moved stealthily toward Bellos.

Whatever it was, it was large—at least six feet long—but thin, insect-like, with long angular limbs not unlike those of a grasshopper, that clung to the vertical side of one of the bookcases. Although Swain couldn't see its face very well, he could see that its sinister-looking head was partially covered by a steel, mask-like object. Its movements were accompanied by a strange mechanical breathing noise.

'What is it?' he whispered.

'It is the Konda,' Selexin said. '*Very* vicious warrior species from the outer regions; remarkably evolved insectoid physique; and, according to those who gamble on the Presidian, highly fancied to take it out. Keep your eyes on its two foreclaws—the tips of each thumbnail secrete a highly poisonous venom. If the Konda punctures your skin and then inserts its thumbnail into the wound, believe me, you will die screaming. Its only weakness: its lungs cannot handle the toxicity of your atmosphere, hence the breathing apparatus.'

The Konda was getting closer to Bellos, an ominous shadow moving steadily along the vertical sides of the bookcases.

Bellos didn't move. He just stood beside the display case, rooted to the spot.

Swain felt a strange sensation as he looked down on the atrium. A kind of voyeuristic thrill to be watching something that no-one else would ever see. That no-one would ever want to see.

The Konda crept cautiously toward Bellos, picking up speed as it closed in—

Suddenly, Bellos held up his hand.

The grasshopper-like Konda stopped instantly.

Swain frowned.

Why had it—?

And then something else caught his eye.

Something in the foreground, something *in between* Swain and the Konda.

It was small and black—a shadow superimposed on the darkness—slinking swiftly and silently across the bare wooden tops of the bookshelves, heading towards the Konda from behind.

From behind.

Swain watched in amazement as another identical creature made its way across the tops of the bookshelves from the other direction. Its movements resembled that of a cat. Menacing in its supreme stealth.

Selexin saw them, too.

'Oh, sweet Lords,' he breathed, '*hoodaya*.'

Swain turned to face the little man. Selexin was staring off into space, wide-eyed and white with fear.

Swain spun back around.

Two more of the small creatures—each about the size of a dog—were creeping on all fours across the tops of the bookshelves, jumping easily from top to top, across the aisles below. Swain saw their jet-black heads—saw their long needle-like teeth and their bony but muscular limbs—saw their thin snaking tails swishing menacingly behind them.

Selexin was whispering to himself: 'He can't do that. He *can't*. Good lord, *hoodaya*.'

The four smaller creatures—hoodaya, Swain guessed—had now formed a wide circle above the aisle containing the insect-like Konda.

The Konda hadn't moved an inch. It hadn't noticed them.

Not yet.

Bellos lowered his hand. And then he turned away.

Swain saw the Konda immediately shift its weight.

It hasn't got a clue, he thought as he gripped the railing. *Hasn't got a prayer . . .*

It was then that the four hoodaya leapt down from their perches.

Into the aisle below.

Hideous, high-pitched, *alien* shrieks filled the atrium. The bookshelves on either side of the aisle shook as the Konda flung itself violently from side to side in the face of the sudden onslaught.

Swain saw Hawkins' face go blank with horror. Selexin was just stunned. Swain pulled Holly close to him, turned her face away from the scene, 'Don't watch, honey.'

146

The godawful shrieking continued.

And then, without warning, the near bookcase fell over and suddenly Swain saw the whole grisly scene— saw the Konda, screaming madly, completely covered by the four hoodaya, its two venom-tipped forelimbs splayed wide, pinned to the ground by two of the hoods, while the other two attack creatures tore ferociously at its face and stomach. In seconds the Konda's steel breathing mask was ripped from its head and the hapless creature's shrieks became desperate, hoarse gasps.

And then, abruptly, the pained gasping stopped and the Konda's body slumped to the ground, limp.

But the hoodaya didn't stop. Swain saw their long needle-like teeth open wide and plunge into its hide. Blood spurted out in all directions as one hoodaya ripped a large chunk of flesh from the Konda's carcass and held it aloft in triumph.

Swain's head snapped left as he heard another noise.

Footsteps.

Rapid footsteps. Soft, barely audible, getting softer. Running away.

One of the hoods heard it, too—lifted its head from its feeding. It leapt from its mount on the Konda's body and raced off into the nearest aisle, heading for the stairwell.

Swain didn't know what was going on until he heard a stumbling noise, like someone being crash-tackled to the floor.

And then he heard another scream—a desperate, pathetic yelp—that stopped no sooner than it had begun.

Swain heard Selexin gulp next to him and he realised.

It had been the guide. The Konda's guide. Swain saw the look on Selexin's face. The other guide had never stood a chance.

Swain looked back at the dead Konda and the hoods on top of it.

'Selexin.'

No reply.

Selexin was simply staring into space, in shock.

'*Selexin*,' he whispered, nudging the little man back to his senses.

'W . . . what?'

'Quickly,' Swain said harshly, trying to get Selexin out of his daze. 'Tell me about them. These hoodaya, or whatever the hell it is you call them.'

Selexin swallowed. 'Hoods are hunting animals. Bellos is a hunter. Bellos uses hoods to hunt. Simple.'

'Hey,' Swain said. 'Just tell me, okay.'

'Why? It won't matter. Not anymore.'

'Why not?'

'Mister Swain, I commend you. Your previous efforts had until now given me some hope of survival. Already you have exceeded any previous human effort in the Presidian. But now,' Selexin was talking quickly, desperately, 'now I have the misfortune to tell you that you have just witnessed the signing of your own death warrant.'

'What?'

'You cannot win. The Presidian is over. Bellos has defiled the rules. If he is discovered, which he won't be because he is too clever, he will be disqualified—killed. But if he isn't, *he will win*. No-one can escape Bellos if he has hoods. They are the ultimate hunter's tool. Remorseless and vicious. With them by his side, Bellos is unstoppable.'

Selexin shook his head.

'Do you remember the Karanadon?' he said, pointing to the green light on Swain's wristband.

'Yes.' Swain had actually forgotten about it, but he didn't tell Selexin that.

'Only one hunter being has ever successfully killed a Karanadon in the wild. And do you know who that was?'

'Tell me.'

'Bellos. *With his hoods.*'

'Great.'

There was an awkward silence.

Then Swain said, 'Okay then, how did he get them here? If he was brought here just like I was, wouldn't you guys have made sure that he didn't bring anything with him?'

'That's exactly right, but there must have been a way . . . something he found that no-one thought of . . . some way to teleport them in—'

'Hey,' Hawkins touched Swain's shoulder. 'He's doing something.'

Bellos was bent over the Konda's body, doing something that Swain couldn't see. When at last he stood, Bellos had the Konda's breathing mask in his hands. A trophy.

He fastened the mask to a loop on his belt, and then he barked a sharp order to the three hoods that were still feasting on the Konda's torso. They immediately jumped off the dead contestant's body and stood behind Bellos, at the same time as the fourth hood returned from the stairwell, large shreds of blood-stained white cloth dangling from its teeth and claws.

Then Bellos walked over to a semi-circular desk in

the middle of the atrium. Swain could just make out the words on the sign hanging above it: INFORMATION.

Behind him, he heard Hawkins take a quick breath.

Bellos bent down behind the Information Desk, picked up something in one of his large black hands and carried it back over to the Konda's body.

As soon as he saw it, Swain knew what it was. It was small, white and limp. Bellos' own guide.

Bellos said something quickly, and the hoods darted behind the Information Desk. Then he draped his guide's lifeless body over his shoulder and pointed it toward the dead contestant.

'*Initialise!*' Bellos said, loudly.

Instantly, a small sphere of brilliant white light appeared above the dead guide's head, illuminating the wide open space of the atrium. Instinctively, Swain bent lower behind the railing, away from the light. The white sphere glowed for about five seconds until it vanished abruptly and the atrium was dark once more.

Selexin turned solemnly to Swain. 'That, Mister Swain, was Bellos confirming his first kill.'

Swain turned to the group gathered around him. 'I think it's time to get out of here.'

'I think you're right,' Hawkins was already moving away from the railing.

Swain grabbed Balthazar and heaved him onto his shoulder. 'Holly,' he whispered, 'quick honey, the elevator.'

'Okay.'

He turned to Hawkins, 'We'll go back to the elevator. Stop it between floors again. That's been the safest place to hide so far.'

'Fine by me,' Hawkins said.

Swain began dragging Balthazar away from the railing, with Holly by his side and Hawkins, Selexin and Balthazar's guide in front. They all headed for the open, darkened elevator.

And then it happened.

The elevator's doors began to close.

Swain shot a look at Hawkins, who immediately dashed forward, trying to get to the doors in time. But the doors joined just as he got there.

'Damn it!' he cursed.

Swain came up beside him, looked up at the numbered display above the elevator doors. The illuminated number was moving down the line from **1** to G and then to SL-**1**.

'The elevator . . .' he whispered.

'Jesus Christ,' Hawkins said, realising, '*they figured out how to use the goddamn elevator.*'

'They're intelligent—' Selexin said.

'They're *animals*, for God's sake,' Hawkins said, perhaps a little too loudly.

'Alien, yes. Animal, no,' Selexin whispered. 'I would say understanding a contraption like your elevator would be regarded as remarkably intelligent.'

Hawkins was about to say something in retort when Swain cut in, 'All right. It doesn't matter. We'll find somewhere else to . . .'

'Hey Daddy, don't be silly,' Holly said, standing next to the elevator call button. 'I can get the elevator back for you.'

Swain's eyes went wide with horror.

'Holly, no!' He lunged to stop her, but it was too late.

Holly pressed the UP button.

Swain closed his eyes and bowed his head. The round UP button glowed brightly in the darkness of the First Floor.

He couldn't believe it. Now, whoever was using the lift wouldn't even have to *guess* which floor they were on. Nor would they even have to figure out how to use the elevator. Because now that Holly had pressed the call button, once the elevator picked up its new passenger, it would *automatically* stop here, on the First Floor.

Holly said, 'What did I do? Didn't I do the right thing, Daddy?'

Swain sighed, 'Yes. Thank you, honey. You did the

right thing.' He handed Balthazar over to Hawkins, and walked quietly back to the balcony overlooking the atrium.

Bellos was still standing behind the Information Desk, putting down his guide, oblivious to their presence.

At least that's good, Swain turned back toward the elevator, head down in thought. They still had to go. Something would be coming up in that elevator very soon and he didn't want to be here when it did.

Finally he looked up toward the elevator.

Holly was staring straight at him.

Selexin and the other guide both stood there with their mouths wide open.

Hawkins was just standing there, too, propping up Balthazar, staring fixedly at Swain.

But it was Balthazar who seized Swain's attention.

The tall bearded man had his left arm draped over Hawkins' shoulder for support. His right was held high, a glistening, evil-looking silver blade in his hand.

Poised.

Ready.

Swain didn't know what to do. What had happened? Balthazar was ready to throw a knife at him and the others weren't doing anything . . .

Balthazar threw the knife.

Swain waited for the impact. Waited to grab his chest and feel the burning pain as the blade lodged deep into his heart . . .

The knife whistled through the air at astonishing speed.

Right past him.

Swain heard a thud as the nasty-looking knife lodged into the railing behind him. The *steel* railing.

Then Swain heard the scream.

A piercing, wailing scream of pure agony.

Swain spun to see that Balthazar's knife had pinned the hood's left foreclaw to the steel railing. The force of the throw was so strong that it had lodged the knife several inches into the steel. It had caught the hood as it had been attempting to climb over the railing from the Ground Floor below—*right behind Swain*.

The hood screamed, and for an instant Swain saw its features up close. Four muscular black limbs, all with long dagger-like claws; a long slashing tail; and strangest of all, the head. It seemed as if the head of this dog-sized animal was nothing more than two gigantic jaws. There were eyes on it somewhere, but all Swain could see were its needle-like teeth, bared wide with the help of its massive lower jaw.

And beyond the hood, Swain caught a glimpse—a split-second glimpse—of Bellos, standing by the Information Desk.

Gazing up at him.

Smiling.

He had known all along . . .

Swain turned away, stumbling away from the railing as the hood wrenched at its pinned foreclaw. It seemed to Swain that the knife fixing the claw to the railing was the only thing holding the hood up.

At that moment there was another whistling through the air and suddenly a *second* knife thudded into the forearm of the hood, slicing right through the narrow bone just above its pinned foreclaw, *cutting the claw clean off!*

With a shriek, the hood dropped instantly out of sight, falling to the atrium way below—leaving in its place a bony five-fingered claw, impaled on the railing by the first throwing knife.

Hawkins yelled to Swain, 'Here! Over here!'

Swain saw the ramshackle group hurrying toward the photocopying room to his right. He ran after them and when he reached the door to the photocopying room, he looked back over his shoulder to see the first of the remaining hoods slink slowly and menacingly over the railing.

Swain shut the door behind him and looked around the photocopying room.

Hawkins was leading the way with Balthazar over his shoulder, throwing open the other door at the far end of the room, the one that read: INTERNET FACILITY. Apart from that door, a solid concrete wall separated the two rooms. Swain followed as Holly and the others hurried through the doorway behind Hawkins.

Swain paused at the threshold. He was standing on a dusty handwritten sign that must have fallen from the door some time ago. It read:

STATE LIBRARY OF NEW YORK
INTERNET/ON-LINE SERVICES FACILITY
CLOSED FOR REPAIRS.
WE REGRET ANY INCONVENIENCE.

'I don't know if this is such a good idea,' he stepped inside, shutting and locking the door after him.

Suddenly, there was a loud *bang* from somewhere behind him and Swain spun around. He peered out through a small rectangular window set into the door—and saw that the hoods were pounding on the *outer* door of the photocopying room.

He turned to face the Internet room.

'Sorry,' Hawkins said, lowering the weary-looking Balthazar to the floor.

The Internet facility of the State Library of New York—a relatively new addition to a relatively old building—was little more than a wide empty room, with open-ended wires hanging down from an unpainted ceiling and bared electrical outlets on the walls. No computers. No modems. Even the light switch next to the doorway was merely a stumpy metal housing with lots of frayed wires. A corner room, there were windows along two of its sides, but no other doors.

There was only the one entrance.

It was a dead end.

Wonderful, Swain thought.

The banging outside continued. He looked back out through the small rectangular window in the door. The photocopying room's outer door was still, except that every few seconds it would vibrate suddenly as the hoods rammed it from the other side.

Hawkins and Holly were standing at the windows, gazing out helplessly over the park outside.

Swain pulled Holly back protectively. 'Don't get too close,' he said, pointing at the window frame, at the tiny blue talons of electricity that lashed out around its edges.

'Uh, excuse me, but I think we have more pressing problems than the *windows*,' Selexin said impatiently.

The pounding of the hoods on the outer door continued.

'Right.' Swain's eyes swept the room, looking for

something he could use. Anything he could use. But there was nothing here. Absolutely nothing. The room was completely bare.

And then, with a sudden, loud crash, the outer door to the photocopying room burst inwards.

'They're inside,' Hawkins said, racing to the door, peering out through its small window.

'Christ,' Swain said.

In an instant, the first hood hit the door. Hawkins stepped back as the whole door shook.

'Get back!' Swain said. 'They'll go for the window!'

The second hood went for the window set into the door.

Shards of glass sprayed everywhere as the window exploded inwards. The hood clung to the broken window, reaching into the room, lashing out indiscriminately with a single claw.

The other hoods were ramming the door, pounding it repeatedly.

'What do we do!' Hawkins yelled. 'It won't hold for long. The other door didn't!'

'I know! I know!' Swain was trying to think.

The hoods continued to pound loudly on the door. The door's hinges creaked ominously. The hood with its arm inside the broken rectangular window was now trying to stick its head through, but the gap was too small. It hissed and snarled maniacally.

Swain spun. 'Everyone to that corner,' he pointed to the far corner. 'I want—'

He stopped—listened to the sound of the soft rain pattering against the windows. Something had changed. Something he almost hadn't noticed. He listened in the silence.

The silence.

That was it.

The pounding had stopped.

What were they doing?

And then Swain looked at the door.

Slowly, almost imperceptibly, the doorknob began to rotate.

Hawkins saw it, too. '*Holy* shit . . .' he gasped.

Swain dived for the door.

Too late.

The knob continued to rotate and then . . .

. . . click!

It was locked. Swain breathed again.

The knob turned again. Clicked again.

Turned. Clicked.

They're testing it, over and over, he thought in horror.

It was at that moment, as Swain was staring up at the door from the floor, that a long black claw slid slowly and silently through the broken window.

The bony black arm reached downward, slowly flexing its jagged razor-sharp fingernails. The lethal black claw was moving across and down to the right when suddenly Swain realised what it was doing.

Swain snapped round to look at Balthazar—to see if the big man could throw another knife at the claw. But, having thrown the two knives earlier, Balthazar was now spent. He just sat on the floor with his head bowed. Swain saw the knives on his baldric, thought about using one, but then decided he didn't want to get too close to the hood's vicious-looking claw.

'Quickly,' he said to Hawkins. 'Handcuffs.'

Puzzled, Hawkins reached for his gunbelt and pulled out a pair of handcuffs. Swain grabbed them.

The clawed hand edged slowly downwards, coming closer to the doorknob.

'It's trying to unlock the door . . .' Hawkins breathed in awe. As soon as it turned the knob from the inside, the door would unlock straight away. Unlock. And open . . .

Swain reached up to the door, trying to prise open the cuffs. But the cuffs wouldn't open.

The doorknob rattled again and Swain jumped, ready for it to burst open.

The door remained shut.

It had come from the outside. One of the hoods outside was trying to turn the knob again. The door was still locked. But the clawed hand on the *inside* was still getting closer to the knob on this side.

'They're locked! The cuffs are locked!' Swain shouted in disbelief, fumbling with the cuffs.

'Shit, of course.' Hawkins pulled some keys from his pocket. 'Here. The smallest one.'

Swain took the keys, hands shaking, and tried to insert the smallest key into the cuffs.

'Hurry up!' Selexin said.

The claw was at the knob now. Feeling.

Swain's hands were shaking so much that the key slipped out of the cuffs' keyhole.

'Quickly!' Selexin yelled.

Swain inserted the key again, turned it. The cuffs popped opened.

'There!' he said, moving across the floor, sliding underneath the doorknob.

The clawed hand was moving over the knob now, trying to get a grip on it.

Swain reached for the light switch next to the door. Its wired remains flowed out from a solid, stumpy metal housing. Swain clamped one ring of the cuffs through a gap in the metal housing.

The clawed hand slowly began to turn the door-knob.

Swain reached up to the knob, sliding the second ring of the cuffs in behind the clawed hand and around the narrowest part of the doorknob—the part closest to the door itself.

Then he clamped the cuff tightly around the door-knob *just as* the clawed hand turned it fully. There was a loud *click!* as the door unlocked. The door swung slightly inward, opening an inch.

And then suddenly, shockingly, the door was rammed from the outside.

The handcuffs went instantly taut, securing the door to the metal housing on the wall.

The door was open six inches now and Swain fell backwards as one of the hoods swiped viciously at him through the narrow gap between the door and its frame.

The hoods were snarling loudly now, scratching at the doorframe, hurling themselves bodily at the door.

But the cuffs held.

The gap between door and frame was too narrow.

The dog-sized hoods couldn't get in.

'Well done,' Hawkins said.

Swain wasn't impressed. 'If they can't open it, they'll soon break it down. We have to get out of this room.'

The hoods kept pounding on the door.

Swain turned around—searching for another way out—when suddenly he saw Holly standing over by one of the windows. She was bent over the window sill as if she were injured.

'Holly? You all right?' He hurried over to her.

'Yes . . .' Distracted.

The pounding continued. The hoods' snarling and hissing filled the room.

'What are you doing?' he said quickly.

'Playing with the electricity.'

Swain stole a glance back at the door as he came up beside her and looked over her shoulder. Holly was holding the broken telephone receiver two inches away from the window sill. As she moved it closer, the small forks of blue lightning seemed to pull *away* from it in a wide circle—away from the phone.

Swain had forgotten Holly still had the phone receiver at all. He frowned at what he saw, though. He didn't know why the electricity should move away from the phone receiver. After all, the phone was dead . . .

The pounding and the grunting of the hoods continued.

The door still held.

'Can I have that?' Swain said quickly. Holly gave him the phone as he looked back at the door.

Then, abruptly, the pounding and the snarling stopped.

Silence.

And then Swain heard the hoods scamper out of the photocopying room.

'What's going on?' Hawkins said.

'I don't know.' Swain moved to look out through the gap in the door.

'Are they coming back?' Selexin said.

'I can't see them,' Swain said. 'Why did they leave?'

Peering out through the gap in the door, Swain saw the outer door to the photocopying room swinging wide open, left ajar by the hoods. Beyond that, quite a way away and shrouded in darkness, the doors to the elevators.

And then he saw the reason why the hoods had left so abruptly.

With a soft *ping* the doors to the far elevator slowly began to open.

Slow night, Bob Charlton thought wryly as he stepped into the bustling offices of the New York Police Department's 14th Precinct.

He had been here a few times before, but this time the main foyer was much less crowded—there were only about eighty people here tonight. He stepped up to the reception desk and shouted above the din: 'Bob Charlton to see Captain Dickson, please!'

'Mr Charlton? Henry Dickson,' Dickson said, extending his hand as Charlton entered the relative silence of his office. 'Neil Peters said you'd be coming down. What can I do for you?'

'I've got a problem downtown that I was told you could help me with.'

'Yeah . . .'

Charlton said, 'Sometime in the last twenty-four hours we lost a main in one of the south–central grids. Lieutenant Peters said that you picked up a guy in that area earlier today.'

'Where's your grid?' Dickson asked.

163

'It's bounded by 14th and Delancey on the north–south axis.'

Dickson looked at a map on the wall next to him.

'Yeah, that's right. We did pick up a fella in that area. Just this morning,' Dickson said. 'But I don't think he'll be much use to you. We picked him up in the old State Library.'

'What was he doing there?'

'Small-time computer thief. Apparently they've just put in a new set of Pentiums down there. But this poor bastard must have stumbled onto something bigger.'

'Something bigger?' Charlton asked.

'We found him covered in blood.'

Charlton blinked.

'Only it wasn't his blood. It was a security guard's.'

'Oh my God.'

'Damn right.'

Charlton leaned forward, serious. 'How did he get inside? Inside the library, I mean.'

'Don't know yet. I've got a couple of babysitters down there now. As you can see, we're pretty busy round here. Site squad'll be going in there tomorrow to determine point of entry.'

Charlton asked, 'This thief, is he still here?'

'Yeah. Got him locked up downstairs.'

'Can I talk to him?'

Dickson shrugged. 'Sure. But I wouldn't get your hopes up. He's been talking gibberish ever since we brought him in.'

'That's okay, I'd like to try anyway. Some of those old buildings have booster valves in funny places. I'm thinking he might have busted something on his way in. That okay with you?'

'Sure.'

Both men stood up and walked toward the door. Dickson stopped.

'Oh, a word of warning, Mr Charlton,' he said. 'Try to hold your stomach, this ain't gonna be pretty.'

Charlton winced as he looked again at the black man in the small cell in front of him.

Quite obviously, they hadn't been able to get all the blood off his face. Perhaps those designated to wash him had retched, too, Charlton thought. Whatever the case, they hadn't finished the job. Mike Fraser still had large vertical streaks of dried blood running down the length of his face, like some bizarre kind of warpaint.

Fraser just sat there on the far side of the cell, staring at the concrete wall, talking rapidly to himself, making darting gestures at some invisible friend.

'That's him,' Dickson said.

'Jesus,' Charlton breathed.

'Hasn't stopped talking to that wall since we put him in here. Blood on his face has dried, too. He'll have to get it off himself later, when he's got sense enough to use a shower.'

'You said his name was Fraser . . .' Charlton said.

'Yep. Michael Thomas Fraser.'

Charlton stepped forward.

'Michael?' he said gently.

No response. Fraser kept talking to the wall.

'Michael? Can you hear me?'

No response.

Charlton turned his back on the cell to face Dickson. 'You never found out how he got into the library, is that right?'

'Like I said, site squad goes in tomorrow.'

'Right . . .'

Dickson said, 'You won't get anything out of him. He hasn't said a word to anyone all day. Probably can't even hear your voice.'

'Hmmm,' Charlton mused. 'Poor bastard . . .'

'*It's hearing your voice,*' Mike Fraser whispered into Bob Charlton's ear.

Charlton jumped away from the cell.

Fraser was right up close to the bars, only inches away from Charlton's head. Charlton hadn't even heard him come across the cell.

Fraser kept talking in an exaggerated whisper, '*Whatever it is, it's hearing your voice! And if you keep talking . . .*'

The black man was pressing his bloodstained face up against the bars, trying to get as close to Charlton as possible. The streaks of dried blood running vertically down his face gave him an aspect of pure evil.

'*Whatever it is, it's hearing your voice! And if you keep talking!*' Fraser hissed crazily. He was starting to wail.

'*And if you keep talking! Talking! Talking! Ah-ah-ah!*' Fraser was looking up at the ceiling, at some imaginary creature looming above him. He held up his hands to ward off the unseen foe. '*Oh my God! It's here! It's after me! It's here! Oh God, help me! Somebody help me!*'

Frantically, he began to shake the bars of the cell. Finally he fell limp, his arms hanging through the bars. At last Fraser looked up at Charlton.

'Don't go there,' he hissed.

Charlton leaned closer, spoke gently. 'Why? What's there?'

Fraser offered a sly, evil grin through his mask of dried blood. 'If you go, you go. But you won't come back alive.'

'He's nuts. Lost it, that's all,' Dickson said as they walked back to the main entrance of the station.

'You think he killed the guard?' Charlton asked.

'Him? Nah. Probably stumbled on the guys who did, though.'

'And you think they messed him up? Scared him to death by painting him in the guard's blood?'

'Something like that.'

Charlton stroked his chin as he walked. 'I don't know. I think I better check out our links with that library. It's worth a shot. Might be that whoever got hold of Michael Fraser decided to hack up my junction line, too. And if they hacked the junction at the booster valve, it would definitely be possible to bring the whole main down.'

They reached the doors.

'Sergeant,' Charlton said as the two men shook hands, 'thank you for your time and help. It's been, well, interesting, to say the least.'

Stephen Swain peered out from behind the handcuffed door of the New York State Library's rather generously named Internet Facility.

The doors of the darkened elevator were fully open now but nothing was happening.

The elevator was just sitting there.

Open and silent.

For their part, the hoods were nowhere to be seen. Having hustled out of the photocopying room, they must have been out on the balcony somewhere. Hiding . . .

Swain watched intently, waiting for something to emerge from the lift.

'Could be empty,' Hawkins whispered.

'Could be,' Swain replied. 'Maybe whoever pressed the button never got in.'

'Shhh,' Selexin hissed, 'something is coming out.'

They turned back to face the elevator.

'Uh-oh,' Hawkins said.

'Oh *man*,' Swain sighed, 'doesn't this guy ever quit?'

The tail emerged first, pointing forward, hovering horizontally three feet above the ground. Swain could easily see the slight kink in the tail a few inches from the tip where he had broken the bone. The antennae came next, followed by the snout, cautiously moving out from the elevator.

'She is not a *guy*,' Selexin said. 'I *told* you that before, Reese is female.'

'How did she figure out the elevator?' Hawkins asked as they watched Reese lower her snout and sniff the floor.

'I imagine,' Selexin said, 'she smelled Mister Swain's residual scent on one of the buttons—'

Abruptly, Reese's snout snapped up and pointed directly at them. Swain and Hawkins ducked instantly behind the door. Selexin didn't move.

'What are you doing? She cannot *see* you,' he whispered. 'She can only smell you. To hide behind the door won't extinguish your scent-trail. Besides,' he added sourly, 'she probably already knows we are here.'

Swain and Hawkins resumed their positions at the door.

Hawkins said, 'So why isn't she coming after us?'

Selexin sighed. 'Honestly, it is a wonder that I bother explaining anything to you. I would think that the reason why Reese has not come directly after us is perfectly obvious.'

'And what is that?' Hawkins said.

'Because she smells something else,' Selexin said. 'Some other creature that I would safely assume is far more worrisome to her than you are.'

'The hoods,' Swain said, not taking his eyes off Reese. She was standing perfectly still at the mouth of the elevator.

'Correct. And since they were out there only very

169

recently, their scent is probably very strong,' Selexin said. 'I would therefore assert that at the moment, Reese is feeling particularly concerned.'

For a long minute they watched Reese in silence. Her long, low, dinosaur-like body didn't move an inch. Her tail was poised high, tensed, ready to strike.

Hawkins said, 'So what do we do?'

Swain was frowning, thinking.

'We get out,' he said finally.

'*What!*' Selexin and Hawkins said at the same time.

Swain was already reaching up for the handcuffs, unlocking them.

'For one thing, we can't stay here,' he said. 'Sooner or later one of those bastards out there is going to break down this door. And when that happens, we'll be trapped. I say we get ready to run as soon as something happens.'

'As soon as *something happens*?' Selexin said. 'A rather inexact plan if you don't mind my saying so.'

Swain put the cuffs in his pocket and shrugged at the little man. 'Let's just say that I've got a feeling something is about to happen out there. And when it does, I want all of us to be ready to make a break for it.'

Several minutes later, Swain had Balthazar draped over his shoulder while Hawkins held Holly by the hand. The door was open a full two feet.

Outside, Reese stood rigidly in front of the elevator, visibly tensed, alert.

They waited.

Reese didn't move.

Another minute ticked by.

Swain turned to face the group. 'All right, when I say go, run straight for the stairwell. When you get there, don't stop, don't look back, just go straight up. When we hit the Third Floor, I'll lead the way from there. Okay?'

They nodded.

'Good.'

Another minute passed.

'It does not look like anything is going to happen,' Selexin said sourly.

'He's right,' Hawkins said. 'Maybe we better put the cuffs back on the door . . .'

'Not just yet,' Swain said, staring intently out at Reese. 'They're out there, and Reese knows it . . . *There!*'

Abruptly, Reese spun to her right, away from them. Something had caught her attention.

Swain tightened his grip on Balthazar. 'All right everybody, get ready, this is it.'

Slowly, Swain pulled the door open and ventured into the photocopying room. The others followed him to the outer door.

Reese was still facing the other direction.

Swain rested his free hand lightly on the outer door, his eyes locked on Reese, praying that she wouldn't turn around and charge.

He opened the door wider, and stepped out.

He could see the stairwell now, off to the left. Reese and the elevators were about twenty feet to the right. Beyond Reese, he could see the wide empty space that fell away to the Ground Floor atrium below. He figured if he could just ease out of the doorway and quietly make his way to the—

Suddenly, Reese whirled around.

For an instant Swain's heart stopped. He felt like a thief discovered with his hands in the till—totally exposed. Caught in the act.

He froze.

But Reese didn't stop to face him.

She just kept turning until she came a full three hundred and sixty degrees. A full circle.

Swain breathed again. He didn't know what was happening until he realised that Reese's quick circling movement wasn't a threatening move at all.

It was a defensive move.

Reese was frightened, agitated, desperately look-ing—no, *smelling*—in every direction.

She's surrounded, Swain thought. *She knows we're here, but she's decided we're not worth worrying about. There's something else out there, something more dangerous . . .*

There was no time to waste.

This was the chance.

Swain turned to the others and whispered, 'Come on! We're moving now.'

Swain half-dragged, half-carried Balthazar out through the doorway, not daring to take his eyes off Reese. The others raced past him and headed for the open stairwell. Swain limped as fast as he could toward the stairwell, straining under Balthazar's dead weight. He was almost at the stairwell when the attack on Reese began.

A hood.

Squealing fiercely, it leapt over the railing from the Ground Floor, claws extended, jaws wide open.

Swain heaved Balthazar into the stairwell, trying as he did to watch what was happening behind him. And as he disappeared into the stairwell, the last thing Swain saw was a fleeting glimpse of Reese, shrieking madly, swinging her tail around to defend herself against the onslaught of incoming hoods.

Feet pounding, Swain hurried up the stairs, Balthazar's weight pressing heavily down against his shoulders.

The others were waiting for him at the fire door marked '3'. When he joined them, Swain passed Balthazar over to Hawkins.

'Why are we stopping here?' the young cop asked. 'Shouldn't we keep going up?'

'We can't go any higher,' Swain said. 'We can't get out there. The door to the roof's electrified.'

'Daddy, what are we doing?' Holly said.

Swain eased the fire door open slightly. 'Looking for a hiding place, honey.'

'Daddy, where are the monsters?'

'I don't know. Hopefully not up here.'

'Daddy . . .'

'Shh. Just wait here,' Swain said. Holly stepped back, silent.

Swain stepped through the doorway and scanned the room.

Yes. He was where he wanted to be.

The wide low-ceilinged study hall stretched away from him, its L-shaped desks creating a waist-high maze that spread right across the room. The whole room was dark, save for the soft blue city light that filtered in through the windows on the far side.

Slowly, Swain bent down to look under the desks. Through the legs he could see all the way across the room. There were no feet—or whatever the hell these creatures walked on—in sight.

The study hall was empty.

He poked his head back through the fire door. 'Okay everyone. Inside, quickly.'

The others filed into the study hall. Swain took Holly's hand and led her through the winding maze of desks.

'Daddy. I don't like it here.'

Swain was looking around the room. 'Yeah, me neither,' he said, distracted.

'Daddy?'

'What, honey?'

'Daddy, can we go now—?'

Swain pointed to a corner near the windows. 'There it is.' He quickened his pace, pulling Holly harder.

Hawkins was walking behind them. 'What is it?' he asked. All he could see was a sign on the wall reading:

QUIET PLEASE.
THIS ROOM IS FOR PRIVATE STUDY ONLY.
NO CARRY BAGS PERMITTED.

'Next to the sign,' Swain said.

Beside the sign on the wall, Hawkins saw a large, solid, grey door. It looked like some sort of maintenance door.

Swain reached for the knob. It turned easily. Unlocked.

The door opened slowly, with the distinctive hiss of a hydraulic valve. Swain didn't think much of it. All the big doors at the hospital needed hydraulics to help people open them, they were that heavy.

He reached for the light switch, but decided against it. Any light would be a certain giveaway.

He surveyed the room before him. Cold grey concrete walls, a janitor's cart filled with buckets and mops, shelves packed with bottles of detergent and floor wax, and several tarps stretched over large mounds of more janitorial equipment.

Diffused white light from the streetlights outside streamed in through two long rectangular windows high up on the left-hand wall. Directly opposite the door, dividing the room in two, was a floor-to-ceiling cyclone fence with a rusted iron gate in its centre. Beyond the fence were more shelves of detergent and a few more piles of equipment covered in dark hessian cloth.

The group moved inside and Swain closed the door behind them. The hydraulic door shut with a soft *whump*.

Holly sat away from the door, up against the cyclone fence. Hawkins put Balthazar on the floor beneath the windows and scanned the maintenance room, nodding. 'We should be safe here.'

'For a while, yes,' Swain said.

Selexin asked, 'How long do you think we should stay here?'

'As long as we can,' Swain said.

'Hooray,' Hawkins said blandly.

'And how long is that?' Selexin again.

'I don't know. Maybe right up till the end. At the moment I'm not quite sure.'

'You cannot forget that there will always be *something* out there,' Selexin said. 'Even when all the contestants are dead, you will still have the Karanadon to face.'

'I don't have to face anything,' Swain said harshly.

'What does that mean?'

'It means, I'm not here to fight. It means I'm not here to win your stupid contest. It means that at the moment all I'm worried about is getting my daughter and the rest of us out of here alive.'

'*But you can't do that unless you win*,' Selexin said angrily.

Swain looked hard at the little man. He was silent for a few seconds.

'I wouldn't be so sure of that,' he said softly, almost to himself.

'What was that?' Selexin said. It was an argument now.

'I said, I wouldn't be so sure of that.'

'You believe you can get out of the labyrinth?' Selexin challenged.

Swain was silent. He looked over at Holly by the cyclone fence, sucking her thumb.

Selexin said again, 'Do you seriously think you can get out of the labyrinth?'

Swain was silent.

Hawkins whispered to him, 'You think we can get out?'

Swain looked at the windows near the ceiling, thinking to himself. At last he spoke. 'Yes.'

'Impossible.' Balthazar's guide stepped forward. 'Absolutely impossible.'

'You stay out of this,' Selexin snapped angrily.

Swain stared at Selexin. The little man had been indignant before, distressed even, but he had never been downright angry.

Balthazar's guide stepped back immediately. Selexin spun back to face Swain.

'*How?*' he demanded.

'How?'

'Yes, how do you propose we get out?'

'You *want* to get out?' Swain couldn't believe it. After the lecture he had received before about the grandeur and honour associated with the Presidian, he found it difficult to believe that Selexin would *want* to get out.

'As a matter of fact I do.'

Balthazar's guide interrupted again, 'Oh, you do, do you? Well forgive me for reminding you of an unpleasant fact, Selexin, but you *can't!*'

Selexin didn't say anything.

Balthazar's guide went on. 'Selexin, the Presidian has begun. It *cannot* and *will not* be stopped until a winner has been found. It is the only honourable way.'

'I think any honour this thing had went flying out the window when your friend Bellos brought his bloodhounds along,' Swain said.

'I agree,' Selexin said, glaring at Balthazar's guide. 'Bellos has broken the rules. And with hoodaya, *he* cannot and will not be stopped. We must get out.'

'And do what?' the other guide sneered, 'use our witnessing teleports to call for help? They transmit vision only, Selexin, not sound.'

'Then *anything*,' Selexin said. 'If two contestants leave the labyrinth and initialise their witnessing teleports and wave for the cameras, the controllers of the Presidian will have to realise that something is amiss.'

The other guide stared at Selexin. 'I do not think our two contestants will last very long outside the labyrinth,' he said smugly.

'Why?'

'As a matter of fact,' the other guide smiled, 'I

would say that they would not last any longer than exactly fifteen minutes.'

'Oh,' Selexin frowned, remembering. 'Yes.'

Swain was bewildered. It was as if Selexin and Balthazar's guide were speaking in another language.

'What does that mean?' he asked Selexin.

Selexin spoke sadly. 'Do you remember what I told you before about your wristband?'

Swain looked down at the heavy grey band around his wrist. He'd forgotten about it entirely.

The little green light still glowed brightly. The display now read:

INITIALISED—6

Six? Swain thought. He remembered the contestant on the Ground Floor—the Konda—that had been killed by the hoods. The wristband, it appeared, was counting *down* now. Striking out a number as each contestant was eliminated. Until only one remained.

And when only one was left, then came the Karanadon that Selexin kept talking about. Whatever *that* was.

'Do you remember?' Selexin said again.

'Yes, I think I remember.'

'Do you recall that if your wristband detects that it is outside the electronic field surrounding the labyrinth, it will automatically set itself to detonate?'

Swain frowned. It all suddenly made sense. 'And I get fifteen minutes to get back inside.'

'*Exactly*.' Balthazar's guide spat.

Nobody spoke. There was silence for a full minute. Someone took a long, deep breath.

178

Balthazar's guide spoke: 'So even if you get out, you are still a dead man.'

Swain looked at him and snorted. 'Thanks.'

'You know, you're a real great help,' Hawkins said to the little man.

'At least I am realistic about my situation.'

'At least I give a shit about somebody else's life,' Hawkins said.

'I would be more concerned about taking care of my own if I were you.'

'Yeah, well you're not me—'

'All right. All right,' Swain said. 'Settle down. We've got to find a way out of this, not fight among ourselves.' He turned to Selexin. 'Is there *any* way we can get this thing off my wrist?'

Selexin shook his head. 'No. It doesn't come off . . . unless you . . .' he shrugged.

'I know, I know. Unless I win the Presidian, right?'

Selexin nodded. 'Only the officials at the other end have the proper equipment to remove it.'

'Can we break it open?' Hawkins suggested.

'Can anyone here break down that door?' Balthazar's guide asked, pointing to the maintenance room's heavy hydraulic door, knowing the answer. 'If not, then no-one here can break open that wristband. It's too strong.'

The group went silent.

Swain looked down at the wristband again. In the last minute it had suddenly begun to feel a lot heavier. He crossed the room and sat next to Holly, resting his back up against the cyclone fence.

'How are *you* doing?' he asked softly.

She didn't answer.

'Holly? What's up?'

Still no answer. Holly was staring vacantly straight ahead.

'Come on, Hol, what is it? Did I do something?' he waited for a response.

This was not unusual. Holly would often refuse to talk to him when she felt rejected or left out or just plain stubborn.

'Holly, please, we don't have time for this now,' Swain shook his head in exasperation.

Holly spoke, 'Daddy.'

'Yes.'

'Be very quiet, Daddy. Be very, *very* quiet.'

'Why—?'

'*Shh.*'

Swain went mute. The others had sat down over near Balthazar, beneath the high windows. Everyone sat in complete silence for ten seconds. Holly leaned over to Swain's ear.

'Do you hear it?' she whispered.

'No.'

'*Listen.*'

Swain looked at Holly. She was sitting dead still, her eyes wide open, her head set rigidly upright, backed up against the cyclone fence. She looked frightened. Frightened out of her mind. She spoke again.

'Okay Daddy, get ready. Listen . . . *now.*'

And then he heard it.

The sound was barely audible, but it was unmistakable. A long, slow inhalation.

Something breathing.

Something not very far away.

Suddenly, there was a snorting sound, like the soft grunting of a pig. It was followed by a shuffling sound.

Then the inhalation came again.

It was slow and rhythmic, like the breathing of someone sleeping.

Selexin heard it, too.

At the grunting sound, his head snapped up immediately. He scrambled silently on all fours across the concrete floor to Swain.

'We have to get out,' he hissed in Swain's ear. 'We have to get out *now*.'

The inhalation came again.

'It's in here,' Selexin said. 'Quickly, give me your wrist.'

Swain offered his wristband for Selexin to see.

The green light was still on.

'Phew,' Selexin breathed.

'It?' Swain asked. 'What is *it*?'

'It's behind us, Daddy,' Holly hissed, her body frozen.

'Oh, Jesus Christ . . .' Hawkins gasped, getting to his feet on the other side of the room. He was looking through the cyclone fence. 'I think it's time to get the hell out of here.'

The inhalation came again, louder this time.

And then slowly, ever so slowly, Stephen Swain turned around.

It was over by the far corner of the cage, under some shelves mounted high up on the wall. In the dark it looked like just another large mound of equipment covered in a tarp.

Only it was moving.

Slowly and steadily.

Rhythmically rising and falling, in time with the deep inhalations.

Swain's eyes followed the outline of the 'mound'. It was big. In the dim light of the storage room he could just make out long spiky bristles on top of an arched back—

There was a loud grunt.

Then *the whole mound* rolled over onto its side and the deep inhalations resumed.

Selexin was tugging on Swain's shirt. 'Let's go! Let's *go!*'

Swain rose to his feet, plucked Holly from the floor, headed for the door. He was reaching for the door's handle when he heard a soft, insistent beeping.

It was coming from his wristband. The little green light was flashing.

Selexin's eyes went wide with horror.

'It's waking up! Get out!' he screamed. *'Get out now!'*

He barged past Hawkins, hauled open the door, pushed Swain through it, screaming, 'Out! Out! Out!'

Swain and Holly were out in the empty study hall again. Hawkins emerged from the janitor's room with Balthazar over his shoulder, the other guide close behind.

Selexin was already charging in among the L-shaped desks of the study hall. 'Don't stop! Don't stop! Keep moving, we have to get as far away from here as possible!'

Swain followed with Holly in his arms—weaving quickly between the desks, away from the janitor's room—the others close in tow.

Up ahead, Selexin was darting between the desks, constantly looking back to see if Swain was still with him.

'The band! The band! Look at your wristband!' he called.

Swain looked down at the wristband. It was beeping horribly loudly now, and quicker, too.

And then he stopped.

The green light on the wristband had gone out.

Now the red one was on.

And it was flashing rapidly.

'Uh-oh.'

Hawkins caught up with them. He was panting desperately. 'What is it?'

'We're about to be in for some serious trouble,' Swain said.

At that moment the heavy hydraulic door to the janitor's room exploded from its hinges and flew out into the study hall, landing with a deafening *bang!*, crushing several desks.

It was followed by a blood-curdling roar that boomed out from within the janitor's room.

'Oh, man,' Hawkins breathed.

'Let's move!' Swain took off, winding through the maze of desks, heading for the stairwell in the opposite corner of the room.

He was glancing over his shoulder when it emerged from the janitor's room.

It was *huge*.

Absolutely huge. It had to double over just to fit through the wide doorway that no longer had a door.

Selexin saw it, too. 'It's the Karanadon!'

They were halfway across the wide study hall, crossing it diagonally, when the Karanadon cleared the doorway and rose to its full height, almost touching the ceiling.

Swain pressed on, carrying Holly toward the stairwell. Hawkins was losing ground behind him, weighed down by Balthazar. Last of all was Balthazar's guide—pushing and shoving—trying desperately to get Hawkins and Balthazar to move faster, constantly looking behind him, to see if the Karanadon was coming after them.

Swain glanced over his shoulder again to get another look at the fearsome beast.

It continued to stand by the door to the janitor's room, watching them.

It hadn't moved yet.

It just stood there.

Despite the noise they were making as they scrambled in a panic through the desks for the stairwell, it just stood in front of the doorway in silence.

Swain rounded another desk. Twenty yards to the stairwell. He looked back again.

Christ, it was big all right—at least fourteen feet tall.

It had the body of an enormous, hairy, broad-shouldered gorilla—all black, hunched forward, with a series of long spiky bristles that flowed over its high arched back. Long muscular arms hung down from its massive shoulders so that the knuckles dragged on the ground.

The head was two-and-a-half feet long, and it reminded Swain of a jackal. High pointed ears. Black, lifeless eyes. And menacing canine fangs that protruded from a dark wrinkled snout, frozen in an eternal snarl.

It moved.

The Karanadon leapt forward and bounded after them at frightening speed. It stomped on the fallen hydraulic door, cracking it in the middle, breaking it in two.

Swain tightened his grip on Holly and bolted for the stairwell. Hawkins struggled to pull Balthazar forward. Balthazar's guide was looking frantically

184

behind them, pounding on Hawkins' back, screaming for him to move faster.

The Karanadon ploughed through the L-shaped desks like an icebreaker through a frozen sea, hurling them in all directions, crushing them under its feet. When they happened to hit the ground, the big beast's footsteps sounded like cannon fire.

Boom. Boom. Boom.

Swain and the others continued to weave in and out between the desks. The Karanadon kept coming in a straight line.

Selexin was at the stairwell, Swain ten yards away. He checked behind him.

Hawkins, Balthazar and the other guide were not going to make it. The Karanadon was closing in on them too quickly.

Better think fast, Steve.

Boom. Boom. Boom.

He let Holly drop to the floor and quickly scanned the wide study hall.

It was roughly square in shape. He and Holly were almost at the stairwell, on the western side of the floor. The janitor's room was roughly opposite them, on the north-eastern corner of the floor. On the south-eastern corner were the elevators.

Boom. Boom. Boom.

'Move faster!' Balthazar's guide was screaming at Hawkins. 'For God's sake, it's getting closer!'

The Karanadon crunched through another desk.

And then Swain pushed Holly *away* from the stairwell, toward the elevators. 'Let's go, honey. We're gonna make a run for the elevators.' He called to Selexin at the stairwell door. 'This way! We're going this way!'

Boom. Boom. Boom.

'*That* way!' Selexin screamed back. 'What about the stairs!'

'Will you just do it, okay!'

The Karanadon was right on top of the others now.

It lunged at Balthazar's guide, swiping at him with one of its long arms. The guide ducked and the massive claw swished over his head and smashed into a nearby desk. The desk shattered and Balthazar's guide stumbled forward, tripping over Hawkins' legs, sending all three of them—the guide, Hawkins and Balthazar—sprawling forward.

Hawkins hit the ground hard, landing heavily on his shoulder. Balthazar fell on top of him. His guide landed helplessly at their feet.

Boom.

There was a sudden, terrifying silence.

The Karanadon had stopped.

Hawkins was sweating profusely. He wriggled desperately, tried to pull himself to his feet, but his right arm was jammed beneath Balthazar. His left wasn't even responding, the shoulder dislocated by the fall.

Down near his feet he saw the little guide frantically clutching at his trouser leg, trying desperately to stand up.

'Help me! *Help me!*' the guide pleaded, petrified.

And then suddenly—violently—the guide was sucked from Hawkins' view.

Over by the wall, Swain watched in horror as his three companions fell below the deskline.

The Karanadon had stopped a few feet short of them. Then it had bent down behind the desks, out of view. When it reappeared, it had the distinctive white shape of Balthazar's guide in one of its massive black claws.

The guide was waving his arms wildly, screaming at the monster. The Karanadon pulled him up to its snout and curiously examined the noisy little creature it had found.

And then, one-handed, the Karanadon held the guide out at arm's length and viciously slashed across the front of his body with its free claw.

Swain's jaw dropped.

Hawkins' eyes went wide with terror.

Three deep slits of red exploded across the guide's chest. One slashing tear sliced across his mouth. The guide's body went instantly limp.

The room was suddenly silent.

The Karanadon shook the body once. It didn't respond. The big beast shook the lifeless body again—like a toy that didn't work anymore—and then flung it away.

Swain still couldn't see Hawkins.

He ducked down to look through the legs of the desks—and he saw him. Hawkins was lying flat on the floor, wedged underneath Balthazar, unable to move, but trying anyway.

Christ, he had to do something for him . . .

Boom.

Hawkins was struggling to free himself when he felt the floor shake beneath him. He froze, and then slowly turned to look upward.

And saw the massive jaws of the Karanadon, wide open, rushing down at him.

He shut his eyes. It was too—
'Hey!'
The Karanadon's head snapped up instantly.
'Yeah, that's right, I'm talking to you!'
Hawkins opened his eyes.
What the hell—?

The Karanadon slowly turned to face Swain. It cocked its head curiously, staring at this bold creature that had dared to interrupt its kill.

Swain was waving his arms, yelling angrily at the fourteen-foot-tall beast that stood barely fifteen yards away from him.

'Yeah, get up! It's okay!' Swain barked, his face twisted in a fierce growl, never taking his eyes off the monster before him.

He raised his voice. It was angry, challenging. *'Move!* I've got it covered! It's looking at me now! Get up and go for the stairwell!' It was like talking to a dog—the beast heard the intonations, but made no sense of the words.

Hawkins suddenly realised what was happening— Swain was talking to him. Immediately, he began struggling again to shift Balthazar off him. In a few seconds, he got him off, and began to drag him across the floor, away from the Karanadon while Swain kept it occupied.

The Karanadon seemed dumbstruck by this challenging display. It roared fiercely at Swain.

'Oh, yeah! Well . . . well, fuck you, too!' Swain yelled back.

Out of the corner of his eye he saw Holly and Selexin reach the elevators over by the southern wall.

In the other direction, he saw Hawkins and Balthazar reach the stairwell.

Unfortunately, the Karanadon was still staring straight at him, totally exposed, halfway between the elevators and the stairs.

Shit. What could he do now? *Nice going, Steve.*

Boom.

The Karanadon took a slow step toward him.

Boom. Boom.

Two more and suddenly the gap was seven feet. Almost within striking distance.

'Hey!'

The Karanadon's head snapped left, toward Selexin and Holly by the elevator.

'Yes! That is right! I am talking to you!' Selexin yelled.

The big creature took a step toward the elevators, growling. It roared.

Selexin braced himself, pointed a finger, and yelled, 'Oh, yeah, well *fuck you, too*!'

Swain coughed back a laugh.

The Karanadon roared in outrage and stepped away from Swain, heading for the elevators. It was gaining speed when a third voice called loudly.

'Hey!'

The Karanadon stopped in its tracks a third time.

'Yeah, you!' It was Hawkins.

Swain swung his head back and forth between the elevators and the stairwell, amazed.

Now totally confused, the Karanadon swung to face Hawkins at the stairwell. Swain took the chance and ran for the elevator. When he got there, he pressed the call button.

Hawkins was waving wildly at the Karanadon as it

approached. When it got to within fifteen feet of him, Swain took over and called again from the elevators.

'Hello there! Hey, buddy! What about me!'

The Karanadon swung around slowly.

It snorted.

Boom.

Swain looked up at the numbered display above the left-hand elevator. The elevator was moving from '1' to 'G'. It was going *down*. What the hell? The right-hand elevator—with its inwardly dented doors and last seen by Swain stopped halfway between the First and Ground Floors—didn't seem to be operating at all.

Boom. Boom. Boom.

'Hey!' Hawkins called again. But this time, the beast didn't respond. It kept moving toward Swain and the elevators.

Boom. Boom. Boom.

'Hey!' Hawkins yelled. The Karanadon didn't stop. It just kept ploughing forward, toward the elevators.

'We have got trouble,' Selexin said flatly.

'We've got deep trouble,' Swain agreed.

Boom. Boom. Boom.

Swain spun around. Options, options. There were none. He checked the numbers above the elevators. Left—still on the Ground Floor. Right—still no movement at all.

He stared at the elevators for a second and suddenly had an idea.

'Quickly,' he said, moving over to the *right*-hand elevator. 'Selexin, Holly, you two grab the other side of this door and pull. We've got to get it open.'

Boom. Boom. Boom.

The Karanadon was closing in—getting faster and faster as it got closer and closer.

The elevator doors slowly came apart. 'Keep pulling,' Swain said. The black elevator shaft opened wide before him.

Boom.

'That's it,' Swain said, easing in between the doors—spreading his legs, holding them apart—while still facing the study hall. The dark elevator shaft yawned wide behind him.

It was then that Swain noticed the silence. No more booming footfalls.

The Karanadon had stopped.

Slowly, ever so slightly, Swain lifted his head.

It was *right there!*

Five feet away.

And it just stood there, looming over the three of them, its enormous black frame dwarfing them all. It tilted its head and glared down at Swain. One of its long pointed ears twitched.

'Holly, Selexin,' Swain whispered, without moving his mouth, 'I want both of you to grab hold of my legs. One each. *Right* now.'

'Daddy . . .' Holly whimpered.

'Just grab my leg, honey.'

There was a scratching sound, and Swain saw that it was the big beast's claws scraping against the marble floor as it flexed its huge black fists.

Getting ready to attack.

Holly clasped onto Swain's left leg. Selexin took the right.

'Hold tight,' Swain said, taking a deep breath as the Karanadon lifted its arm high.

The arm came down fast—but not fast enough. It hit nothing but air as Swain shifted his weight backwards and jumped into the darkness of the elevator shaft.

The elevator cable was greasy, but his grip held.

There were three vertical cables, so Swain held the middle one. Behind him, the elevator doors had shut automatically as soon as he had stopped holding them apart.

The elevator shaft was pitch black and deathly silent. If the Karanadon was roaring, they couldn't hear it in here.

'Selexin,' Swain said, his voice echoing loudly in the empty shaft. 'Grab hold of the cable.'

Selexin reached out from Swain's leg and caught hold of the elevator cable.

'All right now, slide down. Down to the elevator.'

Selexin slid down the cable, disappearing into the murky darkness of the shaft.

'Holly, you okay?'

'Yeah.' A whimper.

'All right, then, it's your turn now. Just reach out and grab the cable.'

'O-*kay*.'

Her hand shaking, Holly reached for the cable. Her fingers hesitated for an eternity just short of the greasy metal rope. She grabbed it.

And then suddenly the elevator doors burst open.

Soft blue light streamed into the elevator shaft, silhouetting the monstrous shape of the Karanadon as it held the doors apart.

It was only a few feet away and Swain was completely exposed, holding onto the elevator cable for dear life, with Holly dangling from his leg.

It roared loudly, leaning out into the shaft, swiping viciously at Swain, only to see him loosen his grip on the cable and drop out of the way a second ahead of the impact.

Swain fell like a stone, whizzing down the greasy cable into the darkness, with Holly hanging from his left leg.

They slid down the cable fast, the grease on the cable preventing Swain's hands from burning, and arrived at the roof of the right-hand elevator. Selexin was there waiting.

The elevator's hatch was still open and the light inside it still on. The lift was exactly where they had left it before, when Swain, Balthazar and the two guides had climbed across to meet Hawkins and Holly in the other one.

'Let's get inside, and see if we can get to another floor,' Swain said, grabbing Holly's hand and lowering her into the elevator. Selexin climbed in next. Swain jumped down last of all.

In the light of the elevator Swain could see how filthy they had become. The black grease from the cable covered their clothes. He felt his cheek. The bleeding had stopped.

'Where do we go now?' Selexin asked.

'I think we should go home, Daddy,' Holly suggested.

'Good idea,' Swain said.

Selexin said, 'Well, we had better figure out somethi—'

Suddenly, the elevator jolted and they were all thrown sideways.

'Oh my God,' Swain said, 'the cable!'

The elevator rocked violently, hurling them all to the ground. A loud *creaking* sound echoed throughout the shaft.

'It's got the cable!'

The elevator swayed dramatically and Selexin was thrown bodily into the side wall, hitting his head, falling to the floor in a heap. Swain tried to fight his way across the swaying lift to reach the button panel, but was jolted backwards. The back of his head banged into one of the elevator's doors, and for a second, he saw spots. The whole elevator groaned again at the tremendous strain being put on the cable.

And then, as quickly as it had begun, the rocking stopped and the elevator was still once more.

Holly was curled up in the corner, vigorously sucking her thumb. Selexin was out cold, face down on the floor. Swain staggered across the lift, rubbing the back of his head, looked up through the hatch.

He had just walked under the open hatch when he felt the elevator move again. Another jolt. But not like the previous ones. It was not as sharp, somehow different.

The elevator swayed again and Swain felt his knees buckle.

And then he realised.

They were going up.

It was *lifting* them up the shaft!

'Okay,' he said to himself, 'how the *hell* are we going to get out of this one?'

The lift continued upward, scraping loudly against the metal lining of the shaft.

Swain looked up through the hatch and could just make out the big arms of the Karanadon heaving on the elevator cable, hauling on it hand over hand, claw over claw.

The lift kept rising, moving higher into the shaft.

There's got to be a way out, he thought, *got to be.*

The Karanadon roared. They were close now, maybe a floor away. The hatch was still open. The Karanadon was glaring down at the elevator with animal fury as it heaved and pulled on the cables.

The cables, Swain thought.

He pondered the idea for a second. It was dangerous, yes. But it *could* work. At the moment it didn't look like he had much choice. He shrugged. Hell, anything was better than nothing.

He looked back at Holly. She was slumped in the corner of the lift, still sucking her thumb.

Yes. It could work.

It had to.

And with that, Stephen Swain reached up and climbed out through the hatch, up onto the roof of the elevator.

The study hall was closer than he thought.

They were about seven feet below the Third Floor doors where the Karanadon stood—and the lift was still moving upward.

The Karanadon saw him. And stopped.

Swain just stood there, on top of the elevator, staring at the beast.

Suddenly the Karanadon lashed out, swiping at

him with its spare claw. Swain stepped back, out of reach. The beast swung again, missed again.

'Come on!' Swain yelled. 'You can do better than that!'

The big beast roared in frustration and lashed out at him again, harder this time, missing Swain, but hitting one of the cables.

The cable snapped like a thread and the elevator lurched. But the Karanadon was still holding it up.

With one hand!

The big beast swung again, and Swain dived to his left. It missed, and cable number two snapped.

One more, Swain told himself. *One more, and we're out of here.*

This was getting to be too much for the Karanadon. It roared again in animal anger, like a dog barking at a cat that it will never catch.

'Come on, big boy,' Swain teased. 'One last swipe, and then you can get me the hell out of here.'

It was then that the Karanadon raised its arm one final time.

But it didn't swing.

It jumped.

Onto the roof of the elevator!

Swain didn't have time for disbelief. The elevator just plummeted straight down!

A piercing metal-on-metal screech attacked Swain's ears as the elevator descended in a freefall down the shaft. Wind whipped all around him as sparks flew out from every corner of the falling elevator.

The big beast stood on the other side of the roof oblivious to what it had done. It glared at Swain.

What sort of stupid creature jumps onto an elevator that it's holding up? Swain's mind screamed.

But Swain didn't have time to think about that now. He dived for the hatch, fell through it, landed heavily on the floor of the elevator.

'Get down!' he called to Holly, above the wail of the falling elevator. 'Get down on the floor! *Flat* on the floor! Rest your *head* on your *arms*!'

The elevator screamed down the shaft.

Holly did exactly as she was told, lay flat on the floor. Swain scrambled alongside her, covering her with one arm, and did the same—lay flat on his belly, spreading his legs wide, burying his head in his other forearm, using it as a cushion.

The last of the cables must have broken by now, he thought as he lay on the floor, waiting for the bone-jarring crash that would come any second now.

The Karanadon poked its huge head through the small hatch—upside-down. It wanted to get inside, but it would never fit.

The elevator roared down the shaft, sparks flying from all sides, its high-pitched wail getting higher and higher and higher.

And then it hit the bottom.

The impact was stunning.

Swain felt his whole body shudder violently as the elevator went from thirty-five miles an hour to zero in a split second.

The muscles on his forearms cushioned his head. And his body, since it was already flush against the floor, stifled most of the force of the impact.

The same happened with Holly. Swain hoped Selexin was all right, since he had already been on the floor, knocked out.

As the elevator hit the bottom of the shaft with a horrendous *bang!*, the roof beneath the Karanadon gave way and the big beast burst right through it, crashing to the floor of the elevator, landing heavily on its back—*right next to* Swain—in a cloud of dust and shattered plastic.

A minute passed.

Slowly, Swain lifted his head.

The first thing he saw was the dark wrinkled snout and the enormous white fangs of the Karanadon, right in front of his eyes.

He started. But the beast did not move.

Swain quickly looked at his wristband and sighed.

The green light was back on. The Karanadon was out cold.

He lifted his body and all sorts of debris fell from his back onto the floor. Half the roof of the old, wide elevator had fallen in under the weight of the big beast, and pieces of the ceiling and shards of fluorescent light bulbs lay strewn all over the elevator.

Christ, he thought, it looked as if a bomb had gone off here: white dust floating through the air, the roof caved in, half the lights flickering, the other half destroyed beyond recognition.

Swain stood up. He touched the large bruise that was forming on the back of his head. His lower back ached from the thunderous impact. He lifted his arm off Holly.

'Holly?' he said, quietly. 'Are you okay?'

She stirred gently, as if coming out of a deep, painful sleep.

'Wha . . . what?'

Swain shut his eyes in relief and gave her a kiss on the forehead.

'Are we there yet, Daddy?' she whimpered, her head still buried in her forearms.

'Yes, honey, we're here,' he smiled.

Across the lift, Selexin groaned. He slowly raised his head and stared, unfocused, at Swain. Then he looked across the lift at the limp—but live—body of the Karanadon.

'Oh my goodness . . .'

'Tell me about it,' Swain said dryly.

'Where are we?'

'We're at the bottom of the shaft, I guess. We took the quick trip down.'

'Oh,' Selexin said absently.

He didn't seem too worried about anything right now, and for that matter, neither did Swain. He figured they could stay here for a while. The Karanadon wouldn't be waking up in the very near future, and no-one would be able to find them here.

He sat up, gently placing his daughter's head in his lap, and leaned up against the wall of the semi-destroyed elevator and smiled sadly at the destruction all around him.

Bob Charlton stopped his Chevy at a red light and dialled his office. It had barely rung once when Rudy answered.

'*Robert Charlton's phone.*'

'Rudy?' Charlton said.

'*Yes, sir. Where are you?*'

'At the moment, stuck in downtown traffic. I'm on my way. I'll be back in about five minutes.'

At the other end of the line, Rudy Baker paused, and glanced nervously around Charlton's office.

'Okay, sir,' he said. 'Is there anything you want me to do in the meantime? Look up something for you?'

Charlton's voice said, '*Good idea, yes. While you're waiting, check the computer. See if the New York State Library was linked up with the main when we did that National Register of Historic Places thing a few months back. If it was, run down to Records and pull the plans. Get the blueprints and see if you can find out where the damn booster valve is.*'

'Uh . . . okay, sure,' he hesitated again.

'*What is it, son?*' Charlton said. '*Something wrong down there?*'

'No, sir. Not here,' Rudy lied. 'I'll see you when you get back.'

'*All right then.*' Charlton hung up.

In the office, Rudy leaned forward and switched off the speakerphone.

'Well done, son,' a voice behind him said. 'Now, why don't you just take a seat with the rest of us, and we can all wait here together until your boss comes back.'

Charlton hurried out of the elevator and walked quickly down the hallway to his office.

He looked at his watch.

It was 7:55 p.m.

He hoped that Rudy had got those files on the State Library. If he had, with a bit of luck they might be able to have the main up and running again by midnight.

Charlton charged into his office and stopped instantly.

Rudy was sitting in the chair behind Charlton's desk. He looked up helplessly.

Five other men, all dressed in dark suits, sat in a neat row in front of the desk.

As Charlton walked in, one of the men stood up and walked over to him. He was short and stocky, with red hair and a big orange walrus-style moustache.

'Mr Charlton, Special Agent John Levine,' he flashed his wallet, revealing a photo ID. 'I'm from the National Security Agency.'

Charlton examined the ID card. He wondered what the NSA would want with Con Ed.

'What seems to be the problem, Mr Levine?'

'Oh, there's no problem,' Levine said quickly.

'Then what can I do for you?' Charlton's eyes wandered warily around his office, scanning the four other men seated there.

They were all big men, broad-shouldered. Two wore sunglasses even though it was nearly eight in the evening. They were very intimidating.

'Please, Mr Charlton, take a seat. We just came by to ask you a few questions about your inquiry into the New York State Library.'

'I'm not looking at the Library itself,' Charlton said, sitting down in a spare chair. Levine sat opposite him. 'I'm just looking for a break in our main electrical line. We've had quite a few calls from that area, complaints about the power cutting out on people.'

Levine nodded. 'Uh-huh. So. Apart from being in the same area, what is the connection between these complaints and the State Library?'

'Well,' Charlton said, 'the Library is on the National Register of Historic Places, you know, one of those lists of old buildings that aren't allowed to be demolished.'

'I know it.'

'Anyway, we linked a few of them up to the main a few months back, and we've found that when they go down, sometimes they take the whole damn system with them.'

Levine nodded again. 'So why have you begun to focus on *this* building? Surely there are others in the area that deserve similar attention?'

'Mr Levine, I've been doing this sort of thing for ten years now and when you get a break in the main it can mean a shitload of problems. And that means you have to check *everything*. Every possibility. Sometimes it's kids hacking at the cables with daddy's chainsaw, sometimes it's just an overload. I've always found it prudent to go down and check with the police and see if they've pulled in someone from that area lately.'

'You went to the police?' Levine raised an eyebrow.

'Yes.'

'And did you find anything?'

'Yes, I did. In fact, it was the police who put me on to the Library in the first place.'

'If you don't mind me asking,' Levine said, 'which police station was this?'

'14th Precinct,' Charlton said.

'And what did they tell you?'

'They told me they picked up a small-time computer thief in the State Library last night, in relation to the murder of a security guard. I saw the fellow, too—'

'A murdered security guard?' Levine leaned forward.

'Yes.'

'A guard from the State Library?'

'Yes.'

'And the police said he was killed last night?'

'That's right. Last night,' Charlton said. 'They found the thief right next to him, covered from head to toe in the guard's blood.'

Levine looked around at his fellow agents. Then he said, 'Do they think the thief did it?'

'No. He was just a scrawny little guy. But they think he must have stumbled upon the guys who did. Then they roughed him up. Something like that.'

Levine stopped for a moment, deep in thought.

Then he asked very seriously, 'Have the police put any men inside the building? Inside the library?'

'The detective I spoke to said they have two officers down there right now,' Charlton said. 'You know, babysitting the building overnight, until some site team can go in tomorrow.'

'So there are police officers inside that building right now?'

'That's what they told me.'

At that, Levine turned to his men and nodded at the nearest one, who stood immediately.

'14th Precinct,' Levine said to him. He glanced back at Bob Charlton. 'Mr Charlton, can you remember the name of the detective to whom you spoke?'

'Yes. Captain Henry Dickson.'

Levine just turned to the standing agent and nodded curtly. The agent didn't reply. He just ran straight from the room.

Levine faced Charlton again. 'Mr Charlton, you have been very helpful. I thank you for your co-operation.'

'Not at all,' Charlton said, rising from his chair. 'If that's everything, gentlemen, I have a main to fix, so if you'll excuse me, I've got to go and check out that library—'

Levine stood, placed his hand on Charlton's chest, stopping him.

'I'm sorry, Mr Charlton, but I'm afraid your inquiry into the New York State Library stops here.'

'*What?*'

Levine spoke calmly. 'This is no longer a matter for you or your company, Mr Charlton. The National Security Agency will take care of it from here.'

'But what about the main?' Charlton objected. 'Or the electricity? I have to get it back on.'

'It can wait.'

'Bullshit, it can wait.' Charlton stepped forward angrily.

'Sit down, Mr Charlton.'

'No, I will not sit down. This is a serious problem, Mr Levine,' Charlton paused. 'I'd like to speak with your superior.'

'*Sit down*, Mr Charlton.' Levine said, a new authority in his voice. Immediately, two agents appeared at Charlton's sides. They didn't touch him, just stood by his shoulders.

Charlton sat, frowning.

Levine said, 'All I will tell you is this, Mr Charlton. In the last two hours, that library has become the focus of a major NSA investigation. An investigation that will not be stopped because one hundred and eighty-seven New Yorkers won't be able to watch *Friends* for one night.'

Charlton just sat there, silent. Levine walked over to the doorway.

'Your inquiry is concluded, Mr Charlton. You will be advised as to when you may proceed.' Levine stepped through the doorway, taking one agent with him, leaving Charlton in the office with Rudy and the other two agents.

Charlton couldn't believe it. 'What? You're *keeping* me here? You can't do that!'

Levine stopped in the doorway. 'Oh yes I can, Mr Charlton, and I will. Under Federal law, it is within the power of an investigating officer to detain anyone concerned in a matter of national security for the duration of that investigation. You *will* remain here, Mr Charlton, with your assistant, under supervision, until this investigation is substantially concluded. Thank you for your co-operation.'

Down the hall, Levine stepped into the elevator and pulled out his cellular phone.

'*Marshall, here,*' a crackled voice said at the other end.

There was a lot of static on the line.

'Sir, it's me, Levine.'

'*Yes, John, what is it? How did it go?*'

'Good and bad, sir.'

'*Tell me the good news first.*'

Levine said, 'It's definitely the State Library.'

A pause, then, '*Yes.*'

'And we got to Charlton just in time. He was just about to go there.'

'*Good.*'

Levine paused, nervously fingering his red walrus moustache.

Marshall's voice said, '*And the bad news?*'

Levine bit his lip. 'We had to detain him.'

There was silence on the other end of the line.

'There was no choice, Mr Marshall. We had to keep him away from the library.'

The man named Marshall seemed to be thinking it over. Finally he spoke, as if to himself. '*No. No. That's okay. Charlton will be all right. Besides, if this thing comes off, any flak the Agency gets from him will be water off a duck's back. What else?*'

Levine held his breath. 'There are two cops inside the building.'

'*Inside?*'

'Yes.'

'*Oh, fuck,*' Marshall's voice said. '*That is a problem.*'

Levine waited in silence. The phone hissed with static. Marshall lapsed into thought again. When he spoke, his voice was soft, deliberate.

'*We'll have to take them with us.*'

'The cops? Can we do that?'

Marshall said, '*They're contaminated. It doesn't look like we have much choice.*'

Levine said, 'What do you want me to do now?'

'Get over to the library and, for the moment, stay out of sight. The boys from Sigma will be there shortly,' Marshall said. 'I'll be landing in a couple of minutes. There's a car waiting on the runway, so I'll be there in about thirty minutes.'

'Yes, sir.'

Levine hung up.

James A. Marshall sat in the executive compartment of the National Security Agency's Director's Lear as it began its descent into Newark.

As the Divisional Agent in Charge of the NSA's ultra-secret Sigma Division, Marshall was officially based in Maryland, but lately he found that he was spending most of his time out in the western states, New Mexico and Nevada.

Marshall was a tall man of fifty-two, mostly bald, with a white-grey beard and hawk-like black eyebrows that narrowed at his nose, giving him a perpetual look of deadly seriousness. He had been in charge of Sigma Division—the NSA's elite high-technology discovery division—for six years now.

Back in the seventies and eighties, the NSA had been the US intelligence community's pride and joy, electronically compressing billions of encryption algorithms that were to become the foundation of its world-renowned code-breaking computers. Then, in the early nineties, Sigma added to this lustre when it utilised semiconductor technology to make the greatest breakthrough in the history of code-making and breaking—it successfully created the world's first quantum computer.

But with the subsequent thawing of the Cold War, code-cracking began to assume a lesser priority in the eyes of the government. Budgets were cut. Money was diverted to other sectors of the intelligence community and the military. The NSA had to find something *new* to excel in—something that would justify its continued existence. Otherwise it would almost certainly get folded into the Army.

James Marshall and Sigma Division were tasked with finding this new expertise.

Within weeks, Sigma's resources were focused upon a new and remarkably different goal. Only this was a goal that did not require the *creation* of new technology, but which rather was centred on the search for, discovery of, and *deciphering* of, a very special kind of technology.

Highly advanced technology.

Technology that man himself could not create.

But technology which the NSA—and the NSA alone, with its new quantum supercomputers—would be in a unique position to decipher and exploit.

Extra-terrestrial technology.

Marshall took it all with a grain of salt. Sure, the Air Force had built underground warehouses in New Mexico and Nevada. But despite the reports of television specials asserting that they had in fact found, captured and studied alien spacecraft and lifeforms— one such special even suggested that the technology behind the Stealth Bomber came from such studies— those warehouses had remained irrefutably and unequivocally empty.

In short, the Air Force had found nothing. And in the ever-competitive quest for budget dollars, that provided the NSA with an opportunity . . .

Like tonight, Marshall thought.

And as his plane made its descent, he looked at the printout in his lap for the hundredth time.

Two hours ago, at 6:01 p.m. Eastern Standard Time, an NSA satellite, *LandSat 5*, during a random sweep over the north-eastern tip of America, detected and quantified an unusually large electronic displacement that seemed to be emanating from Manhattan Island.

The displacement had not been present during any previous sweeps, and its amperage was dangerously similar to that of previously recorded electronic scrambling—or jamming—frequencies used by North African guerilla forces, in particular those used by Libya.

And after the bombing of the World Trade Centre in 1993 by North African extremists and the destruction of two American embassies in Africa in 1998, no-one in the NSA was willing to take any chances.

The response was immediate.

The *LandSat 5* results were bounced immediately to NSA headquarters at Fort Meade, Maryland. A KH-11E counter-intelligence electronic surveillance satellite—more commonly known by its call-sign 'Eavesdropper'—was sequestered from the National Reconnaissance Office, and retasked so that it would pass over New York.

By chance, the Eavesdropper happened to be in the right place at the right time and was on the scene in minutes, and the first set of results were soon in the hands of the NSA's crisis management team in Maryland—a team that had included Marshall.

Once those results had been reviewed, in the space

of nine minutes all records of correspondence between satellite control in Maryland, *LandSat 5* and the Eavesdropper had been destroyed.

LandSat 5 was retasked for immediate splashdown somewhere in the Pacific Ocean, while the Eavesdropper continued to monitor the Manhattan area with every pass.

It was then that the mission had been handed to James Marshall and his boys at Sigma Division.

Time was short, and Marshall had wasted no time.

He had raced to the airport immediately and as he stepped onto the Director's Lear, someone at Sigma was already preparing a press release that would explain the unfortunate and regrettable loss of the two satellites.

And so here he was. On the NSA Director's Lear ready for touchdown in New York.

Marshall reached into his suitcase for a final look at the report from the Eavesdropper.

Judging by the long stretch of time covered in the report, Marshall noted, the Eavesdropper could hold its field of view on a single target for a full fifty minutes. Its orbital velocity must have been much slower than that of the smaller *LandSat 5*.

Marshall read the transcript.

LSAT-560467-S
DATA TRANSCRIPT 463/511-001
SUBJECT SITE: 231.957 (North-eastern seaboard: CT, NY, NJ)

NO.	TIME/EST	LOCATION	READING
1.	18:03:48	CT.	Isolated energy surge/Source: **UNKNOWN**
			Type: **UNKNOWN** / Dur: **0.00:09**

2.	18:03:58	N.Y.	Isolated energy surge/Source: **UNKNOWN**
			Type: **UNKNOWN** / Dur: **0.00:06**
3.	18:07:31	N.Y.	Isolated energy surge/Source: **UNKNOWN**
			Type: **UNKNOWN** / Dur: **0.00:05**
4.	18:10:09	N.Y.	Isolated energy surge/Source: **UNKNOWN**
			Type: **UNKNOWN** / Dur: **0.00:07**
5.	18:14:12	N.Y.	Isolated energy surge/Source: **UNKNOWN**
			Type: **UNKNOWN** / Dur: **0.00:06**
6.	18:14:37	N.Y.	Isolated energy surge/Source: **UNKNOWN**
			Type: **UNKNOWN** / Dur: <u>**0.00:02**</u>
7.	18:14:38	N.Y.	Isolated energy surge/Source: **UNKNOWN**
			Type: **UNKNOWN** / Dur: <u>**0.00:02**</u>
8.	18:14:39	N.Y.	Isolated energy surge/Source: **UNKNOWN**
			Type: **UNKNOWN** / Dur: <u>**0.00:02**</u>
9.	18:14:40	N.Y.	Isolated energy surge/Source: **UNKNOWN**
			Type: **UNKNOWN** / Dur: <u>**0.00:02**</u>
10.	18:16:23	N.Y.	Isolated energy surge/Source: **UNKNOWN**
			Type: **UNKNOWN** / Dur; **0.00:07**
11.	18:20:21	N.Y.	Isolated energy surge/Source: **UNKNOWN**
			Type: **UNKNOWN** / Dur: **0.00:08**
12.	18:23:57	N.Y.	Isolated energy surge/Source: **UNKNOWN**
			Type: **UNKNOWN** / Dur: **0.00:06**
13.	18:46:00	N.Y.	Isolated energy surge/Source: **UNKNOWN**
			Type: **UNKNOWN** / Dur: **0.00:34**

Marshall frowned at the transcript.

At the moment it meant nothing to him.

Twelve strong surges of some unknown kind of energy—the sources of which were also unknown—had all occurred in New York City between 6:03 and 6:46 p.m.

Added to that, the first surge, which had come from somewhere inside Connecticut. Curious also was the last surge—distinctive because it had lasted thirty-four seconds, more than three times longer than any of the others. Not to mention the four consecutive two-second surges that Marshall had underlined.

What it amounted to was a puzzle, a puzzle Marshall wanted to solve.

And Levine's news was good. The taps on Con Edison's phones had been worthwhile, if not altogether legal. The theory that large energy surges would affect local electricity systems had turned out to be correct.

Robert Charlton had led them right to the source of the energy surges.

The New York State Library.

Now they had the location. And they were going to get whatever was there.

James Marshall grinned at the thought as his Lear hit the tarmac at Newark.

Hawkins lowered Balthazar to the floor, resting him up against the concrete wall of the janitor's room. Then he himself collapsed, breathless, alongside the big bearded man.

'You're one heavy bastard, you know that?'

The janitor's room was a complete mess. The cyclone fence cutting across the middle of the room had been crumpled by the Karanadon. The splintered remains of smashed wooden boxes lay strewn everywhere. And without the big hydraulic door, the doorway was nothing more than a gaping hole in the wall.

Hawkins glanced at Balthazar by his side. He wasn't looking good. Eyes still badly bloodshot. A red rash forming on the surrounding skin. Bubbles of saliva still running through his bushy beard.

Balthazar groaned, and then as if testing himself, he put a hand to the floor to get up, but immediately fell awkwardly back against the wall.

They would have to hole up here for a while. But first, Hawkins thought, he had to do something about that doorway.

At last, Selexin got up and walked across the elevator and stared at the massive body of the unconscious Karanadon. He bent down and peered at the long white fangs that protruded from the jet-black snout.

He made a face of pure disgust. 'Hideous,' he said. 'Truly hideous.'

Swain was holding Holly in his lap. She had gone to sleep quickly, complaining of a terrible headache. 'Yeah, not too bright, either,' he said. 'Have you ever seen one before? Up close?'

'No. Never.'

Swain nodded and they both just stared at the gigantic black beast in silence. Then he said, 'So what do we do? Do we kill it? *Can* we kill it?'

'I do not know,' Selexin shrugged. 'No-one has ever done this before.'

Swain offered a crooked smile and spread his hands. 'What can I say?'

Selexin frowned, not comprehending. 'I am sorry, but I am afraid I do not understand. What exactly *can* you say?'

'Don't worry. It's just a saying.'

'Oh.'

'Yeah,' Swain said, 'like "Fuck you".'

Selexin blushed. 'Oh, yes. That. Well, I had to say *something*. My life was in the balance too, you know.'

'Hell of a thing to say to something like *that*,' Swain nodded at the Karanadon.

'Oh, well . . .'

'But it was pretty bold. And I needed it. Thanks.'

'Think nothing of it.'

'Well, thanks anyway,' Swain said. 'By the way, are you allowed to do that? Allowed to help me?'

'Well,' Selexin said, 'technically, no. I am not

supposed to help you physically in any battle—whether against another contestant or the Karanadon. But considering what Bellos has done by bringing hoods into the Presidian, then, to use another of your sayings, I think that all gambling has been cancelled.'

'Huh?'

'Is that not how you say it? "All gambling has been cancelled?" It means that the rules no longer apply.'

'I think what you're trying to say is, *All bets are off*,' Swain said gently. 'But you were close. Very close.'

Selexin preened at that, pleased with himself.

Swain turned back to the Karanadon. The long spiked bristles on the beast's back were rising and falling in time with its loud, strained breathing. It was absolutely enormous.

'So can we kill it?'

'I thought you did not kill defenceless victims,' Selexin said.

'That only counts for people.'

'Balthazar was not a person, and you did not kill him. He is amorphic, remember. As a matter of fact, I am sure that you would be rather surprised at Balthazar's true form—'

Swain said, 'All right. Only for things that *look like* people, then. And besides,' he looked at the Karanadon, 'Balthazar wasn't going to rip my head off if he decided to fight back.'

Selexin looked as if he was about to object but stopped himself. He merely said, 'Okay.'

'So. What do you think? Can we kill it?' Swain asked.

'I don't see why not. But what will you kill it with?'

They surveyed the elevator. There wasn't much to be found by way of weapons. The roof of the lift had been made of thin plasterboard and one whole half of it had simply disappeared, destroyed by the Karanadon's fall. Large jagged shards of frosted plastic from the fluorescent lights lay strewn across the floor. Swain picked one up. In his hand, it looked like a pretty pathetic weapon.

Selexin shrugged. 'It *could* work. Then again, it might not do anything except wake it up.'

'Hmm,' Swain didn't like the thought of that.

He didn't want to rouse the Karanadon. It was fine now. Out cold. But for how long? And killing something that was bigger and stronger than a grizzly bear, by hand, with a shard of plastic, somehow didn't seem very likely.

At that moment, the Karanadon's right claw reached up lazily and swatted at something buzzing around its snout. Then the claw resumed its position by the creature's side and the big beast continued its slumber as if nothing had happened.

Swain watched it intently. Frozen.

The Karanadon snorted loudly, shuffled onto its side, rolled over.

'You know, upon further reflection, I am not so sure that killing it is a very good idea,' Selexin whispered.

'I was just thinking the same thing myself,' Swain said. 'Come on, let's go.' He stood up and lifted Holly.

'Come on, honey. Time to go.'

She stirred groggily, '—my head hurts.'

'Where to?' Selexin asked.

'Up,' Swain said, pointing to the big hole in the roof of the elevator.

After heaving the outer elevator doors open, Swain looked out into the musty yellow gloom to see row upon row of bookshelves stretching away to his left and right.

It was Sub-Level Two.

The Stack.

They were standing on what was left of the roof of the destroyed elevator, five feet below the floor level of Sub-Level Two. The concrete bottom of the elevator shaft, it seemed, was still a fair way below Sub-Level Two.

Swain climbed out first and saw that on this floor, the elevators were embedded in the wall of bookshelves.

He looked out from the doors and immediately realised that they were on one of the long ends of the rectangular floor. The southern wall.

Swain remembered finding Hawkins on this floor, and seeing Reese for the first time, and running blindly through the maze of shelves to the safety of the stairwell. But that, he remembered, had happened on the other side of the floor.

He turned back to the elevator shaft and pulled Holly and Selexin out.

'I remember this part of the labyrinth,' Selexin said, seeing the bookshelves around him. 'Reese.'

'That's right.'

'Daddy, I have a headache,' Holly said wearily.

'I know, honey.'

'I want to go home.'

'So do I,' Swain said, reaching down, touching her head. 'We'll see if we can find something for your headache, and at the same time, somewhere to hole up. Come on, let's go.'

They began walking left, down the southern wall of the Stack. After walking some distance, their aisle turned sharply to the right, and they headed up the shorter western wall of the floor. They had gone about twenty yards along the wall when Swain noticed something odd.

Just ahead of them, flush against the outer wall of shelves, something was ajar, sticking slightly out into the aisle. Something red.

As they came closer, Swain realised what it was.

It was a door.

A small red door, slightly opened. It was tucked into the outer wall of shelves, very unobtrusively. Indeed, Swain had seen it only because he had almost walked right past it. Anyone conducting a cursory examination of the Stack would almost certainly miss it.

The small red door had writing on it.

'"No Staff Access Permitted",' Selexin read aloud. 'What is that supposed to mean?'

But Swain wasn't paying any attention to Selexin. He was already kneeling in front of the door, peering down at its base.

Selexin said, 'I thought the staff were allowed to go everywhere in a place like this—'

'Shh,' Swain said. 'Look at this.'

Selexin and Holly crouched beside him and stared down at the book lying on the floor, wedged in between the door and its frame.

'It looks like it is holding the door open . . .' Selexin said.

'It *is* holding the door open,' Swain said, 'or at least stopping it from closing.'

'Why?' Holly asked.

Swain frowned. 'I don't know.' He looked at the door handle. On the library side, it had a keyhole in the middle of a plain silver knob. On the other side, though, he could not see any lock or keyhole. High up near the hinges he saw the closing mechanism.

'It's spring-loaded,' he said. 'To make sure it shuts every time. That's why someone used the book.'

'Why is no staff access permitted?' Selexin asked.

'Probably because this door has nothing to do with the library. And only staff are allowed in the Stack. I'd say it's probably a gas or electricity meter. Something like that,' Swain said. 'Something the staff are not supposed to touch.'

'Oh.'

Holly said, 'Can we get out through there?'

Swain looked to Selexin. 'I don't know. Can we?'

'The labyrinth was *supposed* to be sealed at the time of electrification. I cannot know what would happen if one entrance was not fully closed at that time. But I can guess.'

'So guess.'

'Well,' Selexin peered around the rim of the small red door marked NO STAFF ACCESS PERMITTED. 'I see no visible sign of electrification here. And unless there is another door *beyond* this one that was closed at the time of electrification, my guess is that we may have just found a way out of the labyrinth.'

'A way out?' Holly said hopefully.

'Yes.'

'Are you sure?' Swain whispered.

'There is only one way to find out,' Selexin said. 'We have to see if there is another door beyond this one.'

'Do we?' Swain said, thinking.

'Why, yes,' Selexin said. 'Unless you can think of another way.'

Crouching on the floor, Swain looked up at the little man, and said, 'As a matter of fact, I think I can.'

And with that, Stephen Swain thrust his left arm—with the thick grey wristband attached to it—*through* the gap between the small red door and its frame.

Immediately they heard a loud, insistent beeping coming from outside the door, and after a couple of seconds, Swain pulled his wrist back inside.

The beeping stopped instantly.

They all looked at the thick grey wristband. Its display now read:

INITIALISED—6
DETONATION SEQUENCE INITIALISED.
AT * 14:57 * DETONATION SEQUENCE CANCELLED
RESET.

14:57 was flashing.

Swain smiled at Selexin. 'There's no outer door. This is the last one.'

'How do you know, Daddy?' Holly asked.

'Because,' Selexin said, 'your father's wristband is set to initialise an automatic detonation sequence of fifteen minutes as soon as it senses that it is outside the energy field of this labyrinth.'

'What?' Holly said.

Swain said, 'He means that if I move outside the electric field that's all around this building, this wristband will explode unless I get back inside in fifteen minutes.'

'And do you see that?' Selexin pointed to the readout, the flashing 14:57. 'The countdown started when he put his wrist outside the door.'

'Which means,' Swain continued, 'that once we're

outside this door, we're outside the electrical field, and outside the labyrinth.'

'Right,' Selexin said.

'So let's go,' Holly said. 'Let's get out of this place.'

'We can't,' Swain said sadly, 'or, at least, *I* can't. Not yet.'

'Why not?' Holly said.

'Because of the wristband,' Selexin sighed.

Swain nodded. 'I can't get it off. And if I don't, I'll only last fifteen minutes before this thing explodes.'

'Then we had better find a way to get it off,' Selexin said.

'How?' Swain said, shaking his wrist. The wristband was hard and strong, a thick steel clamp. 'Look at it. It's as solid as a rock. We'd need an axe or a hammer to break it open, *and* someone strong enough to crack it.'

'I bet Balthazar could do it,' Holly said. 'He's really big. And I bet he's really strong, too.'

'And when we last saw him, he was not strong enough to stand up by himself,' Selexin said sourly.

'We don't even know if he and Hawkins are still alive,' Swain said. 'There has to be another way.'

Selexin said, 'Maybe they have a vice around here that we could squeeze it in. Snap it open with the pressure.'

'In a library? Not likely.'

Frustrated, Selexin sat down next to the semi-opened door, staring at the escape he couldn't use. Swain was also gazing at the door, deep in thought. Holly held him tightly by the arm.

'Well, first of all,' Swain said, 'we have to get you guys out. After that, I'll just have to find a way to get this thing off and then meet you outside.' He snorted.

'Hmph. Maybe I should go and ask Bellos if he'd like to have a try. I'm sure he'd like that.'

'He'd definitely be strong enough,' Selexin said.

'But would he do it?' Swain scoffed.

'Gladly,' a deep baritone voice said from somewhere behind him.

Swain spun.

There, right in front of him, standing in one of the aisles perpendicular to the western wall, stood Bellos.

Swain felt a chill at the sight of the man. His body, his face, his long tapering horns, everything about him was black. Except for his breastplate, which Swain now clearly saw to be beautifully crafted in gold.

And he was tall, taller than he had seemed before. At least seven feet.

'Greetings, fellow competitor. Before you stands Bellos—'

'I know who you are,' Swain said softly.

Bellos cocked his head in astonishment.

'Where are your hoods?' Swain asked calmly, as Selexin and Holly slowly got to their feet beside him. 'You don't fight without them, do you?'

Bellos chuckled evilly. As he did so, Swain saw something jingle at his side—something attached to his belt.

It was the Konda's breathing mask.

With a tinge of horror, Swain recalled Selexin's earlier description of Bellos: *the trophy collector*.

And then suddenly he caught sight of a second

object clipped to Bellos' belt, something that glinted dull gold in the mouldy yellow light of the Stack. Swain's eyes widened when he saw what it was.

It was a New York Police Department badge.

Hawkins' partner . . .

Bellos spoke, releasing Swain from his thoughts. 'You attempt to show courage you do not possess, little man. There are no hoods here. Just you. And me.'

'Really,' Swain said. 'I don't believe you.'

Bellos stepped forward. 'You use strong words for a man who is *moriturum esse*.'

'*Moriturum esse*,' Swain repeated. Out of the corner of his eye, he watched for the hoods, expecting one of them to spring from one of the nearby aisles at any moment now. 'About to die, huh. If that's the case, why don't you just *osci assinum meum* then,' he said.

Bellos frowned, not understanding.

'*Osci assinum meum*?' he repeated, perplexed. 'You want me to kiss your mule, your ass?'

Swain surreptitiously kicked the book wedged in the doorway clear from the small red door. The spring-loaded door immediately began to close and he caught it in his hand—behind his back.

'When they attack,' he whispered to Selexin and Holly, 'I want you two to run straight through the door. Don't worry about me.'

'But—'

'*Just do it*,' Swain said, never taking his eyes off Bellos.

Bellos sneered, 'Do you just stand there, little man, *or do you fight*?'

Swain said nothing, just looked left. Then right. Waiting for the hoods.

They attacked.

Suddenly. Without warning. From the front. Not the sides. From *behind* Bellos's shoulder.

It was a single hood, springing forward, claws bared. Straight at Swain.

With his free hand Swain swiped at the creature backhanded, hitting it squarely in the head, sending it crashing to the floor with a squeal.

Swain immediately opened the door behind him. 'Go!' he yelled to Selexin and Holly. 'Go! Go!'

And then the second hood attacked.

This one came from the left, slamming into Swain's back, knocking him to the floor, making him let go of the door.

The spring-loaded door began to close.

The second hood leapt at Swain again as he rolled onto his back. Swain threw a desperate arm up at the approaching hood and caught its narrow throat in his hand. Its massive jaws clamped viciously open and shut, trying madly to reach his face, as Swain held it out at arm's length.

Its claws swatted wildly, lashing out at his chest— but they weren't long enough. So it went for his arm instead—slashing ferociously. Five bloody gashes appeared instantly across Swain's forearm.

It was then that Swain saw the door closing.

'The door! *Get the door!*' he yelled to Holly and Selexin.

But Holly and Selexin just stood there. Dead still. Staring off to the right, down the western wall.

Swain was looking desperately at the rapidly closing door. It was almost shut when, as a last resort, he thrust his leg out and wedged his foot between the door and its frame.

'Go!' he yelled, kicking the door open again as he wrestled with the hood.

But Selexin and Holly weren't moving.

They were watching the third and fourth hoods as they stalked ominously out into the aisle.

Swain got up on one knee, still holding the second hood at arm's length. The animal decided on a new tactic. Instead of writhing about maniacally in his grip, lashing out with its claws, it grabbed hold of Swain's forearm with both its claws, clinging to him, and started *squeezing*, hoping to break his grip on its neck.

'Jesus! Go! Get out!' Swain yelled, his foot holding the door wide open. 'I can't hold it open much longer!'

But Holly and Selexin didn't move, and when at last he saw what they were looking at, Swain had a fleeting thought that came a second too late.

Where did that first hood go?

The first hood slammed into Swain at a crunching speed—hurling itself, Swain and the second hood into the open door. Swain bounced off the door and into the dark corridor beyond it, the two hoods with him.

'*No!*' he cried, as he saw the door behind him start closing again.

He still had the second hood's throat gripped tightly in his hand—just as it still held his forearm. Ruthlessly, he banged its head twice against the hard concrete floor and the hood immediately released its grip and its body went limp and Swain threw it aside and dived for the closing door.

There was noise everywhere. The hoods squealing, a loud electronic beeping coming from his wristband, and then—worst of all—the sound of Holly screaming inside the library.

Still diving, Swain landed a few feet short of the door and slid the rest of the way on his chest, arms outstretched . . .

Too late.

The door shut.

The lock clicked.

And a blinding burst of sizzling blue electricity exploded out from the hinges and the handle.

Electrified.

There was a sudden, terrifying silence, broken only by the loud insistent beeping noise that came from Swain's wristband. Swain looked down at it. It read:

INITIALISED—6
DETONATION SEQUENCE INITIALISED.
* 14:55 *
AND COUNTING

Stephen Swain looked up at the electrified door in horror.

He was now outside the labyrinth.

FOURTH MOVEMENT

30 November, 8:41 p.m.

Holly and Selexin ran flat out down one of the aisles of Sub-Level Two.

Holly could hear nothing but her own rapid breathing as they raced down the narrow canyons of bookshelves. Beside her, Selexin was holding her hand, pulling her along, constantly looking behind them.

They came to a junction of aisles and made a quick right-left, zig-zagging their way toward the stairs at the centre of the massive subterranean floor.

Holly had started screaming as soon as she'd seen Swain tumble backwards through the doorway under the weight of the two hoods, but Selexin had suddenly come to life, seizing her hand, pulling her down the nearest aisle.

Behind them, they could hear the snarls and grunts of the hoods in hot pursuit.

Not far behind.

And gaining. Fast.

Selexin pulled Holly harder. They had to keep running.

Swain surveyed the dark passageway around him. Mouldy yellow fluorescent lights illuminated the tiny corridor.

The hood by his feet groaned softly. It lay on the floor, dazed by the two pounding blows Swain had given it against the hard concrete floor.

The other hood was nowhere in sight.

Swain crouched beside the hood on the floor. It hissed defiantly at him, but it was too badly injured to move.

Swain looked at his wristband, at the countdown in progress.

14:30

14:29

14:28

There was no time to waste. He had fourteen minutes to get back inside before his wristband exploded.

No. More important than that. He had fourteen minutes to get back to Holly.

Swain grimaced and picked up the injured hood by its narrow throat. It wriggled weakly in his grip—a futile gesture. Then Swain closed his eyes and banged the creature's head a final time against the concrete floor. The body went limp immediately. Dead.

Swain discarded the carcass and headed cautiously down the narrow corridor.

The other hood was still nowhere to be seen.

At the end of the passageway, he came to a small room filled with large box-like electricity meters attached to the walls. A big sign above one of the meters read: BOOSTER VALVE.

Swain noticed a small talon of jagged blue electricity licking intermittently out of a gap in the ceiling, touching the booster valve meter, causing it to short. Con Ed would love that, he thought.

There was a small doorway on the other side of the room.

With no door.

With his wristband still beeping insistently, Swain eased his way through the doorway and found himself standing beside the train tracks of the New York Subway.

It was quiet in the train tunnel. The walls were all painted black, with long white fluorescent tubes spaced every fifteen yards or so. An old wooden door swayed from a sturdy padlock by the side of the doorway. Swain wondered how the door had come to be pulled from its hinges.

There was a rustling sound from his right.

Swain turned.

The second hood was *right there!*

Three yards away, its back turned, its head shaking violently from side to side. In its mouth, the remains of what was once a rat.

Swain was about to move away from the hood when there came a soft rumble from deep within the tunnel. The tracks beside him began to hum.

Vibrating.

A soft white glow appeared around of the corner of the tunnel.

Suddenly a subway train burst through the silence, its wheels screaming a deafening, high-pitched wail, its brightly lit windows flashing rapidly by.

Immediately, Swain dropped to the black sooty ground of the tunnel, and in the flashing light of the train saw the hood's head snap up and see him.

The train roared by, kicking up specks of dust and dirt, throwing them at Swain's face. He squeezed his eyes shut.

And then, in an instant, the train was gone, and the tunnel was silent once more. The wristband continued beeping.

Slowly, Swain raised his head.

The tunnel was empty. He glanced over to where the hood had been—

It was gone.

Swain spun around.

Nothing.

He could feel his heart thumping loudly inside his head now. His right forearm stung like crazy where dust from the passing train had fallen inside the five deep claw-marks. He began to sweat.

13:40

13:39

13:38

He didn't have time for this. He rolled onto his side, and—strangely—felt something in his left jeans pocket.

It was the broken phone receiver. He had forgotten all about that. Holly had given it to him back on the First Floor. He checked his other pocket.

The handcuffs.

And Jim Wilson's useless Zippo lighter.

He checked the time again.

13:28

AND COUNTING

The words were flashing.

Christ, he thought, *and counting. I know that. I know that!*

Shit.

Fearfully, Swain scanned the tunnel around him,

searching for the hood. Time was running out. He had to get back inside.

And then, without a sound, the hood attacked him from behind, slamming into his back, sending them both sprawling onto the train tracks. The handcuffs fell to the ground; the lighter, too.

The hood leapt onto his back, but Swain rolled quickly, hurling it clear.

Like a cat, the hood landed smoothly on its feet and immediately spun around and launched itself again at Swain. Swain caught it by its narrow throat, and fell onto his back in between the train tracks.

The hood hissed and squealed and writhed madly about, desperately trying to break Swain's grip. It flailed its razor-sharp claws in every direction—one claw slashing down Swain's chest, ripping the buttons off his shirt, drawing blood, the other swiping viciously at his arm.

Swain lay on his back, on the concrete sleepers *in between* the train tracks, holding his hand outstretched, keeping the frenzied hood at arm's length. Better to let it cut his forearm a few times than let it get at his body—

And then he froze.

He heard it.

A soft, distant rumble.

The hood paid no attention, it just kept jerking its body about fitfully.

And then, on either side of Swain, the train tracks began to hum.

Vibrating.

Oh, no . . .

Oh, no!

Swain's face was right next to the railway track,

his eyes level with one of the large circular hooks—on the inside of the tracks—that held the rails to the sleepers.

The hooks, he thought.

The hood was still twisting and turning as Swain rolled suddenly.

Searching.

The hum of the tracks grew louder.

Swain looked desperately about himself. *Where were they?*

Louder still.

Where . . .

This side. That side. Searching. Searching . . .

He could hear the metallic rattling of the approaching train. It would be on them any second now—

There!

The handcuffs lay on the ground, beside another of the big round hooks on the inside of the tracks.

Swain reached over with his free hand and grabbed the cuffs and in one swift movement brought them up to the hood's throat and snapped them around its narrow neck.

Calick!

The hood was momentarily startled by the single handcuff locked around its throat.

Swain looked up and saw a hazy white light growing around the corner of the tunnel. The rumbling was very loud now.

Then he quickly dropped the hood and latched the other cuff around the nearest hook on the inside of the track.

Calick!

The scream of steel wheels filled the air. The train rounded the corner.

Swain grabbed the hood by its tail, and dived clear of the tracks, yanking the animal with him.

The handcuffs went instantly taut.

And the hood was left with its head cuffed to the hook on the *inside* of the track, and its body held to the *outside* by Swain.

The train shot past Swain, and there was a loud, sickening *crunch!* as its steel wheels carved through the bone of the hood's neck, decapitating it.

The train roared by, windows flashing, and then disappeared into the tunnel.

There was silence again, except for the wristband's incessant beeping.

Slimy black ooze dripped slowly from the hood's headless body. Swain touched the large droplets of blood that had splattered all over him as the train had sliced the hood's head off.

He dropped the body and looked at his wristband.

11:01
11:00
10:59
AND COUNTING

Only eleven minutes to get back inside.

There wasn't much time.

Swain hurriedly picked up the lighter and leapt from the black floor of the subway tunnel and began to run down the tracks into the darkness.

John Levine sat in the passenger seat of a black Lincoln sedan parked across the street from the main entrance to the State Library of New York.

The building looked peaceful. Quiet. Dead.

Levine looked at his watch. 8:30 p.m. Marshall should have been here by now.

His cellular rang.

'Levine,' the voice said. *'It's Marshall. Are you at the library?'*

'Yes, sir.'

'Is it secure?'

'Affirmative, sir,' Levine said, 'as quiet as a mouse.'

'All right, then,' Marshall said, *'the insertion team is en route. They'll be there in five minutes. I'll be there in two. Break out the tape. I want a thirty-yard perimeter set all the way around that building, okay. And Levine . . .'*

'Yes, sir?'

'Whatever you do, don't touch the building itself!'

Selexin and Holly could see the stairwell now.

Up ahead. Thirty yards away.

Panting madly, they kept running down the narrow aisle.

They were approaching the intersection of two aisles when suddenly a hood leapt across their path, its claws raised, its jagged teeth bared wide.

Holly and Selexin skidded to a stop and the hood crashed down onto the hard wood floor in front of them.

It got to its feet again, quickly blocking their path down the aisle. Not far beyond the animal, they could see the open door to the stairwell.

Selexin spun to go back the other way but stopped instantly.

There behind them, stepping slowly into the narrow aisle, was the second hood.

Swain ran down the tunnel, toward a light around the bend.

It was a subway station. Which one, he didn't care.

10:01

10:00

9:59

Swain burst into the white light of the subway station and heaved himself up from the tracks onto the platform.

A murmur arose among the commuters standing on the platform. They all stepped back in horror as Swain pushed past them, oblivious to how he must have looked.

His jeans were covered with black streaks of grease, and his shirt—filthy black with subway soot, elevator grease and hoodaya blood—was ripped from neck to navel. A single vertical line of blood stretched down

241

his chest, while his right forearm was soaked red from the deep gashes inflicted by the hood. The bloody red scar across his left cheek was indistinguishable on his black sooty face.

Swain barged through the crowd and raced up the stairs toward the surface.

'What do we do now?' Holly whispered fearfully.

'I don't know, I don't know,' Selexin said.

The two hoods stood at both ends of the aisle, trapping Holly and Selexin in the middle.

Selexin, four feet tall, and Holly, about the same, were scarcely bigger than the two hoods.

Selexin looked anxiously around himself, at the bookshelves that stretched up to the ceiling. They seemed to form an impenetrable wall on either side of the aisle.

The hood in front of them edged closer. The other didn't move.

Holly noticed why.

The second hood, the one preventing their retreat, had no left foreclaw. Just a bloody stump at the end of its bony black arm. It must have been the one that Balthazar had pinned to the railing with his knife up on the First Floor.

Holly jabbed Selexin with her elbow and pointed at the hood and he saw it, too.

Selexin edged away from the first hood, toward the injured one, still eyeing the impenetrable walls of shelves on either side of them.

Wait a minute, he thought.

He scanned the bookshelves again.

They weren't *impenetrable* at all.

'Quickly,' he said. 'Grab the books. The ones here,' he pointed to a low shelf. 'Grab them and start throwing.'

He reached down to the bottom shelf and grabbed a large hardback and hurled it at the able-bodied hood, striking it in the face. The hood snarled angrily back at him.

A second book hit it again. Then a third. The fourth book hit the injured hood.

'Keep throwing them,' Selexin said.

They kept hurling books at the hoods, who backed off slightly. Holly threw another and was reaching down for more when suddenly she understood what Selexin was doing.

He wasn't just using the books to keep the hoods at bay. He was using them to create a hole in the book-shelf. The more books they threw from the shelf, the bigger the gap in the shelf became. Soon Holly could see through to the next, parallel aisle.

'Are you ready?' Selexin said, throwing a book, hitting the injured hood on its wounded forelimb. The black creature howled in agony.

'I think so,' Holly said.

The able-bodied hood began to move in.

'All right,' Selexin said. 'Go!'

Without a second thought, Holly dived cleanly through the gap in the bookshelf and landed with a thud in the next aisle.

But Selexin continued to stand in the original aisle.

The injured hood stepped cautiously forward.

The two hoods closed in on either side of the little man.

'Come on!' Holly said from the next aisle. 'Jump through!'

'Not yet,' Selexin didn't take his eyes off the approaching hoods. 'Not *yet*.' He threw another book at the injured hood. It hit. The hood hissed angrily.

'Come *on!*' Holly said.

'Just get ready to run, okay,' Selexin said.

Holly looked frantically down her aisle. On one side she could see the stairwell. On the other . . .

She froze.

It was Bellos.

Striding down the aisle toward her with long strong powerful steps.

'Selexin, jump! Jump *right now!*' she screamed.

'They're not close enough yet . . .'

'Just *jump!* He's almost here!'

'He . . . ?' Selexin was momentarily startled. The hoods were very close now.

'Oh! *Him!*' Realising, Selexin immediately dived through the gap in the shelf, landing in a heap at Holly's feet. She pulled him up and they ran for the stairwell.

Behind them, Bellos began to run.

They bolted down the aisle. Holly could hear the able-bodied hood grunting and snorting as it ran down the parallel aisle.

They hit the stairs running and climbed them two at a time.

Behind them they heard the distinctive scratching sound of claws on marble as the hood charged into the stairwell. That sound was quickly followed by a sudden thudding, crashing sound as the hood lost its footing on the slippery marble floor and slammed into the concrete wall.

Breathlessly, Holly and Selexin kept climbing and climbing until they could hear nothing behind them.

The stairwell was silent.

They kept hurrying upward.

And then there came a voice, from way down at the bottom of the shaft, echoing loudly through the stairwell.

'Keep running!' Bellos's voice boomed. 'Keep running, tiny man! We will find you! We will *always* find you! The hunt has begun, and you are the game. I will hunt you, and I will find you, and when I do, tiny man, you will wish to God that somebody else *had found you first!*'

The voice stopped. And as Holly and Selexin climbed higher, an evil laugh resounded throughout the stairwell.

'Here they come,' Levine said to Marshall as they stood beside his car.

A massive blue van rounded the corner and stopped behind Levine's Lincoln. It looked like a big TV van, with a revolving satellite dish on the roof and flashing blue police lights.

Levine shielded his eyes from the glare of the van's headlights as a barrel-chested man dressed completely in blue stepped down from the passenger-side door and stood to attention before Marshall.

It was Harold Quaid.

Commander Harold Quaid.

Levine hadn't actually worked with Quaid before, but his reputation was legendary. Apparently Quaid had given himself the title of 'Commander'—there was no such rank in the NSA—when he had assumed command of Sigma Division's field team. Rumour had it that he had once killed a civilian by mistake while following up a bogus alien sighting. No investigation into the incident was ever held.

Tonight he was dressed exactly like a SWAT team member: blue fatigues, bulletproof vest, boots, cap and gunbelt.

'Sir,' Quaid said to Marshall.

'Harry,' Marshall nodded. 'You made good time.'

'As always, sir.'

Marshall turned to Levine. 'You've cordoned off the site?'

'They're finishing now,' Levine said. 'Tape's set up all around the building. Thirty yards. Even in the park.'

'Nobody's touched the building?'

'They were given strict instructions.'

'Good,' Marshall said. On the Eavesdropper satellite's last pass—now targeted directly at the New York State Library—an unusually large amount of electromagnetic energy had been detected surging through the outer surface of the building. Marshall didn't want to take any chances.

He turned to Quaid. 'I hope your boys are ready. This is the big one.'

Quaid smiled. It was a cold, thin smile. 'We're ready.'

'You'd better be,' Marshall said, 'because as soon as we figure out how to bring down the electric field around that building, you're going in.'

For the first time that night, Stephen Swain beheld the exterior of the New York State Library.

It was a beautiful building. Four storeys high, square-shaped, flat-roofed, with six majestic Corinthian columns stretching all the way up from the front steps to the roof.

In fact, it looked like an old Southern courthouse, grandly situated in the middle of a beautiful inner-city park, as if part of a town square. Only this was a dated town square, dwarfed by the skyscrapers that had grown up around it.

Swain watched the library from across the street, from the entrance to the subway station. He was breathing hard, and the wounds to his chest and forearms burned.

His wristband was still beeping.

8:00

7:59

7:58

Time was running out and the situation didn't look good.

The library had been sealed off.

A single ribbon of bright yellow police tape stretched

from tree to tree in the park surrounding the big dark building, leaving at least thirty-odd yards of open ground between the tape and the walls of the library.

Half a dozen unmarked cars—their headlights still on—formed a tight circle in front of the main entrance to the library. And in the centre of the circle, towering above the cars, stood a big blue police van with a revolving dish on its roof. Next to the dish, flashing blue police lights spun crazily, splashing the park around the library in a strobe-like blue haze.

Damn it, Swain thought, as he watched the big blue van.

For the last two hours all he had wanted to do was get *out* of the library—to get himself and Holly away from Reese and Bellos and the Karanadon—to get out of the electrified cage the library had become.

And now?

Swain smiled sadly.

Now he had to get back *in*.

To get back in and stop this bomb on his wrist from going off. To get back inside the cage, where Reese and Bellos and the Karanadon were waiting for him, waiting to kill him.

But most importantly of all, to get back inside and save Holly. The mere thought of his only daughter trapped inside the library with those monsters made him feel ill. The thought of her being trapped in there *after he was dead*, made him feel terrible. She'd already lost one parent. She wasn't going to lose another one.

But he still had to penetrate the electrified walls.

And who were these new people?

7:44

Swain's gaze came to rest on some shadows at the

249

rear of the library building. Darkness there. Good. It was a chance.

Swain ran across the street.

The park surrounding the State Library was a pretty one, flat and grassy, with evenly spaced oaks spread around three sides of the central building— only now, the oak trees were joined by the bright yellow tape.

Outside the perimeter of oaks, on the eastern side of the building, stood a splendid white rotunda. It was essentially an elevated circular stage, free-standing, with six thin pillars supporting a beautiful domed roof twenty feet above the stage itself. A lattice handrail circled the stage.

It was a beautiful structure, popular for outdoor weddings and the like. Swain even remembered taking Holly to the pantomimes they held here in the summer—*Wizard of Oz*-type shows that involved clouds of coloured smoke and the deft use of a trapdoor in the centre of the stage.

Swain scampered across the open grass and ducked behind the rotunda's stage, out of sight.

Twenty yards to the nearest oak.

Thirty yards from the oak to the library.

He was about to run for the treeline when he saw a garbage bin next to him.

He stopped. Thinking.

If they had set up police tape around the library, it was likely they would have someone patrolling the building, warding off any would-be intruders. He had to find a way . . .

Swain rummaged through the bin and found some crumpled old newspapers. He was grabbing a handful of them when he caught sight of something else.

A wine bottle.

He picked it up and heard the sloshing of liquid still inside it. Excellent. Swain upended the bottle and poured the excess wine onto his hands. The alcohol stung the scratches on his hands.

Then, with bottle and newspapers in hand, he bolted for the treeline.

7:14

7:13

7:12

Swain thrust himself up against the thick trunk of the tree and felt his pockets.

The broken phone receiver and the equally broken lighter were still there. He cursed himself for leaving the handcuffs back at the train tracks.

In the flashing blue light of the van, he saw the nearest corner of the building.

Thirty yards.

He took a deep breath.

And ran out into the open.

Levine yawned as he leaned on the bonnet of the Lincoln. Marshall and Quaid had gone off to check out the parking lot while he had been left to watch the front of the building.

His radio crackled. It would be Higgs, the agent in charge of the surveillance team he had just sent out.

'Yeah,' Levine said.

'We're on the western side of the building and there's nothing here, sir,' Higgs' tinny voice said.

'Okay,' Levine said. 'Just keep circling the building, and let me know if you find anything.'

'Roger that, sir.'

Levine clicked off the radio.

Swain reached the south-eastern corner of the building and ducked into the shadows of the southern wall.

He was breathing hard now, his heart pounding loudly inside his head.

He scanned the wall.

7:01

7:00

6:59

There. Near the far corner.

Swain ran forward and dived to the ground.

The radio crackled again. Higgs' voice.

'We are approaching the south-west corner, sir. Still nothing to report.'

Levine said, 'Thank you, Higgs.'

Swain lay on the grass next to the southern wall of the State Library, still holding the newspapers and the wine bottle.

He was peering at a small wooden window set into the wall at ground level, not far from the south-western corner of the building. The window was old and dusty, and it looked like it hadn't been opened in years. His wristband still beeped softly.

6:39

Swain leaned close and saw a jagged fork of tiny blue lightning lick out from the old window's frame—

A twig snapped.

Somewhere close.

Swain pulled the newspapers to his body and immediately rolled up against the library wall, his eyes inches away from the tiny sparks of electricity that licked out from the window.

Silence.

And then a soft *beep . . . beep . . . beep*.

The wristband!

Swain thrust his left wrist under his body to muffle the sound of the beeping just as he saw three sets of black combat boots step slowly around the corner.

NSA Special Agent Alan Higgs lowered his M-16 and winced at the figure lying huddled up against the wall before him.

A filthy body, curled up in the foetal position, wrapped in crumpled newspapers in a vain attempt to counter the cold. His clothes were filthy rags and the man's face was covered in black grime.

A bum.

Higgs put his radio to his mouth. 'Higgs here.'

'What is it?'

'Just a bum, that's all,' Higgs said, nudging the body with his boot. 'Rolled up tight next to the building. No wonder nobody saw him when they set up the perimeter.'

'Any problem?'

'Nah,' Higgs said. 'This guy probably never even noticed the perimeter going up himself. Don't worry about it sir, we'll have him out of here in no time. Higgs out.'

Higgs bent down and shook Swain's shoulder.

'Hey, buddy?' he said.

Swain groaned.

Higgs nodded to the other two agents—like himself, they were dressed in full SWAT gear—who slung their M-16s and bent down to pick up the man.

As they did so, the bum grunted loudly and rolled sleepily toward them, feebly stretching out with one hand, pressing it against the face of one of the agents, as if to say, 'Go away, I'm sleeping here.'

The agent made a face and pulled back. 'Oh, man, does this guy *stink*.'

Higgs could smell the wine from where he stood. 'Just pick him up and get him the hell out of here.'

Swain kept the beeping wristband pressed tightly against his stomach and covered in newspapers as he was carried away from the library building, back into the park.

To his ears it was beeping louder than ever, almost certain to be heard.

But the two men carrying him didn't seem to notice. In fact, they seemed to be trying to keep their bodies as far away from his as possible.

Swain began to sweat.

This was taking too much time.

He desperately wanted to look at the wristband. To see how much time was left.

They couldn't take him away.

He had to get back inside.

'Ambulance?' one of the two carriers asked the third—and presumably superior—man walking in the lead.

Swain's body tensed as he waited for the response.

'Nah,' the third man said. 'Just get him outside the perimeter. Let the police pick him up later.'

'Roger that.'

Swain breathed a sigh of relief.

But if they weren't taking him to a hospital to clean him up, and if they weren't police officers, then there were still two questions to answer: where *would* they take him, and *who the hell were they*?

The heavily armed men carried Swain through the treeline and across the park, toward the rotunda.

Okay. You can put me down now, Swain willed them. *You're taking too long . . .*

They carried him up the steps of the rotunda and laid him down on the circular wooden stage.

'Here will do,' the senior one said.

'Good,' the one whom Swain had rubbed in the face said as he released Swain's arm.

'Come on, Farrell, he doesn't smell that bad,' the senior one said.

Swain breathed again, and his body relaxed.

There would still be time.

Now go, boys. That's good. Keep going . . .

'Wait a minute . . .' the one named Farrell said.

Swain froze.

Farrell was looking down at his gloves. 'Sir, this guy is bleeding.'

Oh shit.

'He's what?'

'He's bleeding, sir. Look.'

Stay calm. Stay calm.

They are not going to come over.

They are not going to look at your arm . . .

Swain's whole body tensed as Farrell held out his gloved hands and the senior man came over.

Higgs examined the blood on Farrell's gloves. Then he looked down at Swain, at the newspapers covering his arms, at the tiny splotches of red that had seeped through the newsprint on his right arm. The strong odour of wine pervaded it all.

Finally, he said, 'Probably just a cut he got falling into a gutter. Leave him be, I'll radio it in. If they think it's necessary, the others can come by later and check him out. I don't think this guy will be going anywhere fast. Come on, let's get back to work.'

They headed back towards the main entrance.

Swain didn't dare move until the sounds of the foot-steps had faded off into the night.

Slowly, he lifted his head.

He was in the rotunda, on the stage. He looked at his wristband:

2:21

2:20

2:19

'Why don't you take your time next time, boys?' he said aloud. He couldn't believe it had taken only four minutes. It had felt like an eternity.

But now he only had two minutes left. He had to move.

Fast.

With a final look through the white lattice handrail of the rotunda stage, Swain leapt to his feet, and ran down the stairs.

2:05

Into the treeline, and he stopped beneath one of the heavy oaks.

He reached up and grabbed a thick low-hanging

branch and snapped it from the tree. Then he ran out onto open ground again, toward the library building.

1:51

1:50

1:49

In the shadows of the southern wall, Swain came to the ground-level window he had seen before and dropped to his knees. He tightened his grip on the long thick branch and prayed to God that this would work.

He swung the branch down hard at the window. The small window shattered instantly. Glass exploded everywhere.

Instantly, however, a crackling grid of silver-blue electricity burst to life across the width of the window.

Swain's eyes went wide with dismay.

Oh, no. Oh . . . *no*.

1:36

Swain swallowed.

He hadn't thought that *that* would happen. He had hoped that the gap would be too wide, that the electricity would not be able to jump the width of the small window.

But the window was too small.

And now he was left with a wall of jagged, criss-crossing lines of pure electricity in front of him.

1:20

1:19

1:18

Only a minute left.

Think, Swain! Think! There has to be a way! There *has* to be!

But his mind was now a blur of panic and incredulity. To have got so far, and to end it all like this . . .

Images of the night flashed across his mind.

Reese in the Stack. Meeting Hawkins. The parking lot. Balthazar. Up to the First Floor. Bellos and the hoods and the Konda in the atrium . . .

1:01

1:00

0:59

. . . the Internet Facility and the handcuffs on the door. Up to the Third Floor. The janitor's room. The Karanadon. The elevator shaft. Back down to the Stack. The small red door. Falling through the door with the hoods.

Outside. In the tunnel. The subway train.

0:48

0:47

0:46

Wait.

There was something there.

Something he had missed. Something that said there was a way in.

0:37

0:36

0:35

What was it? *Shit!* Why couldn't he remember? Okay, slow down. Think. Where did it happen?

Downstairs? No. Upstairs? No. Somewhere in between.

The First Floor.

What had happened on the First Floor?

They had seen Bellos, seen the hoods attack the Konda. Then Balthazar had thrown a knife and pinned one of them to the railing . . .

0:29

0:28

0:27

Then Holly had pressed the elevator button and they had run into the Internet room.

Holly . . .

Then the door. And the handcuffs.

0:20

0:19

0:18

What was it?

Holly . . .

It was there! Somewhere in the back of his mind. A way in! Why couldn't he remember it?

0:14

0:13

0:12

Think, Goddamn it, think!

0:11

0:10

Swain pursed his lips, frowning.

0:09

He swung his head from right to left. No other windows. Nowhere else to go.

0:08

Think back. First Floor. Bellos. Hoods.

0:07

Balthazar. Knife.

0:06

Elevator. Holly pressing the button. *Holly* . . .

0:05

Holly? Something about Holly.

0:04

Something Holly *said*?

0:03

Something Holly *did*?

0:02
And with the expiration of the countdown came the horror of the realisation.

Stephen Swain was dead.

FIFTH MOVEMENT

30 November, 8:56 p.m.

In the janitor's room on the Third Floor, Paul Hawkins sat down against the wall beside Balthazar, and nodded, satisfied.

Across the floor from him, in front of the open doorway of the room, lay a large puddle of highly flammable methylated spirits—and next to him, a box of old-fashioned phosphorus-tipped matches. He had been pleasantly surprised at what he had been able to find on the shelves of the old janitor's room.

He felt a little safer now. Any unwanted guests passing through that doorway would be in for a big—

And then, abruptly, he heard it.

The windows above him rattled slightly, while the floor shook gently.

Hawkins couldn't quite guess what it was.

But it sounded like a muffled explosion.

Selexin and Holly stopped at the top of the stairwell as the wooden banister beside them began to shudder.

'Did you hear that?' Selexin asked nervously.

'I felt it,' Holly said. 'What do you think it was?'

'It sounded like a blast of some sort. An explosion. From somewhere outside—'

He cut himself off.

'*Oh no . . .*'

'*Clear!*' 'Commander' Harry Quaid called again.

Marshall ducked behind the wall at the top of the ramp as Quaid rounded the corner and joined him.

The second blast rushed outward from the bottom of the concrete entry ramp. A billowing cloud of grey smoke raced up the ramp and shot out onto the street, thundering past Marshall and Quaid.

Fragments of metal—the remnants of what had been the steel grating that closed off the library's parking lot—clattered loudly to the ground.

The smoke cleared and Marshall, Quaid and a small cohort of NSA agents made their way down the charred ramp, stepping over the gnarled pieces of steel that now littered the slope.

Marshall stopped at the bottom of the ramp and stared in awe at the sight before him.

Across the wide rectangular opening of the parking lot—filling the exploded round hole in the middle of the steel grating—was an enormous grid of bright blue electricity, crackling and sizzling, lashing out every few seconds with long fingers of high-voltage lightning.

Marshall folded his arms as Quaid stood beside him, gazing at the criss-crossing grid of light before them.

'We knew it,' Quaid said, not taking his eyes off the wall of blue light.

'We did indeed,' Marshall said. 'So. They electrify the whole building, cutting it off, sealing it so that nothing can get in or out . . .'

'Right.'

'So, why have they done it?' Marshall asked. 'What the hell is going on inside this building that we're not supposed to see?'

Holly tapped her foot impatiently as she waited on the Third Floor landing of the stairwell. Selexin was peering around the open fire door into the study hall.

The room was a mess.

An absolute mess.

A diagonal line of pure destruction ran all the way across the study hall—from the doorway to the janitor's room in the far corner, right up to the stairwell door. Desks crushed beneath the weight of the Karanadon lay in splinters, strewn all over the floor.

In the dim blue city light, Selexin could just make out the doorway to the janitor's room on the far side of the room. There didn't seem to be anybody there at the moment. In a dark corner of his mind, Selexin wondered what had happened to Hawkins and Balth—

Suddenly a shadow cut across his view of the janitor's room.

A dark shape, barely distinguishable in the hazy blue darkness, about the size of a man, but much, much thinner, moving stealthily between the desks of the study hall, heading toward the janitor's room.

Selexin ducked back behind the stairwell door, hoping that it hadn't seen him.

Then he grabbed Holly's hand and they began to descend the stairs.

In the janitor's room, Hawkins leaned back wearily against the concrete wall. He was watching Balthazar walk gingerly around the room.

Now that his eyes were clear of Reese's saliva and his vision seemingly restored, Balthazar seemed to be getting his strength back. A few minutes before, he had managed to stand up on his own. Now he was walking.

Hawkins looked out through the doorway—over the wide puddle of methylated spirits he had poured—into the study hall.

Everything was silent.

Nobody was out there.

He turned back to watch Balthazar pace awkwardly around the room, and as he did so, he failed to notice a sharp triangular head loop itself smoothly and silently around the doorway.

It looked inside, slowly tilting its head from side to side, alternating between Balthazar and Hawkins.

It never made a sound.

Hawkins turned idly and saw it. He stopped cold.

The head was a long, sharp, flat isosceles triangle, pointing downwards. No eyes. No ears. No mouth. Just a flat, black triangle, slightly larger than a man's head.

And it just hovered there, in the doorway.

The body was still out of view, but Hawkins could clearly see its long thin 'neck'.

Now, inasmuch as everything he had seen so far was basically 'animal'—with eyes, limbs and skin—this thing, whatever it was, was *totally* alien.

Its 'neck' was like a string of white pearls flowing down from the flat, two-dimensional triangular head. Presumably it flowed into a body that was still out of his sight.

Hawkins continued to stare at the creature—just as it seemed to stare curiously back at him.

And then Balthazar spoke. A deep, husky voice.

'Codex.'

'What?' Hawkins said. 'What did you say?'

Balthazar pointed at the alien. 'Codex.'

The Codex moved forward—effortlessly, smoothly—floating through the air.

It crossed the threshold of the room and Hawkins saw that it had no body at all. The string of pearls that formed its neck was, in fact, about five feet long. And it dangled down from the head, curling upward at the tip, never touching the ground.

And at the tip of the tail, burning brightly, was a green light that glowed from a tight grey metal band. The Codex was another contestant.

The tail slithered back and forth like a snake's, hovering upright, one foot above the ground.

'Oh man,' Hawkins grabbed the matchbox and pulled out a phosphorus-tipped match. He struck it on the floor.

The flare of white light made the Codex hesitate. It stopped above the pool of methylated spirits.

Hawkins held the match aloft, the flame slowly burning its way down the white wood of the match-stick, blackening it.

He swallowed.

'Aw, what the hell,' he said. And he dropped the match into the pool.

Levine was standing out in front of the library when his radio sputtered to life.

'Sir! Sir! We have a light! I repeat: we have a light! Looks like a fire. Third floor. North-east corner.'

'I'm on my way,' Levine said. He switched channels on his radio. 'Sir?'

'What is it, Levine?' James Marshall sounded irritated by the interruption.

'Sir,' Levine said, 'we have confirmation of activity inside the library. I repeat, confirmation of activity *inside* the library.'

'Where?'

'North-east corner. Third Floor.'

Marshall said, *'Get over there. We're on our way.'*

The walls of the janitor's room flared bright yellow as a curtain of fire burst upward from the pool of methylated spirits, engulfing the Codex.

Hawkins and Balthazar stepped back from the flames, shielding their eyes. The Codex could not be seen through the blazing wall of fire.

And then it emerged.

Floating forward. Through the flames. Oblivious to the heat.

It moved inside the janitor's room, clear of the fire.

'Oh, *man*,' Hawkins said, edging backwards.

Balthazar spoke—again, just one word in a flat monotone.

'Go.'

Hawkins said, 'What?'

Balthazar was staring intently at the Codex. 'Go,' he repeated solemnly.

Hawkins didn't know what to do. The Codex was hovering right in front of them. And even if he got past it, he still had to get through the fire—the fire that he had set up to keep intruders *out*. It had never occurred to him that that same fire might serve to keep him *in*.

There was no way out. There was nowhere *to* go.

Balthazar turned to Hawkins and looked him squarely in the eye. 'Go . . . *now!*'

And with that Balthazar launched himself at the Codex.

Hawkins watched in astonishment as the Codex leapt forward at the same moment and coiled its thin body three times around Balthazar's throat.

With both hands, the big man pulled desperately at the Codex's stranglehold around his neck. He stumbled backwards into the remains of the cyclone fence that divided the room, tripped, and fell to the floor beneath the shelves packed with detergents and cleaning agents.

Hawkins was still just standing there, stunned, watching the battle in awe, when Balthazar cried, 'Go!'

Hawkins blinked and turned immediately. He saw the fire, spreading across the room, creeping across the floor toward him. He saw the dusty methylated spirits bottle he had used, lying on the floor, inches away from the approaching flames.

Too late.

The flames devoured the bottle as Hawkins dived over the nearest pile of wooden boxes.

Under the intense heat, the glass bottle—still half full—exploded like a Molotov cocktail, shooting out missiles of glass and fire in every direction.

Beyond the cyclone fence, Balthazar was back on his feet again, struggling with the Codex.

He fell back heavily against the wooden shelves and they collapsed under him. Glass spirit bottles, plastic detergent bottles and a dozen aerosol spray cans crashed to the floor.

Hawkins saw the shelves collapse, saw all the bottles hit the floor—cleaning agents and detergents that carried conspicuous red warning signs: DO NOT MIX WITH DETERGENTS OR OTHER CHEMICALS, and highly flammable aerosols with their own glaring warning labels.

The fire moved inexorably forward, across the room.

'*Oh my God,*' Hawkins' eyes darted from the fire on the floor to the chemicals lying in its path.

Behind the cyclone fence, the Codex's body was still coiled tightly around Balthazar's throat. Balthazar's face was twisted in a tight grimace, his cheeks beetroot red.

Hawkins spun to warn him about the fire and in that instant their eyes met, and Balthazar, staring intently at Hawkins, tightened his grip on the Codex's snake-like body.

Hawkins saw it in the big man's eyes. Balthazar knew what was going to happen. The fire. The chemicals. He was going to stay in the room. And keep the Codex with him.

'No!' Hawkins cried, realising. 'You can't!'

'Go,' Balthazar gasped.

'But you'll—' Hawkins saw the flames creeping steadily across the floor. He had to make a decision fast.

'*Go!*' Balthazar yelled.

Hawkins gave up. There was no more time. Balthazar was right. He had to go.

He turned back to face the fast-approaching wall of fire, and, with a final glance back at Balthazar—locked in battle with the Codex—Hawkins said softly, 'Thank you.'

Then he covered his face with his forearm and plunged into the fire.

Levine arrived at the north-east corner of the library building just as Quaid and Marshall came running up. The agent in charge of the perimeter, Higgs, was there waiting.

'Up there,' Higgs said, pointing at two long rectangular windows up on the third floor, just below the overhang of the library's roof.

The two windows glowed bright yellow, with the occasional flash of orange flames.

'Jesus Christ,' Marshall shook his head. 'The goddamn building is *on fire*. That's just what I need.'

'What do we do?' Levine said.

'We get inside,' Harry Quaid said flatly, gazing up at the glowing windows. 'Before there's nothing left.'

'Right,' Marshall scowled, thinking. 'Damn it. *Damn* it!' Then he said, 'Levine.'

'Yes, sir.'

'Call the fire department. But when they get here, tell them to hold off. We don't want them going in there until we've had a good look inside. I just want them here in case that fire gets out of con—'

'Hey. Hold on a minute . . .' Quaid called. He had wandered off down the side of the building and was now standing at the south-eastern corner.

'What is it?' Marshall said.

'*What the fuck . . . ?*' Quaid disappeared down the southern side of the building.

'What is it?' Marshall followed, rounding the corner after Quaid.

Quaid was thirty yards down the southern wall,

almost at the south-western corner of the building. He called back to the group. 'Special Agent Higgs, you in charge of surveillance tonight?'

'Yes, sir.'

'Tell me, did you find anybody around here earlier? Anybody near this wall?'

Higgs didn't understand what was going on. Quaid was peering at the base of the wall, at what appeared to be a small window down near the ground.

'Well—uh—yes, sir. Yes, we did,' Higgs said. 'We found a drunken bum asleep up against this wall not long ago.'

'Was he down near this corner? Near the window down here?' Quaid asked.

'Uh, yes. Yes he was, sir.'

'And where is this drunken bum now, Higgs?' Quaid asked, kneeling on the grass, still looking at the base of the building.

Marshall, Levine and Higgs came closer.

Higgs swallowed. 'We put him in the rotunda over there, sir.' He pointed back over his shoulder. 'I was going to call it in, but I didn't think there was any hurry.'

'Special Agent Higgs, I want you to go straight to that rotunda and find that bum for me, right now.'

Higgs hurried off immediately.

Quaid glanced up at the others as they saw what he had been looking at.

'What the . . .?' Levine gasped.

'Well would you look at that,' Marshall said as he saw the spiderweb of electricity that spread across the small ground-level window. Tiny shards of glass lay strewn on the grass around the base of the window.

There was nobody in sight.

Quaid leaned close to the window. It was just big enough for a man to fit through. But why would somebody break it? That would serve no purpose whatsoever.

Unless they wanted to get in . . .

Higgs came running back. He spoke breathlessly.

'Sir, the bum is gone.'

Hawkins burst through the flames and fell out of the doorway and dropped to the floor of the study hall.

He checked his body. His police trousers and parka had survived the dash through the fire intact and unharmed. But for some reason his head stung like crazy.

He reached up to touch the crown of his head and suddenly felt the searing heat.

His hair was on fire!

Hawkins frantically took off his parka and smothered the tiny flames on his head with it. The heat died down quickly, and he began breathing again.

The janitor's room was glowing bright yellow now, lighting up the study hall outside. Flames flared out through the doorway.

It wouldn't be long now, he thought.

Hawkins crawled to the side of the doorway, pushed his back up against the wall.

He only had to wait a few seconds.

The chemicals inside the janitor's room combined well. After the first aerosol can exploded in a ball of gaseous blue flame, a chain reaction of chemical explosions was set in motion.

The concrete wall behind Hawkins cracked under the weight of the shock wave as a golden fireball blasted out through the doorway, rocketing past Hawkins, setting the study hall aglow in a flash of brilliant yellow light.

Marshall, Levine and Quaid all looked up at the same time as the entire third floor of the building flared like a fiery flashbulb, lighting up the night.

Voices came in over their radios:

'—*fire is spreading!*—'

'—*corner room just exploded*—'

'Holy shit,' Levine breathed.

It sounded like thunder.

Close, booming thunder.

The whole building rocked under the weight of the explosions.

On the Second Floor of the library, Holly and Selexin reached desperately for handholds as they tried to stay on their feet.

The Second Floor of the New York State Library was comprised mainly of two large computer rooms. In the centre of each room, long wooden tables were covered with PCs. A tangle of air-conditioning units and aluminium air ducts hung from the ceiling, providing much-needed humidity control for the computers. Glass-walled reading rooms lined the perimeter of the floor.

The explosions from the Third Floor were growing in intensity, and on the Second Floor they were received with all their violent force.

The glass walls of the reading rooms shattered all around Holly and Selexin. Computers fell from the edges of the tables, crashed to the floor.

Selexin pulled Holly under one of the long tables in the centre of the floor and they huddled together, covering their ears, as the building shook and the explosions boomed and monitors and keyboards fell from the tables all around them, smashing down onto the floor.

Chaos. Absolute chaos.

In the study hall, Hawkins pressed his hands tightly against his ears as waves of flames lashed out from the doorway next to him.

Several of the L-shaped desks around him were on fire—ignited by the initial flamethrower-like finger of fire that had blasted out from the janitor's room.

The explosions were bigger now—bigger than he had expected them to be, bigger than any chemical fire he knew.

They were almost, well . . . *too* big.

Why had that—?

Hawkins froze. Something else must have happened. *But what?*

And then he saw it.

A small pipe, running horizontally, high up on the wall near the ceiling.

It ran out from the janitor's room, across the wall of the study hall—above the northern windows—and then, halfway across, it turned abruptly downwards and ran down to the floor, and then *through* the floor down to the other floors below . . .

A gas pipe.

There must have been a gas valve in the janitor's room that he hadn't seen. A gas water heater or a gas—

The small pipe ignited.

277

Hawkins watched in horror as a yellow-blue flame sped in a thin line across the pipe's horizontal length, and then turned as the pipe did, darting downwards, heading for the lower floors.

Hawkins watched as a droplet of fire fell from the gas pipe and landed on one of the wooden desks. With a sudden *whoosh*, the desk went up in flames.

Hawkins leapt to his feet. The explosions from the janitor's room were finally beginning to die, but that didn't matter anymore.

A fire was spreading through the gas piping.

Soon the whole building would be alight.

He had to find a way out.

In a small toilet on Sub-Level One, somebody else was feeling the shuddering explosions that were rocking the New York State Library.

Stephen Swain MD sat with his back pressed up against the white-tiled wall of a cubicle in the ladies' room of Sub-Level One. The water in the toilet bowl next to him splashed about wildly as the building around it tilted and swayed.

Another explosion boomed and the building shook again, although not as drastically as it had before. The explosions seemed to be losing their muscle.

Swain checked his wristband. It read:

INITIALISED—6
DETONATION SEQUENCE TERMINATED AT:
* 0:01 *
RESET

The top line flickered, then changed to:

INITIALISED—5

High above Swain's head, just below the ceiling,

the grid of blue electricity was still sizzling. Beyond the glowing window he could hear the faint voices of the NSA agents.

He pressed himself closer against the tiles and breathed deeply.

He was back inside.

It was the thought of Holly that had done it.

Holly on the First Floor, in the dilapidated Internet Facility. When the hoods had been pounding on the door and Swain had handcuffed it shut, he had found Holly over by the window.

She had been holding the broken telephone receiver up against the electrified window. When the phone was brought in close to the window, the electricity seemed to pull back in a wide circle.

Away from the phone.

At the time, Swain hadn't realised what was happening, but he knew now.

It wasn't the phone that the electricity had been pulling away from, but the *magnet* inside the phone. The earpiece of a telephone is like a common stereo speaker: at its centre one will find a relatively high-powered magnet.

And as a radiologist, Stephen Swain knew all about magnetism.

People commonly associate radiologists with X-rays, but in recent years radiologists have been endeavouring to discover new ways to obtain cross-sections of human bodies—views taken by looking *down* on the body from above the head.

There are a number of techniques used to obtain these cross-sections. One well-known method is the CAT-scan. Another more modern method involves the splicing and ordering of atomic particles and is called Magnetic Resonance Imaging.

Basically—as Swain had explained to the troublesome Mrs Pederman earlier that day—MRI works on the principle that electricity reacts to magnetic interference.

And that was exactly what had happened when Holly had held the receiver to the window—the *magnetic* waves disrupted the very structure of the *electronic* waves and, hence, made the wall of electricity pull away from the magnet in order to maintain their frequency.

To get inside again, Swain had grabbed the receiver from his pocket and held the ear-piece to the window. The electricity had instantly pulled back from the receiver, forming a wide two-foot hole in the grid, and Swain had simply thrust his arm in through the hole.

The wristband, once detecting itself to be inside the electric field again, stopped its countdown immediately.

Just in time.

After a minute's careful wriggling and squirming—to make sure he did not move his body beyond the two-foot magnetic circle in the electric grid—Swain was back inside.

In fact, he had just pulled his right foot inside the window when he fell from the high window sill. The electric grid sizzled immediately back into place and Swain fell clumsily onto the toilet seat below.

Inside.

Paul Hawkins was halfway across the study hall when the explosions ceased.

Only the loud crackling sounds of a fire out of control remained. The desks over by the janitor's room were now blazing wildly. The janitor's room itself was still glowing bright yellow. The whole study hall was bathed in a flickering golden haze.

Suddenly there came a crashing sound from behind him and Hawkins spun.

There, hovering in the doorway to the janitor's room, silhouetted by the flickering yellow flames behind it, was the Codex.

Hawkins froze.

Then he saw it wobble slightly.

The Codex was hovering unsteadily. It began to swirl dizzily. And then, abruptly, its flat triangular head snapped upward and the Codex fell, crashing down on top of a crumpled desk.

After that, it didn't move.

Hawkins sighed with relief.

He was about to turn back for the stairwell when he caught sight of something on the floor not far from the door to the janitor's room. Something white. Slowly,

Hawkins stepped forward until he could see what it was . . .

He stopped cold.

It was a guide. Or at least what was left of him.

It had probably been the Codex's guide, stationed outside the janitor's room while the Codex had gone inside for the kill.

The guide's body lay in a wide pool of blood underneath one of the L-shaped desks and it had been mangled beyond recognition.

Small clusters of parallel red slashes ran across its face, arms and chest—one of which had broken its nose, making for an especially gruesome excess of blood. Deep scratches on the little man's palms suggested futile defensive efforts. His eyes and mouth were wide open—frozen in eternal terror—a snapshot of his horrifying final moments.

Hawkins winced at the sickening sight—it was disgusting, brutal. And then, as he looked more closely at the clusters of slashing cuts all over the guide's body, he had a sudden, terrifying realisation. Parallel cuts indicated claws . . .

Bellos' hoods had done this.

It was time to get out of here.

Hawkins immediately turned back for the stairwell—

—only to see a big black hand rush toward his face.

And then he saw nothing.

Stephen Swain stepped cautiously out from the ladies' room and saw the familiar glass-walled offices of Sub-Level One.

He checked his wristband and found that the screen had changed again.

INITIALISED—4

Another contestant was dead. Only four were left now.

Swain wondered which contestants were still alive. He shrugged off the thought. Hell, he only really knew of three others—Balthazar, Bellos and Reese. Including himself, maybe they were the only four left.

Got to find Holly, he told himself. *Holly*.

He stepped out among the offices. Across the floor, through the glass partitions, he saw the elevator bay. He also saw the heavy blue door that led out to the parking lot. It was open.

Swain hastened over to the door and examined it. It had been torn from its hinges, presumably by Reese when she had been chasing them before.

He remembered the chase into the parking lot, remembered Balthazar coming up the concrete ramp from the floor below . . .

The floor below.

Sub-Level Two, the Stack.

That was where he had been separated from Holly and Selexin, so it was the obvious place to start looking for them.

He had to get down there.

Go down the stairwell?

No. There was another way. A better way.

He remembered Balthazar again, coming up the ramp in the parking lot. *That* was the way in. Balthazar had come from another, lower, parking level. And that level had to have an entrance of some sort, a door that would open onto Sub-Level Two.

With that Swain ran through the big blue door and out toward the parking lot.

From the outside it looked like a scene from *The Towering Inferno*. The State Library of New York—standing proudly in the centre of a beautiful inner city park—with long flaming tentacles spraying out from two flat rectangular windows up near its roof, while rows of windows on the third and second floors were illuminated by a glowing golden haze.

John Levine was back at the front of the library, watching as the building before him burned.

Behind him, the big blue NSA van pulled out from the kerb and headed for the western side of the library building.

Levine watched as the van jumped the kerb and drove straight onto the grass lawn surrounding the library. Then it disappeared around the corner.

He turned back to see headlights—lots of headlights—and he knew what that meant. The fire department was arriving—closely followed by the media.

Multi-coloured vans screeched to a halt just outside the perimeter of yellow tape. Sliding doors were flung open and cameramen charged out. Behind them, pretty reporters emerged from their vans, fluffing and primping.

One bold young reporter hustled straight over from her van, ducked under the yellow police tape and walked straight up to Levine and thrust a microphone into his face.

'Sir,' she said, in her best, most serious voice, 'can you tell us *exactly* what is happening here? How did the fire start?'

Levine didn't answer. He just stared at the young woman, silent.

'Sir,' she repeated, 'I said, can you tell us—'

Levine cut her off, speaking softly and politely, facing the young reporter, but clearly addressing the three NSA agents standing nearby.

'Gentlemen, please escort this young lady outside the perimeter and inform her that if she or anyone else crosses that line again they will be arrested on the spot and charged with Federal offences relating to interference with matters of national security, sentences for which range between ten and twenty years, depending on what sort of mood I'm in.'

The three agents stepped forward and the reporter, mouth agape, was led ignominiously back to the perimeter.

Levine was watching her legs as she walked off when his radio came to life. It was Marshall.

'Yes, sir?'

'*Quaid and I are at the entrance to the parking lot,*' Marshall said. '*TV there yet?*'

'They're here all right,' Levine said.

'*Any trouble?*'

'Not yet.'

'*Good. We'll be down here from now on. This fire has raised the stakes. Now we have to get inside before the whole place burns down. Is the truck on the way?*'

'It just left,' Levine said. 'You'll be seeing it any second now.'

The ramp leading down from the street to the underground parking lot was on the western side of the library building.

Marshall was standing at the base of the ramp, not far from the metal grille that closed off the parking lot. In the centre of the grille, just touching the ground, was the large circle of criss-crossing blue electricity.

Behind him, the big NSA van reversed around the corner and backed slowly down the ramp.

'Okay,' Marshall said into his radio, seeing the van, 'it's here. I'll call you back soon. For now, you just keep those firemen and reporters behind the tape. Okay?'

'*Okay*,' Levine's voice said as Marshall hung up.

The van stopped and the back doors burst open and four men dressed in SWAT gear jumped down onto the ramp. The first of them—a young technician—came straight up to Quaid and they spoke quietly. Then the technician nodded vigorously and disappeared inside the van. He re-emerged several seconds later carrying a large silver box.

Quaid walked over to Marshall, standing in front of the electrified metal grille.

Marshall said, 'How long will it—?'

'We'll be in there soon,' Quaid said calmly. 'We just have to do the math first.'

'Who are you going to get to do it?'

'Me,' Quaid said.

The technician placed the heavy box down on the concrete next to Quaid, then bent down and flipped open its silver lid to reveal three digital counters. Each counter displayed red numbers, which at the moment read: **00000.00.**

Quaid then pulled a long green cord out from the box and led it over to the metal grille. The cord had a shiny steel bulb at the tip.

Another heavily armed agent came over and handed him some insulated black gloves and a long pole with a loop of rope attached to its end. Quaid put the gloves on and inserted the steel bulb into the loop at the end of the pole.

He took a long, slow breath. Then he pointed the pole away from his body, toward the wall of criss-crossing blue lightning.

The steel bulb at the end of the pole glistened as it edged closer and closer to the wall of blue light.

Marshall watched tensely. Quaid swallowed.

The NSA team stared in anticipation.

None of them knew what would happen.

The bulb touched the electricity.

The counters in the steel box immediately began to tick upward slowly, measuring the voltage. They sped up slightly, the numbers getting larger and larger.

And then they went into overdrive.

On the Second Floor of the library, Holly and Selexin huddled together underneath one of the large central tables. On the floor all around them lay the crumpled remains of a dozen shattered computers.

The glass walls of the Reading Rooms had once been like the glass partitions on the First Floor—glass from the waist up, wood from the waist down—only now they had been shattered beyond recognition by the explosions, reduced to little more than gaping windows with jagged edges.

Worse still, on the eastern side of the floor, in two of the reading rooms, fires had started.

Selexin sighed sadly. Next to him, Holly was sobbing.

'Are you all right?' he asked, concerned. 'Are you hurt?'

'No . . . want *Daddy*,' she whimpered. 'I want my Daddy.'

Selexin looked over at the doorway leading to the stairwell. It was shut. 'Yes. I know. I do, too.'

Holly stared at him, and Selexin could see the fear in her eyes. 'What's *happened* to him?' she sniffed.

'I do not know.'

'And those *things* that pushed him out through the door? I hope they die. I *hate* them.'

'Believe me,' Selexin said, still eyeing the door, 'I dislike them intensely, too.'

'Do you think Daddy's coming back inside?' Holly asked hopefully.

'I am *sure* he is already back inside,' Selexin lied. 'And I would wager that at this very moment he is probably somewhere in the building looking for us.'

Holly nodded, wiping her eyes, encouraged. 'Yeah. That's what I think, too.'

Selexin smiled weakly. As much as he wanted to believe that Stephen Swain was still alive, he was extremely doubtful. The labyrinth was electronically sealed for the sole purpose of keeping the contestants *in*. Only an inexplicable fluke had created an opening in the building at the time of electrification—it was highly unlikely that another existed.

And besides, he had *heard* the explosion himself. Stephen Swain was most certainly dead . . .

And then, out of the corner of his eye, Selexin saw movement.

It was the stairwell door.

It was opening.

Swain hurried down the grey corridor and stepped out into the white fluorescent light of the car park.

It was exactly as he remembered it. Clean, shiny concrete, white floor markings, the DOWN ramp in the centre.

And it was quiet. The carpark was totally empty.

Swain hurried over to the DOWN ramp and had just started to descend it when he heard someone shouting.

'Hello! *Hey!*'

Swain turned around, puzzled.

'Yes, you! The guy at the top of the ramp!'

Swain searched for the source of the shouts. His gaze fell on the entry ramp. It was off to the left, down a long, narrow passageway, closed off to the outside world by a big steel grille. At the bottom of the grille was a round exploded hole that glowed blue with criss-crossing lines of electricity.

Beyond the hole in the grille, however, was a man, dressed in blue combat attire.

And he was shouting.

Holly sat frozen underneath the long wooden table. Selexin stared at the slowly opening door.

Apart from the muffled crackling of flames that came from the fire in the reading rooms, the Second Floor of the New York State Library was completely silent.

The door to the stairwell continued to open.

And then slowly—very slowly—a big black boot stepped through the doorway.

The door opened wide.

It was Bellos. He was alone. The two remaining hoods were nowhere to be seen.

Selexin raised a finger to his lips and Holly, her eyes wide with fear, nodded vigorously.

Bellos walked into the open central area of the Second Floor.

His boots crunched softly on the broken glass of the computer monitors as he passed within a foot of the table under which Holly and Selexin hid.

He stopped.

Right in front of them!

Holly held her breath as the big boots swivelled on the spot, the body above them looking around in every direction.

Then the knees began to bend and Holly almost squealed at the prospect of it: Bellos was going to look under the table!

Bellos' legs crouched and a wave of terror swept through Holly's body.

The long tapering horns appeared first.

Then the evil black face. Upside down. Peering at them.

And at that moment, a wicked grin broke out across Bellos' face.

In the parking lot, Swain edged cautiously toward the exit ramp.

'*Hellooo!*' the man behind the grille called. 'Can you hear me?'

Swain didn't reply. He moved forward, toward the grille, focusing on the man on the other side.

He was a stocky man, dressed in blue fatigues and a bulletproof vest, like a member of a tactical response team.

The man called again. 'I said, *can you hear me?*'

Swain stopped, twenty yards away from the electrified grille.

'I can hear you,' he said.

At the sound of Swain's voice, the man behind the grille turned instantly and spoke to someone else, someone Swain could not see.

The man turned back, held up his palms and spoke very slowly. 'We mean you no harm.'

'Yeah, and I come in peace,' Swain said. 'Who the hell are you?'

The man continued to speak in that kind of slow, articulate voice one uses with an infant.

Or, perhaps, an alien.

'We are *representatives* of the government of the *United States of America*. We are'—the man spread his arms wide—'*friends*.'

'All right, friend, what's your name?' Swain said.

'My *name* is *Harold Quaid*,' Quaid said earnestly.

'And what department are you from, Harold?'

'The *National* Security *Agency*.'

'Yeah, well, I've got some bad news for you, Harold Quaid of the National Security Agency. I'm not the alien you're looking for. I'm just a guy who was in the wrong place at the wrong time.'

Quaid frowned. 'Then who are you?'

Something inside Swain's head told him not answer that question.

'I'm just a guy.'

'And where are you from?'

'Around.'

'And what are you doing in a building that's got a hundred thousand volts of electricity running through its walls?'

'Like I said, Harold, wrong place, wrong time.'

Quaid changed tack. 'We can help you, you know. We can get you out of there.'

'I've already been out, thanks,' Swain said. 'It's hazardous to my health.'

Quaid turned away for a second and conversed briefly with the man behind him. He turned back to Swain. 'I'm afraid I didn't catch that last thing you said,' he called. 'What was it again? Something about your health?'

'Forget it,' Swain said, rapidly losing interest in this conversation.

The NSA was not so selfless as to come all the way out

here to save innocent humans caught up in an electrified library. It was bigger than that, it had to be. The NSA was here for contact—*extra-terrestrial* contact. Somehow they must have figured out that something was going on inside the library and now they wanted the aliens.

And, presumably, anyone who had come into contact *with* the aliens.

'No, I mean it,' Quaid said reasonably, 'come a little closer and say it again.'

Swain took a step back. 'I don't think so, fellas.'

'No, no. Please! Listen. We're not going to hurt you. I promise.'

'Uh-huh.'

'But if you'll just step a little closer ...'

The dart whizzed by Swain's head, missing it by inches.

It had come from behind Quaid—from somebody who must have crept up behind him while he had kept Swain occupied. They must have shot the tiny dart *through* a gap in the electric field.

Swain didn't wait to think about it. He turned and ran, bolting for the DOWN ramp in the centre of the parking lot.

And as he raced down the ramp toward Sub-Level Two, the last thing he heard was the echoing voice of Harold Quaid of the National Security Agency shouting fiercely at some poor unseen subordinate.

At the base of the outer ramp, Quaid swore.

'*Fuck!* We had him!'

He turned to the Lab agent holding the tranquilliser gun. 'How the *fuck* did you miss? I can't believe you could miss him from—'

'Hold on, Quaid,' Marshall said, resting a hand on his shoulder. 'We may have lost the guy, but I think we just hit the jackpot. Take a look at that.'

Quaid turned. 'Take a look at what?'

Marshall pointed at the parking lot and Quaid followed the line of his finger. His jaw dropped immediately.

'What the hell is *that*?' he breathed.

'I don't know. But I want it,' Marshall said.

Through the grid of blue electricity they could see it clearly, whatever it was.

It looked monstrous, like a large, low-bodied dinosaur—at least fifteen feet long, with a rounded, blunt snout and two long antennae that clocked rhythmically from side to side above its head.

Quaid and Marshall watched, entranced, as the creature limped slowly across the parking lot. It stopped at the top of the DOWN ramp, where it seemed to sniff the ground for an instant.

Then it slithered quickly down the ramp and out of sight.

'Well, well, well. What *do* we have here?' Bellos said, peering under the table.

Selexin was trying hard to keep his body from shaking—and obviously not succeeding. Holly sat frozen beside him.

'Why, tiny man, your memory is as short as you are. I told you I would find you. Or did you forget?'

Selexin swallowed. Holly just stared.

'Perhaps your memory needs a little . . . *refreshing*.' Bellos began to stand. 'Get out from under there.'

Holly and Selexin scrambled out to the far side of the table. Bellos stood on the other side, his wounded guide draped over his shoulder. The flickering fires in the nearby reading rooms were now looking decidedly out of control.

Bellos cocked his head mockingly, 'Where will you run to now, tiny man?'

Selexin glanced over toward the stairwell, and saw the two hoods step menacingly into the open doorway, cutting off their only escape.

'Uh-oh,' he whispered.

When he looked at Bellos again, he saw that his golden breastplate was now smeared with thick red streaks of blood. On the black background of Bellos' forearm, Selexin saw his grey wristband clearly.

And saw the glowing green light suddenly flicker off.

The red light next to it blinked to life.

'*Uh-oh*,' Selexin said again.

Bellos began to strut around the long table. He seemed to be in no hurry. Savouring the moment. He didn't appear to notice the red light now illuminated on his wristband.

'Why have you done this?' Selexin asked.

'Done what?'

'Broken the rules of the Presidian. Cheated. Why have you done this?'

'Why not?'

'You have broken the rules of the contest in order to win it. How can you respect the prize if you cannot respect the tournament? You have cheated.'

'When one is *caught* breaking the rules, one is a cheat,' Bellos said, walking around the end of the table. 'I do not plan to be caught.'

'But you *will* be caught.'

'How?' Bellos asked, as if he already knew the answer to the question.

Selexin spoke quickly. 'A contestant can expose you. He can say 'Initialise' and show those watching at the other end that you have hoods with you.'

'It would be a brave man who would attempt such a thing *while he was running for his life*. Besides,' Bellos said, 'who here knows that I have hoods?'

'I do.'

'But *your* master was last seen falling out of the labyrinth. And he is the only one who can initialise the teleport on your helmet.'

Selexin paused for a moment. Then he said, 'Reese.'

'What?'

'Reese knows,' Selexin said, remembering the hoods attacking Reese back on the First Floor.

'But you do not know if Reese is still alive.'

'Is she still alive?'

'Amuse me,' Bellos said. 'Let us suppose for the moment that Reese is still alive.'

'Then she can report you. She can initialise the teleport on her guide's helmet and expose you.'

'And what about her guide?'

'Excuse me?' Selexin frowned.

'Her *guide*,' Bellos said smugly. 'Surely you cannot believe that if I let Reese live, I would also allow her guide to do so.'

'You killed Reese's guide *before* you attacked Reese?'

Bellos smiled. 'All's fair in love and war.'

'Clever,' Selexin said. 'But what about the hoods? How did you plan to get the hoods out of the labyrinth. Surely you were not just going to leave them here.'

'Trust me, the hoodaya will be long gone from the labyrinth by the time I step through the final teleport,' Bellos said.

Selexin frowned. 'But how? How can you remove them from the labyrinth?'

'I will simply use the same method I used to bring them here.'

'But that would require a teleporter . . .' Selexin said, '*and* the co-ordinates of the labyrinth. And no-one but the organisers of the Presidian knows the location of the labyrinth.'

'On the contrary,' Bellos looked down at Selexin, 'guides like *you* know the co-ordinates of the labyrinth. You have to, because you are teleported with each contestant into the labyrinth.'

Selexin thought about that.

The process of teleportation involved a guide being sent to the contestant's home planet. There, the guide and the contestant would enter a teleporter, *alone*. Once inside, the guide would enter the co-ordinates of the labyrinth and the two of them would be teleported.

Selexin's case had, of course, been different, since humans knew nothing of teleporters and teleportation. He and Swain had been teleported separately.

'But you would still need a teleporter to get the hoods out of here,' Selexin said. 'And there are no teleports to be found on Earth.'

Bellos offered an indifferent shrug, conceding the point. 'I suppose not.'

Selexin was angry now. 'You forget that this is all based on the assumption that you will be the last contestant remaining in the labyrinth. And *that* is yet to be determined.'

'*That* is the risk I take.'

'Your great-grandfather won the Fifth Presidian with no need for treachery,' Selexin said spitefully. 'Imagine what he would think of you now.'

Bellos waved a dismissive hand. 'You do not realise, do you? My people *expect* me to win this contest, just as they expected my great-grandfather to do so, too.'

'But you are not the huntsman your great-grandfather was, are you, Bellos?' Selexin said harshly.

Bellos' eyes narrowed. 'My, my. How boldly we speak when we are about to meet our maker, tiny man. My great-grandfather did what he had to do to win the Presidian. So will I. Different methods, for sure, but tiny man, you must realise that the end does justify the means.'

'But—'

'I think I have had enough of your talk,' Bellos cut him off. 'It is time for you to die.'

Slowly, Bellos rounded the near corner of the table, moved toward Selexin and Holly. Selexin looked desperately about himself. There was nowhere to run to now. Nowhere to hide.

He stood there rooted to the spot, in front of Holly, watching Bellos come closer.

And then—slowly, silently—something behind Bellos caught Selexin's eye.

Movement.

From above.

From behind one of the air-conditioning ducts in the ceiling.

Slowly, ever so slowly, a spindly black body began to unfold itself from the ceiling *behind* Bellos.

It made no sound.

Bellos hadn't noticed it. He just kept approaching

Selexin and Holly—while behind him, the large spindly creature assumed its full, ominous, nine-foot height.

Selexin was dumbstruck.

It was the Rachnid.

The seventh and last competitor in the Presidian. It looked like a giant stick insect, small-headed, multi-limbed. He saw its eight bone-like limbs slowly expand, preparing to wrap themselves around Bellos' body and squeeze him to death.

Then suddenly the Rachnid struck—quickly, violently—closing its arms around Bellos with stunning speed, wrenching him off his feet, lifting him high into the air.

At first, Selexin and Holly were stunned by the sheer rapidity of the attack. It had happened so fast. The slow ominous descent of the Rachnid had instantaneously transformed itself into brutal violence. And now all of a sudden Bellos was in the air, in the grip of the Rachnid, struggling with this new opponent.

The hoods moved immediately.

The able-bodied one galloped from the doorway, leapt up onto the table and flung itself at the Rachnid, jaws bared, defending its master. The second, injured hood moved more slowly, but with equal fervour, clambering up onto the table and diving into the fray.

The element of surprise now appeared completely worthless as the Rachnid—confronted by the unexpected appearance of the two hoods—dropped from the ceiling, shrieking. It landed with a loud *smack!* on the table below, its eight spindly limbs flailing wildly in a desperate attempt to ward off the three-pronged attack.

Holly and Selexin were both staring at the scene in

amazement when suddenly they both had the same thought.

Get out of here.

They bolted for the stairwell door and burst into the darkened stairway.

'Up or down?' Holly asked.

'Down,' Selexin said firmly. 'I saw another contestant up on the Third Floor before.'

They had barely taken five steps down the stairs when there came a deafening—but familiar—roar from the bottom of the stairwell.

'The Karanadon,' Selexin said. 'It's awake again. I saw the red light on Bellos' wristband. Come on,' he grabbed Holly's hand. 'Upstairs.'

They started up the stairs again, and as they ran past the door to the Second Floor, Selexin glanced inside and saw a flashing glimpse of Bellos on the table, kneeling astride the Rachnid, locked in combat.

But now Bellos clearly had the upper hand.

The hapless Rachnid was pinned beneath him, flat on its back, squealing insanely as one of the hoods ripped one of its arms clean off. The Rachnid shrieked. Off to one side, the other hood—the injured one—was busy mauling the Rachnid's guide.

And then Bellos coldly broke the Rachnid's neck and in an instant the squealing stopped. Then Bellos stood and called the hoods to stand behind him, and pointed his guide's head toward the dead body on the table.

'Initialise!' he said loudly.

A small sphere of brilliant white light appeared above the guide's head and Selexin was suddenly captivated.

Holly pulled on his arm. 'Come on, let's go!'

Selexin ducked back behind the door and the two of them hurried up the stairs.

The first thing that struck Stephen Swain about the lower parking level was its size. It was smaller than the parking floor above it. And it had no exit for cars. You could park down here, but you had to go back up to the floor above to get out.

There were three doors, each set into a different wall. One, leading east, had emblazoned across it, EMERGENCY EXIT. Opposite that door was another that read TO STACK. A third door—an older one—lay on the southern side of the parking lot. A few letters were missing from its nameplate. It simply read: —LER ROOM—NO ENTRY.

And there was a car in this parking lot.

A single, solitary car.

A tiny Honda Civic turned silently into the north-west corner, waiting patiently for its owner to return.

Swain tensed at the sudden thought that perhaps there was someone else inside the library. The owner of the car, somebody they had not seen yet.

No, he told himself. *Couldn't be.*

Then he began to think of the other possibilities—like sending the little hatchback blasting through the electrified grille in a fiery blaze of glory, and maybe getting out of the library.

But as he came closer to the little Civic, all his grandiose thoughts faded to nothing.

He sighed.

The car's owner would not be here.

And the car itself would not be blasting through any electrified grille.

This car wouldn't be going anywhere.

Swain looked sadly at the two heavy yellow clamps that held the little car firmly to the concrete floor of the parking lot, and then at the painted blue stripe on the concrete beneath it.

The car had been parked in a handicapped zone, and since it didn't have a sticker on the windshield, the authorities had put the clamps on it.

Swain smiled sadly at the useless car in front of him. At the hospital he'd seen it happen a thousand times, and he always felt that the creeps who parked in the handicapped zones deserved to get clamped.

But now, in the parking lot of the New York State Library, this car offered him absolutely nothing. A gun without any bullets.

It was then that Swain noticed the low hissing noise.

He turned around.

'You never give up, do you?' he said aloud.

For there, standing at the base of the DOWN ramp—her tail slinking back and forth behind her, her antennae clocking from side to side, and her four-sided jaw salivating wildly—stood the very first contestant Stephen Swain had met that night.

Reese.

Holly and Selexin clambered up the dark stairwell and stopped once again on the Third Floor landing. From the bowels of the stairwell came another deafening roar.

The Karanadon.

Somewhere down there.

Selexin stopped in front of the closed door to the study hall, remembering the thin shadow he had seen in there before—the shadow of the Codex.

'The door's closed,' Holly whispered.

'Yes . . .' Selexin said as if it were quite obvious.

'Well—'

'Well what?'

Holly leaned close. 'Well, *we* didn't close it. When we were here before, we just left. We didn't close the door. Remember?'

Selexin didn't remember, but at the moment he didn't care whether the door had been closed or not, they had to go somewhere.

'You are probably right,' he said, gripping the door handle. 'But right now, there is nowhere else to go.'

The little man turned the handle and opened the fire door. He pulled it wide.

And then he fell instantly backwards.

Beside him, Holly turned and vomited explosively.

'Bring it over! Bring it over!' Quaid called. It had started to drizzle softly and a light rain now fell on his head. Quaid didn't even notice it.

The four NSA agents carrying 'it' heaved and grunted as they lowered it to the ground beside the electrified grille.

As they did so, Quaid looked down at the silver box with the counters.

The middle counter read: **120485.05**.

One hundred and twenty *thousand* volts. One hundred and twenty thousand volts of pure, borderless electric current. Kind of like an electrified fence, only without the fence.

Quaid turned his attention to the object that the four agents had just put down beside him. 'It' was the thick lead casing for Sigma Division's portable Radiation Storage Unit.

A portable RSU is basically a pressurised vacuum set inside a four-foot-high lead cube. It is used to contain any radioactive object discovered in the field until it can be brought back for study at the huge electromagnetic Radiation Storage Facility in Ohio.

In other words, it was a glorified thermos flask, surrounded by a thick, waist-high lead casing.

Quaid had ordered that the portable RSU in the van be dismantled and the heavy lead casing be brought out.

'It won't work,' Marshall said, looking down at the big lead cube, which now had its top and bottom faces removed.

'We'll see,' Quaid said.

'That electric field will cut right through it.'

'Eventually, yes, but maybe not right away.'

'What does that mean?'

'That means that it might buy us enough time to get a couple of men inside.'

Marshall frowned. 'I'm not sure . . .'

'You don't have to be sure,' Quaid said roughly. 'Because you are not the one who'll be going in.'

Selexin never took his eyes off the doorway. Beside him, Holly was still retching over a puddle of vomit, tears welling in her eyes.

Slowly, clumsily, Selexin got back to his feet, all the while staring wide-eyed up into the doorway.

There, silhouetted grimly by the blazing yellow flames inside the study hall, hanging upside down from the ceiling, drenched in glistening blood, was the horribly mutilated body of New York Police Officer Paul Hawkins.

In the lower parking lot, Swain kept his eyes fixed on Reese's tail, trying to avoid eye contact with her paralysing antennae.

She moved forward.

Toward him.

Slowly.

Then abruptly her forefoot tripped and she stumbled slightly.

It was only then that Swain remembered where he had last seen Reese. It was back on the First Floor, when the hoods had attacked her, and he and the others had fled for the stairs.

There was no doubt about it. Reese was injured. Battered and bruised from a fight with the hoods that she had only just survived.

Swain looked at himself, covered in the filthy black grime of the elevator shaft and the subway tunnel. He glanced at his wristband.

INITIALISED—3

Another contestant was dead. There were only three

of them left now. The Presidian was nearing completion and the remaining contestants were injured and dirty and exhausted. It was now a battle of endurance.

There was a sudden flare of yellow from the right and Swain saw a gas pipe near the ceiling catch fire.

He stole a glance back at Reese—still trudging wearily forward—then at the little Honda Civic next to him—still utterly useless.

Then back up at the gas pipe. At the soft blue-yellow flame that began to shoot along its length. Swain's eyes followed the pipe, ahead of the flame. The pipe disappeared into the wall, right above the mysterious door marked —LER ROOM—NO ENTRY.

Then Swain had a sickening thought.

Gas. Gas mains.

'—LER ROOM.'

Boiler room.

Oh my . . .

The racing blue-yellow flame scooted across the ceiling, following the path of the gas pipe. Then it disappeared into the wall above the door.

A long silence ensued.

Then . . .

The explosion was huge. It sounded like a cannon going off as the door to the boiler room blasted outward in a thousand pieces, followed by a billowing cloud of smoke and flames. Swain was thrown backwards onto the bonnet of the Civic.

Quaid wobbled slightly as the ground shook. An explosion somewhere.

'We have to go in now,' he said to Marshall.

'How many—?'

'As many as we can.'

'How do you know you'll get through?' Marshall asked.

'How do you know we won't?' Quaid said.

Marshall pursed his lips. 'No-one has ever seen anything like this before . . .'

Quaid just stared at him, waiting for him to make the call.

Then Marshall's eyes narrowed. 'Okay, do it.'

Swain rolled off the bonnet of the little Honda to see Reese turn to face the blazing boiler room.

Overhead sprinklers came instantly to life, dousing the whole parking lot with streams of water. It was like standing in a thunderstorm—booming explosions from the boiler room amid the pouring rain of the sprinklers.

Swain brushed the torrents of water from his eyes as he tried to see what Reese was doing. To his right— halfway between Reese and himself—he caught a glimpse of the door on the western wall of the lot, the door he wanted.

The door that read: TO STACK.

'Ready? Okay, push!' Quaid yelled.

The NSA team heaved on the big lead casing, pushing it toward the electrified grille of the parking lot.

Quaid had got them to turn the big lead cube onto its side, so that the open ends—the top and bottom— were now pointed sideways, toward the crackling grid of blue electricity.

When the lead cube was a foot away from the blue lightning, Quaid, now dressed in full assault gear— helmet, bulletproof vest—called them to a halt.

Marshall handed him an M-16 assault rifle, equipped with a high-tech-looking underslung unit. It looked like an M-203 grenade launcher, except that it had two sharp silver prongs at its end instead of a wide gunbarrel. It was a Taser *Bayonet*—a modern version of an ancient weapon. Instead of attaching a long dagger to the end of your rifle, you attached a couple of thousand volts.

'Some firepower,' Marshall said.

'Don't leave home without it,' Quaid said, taking the weapon.

Marshall reached into his coat.

'One more thing,' he said, pulling a sheet of paper from his pocket. It was the list of times and energy recordings taken from the Eavesdropper satellite. 'Have you got your copy?'

Quaid patted his back pocket. 'Don't you think I know the damn thing off by heart by now? Thirteen surges of energy after we picked up the initial electricity field in the city. That's the starting point. Thirteen things for us to find.'

'If you get in,' Marshall said.

'Yeah,' Quaid said grimly, 'if I get in. You just make sure you're ready for whatever I bring out.'

'If we're not ready, it'll be because we're already inside with you.'

'Good,' Quaid turned to the agents around him. 'Okay, boys. Let's do it.'

The agents began pushing the lead cube toward the wall of criss-crossing blue electricity. Quaid walked slowly behind it, waiting at the open rear end of the cube.

The front end of the cube touched the electricity.

Sparks flew.

Quaid ducked instantly to look through the open rear end of the lead cube. He could see right through it. The electricity wasn't able to cut through the lead.

The NSA agents kept pushing until the cube was half inside, half outside the blue wall of light.

The lead was still holding.

They now had a tunnel through which Quaid could crawl *through* the electrified wall.

Gun in hand, Quaid dived inside the cube—and for a moment, disappeared from sight—and then he emerged on the other side of the electric grid, thumbs up.

'All right,' he called back. 'Send the others through.'

The rest of the NSA entry team—all of them armed with Taser-equipped M-16s—were lined up behind the cube.

The first agent in the line, a young Latin-American named Martinez, immediately dived head-first into the cube.

There came a sudden gut-wrenching *crack!* just as Martinez's legs disappeared inside the tunnel.

'Quickly, move! Before she goes!' Marshall yelled.

And then, without warning, the thick lead cube snapped like a twig under the weight of the surging electric wall *just as* Martinez emerged from the other side, his gun hand trailing behind him. The cube collapsed instantly, cut clean across its middle—likewise Martinez's M-16, which was sheared right through its trigger guard, the lethal electricity missing the young commando's fingers by millimetres.

The wall was back in place.

Quaid and Martinez were cut off.

'You guys all right?' Marshall asked through the grille.

'One gun down, but we're okay,' Quaid said, handing Martinez his own SIG-Sauer pistol, to replace the younger man's ruined M-16. 'Guess we're on our own from here. Be back soon.'

Quaid and Martinez hustled off into the parking lot, heading toward the DOWN ramp.

Marshall watched them go. When finally they were gone, his face creased into a smile.

They were inside the library.

Yes.

Swain stood in the corner of the lower parking lot, drenched in the pouring rain. On the other side of the floor, billowing flames lashed out from the boiler room, impervious to the relentless downpour of the ceiling sprinklers.

Reese continued to limp toward him.

Somehow, she seemed determined to reach him despite the protests of her aching body; consumed by an obsession that would not rest until Stephen Swain was dead.

Swain began to think. He couldn't kill Reese, she was just too big, too strong. And even if she was injured, she would still rip him apart in a fight.

How do you do it? he thought. *How do you kill a thing like that?*

Easy. You don't.

You just keep running.

Swain took a step backwards and felt his legs touch the little Honda.

He was in the corner.

Wonderful.

He stepped out along the wall of the parking lot,

away from the car, toward the door leading to the Stack.

Reese moved quickly, paralleling the move, cutting off his escape.

Swain stopped about ten feet from the Honda, his back to the wall. He could feel the thick spray of the sprinklers hammering down against his head.

He looked at his feet, at the thick pool of water that seemed to be growing around him. It wasn't even a centimetre deep, but it stretched nearly all the way across the vast concrete floor, constantly expanding as the overhead sprinklers supplied it with a constant rain of water.

He was standing in it. Reese was, too.

His eyes followed the path of the spreading pool of water.

The pool seemed to be branching out in every direction, even over toward the eastern wall, toward the door marked EMERGENCY EXIT.

The Emergency Exit.

Swain's mind began to race.

The Emergency Exit would have to be an exterior door, a door leading directly outside.

And if it was, then . . .

He froze in horror. Reese still stood opposite him. The expanding pool of water crept slowly toward the Emergency Exit.

If it was an exterior door, *then it would be electrified.*

And if the pool of water reached it . . .

'Oh dear,' Swain said aloud as he looked at the water in which he was standing. 'Oh *dear* . . .'

Run! his mind screamed. *Where? Any—*

'*Don't move!*' a voice shouted.

Swain's head jerked upright.

Reese snapped around.

Two men stood at the base of the ramp in the centre of the parking lot.

It was Harold Quaid of the National Security Agency and another agent, both dressed in SWAT gear. Quaid held a strange-looking M-16 assault rifle in his hands. The other agent held a silver semi-automatic pistol.

Swain froze.

He glanced over at the Emergency Exit—at the sprinklers on the ceiling that showed no sign of stopping—at the growing pool of water that continued to edge closer to the door.

It was three feet away.

He must have made to move because Quaid called again. 'I mean it! *Don't move!*'

Swain stood stock still.

The water edged closer to the door.

Reese scuttled off to Swain's left, away from Quaid.

Quaid and his partner edged out from the ramp, their respective guns up, eyeing Reese, eyeing Swain. They stepped out into the water.

The spreading pool was now two feet from the door.

Rain from the sprinklers kept falling.

Swain wanted to run—

'Just stay there!' Quaid barked, aiming his gun threateningly at Swain. 'I'm coming over!'

One foot . . .

The water was almost at the door . . .

Screw it, Swain thought. *Either way, I'm going to die.*

'*Don't move*—' Quaid yelled as Swain broke into a run, racing for the Civic in the corner, every step splashing in the water.

Gunfire erupted.

Swain sprinted along the concrete wall, inches ahead of a line of bulletholes.

I'm not going to make it, he thought as heavy drops from the sprinklers pounded against his face. *Not going to make—*

He dived for the car.

The water touched the door.

Swain landed on the bonnet of the little Honda with a loud thud and covered his head with his hands. At the same moment, Quaid's gunfire ceased.

Swain wasn't sure what he expected to hear. The sizzling of electrostatic currents shooting through the water. Maybe even a scream from Quaid, whom he had last seen standing in the middle of the pool of water, firing at him.

But nothing happened.

Nothing at all.

The parking lot remained dead silent, save for the constant *shoosh* of the sprinklers.

Swain slowly lifted his hands from his head and saw Quaid and the second NSA agent—still standing near the central concrete ramp, their feet still in the pool of water—staring curiously at him as he lay on the car bonnet.

Reese, however, was nowhere in sight.

The pool of water had reached the Emergency Exit and flowed right under it without incident.

Swain could think of only one explanation. It wasn't an exterior door. It hadn't been electrified. There must be another door beyond it.

Sprinkler rain continued to fall.

And then suddenly—*ferociously*—Reese burst forward from behind the second NSA agent, and abruptly, the man's ribcage exploded, replaced in an instant by the pointed tip of her tail, protruding grotesquely from his chest.

Quaid spun but he was too slow.

Reese was already moving—extracting her tail from Martinez's body, letting the corpse drop to the floor like a rag doll—and then trampling roughly over the body and hurling herself at Quaid, bounding into him, pitching him forward, knocking him to the floor with a splash.

She must have circled the central ramp, Swain realised, and then come up *behind* the two NSA agents, who had been threatening him.

Threatening *her* kill.

But Quaid was not giving in without a fight. He rolled onto his back just as Reese leapt onto his chest, jaws salivating, antennae swaying. Quaid reached up with his M-16, holding it above the water, and vainly sprayed the ceiling with automatic gunfire. At the same time, Swain thought he saw a flicker of white light flash out from the high-tech-looking unit attached to the barrel of Quaid's assault rifle.

The struggle continued in the pouring indoor rain—but Reese was too strong, too heavy.

Her thick right forelimb came crashing down on Quaid's right arm—his gun arm—and Swain heard the nauseating crunch of breaking bone.

The gun stopped firing instantly, and as Quaid's arm broke horribly in two, the M-16 flew from his grasp, skittling across the water-covered floor of the parking lot, landing a few feet away from Swain's Civic.

His face covered with saliva, Quaid screamed madly as blood streamed out from his cracked right elbow. With his other arm he tried pathetically to hold Reese at bay.

And then Swain saw Reese's tail arch.

Smoothly and gracefully, behind her flailing antennae. Out of Quaid's sight.

Swain didn't have time to move.

The tail came down hard.

Viciously hard.

The pointed tip penetrated Quaid's head in an explosion of red, shooting straight through the skull, emerging on the other side. Quaid's body spasmed violently with the impact, his feet lifting off the ground, and then abruptly his body went completely limp.

Swain watched in horror as Reese coldly withdrew her tail from the dead man's skull. Her tail came clear and the bloodstained head dropped to the floor with a soft splash.

Then she looked up at Swain.

And hissed at him fiercely.

Your turn.

Reese stepped clear of Quaid's body, her whole body coiled, tensed, invigorated by the scent of battle.

Sprinkler rain hammered down on her pebbled dinosaurian back.

Swain stepped off the little Honda, eyeing her cautiously, wondering what the hell he was going to do now. And then, out of the corner of his eye, he saw it.

Quaid's M-16.

Lying in the water to his right, five yards away. Lifeless. Abandoned.

Swain didn't waste a second. He dived for the gun.

Reese leapt forward.

Swain's fingers slapped hard against the water as he grabbed the gun, lifted it clear of the pool and whirled it around to face the charging Reese.

He jammed down on the trigger.

Click!

No bullets! Quaid must have run it dry.

Not fair!

Reese was close now. She leapt at him in the driving rain, flying through the air, forelimbs raised, jaws bared—a giant attacking alligator.

Swain somersaulted left, just as Reese came crashing down on the spot he had just occupied, landing in the shallow water with a massive splash.

Swain got to his feet, turned to see where Reese was—

Thwack!

An immense weight crunched into his chest, driving him backwards. It was Reese's shoulder, slamming into him.

Swain was lifted fully off the ground by the impact and then suddenly—*whump*—he landed with a thud on the bonnet of the parked Honda.

The car beneath him shuddered violently on its suspension and then before he knew it his ears were filled with the most terrifying sound he had ever heard in his life and he opened his eyes to find that he was looking into Reese's wide-open jaws from a distance of six inches.

It made for a very peculiar sight: Swain—on his back, on the bonnet of the Civic, his arms splayed wide, dangling over its sides—with Reese, standing upright, her hind legs resting on the parking lot floor, her stubby forelimbs planted firmly on the bonnet of the car on either side of him.

She lowered her snout over his chest, as if sniffing him, smelling him, savouring her victory over him.

Swain kept his eyes averted—not daring to look at her antennae—while also keeping them clear of the torrent of saliva that now splattered down onto his chest.

Through the sprinkler rain, he could see their combined shadows on the wall nearby—her body bent over his—resting on the shadow of the car.

She had him.

Reese hissed fiercely.

And at that moment, on the wall, Swain saw the shadow of her tail rise behind her back.

This was it.

This was the end.

Reese knew it. Swain did, too.

And then suddenly he felt it—*somehow* it was still in his hand, hanging over the edge of the bonnet—and like the dawn of a new day, a new realisation hit him and Swain looked up into Reese's eyeless face and said, 'I'm sorry.'

And with that Swain jammed down on the *second* trigger of the M-16 he was still holding—the trigger that was attached to the gun's barrel-mounted Taser—and fired it into the pool of water beneath the car.

A bolt of electricity flashed out from the prongs of the *Bayonet* and slammed into the water at the base of the Honda.

Instantly, a blinding flare of light illuminated the parking lot as a thousand branches of jagged white lightning snaked out across the surface of the water at astonishing speed.

Reese shrieked in agony as the electricity from the M-16's underslung Taser shot through the water and up into her body—via her hind legs which were still planted in the shallow pool.

She shuddered violently, her whole lizard-like frame convulsing and spasming, causing the Honda beneath her to rock.

Swain just tried to keep himself clear of her body as it absorbed the stunning surge of electricity.

And then, in a final, lurching fit of electrocution, Reese vomited all over his chest—a disgusting greeny-brown slime—before she reared up on her hind legs and fell to the ground, splashing into the pool of water.

Dead.

For its part, the little Honda Civic—with Swain still on it—stood its ground as the electricity from the *Bayonet* hit its tyres but proceeded no further, its attempts to climb the car frustrated by the rubber.

Moments later, the sprinklers stopped.

The parking lot was silent once more.

Flat on the bonnet of the Civic, Swain breathed again. The initial flare of white light was gone and now only weak glints of electricity flickered up from the water.

The surge of power from the M-16's *Bayonet* had dissipated. The water was back to normal. The *Bayonet* itself was spent, sizzling, shorted out by the water contact. Swain let the gun splash to the ground.

He looked down at Reese. Strangely, in death her bulky dinosaurian body seemed even larger than it had in life. He also saw the bodies of the NSA agents, Quaid and Martinez, lying motionless on the watery floor.

He shook his head in astonishment, wondering how the hell he had managed to survive this confrontation.

And then his wristband beeped.

INITIALISED—2

Now there was only one other contestant left—and he still hadn't found Holly and Selexin.

Swain took a deep breath and heaved himself off the car. His feet hit the concrete with a soft splash.

It wasn't over yet.

'We have to,' Selexin said urgently.

'You can. But I'm not,' Holly said.

'I am not going to leave you here.'

'Then we can just stay here together.' Holly folded her arms resolutely.

They were still standing on the Third Floor landing of the stairwell, outside the study hall.

After seeing Hawkins' mutilated body suspended from the ceiling and throwing up, Holly had slumped down against the nearest wall and stared off into space. Now she was flatly refusing to enter the study hall, which meant walking past the body, and—worse still—through the blood.

Selexin looked about himself nervously. Down the stairs, he could see the open door to the Second Floor. Inside the study hall, upside down, he saw Hawkins' body swaying gently from the ceiling.

Whatever had done this—Selexin suspected it had been Bellos and his hoods—it had ripped his arms right out of their sockets and torn off his head, accounting for the enormous pool of blood underneath the swinging body. Clusters of parallel gashes cut across Hawkins' body—claw marks. Hood marks.

When combined with the ominous yellow glow of the fire in the study hall, it made for a particularly grisly sight.

'You can shut your eyes,' Selexin suggested.

'No.'

'I can carry you.'

'No.'

'You must realise, we cannot stay here.'

Holly remained mute.

Selexin shook his head in frustration and again looked down the stairs.

He froze.

And then he turned back to Holly, picking her up roughly whether she liked it or not.

'Hey—'

'*Shh!*'

'What are you doing—?'

'We're going inside. *Right now*,' Selexin said, pulling her toward the door, looking over his shoulder.

Resisting, Holly followed his gaze down the stairwell. '*I said*, I don't want—'

Her voice trailed off as her eyes came to rest on the door to the Second Floor. She fell silent.

A faint rectangle of light stretched out onto the Second Floor landing, and slowly—very slowly—Holly saw a dark shadow extend into it.

The source of the shadow appeared and Holly watched in terror as a hood stepped out onto the landing and looked up into her eyes.

The M-16's underslung unit had writing on it: TASER BAYONET-4500.

Jesus, Swain thought, as he stood over the body of

Harold Quaid, it made it sound like a new model motorcycle.

Swain had seen Taser shock victims before. Usually you recovered with a monster of a hangover, chiefly because police Taser sticks were unchangeably set at minimum voltage.

But this rifle-mounted Taser unit was *not* standard police issue. And if Quaid really was NSA, who knew what sort of voltage it was packing.

Swain looked down at Reese, lying face down in the shallow pool of water. One thing was certain: NSA Tasers weren't set to simply stun. This one had carried enough voltage to kill Reese.

Swain held the M-16 in his hands. With its magazine empty and the Taser shorted out, it was useless. He discarded the assault rifle and bent down to examine the bodies of Quaid and Martinez. They might have something else on them.

Martinez's SIG-Sauer pistol, or what was left of it, lay half-submerged in the water. It had been completely flattened—Swain guessed Reese must have stepped on it—and now it was little more than a collection of bent metal and broken springs.

Swain rummaged through the pockets of the two NSA men's uniforms. He found a pair of small Motorola walkie-talkies, four extra batteries for the Taser unit, extra clips for the SIG-Sauer, two telescoping truncheon sticks, and each man had two CS tear-gas grenades.

Swain wondered if Karanadons were susceptible to tear gas—probably not. Hell, if he used the grenades, Swain thought, he'd probably only succeed in incapacitating himself. The radios were no help—after all, who was he going to call? And he didn't like his chances with the truncheons against someone like Bellos. No, Harold Quaid and his partner had little to offer him.

He wondered how they had got inside the library in the first place. The parking lot presumably. But something must have gone wrong—otherwise they would have had ten more guys with them, and much more artillery. Surely they wouldn't come searching for aliens with only two guns between them.

Then Swain found something.

In Quaid's back pocket. A sheet of paper. A list:

LSAT-560467-S
DATA TRANSCRIPT 463/511-001
SUBJECT SITE: 231.957 (North-eastern seaboard: CT, NY, NJ)

NO.	TIME/EST	LOCATION	READING
1.	18:03:48	CT.	Isolated energy surge/Source: **UNKNOWN** Type: **UNKNOWN** / Dur: **0.00:09**
2.	18:03:58	N.Y.	Isolated energy surge/Source: **UNKNOWN** Type: **UNKNOWN** / Dur: **0.00:06**
3.	18:07:31	N.Y.	Isolated energy surge/Source: **UNKNOWN** Type: **UNKNOWN** / Dur: **0.00:05**
4.	18:10:09	N.Y.	Isolated energy surge/Source: **UNKNOWN** Type: **UNKNOWN** / Dur: **0.00:07**
5.	18:14:12	N.Y.	Isolated energy surge/Source: **UNKNOWN** Type: **UNKNOWN** / Dur: **0.00:06**
6.	18:14:37	N.Y.	Isolated energy surge/Source: **UNKNOWN** Type: **UNKNOWN** / Dur: **0.00:02**
7.	18:14:38	N.Y.	Isolated energy surge/Source: **UNKNOWN** Type: **UNKNOWN** / Dur: **0.00:02**
8.	18:14:39	N.Y.	Isolated energy surge/Source: **UNKNOWN** Type: **UNKNOWN** / Dur: **0.00:02**
9.	18:14:40	N.Y.	Isolated energy surge/Source: **UNKNOWN** Type: **UNKNOWN** / Dur: **0.00:02**

10.	18:16:23	N.Y.	Isolated energy surge/Source: **UNKNOWN**
			Type: **UNKNOWN** / Dur: **0.00:07**
11.	18:20:21	N.Y.	Isolated energy surge/Source: **UNKNOWN**
			Type: **UNKNOWN** / Dur: **0.00:08**
12.	18:23:57	N.Y.	Isolated energy surge/Source: **UNKNOWN**
			Type: **UNKNOWN** / Dur: **0.00:06**
13.	18:46:00	N.Y.	Isolated energy surge/Source: **UNKNOWN**
			Type: **UNKNOWN** / Dur: **0.00:34**

Swain stared at the list, bewildered.

Numbers and times and energy surges and the constant repetition of the word UNKNOWN. And presumably it all had something to do with the library.

Thirteen surges of energy in all. One in Connecticut and twelve in New York.

Okay.

Swain looked at the times of the first few surges.

18:03:48. A surge—source unknown, type unknown—detected in Connecticut, lasting *nine* seconds.

Exactly *ten* seconds after that initial surge began, at 6:03:58 p.m., a surge appeared in New York.

All right. That was easy. That was Swain himself and Holly being teleported from his home in Connecticut to the library in central Manhattan.

Six other surges of roughly the same duration—five to eight seconds—accounted for the other contestants and their guides being teleported into the library for the Presidian.

Swain remembered that Selexin had already been inside the library when he had arrived. His teleportation must have occurred too early to be on this list.

But that still left five other surges.

Swain scanned the list further and saw the entries numbered 6 through 9—the four two-second surges that had come in rapid succession one second after the other. They had been underlined.

Swain frowned at the fifth surge.

18:14:12. A six-second surge. Nothing special about that, just another contestant and his guide being teleported inside. But twenty-five seconds after that surge came the four rapid surges in quick succession.

The hoods! he thought, realising.

They were small, so teleportation must not have taken very long. Only two seconds each.

And that explained the variation in the times needed for the other teleportations—some contestants were bigger or smaller than others, so they required more or less time to be teleported into the labyrinth, somewhere between five and eight seconds.

Swain smiled, this was coming together nicely.

Except for one thing.

The last energy surge.

It had come more than *twenty-two minutes* after all the other surges, which themselves had all occurred *within* twenty minutes.

And it had lasted thirty-four seconds. The longest surge before that had lasted only nine seconds.

What was it? An afterthought perhaps? Was it something the organisers of the Presidian had forgotten to put inside the labyrinth?

It wasn't the Karanadon. Selexin had told Swain that the Karanadon had been placed inside the labyrinth almost a day *before* the Presidian was to commence.

Swain couldn't figure it out now, so he let it be for the moment. It was time to go.

He put the sheet of paper in his pocket and with a final glance at Reese's motionless body, he headed for the door marked TO STACK.

The study hall was bathed in the yellow glow of a fire out of control.

In the far corner of the wide room, beyond the flames, the janitor's room stood sombrely—dark and charred, the fire inside it having burned itself out.

Holly shut her eyes as Selexin led her around the bloody corpse swinging from the ceiling. Her feet slipped suddenly on the pool of blood, but Selexin steadied her before she fell.

They could hear the hoods climbing the stairs behind them, grunting, snorting.

Selexin pulled harder, guiding Holly in among the L-shaped desks of the study hall.

'The elevator!' Holly whispered. 'Go for the elevator!'

'Good idea,' Selexin said, pressing on through the tangle of standing and fallen desks.

There must have been hundreds of desks in the study hall, half of which still stood, undisturbed. The other half had not been so fortunate, crushed or thrown by the Karanadon, torn to pieces, smashed beyond recognition.

The elevators were close now.

The doors to the left-hand elevator were still pulled wide, revealing the black abyss of the elevator shaft. The Karanadon must have pulled them open so hard that they had stayed open.

Selexin hit the call button on the run, slammed into the wall, spun around.

In the flickering glow of the fire, he saw Hawkins' body spinning slowly from the ceiling above the entrance to the stairwell.

And beneath the body, stepping slowly and cautiously into the study hall, was a hood.

Through the tangled forest of desk legs, Selexin saw the second hood join its partner and he felt a chill.

They were scanning the study hall very slowly, peering across the room, under the desks.

Selexin watched intently. It was as though the hoods were more resolved now, more serious. It was time to kill. Play was over. The hunt had begun.

Holly snapped to look at the open elevator shaft behind them.

The cables that had run vertically down the shaft were all gone now, snapped by the Karanadon, probably resting at the bottom with the rest of the battered lift. They couldn't slide down this time.

The numbered display above the other elevator was still working though: one number after the other slowly ignited as the elevator crawled upwards.

LG glowed yellow. Then faded.

G glowed yellow, faded.

1 glowed—

Holly felt Selexin tug on her shoulder. 'Come on,' he said. 'We can't stay here.'

'But the lift . . .'

'It will not get here in time.' Selexin grabbed her arm and pulled her away from the elevators just as she caught a glimpse of the hoods moving in from the left.

Selexin pulled hard, dragging Holly to the right, watching the hoods through the legs of the desks.

The hoods were twenty feet away, moving with the cold stealth of seasoned hunters.

In the strobe-like light of the fires, Selexin could see them clearly. The needle-like teeth protruding from the spherical head; the bony black forelegs with their blood-ied claws scraping on the floor; the powerful, muscular hind legs; and the long scaly tail that swished menac-ingly behind the black torso as if it had a mind of its own.

The perfect hunter.

Remorseless. Relentless.

Selexin swallowed as he jumped over a fallen desk and found himself standing before the janitor's room. In the corner.

Dead end.

He looked back. The hoods had stopped now, still twenty feet away. They were just standing there, star-ing at their diminutive prey.

A moment later, they moved again.

In opposite directions.

They were splitting up.

'Not good,' Selexin said, 'this is not good.' It was better when they were together, because at least then he could see them both at the same time. But now . . .

'Quickly,' he said to Holly, 'get on the desks.'

'What?'

'*Get on them*,' Selexin insisted. 'They are seeing us through the legs. If we get onto the desks, they will not know where we are.'

Holly climbed like a monkey onto the nearest L-shaped desk. Selexin jumped up quickly behind her.

'Let's go,' she whispered, obviously in her element now, jumping easily across to the next desk.

'Just be careful,' Selexin said, stumbling after her. 'Do not fall off.'

Holly danced nimbly from desk to desk, skipping over the gaps with ease. Behind her, Selexin did the same.

Beneath them, they could hear the snorting and grunting of the hoods.

There was a sudden *bing!* and Selexin looked over his shoulder and saw—across the sea of desks—the upper half of the elevator doors.

They were opening.

'Oh no,' he said, running across the desk tops.

Holly saw them, too. 'Can we get there?'

'We have to try,' Selexin said.

Holly changed her course, turning in a wide semi-circle, jumping across the desks. She was about to leap across a wide gap between two desks when the able-bodied hood, claws raised to attack, sprang up from the floor into her path.

Holly fell backwards onto the desk and the hood dropped from sight.

Selexin caught up with her. 'Are you—?'

With a loud squeal, the hood leapt up again, onto an adjacent desk, and lashed out at Holly with a scythe-like foreclaw.

Holly screamed as she rolled clear, *off the desk*, falling to the floor. Selexin watched her fall out of sight.

'No!'

The hood swung viciously at Selexin—back-handed—hitting him squarely in the face. He recoiled sharply, losing his balance, falling backwards onto his desk.

With frightening speed, the hood leapt at him as he landed, but Selexin rolled and the hood smashed into the upright partition of the L-shaped table.

The weight of the impact rocked the desk, and in an instant Selexin's horror became complete as he saw the world tilt crazily and felt the desk he was sitting on keel over backwards.

From the floor, Holly watched fearfully as the desk on which Selexin and the hood fought lurched backwards and tipped over. It seemed to fall in slow motion.

Selexin fell first, hitting the floor hard, his white eggshell hat flying from his head. He rolled clear of the falling desk.

The hood slid off the tilting desk, landing on its feet like a cat, right in front of Selexin.

Selexin was totally exposed, and the hood was tensing itself to attack when abruptly the desk came crashing down on its back.

Pinned to the floor, shrieking like a mad animal, the hood writhed about in a frenzy, attempting to free itself. Its jaws snapped and snarled as it still tried—despite its own predicament—to get to Selexin.

Selexin was scrambling backwards on his butt, away from the wailing creature when, from behind him, Holly tipped over a second desk.

This time the L-shaped table fell forward, and the hood looked up in horror at the desk rushing down toward it.

The leading edge of the desk landed with a loud crunching sound on the hood's upturned head, shattering the animal's long needle-like teeth as it crushed its skull against the floor.

The hood's body jerked and spasmed beneath the two fallen desks, until at last it lay still. Dead.

Silence.

Then Holly heard a soft *bing!* followed by the grinding sound of the elevator doors closing again.

She knelt beside Selexin, looking quickly in every direction. 'Where's the other one?'

'I . . . I do not know,' Selexin was badly shaken. 'It could be anywhere.'

Now it was Holly who grabbed Selexin by the arm and pulled him to his knees. 'We missed the elevator,' she said, determined. 'Come on, we've got to get out of here.'

'But . . . but,' Selexin mumbled feebly.

'Come *on*. Let's move.'

'But my . . . my hat!' Selexin clawed at his bald head. 'I need my hat.'

Holly spun around quickly and saw the hat. The small white hemisphere was sitting on the floor, jutting out from behind a nearby upturned desk.

She crawled toward the fallen desk on her hands and knees, rounded the upturned legs, and reached out to grab the hat . . .

Holly paused.

Then she froze.

Beside the hat stood two bony black forelegs—one with a bloodstained claw; one with no claw at all.

Her eyes lifted, rising up the forelegs, following them until she came face to face with the second hood.

The hood's jaws opened wide, salivating in evil anticipation, inches away from her face.

Selexin watched helplessly from the floor ten feet away. Too far.

Holly was still on all fours, almost nose-to-nose with the hood.

Totally defenceless.

The hood stepped forward and stood over the hat.

It was so close now that all Holly could see was its teeth. Its long, pointed, bloody teeth. She felt the warmth of its hot breath blowing on her face; smelled the foul odour of rotting flesh.

Holly shut her eyes and clenched her fists, waiting for the animal to strike, waiting for the end. Her terror was extreme.

Suddenly, the hood hissed fiercely and Holly wanted to scream and then, as her horror hit fever pitch, she had the strange sensation of hearing her father's voice.

'Initialise!'

There was a sudden, glorious flare of white that shot through Holly's eyelids.

Then she heard the hood shriek in total, rabid agony and she opened her eyes and was instantly blinded by the small sphere of dazzling white light that had flared to life above Selexin's hat.

The hood's shrieking cut off abruptly and Holly heard her father's voice again.

'Cancel.'

The blinding white light vanished instantly and for a moment Holly saw nothing but kaleidoscopic spots of colour.

Then suddenly there were two strong arms wrapped around her, holding her tightly, and still blind, Holly's first thought was to break free.

But the grip was firm and gentle.

A hug.

Holly blinked twice as her eyesight slowly returned and she found herself in the warm embrace of her father.

Her muscles drooped with relief and she let her body fall limply into his.

Then she began to cry.

As he held his daughter tightly in his arms, Stephen Swain closed his eyes and sighed. Holly was safe, and they were back together again. He didn't want to let her go.

Still holding her, he turned to look at the remains of the hood.

The body had been cut perfectly in two—only the hind legs and the tail remained. The head, forelimbs and upper torso had simply disappeared, teleported to God-only-knew-where. Thick black blood oozed out from the exposed cross-section of the animal's torso.

Selexin limped to Swain's side and grimaced at the sight of the half-bodied hood.

'"Initialise". "Cancel",' Selexin laughed softly to himself. 'It is nice to know,' he said wryly to Swain, 'that you do not forget *everything* I tell you.'

Swain smiled sadly, still hugging Holly. 'Not everything.'

Holly looked up at her father. 'I knew you would come back.'

Swain said, 'Of course I came back, silly. You didn't think I'd leave you here all by yourself, did you?'

'Ah, ahem,' Selexin coughed, 'I beg your pardon but the young lady was certainly not *all* by herself.'

'Oh, excuse me.'

Holly said, 'He was very brave, Daddy. He helped me a lot.'

'He did, huh?' Swain looked at Selexin. 'That was very noble of him. I really should thank him.'

Selexin bowed modestly.

'Thanks,' Swain said softly to the little man.

Selexin, proud of his new-found hero status, shook it off. 'Oh, it was nothing. All part of the service, right?'

Swain laughed. 'Right.'

'I knew you'd come back. I knew it.' Holly nestled into Swain's arms. Then she looked up suddenly, made a mock-angry face, and adopted a severe adult tone. 'So where have you been all this time? How did you find us?'

Actually, in the end, finding Holly and Selexin had been rather lucky.

From the parking lot, Swain had run into the Stack and arrived at the small red door through which he had been bowled out by the hoods. When he found nothing there, not even a trace of Holly and Selexin, he was at a total loss.

And then, in the silence, he had heard the nearby elevator ping.

It must have just been sitting there on Sub-Level Two when somebody on another floor had pressed the call button.

Swain raced for the elevator and reached it just as the doors were about to meet. He jumped inside and rode the lift to whichever floor the call had come from. It was better than nothing. And besides, who knew? Maybe Holly or Selexin had pressed the call button. Then again, it might not have been them, but by then Swain didn't care. It was a risk he had to take.

The elevator had opened onto the Third Floor and Swain had been confronted with the burning study hall.

He had ducked and crawled out of the lift on his hands and knees, trying to stay out of sight.

Then he had heard voices and the grunts of the hoods, and then the crash of a falling desk, and then another.

He jumped to his feet, and followed the noise, rounded a clump of desks and saw his daughter crouched on her hands and knees, nose-to-nose with one of the hoods.

Swain was too far away, and didn't know what to do, when he realised that the hood was standing over Selexin's white, egg-like hat.

And at that moment, a single word had leapt into his mind—'Initialise'.

'Can you get them?' Marshall asked the radio operator inside the NSA van.

'Negative, sir. There's no response from Commander Quaid or Agent Martinez.'

'Try again.'

'But, sir,' the operator insisted, 'all I'm getting is static. We can't even tell whether Commander Quaid has his radio turned *on*.'

> Status Report: Station 4 reports detection of
> contaminant inside labyrinth.
> Awaiting confirmation.

'Just keep trying,' Marshall said, 'and call me as soon as you pick up anything.'

Marshall climbed out of the van onto the parking lot ramp. He looked up at the electrified grille, at the crumpled lead cube at its base, at the surging blue grid of electricity.

What the hell had happened to Quaid?

In the study hall, Swain stood up, holding Holly in his

arms. 'We better get going.'

Selexin was putting his white, dome-like hat back on. It was stained with the black blood of the hood. 'You are right,' he said. 'Bellos cannot be far away.'

'Bellos,' Swain thought aloud. 'It had to be.'

'What are you talking about?'

'Bellos is the other one,' Swain said. 'The only other contestant left.'

'There are only *two* contestants remaining in the Presidian?' Selexin asked.

'Yep,' Swain offered him the wristband.

Selexin perused it for a moment, then looked up at Swain. His face was grim. 'We have a serious problem.'

'What?'

'Look at this.' Selexin held Swain's wristband up to him. It read:

INITIALISED—2
STATUS REPORT: STATION 4 REPORTS DETECTION OF
CONTAMINANT INSIDE LABYRINTH.
AWAITING CONFIRMATION.

'What the hell does that mean?' Swain said.

'It means,' Selexin said, 'that they have discovered the hood.'

'Which hood?' Swain asked. 'And who on earth are *they*?'

'The hood that you just killed using the teleport in my hat.'

'And *they*?'

'*They* are the officials watching at the other end of that teleport, who I imagine received quite a shock when half a hoodaya was teleported into their laps. They are in Station Four, the teleport station assigned to monitor the progress of contestant number four—you.'

'So what does the message mean?'

Selexin said, 'This contest is for seven contestants only. It is a fight to the death between the seven intelligent beings of the universe. Outside assistance is strictly forbidden. Hoods are like dogs. They are not intelligent beings. Wherefore, they do not compete in the Presidian. And they most surely do not live on Earth. So when the officials in Station Four received a hood teleported from the labyrinth on Earth, they immediately realised that the Presidian had been compromised, contaminated by an outside agent.'

Swain was silent for a moment. Then he said, 'So what are they doing now?'

'They are awaiting confirmation.'

'What's confirmation?'

Selexin said, 'An official must go to Station Four and visually confirm the existence of the contaminant.'

'And what happens when it's confirmed?'

'I do not know. This has never happened before.'

'Can you guess?'

Selexin nodded slowly.

'Well?' Swain prompted.

The little man bit his lip. 'They will probably annul the Presidian.'

'You mean call it off?'

Selexin frowned. 'Not quite. What they will probably do—'

'Daddy . . .' Swain heard Holly's soft voice come from his chest. He was still holding her in his arms.

'In a minute, honey,' Swain said. Then to Selexin, 'What will they do?'

'I think they'll—'

'*Daddy!*' Holly whispered insistently.

'What is it, Holly?' Swain said.

'Daddy. *Someone's here . . .*' she spoke in such a low, hissing whisper that it took Swain a couple of seconds to realise what she had said.

He looked down at her. She was staring fearfully out over his shoulder.

Slowly, Stephen Swain looked behind him.

Across the wide room, he saw a body—bloodied and mutilated—hanging upside down from the ceiling, just inside the stairwell door.

And standing beside the body was Bellos.

Swain spun and saw the body next to Bellos swing around lazily. A wave of sadness shot through him as he saw the police uniform.

Hawkins.

Without a word, Bellos began to walk through the tangle of L-shaped desks toward them.

Toward them.

'Let's *go*!' Holly said loudly in his ear.

Swain moved laterally to his left, trying to keep as many desks as possible between him and Bellos.

Bellos did the same, moving in a peculiar, wide arc from left to right, threading his way calmly and quickly between the desks. He still had his white guide draped over his shoulder.

Swain stumbled away from the big man, toward the elevators, Holly in his arms, Selexin by his side.

'Nowhere to run!' Bellos boomed from across the study hall. 'Nowhere *to hide*!'

'They've found you out,' Swain called, walking backwards. 'They know you brought hoods into the contest. You cheated, and you got caught.'

Bellos continued to move forward in wide arcs, left and right. It was an odd movement, a movement that seemed to force them back. Back toward the—

'Their discovery will be of no help to you,' Bellos said.

Swain looked over his shoulder and saw the gaping black hole that was the left-hand elevator. The doors to the right one were closed.

Swain moved sideways until his back was pressed up against the call button panel.

'The Presidian is over, Bellos,' Swain said. 'You can't win anymore. They know you cheated.'

Behind his back, Swain's free hand searched for the call button, found it, pressed it.

'Perhaps they know,' Bellos said whimsically. 'Perhaps they don't. It does not matter now.'

'You have disgraced yourself!' Selexin blurted.

'And I don't *care*,' Bellos said defiantly. 'I did what I had to do to win. And even if they do find out about the hoodaya, I will still prove to them all that I have won this Presidian.'

'And how will you do that?' Selexin said.

Swain grimaced, knowing the answer.

'By being the only surviving contestant,' Bellos said.

Swain groaned.

Then he heard Holly's voice again. It was loud, close to his ear. 'Daddy, it's here.'

'What?'

'The elevator.' She pointed up at the numbered display above the elevator doors. The number 3 glowed yellow.

There was a soft *ping*.

The doors opened. The darkened interior of the elevator yawned before them.

'Inside,' Swain said quickly to Selexin. 'Now.'

Swain and Holly stepped back into the elevator as Selexin ran to the button panel and pressed a button.

Bellos didn't react quickly. In fact, he didn't react at all.

He just kept walking forward. Toward the elevator.

The doors began to close.

Bellos walked casually toward the lift.

As Swain watched, he got the impression that Bellos was in no hurry to get to them. It was as if he had all the time in the world.

As if he knew something that they did not. As if he had calculated . . .

But then the doors closed and they were swallowed by darkness and the elevator began its descent.

Two long cylindrical fluorescent light tubes lay on the floor of the lift—they were the tubes that Hawkins had removed from their sockets when Swain and his group had been hiding on the First Floor earlier that night.

Swain put one of the tubes back into its socket, bathing the elevator in a dull white glow.

'Well, that was easy,' Selexin said.

'Too easy,' Swain said.

'Why didn't he follow us, Daddy?' Holly said. 'Before, he chased us all over the place. *All* over the place.'

'I don't know, honey.'

'Well, we are away now,' Selexin said. 'And that is all that matters.'

'That's what worries me,' Swain said.

And then it happened.

Suddenly. Without warning.

A loud, heavy *thump!* on the roof of the elevator.

They all froze. And then slowly, very slowly, looked up at the ceiling.

Bellos had jumped down onto the roof of the elevator!

He must have jumped across from the open doors of the other elevator.

Swain realised his mistake immediately. 'God*damn* it!'

'What?' Selexin said.

'You'll be happy to know,' Swain said wryly, 'that we've just managed to trap ourselves.'

He cursed himself. He should have seen it. While they were running away from Bellos, he had been moving in those strange arcs, virtually guiding them to the elevators. When they thought they were escaping, they were actually going exactly where he wanted them to go. *Shit.*

Suddenly, the hatch in the roof opened.

Swain pulled Holly and Selexin to the rear corner of the lift.

Bellos' head appeared through the open hatch upside down, his long tapering horns pointing downward.

He smiled menacingly.

Then his head disappeared from view, back outside the lift. A moment later Bellos swung down through the hatch, landing on his feet.

Inside the lift.

Right in front of them.

'Nowhere to run now,' he sneered. 'Finally.'

Swain pushed Holly into the corner behind him. Selexin stood by his side. Bellos was standing in the opposite corner of the elevator, beside the button panel. He didn't have his guide with him anymore.

Swain saw the panel next to Bellos and wondered which button Selexin had pressed. He hoped the little man had pressed the next floor. Then they might be able to make a run for it.

He saw the illuminated button and closed his eyes in dismay.

SL-2 was glowing.

That was Sub-Level Two, the Stack. The bottom floor. They were in for a long ride.

'You pressed the *bottom* floor?' he whispered to Selexin in disbelief.

'To get as far away as possible,' Selexin whispered back. 'How was I supposed to know he would jump on top of the—'

'*Silence!*' Bellos boomed.

'Oh, shut up,' Swain said.

'Yes. And fuck you, too,' Selexin added.

Bellos cocked his head, amazed at this display of impertinence. His face tightened, angry.

He began to walk across the elevator.

It was then that Swain realised just how big Bellos was—he had to bend so that his horns wouldn't hit the ceiling. And he was built like a house, too. Swain eyed the golden breastplate on his chest. It was dazzling.

He also saw that Bellos had added several more trophies to his belt. He still had the Konda's breathing mask and the NYPD badge clipped to it, but now he had two more-recent additions: first—and most grue-somely—the severed head of a thin, stick-insect-like creature; and second—a more earthly object—a small canister of police-issue chemical Mace, still in its belt-pouch.

Swain froze at the sight of the Mace.

It was Hawkins' Mace.

It was Bellos' trophy from killing the young policeman.

Bellos caught Swain looking at his newly acquired trophy. He touched the small canister on his belt.

'A curious weapon,' he mused. 'As his dying act, your companion sprayed it into my eyes, but to no effect. You humans must truly be fragile beings if something so pathetic as this injures you.'

'You are a coward, Bellos,' Selexin spat.

Bellos rounded on him, took a step toward him, extended his arm toward the little man's head.

Selexin leaned back against the wall, trying to pull away.

Then, roughly, Swain swatted Bellos's arm away. 'Get away from him,' he said flatly.

Bellos pulled his arm back—away from Selexin— dutifully obeying Swain's command. And then suddenly he thrust his arm viciously forward, hitting Swain hard in the face.

Swain fell to the floor, clutching his jaw.

'And fuck you, too,' Bellos said with a sneer. 'Whatever that means.'

Then the big man moved quickly, grabbing Swain by the collar and hurling him into the far wall of the elevator.

Swain banged hard against the wall, fell to the floor again, wheezing.

Bellos strutted across the elevator, following him.

'Pathetic little man,' he said. 'How *dare* you touch me. My great-grandfather also killed a human once. In another Presidian, two thousand years ago. And this human cried, begged, pleaded for mercy.'

Bellos picked Swain up by the hair and threw him against the doors of the lift.

'Is that what you will do, little earth man? Cry for clemency? Beg me to be merciful?'

Swain was lying face down on the floor. He picked himself up slowly and sat with his back up against the doors. The cut on his lip had been reopened and now it was bleeding profusely.

'Well, little human?' Bellos jeered. 'Will you beg for your life?' He paused, and then turned to face Holly in the corner. 'Or perhaps, you would rather beg for hers?'

'Come over here,' Swain said evenly.

'What?' Bellos said.

'I said, *come over here.*'

'No,' Bellos smiled. 'I think I'd like to acquaint myself with this young lady first.' He stepped across the elevator, toward Holly.

Selexin took a step sideways, blocking him. 'No,' he said firmly.

It was a strange sight. Selexin—four feet tall, dressed completely in white—protecting Holly from Bellos—seven feet tall and clad entirely in black.

'Goodbye, tiny man,' Bellos said, delivering a heavy blow across Selexin's head, sending the little man crashing to the floor.

Bellos towered over Holly. 'Now . . .'

'I said,' a voice said in Bellos' ear, '*come over here.*'

Bellos turned to see Stephen Swain and a long white fluorescent light tube come rushing at his face.

Swain held the fluorescent tube like a baseball bat and he swung it hard.

The swing connected. The tube smashed against Bellos' face, sending glass shards flying everywhere, and showering the big man's face with a strange white powder that had been inside the fluorescent tube.

Bellos jolted slightly with the impact. But despite the spectacular explosion of the tube across his face, he remained unmoved—uninjured by the blow, save for the layer of powder on his jet-black face—and simply stared coldly down at Swain.

'Uh-oh,' Swain said.

Bellos hit him.

Hard.

Swain bounced into the elevator doors, just as the elevator stopped and the doors themselves opened. He stumbled backwards, out onto the floor of the Stack. Bellos stepped out of the lift after him, walked over to him, and picked him up by his shirt.

'Yes, yes,' Bellos said. 'Begged for mercy, that's what he did. And do you know what my great-grandfather did when this human begged?'

Swain didn't answer.

'He decapitated him,' Bellos moved his powder-covered face close to Swain's. 'Tore his arms from his body, too.' Bellos stroked his golden breastplate. 'And then he took this. A glorious trophy from such an inglorious creature.'

Swain looked at the breastplate more closely. Indeed, upon closer examination, it looked like . . . like the gilded armour of a Roman centurion.

A Roman centurion? Swain thought. *In a Presidian? Two thousand years ago? My God . . .*

Bellos raised Swain higher so that his sneakers were a full foot above the floor. He carried him over to the crumpled outer doors of the other elevator. When the Karanadon had climbed out of the broken elevator at the bottom of the shaft, it must simply have crashed through the outer doors to get out.

Bellos threw Swain through the open outer doors and he landed heavily on what was left of the roof of the destroyed elevator, resting at the base of the shaft. The roof was a good five feet below the floor level of the Stack.

Bellos leapt down onto the roof after him. 'Well, human?' he said. 'Do you beg?'

350

Swain coughed. 'Not in this life.'

'Then perhaps in the next,' Bellos said, picking him up again and hurling him into the concrete wall of the shaft. Swain hit the wall and fell to his knees, aching, coughing.

'Are you thinking of yourself now, little man?' Bellos said, circling Swain. 'Or are you thinking of what I will do when you are dead? Which is worse? Your death, or the prospect of what I will do to your little one *after* you are dead?'

Swain clenched his teeth, felt the warmth of his own blood in his mouth.

He had to do something.

He looked up and saw the other lift, hanging above them like a big square shadow in the blackness of the shaft. There was a dark gap beneath it. *Maybe . . .*

Bellos moved in close again—and suddenly Swain came to life, launching himself quickly forward, tackling the big man around the ankles, throwing Bellos off balance, sending them both falling toward the edge of the roof.

They fell.

Both of them.

Off the roof of the destroyed lift, out into the shaft *underneath* the working elevator.

The drop was about ten feet and Bellos landed heavily on the concrete base of the elevator shaft. Swain landed on top of him, the big man's body cushioning his fall.

Swain got to his feet immediately and looked around the base of the shaft.

Solid concrete walls on two sides—a series of counterweight cables on one of them. Opposite the counterweight cables was the battered side wall of the destroyed elevator, lying crumpled at the bottom of the shaft. On the fourth side of the shaft, however, Swain saw the most unexpected sight of all.

A pair of outer doors.

There was another floor down here.

The working elevator could come down.

And if it could, then . . .

'Holly! Selexin!' he called desperately. 'Are you still up there! If you are, go to the buttons! *Press anything below SL-2!*'

Inside the elevator, Selexin was still sprawled on the floor, bloodied and dazed. Holly was huddled in the corner.

Then strangely she heard her father's echoing voice and she blinked back to life. '—*anything below SL-2!*'

What?

She ran over to the button console and scanned the buttons there:

3	2
1	g
sl-1	sl-2

SL-2 was the lowest it went. There *was* nothing below SL-2!

What was he talking about?

Groggy, Bellos got slowly to his feet. The fall had hurt him.

Swain called up again. 'Anything below Sub-Level 2! Just press it!'

Holly's voice floated down the shaft. 'There isn't anything! There's nothing below that one!'

Christ, Swain thought. *I can see the doors. There has to be!*

He called again, 'Look below the buttons! Is there a small door in the wall! A panel of some sort! Something like that! Anything like that!'

A few seconds.

Holly's voice. 'Yes. *I see it!* I see a little panel!'

Beside Swain, Bellos staggered against the side wall of the destroyed elevator. On the other side of the shaft, Swain saw the five or so counterweight cables running vertically up the concrete wall. They were taut and greased and they appeared to run all the way up the shaft, past the elevator hovering above them. 'Holly!' he called urgently. '*Open the panel!* If there's another button there, *just press it!*'

Holly opened the small white door set into the wall beneath the button console. Inside she saw several switches that looked like regular light switches.

Underneath them, though, was a mouldy green button, beside which was scrawled in white chalk the words: ACCESS TO STORAGE BASEMENT.

'I found one!' she called.

'*Press it!*'

Holly pressed the green button and immediately felt her stomach lurch.

The lift was going down.

The cables running up the wall of the shaft suddenly came to life, some going up, some going down—all moving too fast to tell—as the complex pulley system of counterweights burst into action.

Swain looked up as the elevator fourteen feet above him began to move.

Downward.

Toward them.

That was good. He'd needed to do something, to provide some sort of—

And then abruptly he was slammed onto the concrete floor. Bellos had thrown himself into him and both of them went sprawling to the ground.

Swain hit the floor hard and rolled quickly just as a big black fist came plunging down into the concrete right next to his head.

Bellos roared in pain, clutching his fist.

Swain leapt to his feet. He looked up at the slowly descending elevator. It was close. There wasn't much time.

You can't fight Bellos. You have to find a way out of—

Then suddenly Bellos was on his feet again and he launched himself at Swain, driving him back against the side wall of the destroyed elevator.

The moving elevator edged downward.

Twelve feet off the ground.

Bellos punched Swain in the stomach. He buckled over.

Eleven feet.

Bellos hit him again. Swain gagged. Bellos was just too damn big to fight.

Ten feet.

Bellos glanced up quickly at the descending elevator and then all around himself for an escape. He saw the rapidly moving counterweight cables by the wall. There seemed to be enough space there to stand . . .

354

Nine feet.

The bottom of the lift scraped Bellos' horns and he ducked.

Eight feet.

And Swain saw the speeding cables, too. Beside him, Bellos was crouching now, bent over at the waist, facing the other way, looking at the cables.

It was a chance.

Swain seized it.

He moved in quickly behind Bellos and kicked him hard in the back of one knee. Bellos dropped immediately, fell to his knees.

Seven feet.

Swain dived in front of Bellos, scrambled for the counterweight cables.

Got to get out.

Have to get out.

Going to die.

He was almost at the cables when suddenly—violently—a big black hand clasped his ankle. Bellos had his foot in a vice-like grip, and was *dragging* him away from the cables!

Six feet.

Swain broke out in a cold sweat.

Bellos was holding him tightly, pulling him bacwards—so that now *Bellos* was closer to the counterweight cables.

There was nothing Swain could do! It was obvious Bellos was going to hold him until the last moment and then roll to safety near the cables, leaving Swain to be crushed underneath the elevator. There was no way out this time, no way to break Bellos' grasp. The elevator came slowly down.

It was then that Swain saw Bellos' trophy belt right

next to his eyes—saw Hawkins' chemical Mace canister hanging from it.

The Mace . . .

But it hadn't worked for Hawkins before . . .

Five feet.

And then Swain saw the white powder on Bellos' face. The white powder from the fluorescent light tube that Swain had smashed across his face.

It was oxidised fluorine.

And fluorine added to Mace would make . . .

Don't think! No time. Just do it!

Swain wrenched the Mace canister clear of Bellos' belt and aimed it at Bellos' face.

But Bellos saw him move and in response, the big man lashed out at the Mace canister with his fist and hit it a glancing blow, snapping its spray nozzle clean off!

No! Swain's mind screamed. *Now he couldn't spray it!*

And then he saw another option.

Gritting his teeth with determination, Swain slid in close to Bellos' head and then, in one fluid movement, holding the Mace canister tightly in his fist, he banged the base of the canister down on the *point* of one of Bellos' horns—puncturing the canister in an instant.

Blinding chemical Mace sprayed downwards—out from the puncture hole in the base of the canister. Swain then whipped the canister up so that the spray jetted directly into Bellos' powdered face.

The chemical reaction was instantaneous.

The active ingredients of chemical Mace—chloroacetophenone and diluted sulphuric acid—combined with the oxidised fluorine immediately to create hydrofluoric acid, one of the most corrosive acids known to man.

Bellos roared in agony as bubbles of burning acid rippled across his face. He squeezed his eyes shut *and released Swain's ankle instantly*.

Four feet.

Swain was free!

But he wasn't finished yet.

As Bellos recoiled, Swain rolled onto his back and let fly with an upwardly directed kick.

The kick hit its mark—slamming into the underside of Bellos' jaw, causing the big man's head to jolt sharply upward.

The big man's head snapped up—and his sharp horns penetrated the *floor* of the descending elevator—and in a moment of pure terror Bellos realised what had happened.

He was stuck!

His horns were jammed into the floor of the descending elevator, and he didn't have enough room beneath it to manoeuvre himself out!

Three feet.

Swain was flat on his stomach now, crawling away from Bellos, across the base of the shaft.

Two feet.

And he could feel the bottom of the elevator touching his back. It was like crawling underneath a car.

He reached out for one of the speeding counterweight cables running up the far wall. His hand closed around the cable.

Behind him, Bellos now lay on the ground, his neck bent upwards at an awkward angle, wrenching desperately at his horns. He let out a piercing high-pitched wail. '*Arrrrrrggghhhh!!!*'

One foot.

And Swain felt the cable yank on his arm and he

was pulled into the air, his feet sliding out from under the elevator just as it hit the bottom with a resounding *boom!* and Bellos' hideous wail cut off abruptly and Swain flew up into the darkness of the shaft.

Swain swung to a sudden halt.

The counterweight cable stopped dead as the elevator came to rest at the base of the shaft.

Everything was silent.

There was no light, save for the weak yellow haze coming through the crumpled outer doors that led to the Stack.

Swain was hanging by his arms six feet above the roof of the working elevator, dangling against the wall. He looked down at the elevators.

It was a peculiar sight—both elevators, side by side, resting on the bottom of the shaft, one totally destroyed, the other just sitting there, silent.

Suddenly the hatch of the working elevator burst open and Swain's heart jumped. Bellos couldn't have . . .

Holly's head appeared through the hatch and Swain sighed with relief. Her head swung around anxiously, searching. Finally she saw him, hanging above her, swinging gently from the counterweight cables on the side of the shaft.

'Daddy!' Holly climbed out onto the roof of the elevator.

Swain let go of the cable and dropped down onto the roof beside her. She leapt into his arms and held him tightly.

'Daddy, I was so scared.'

'So was I, honey. Believe me, so was I.'

'Did I do the right thing? Did I press the right button?'

'You pressed the right button, all right,' Swain said. 'You were great.'

Holly nodded to herself, satisfied, and hugged him harder.

Selexin's head popped out through the hatch. He saw Swain and Holly and then looked around the dark, empty shaft.

'It's okay,' Swain said. 'Bellos is dead.'

'I, uh, gathered as much,' Selexin said.

Swain frowned. Selexin nodded back at the elevator's hatch. Swain looked down through it.

'Oh, yuck . . .'

Sticking up through the floor of the elevator were two high-pointed horns—Bellos' horns. Having pierced the underside of the lift, they now appeared *inside* it— unmoving, still—like the hood ornament of a Cadillac. The only remnant of Bellos.

'What happened?' Selexin asked.

'Crushed,' Swain said.

'*Crushed?*'

'Uh-huh.'

Selexin winced. 'Not a very nice way to die.'

Holly said, 'He wasn't a very nice kind of person.'

'This is true.'

At that moment Swain's wristband beeped softly.

Swain checked it to find that its rectangular display was now filled with scrolling lines of type:

PRESENCE OF CONTAMINANT CONFIRMED AT STATION 4.
* PRESIDIAN HAS BEEN COMPROMISED *
REPEAT.
* PRESIDIAN HAS BEEN COMPROMISED *
DECISION TO ABORT PENDING.

The screen flickered and a new line appeared.

INITIALISED—1
OFFICIALS AT EXIT TELEPORT REPORT ONE
CONTESTANT REMAINING INSIDE LABYRINTH.
AWAITING INSTRUCTIONS.

There was a pause.

'What does that mean?' Swain asked.

'When only one contestant remains,' Selexin said, 'the Karanadon is awakened, if it is not already awake, and then—'

'And then the exit teleport is opened,' Swain said, remembering. 'And if you can avoid the Karanadon and get to the teleport, you win the Presidian.'

'Right,' Selexin said. 'Only now that Bellos has compromised the Presidian, the officials are deciding whether or not they should abandon the Presidian completely. Because if they do decide to abandon it, they will not open the exit teleport. And we will be left here, *with* the Karanadon. And as I wanted to tell you before, they will also probably . . .'

The wristband beeped loudly and Selexin immediately stopped speaking.

OFFICIALS AT EXIT TELEPORT BE ADVISED THAT
A DECISION HAS BEEN MADE TO ABORT PRESIDIAN.

* DO NOT INITIALISE EXIT TELEPORT *
REPEAT.
* DO NOT INITIALISE EXIT TELEPORT *

'They're calling it off,' Swain said flatly.

Selexin didn't reply. He just stared at the wristband in disbelief.

Swain shook him gently. 'Did you see that? They're calling the whole thing off.'

Selexin said softly, 'Yes. I saw it.' He looked up at Swain. 'And I know what it means. It means that you and I are most certainly going to die.'

'What?' Swain said.

'*Die?*' Holly said.

'*You* will certainly die,' Selexin said to Swain, 'and without the exit teleport, I cannot leave this planet. And what do you think my chances of survival on Earth are?'

Swain knew the answer to that. The NSA were outside the library right now and they weren't here to borrow some books. Selexin didn't have a prayer outside the library. And now there was no way he could leave.

Swain said, 'So why do I have to die? Why is that so certain? There's no guarantee that the Karanadon will find us.' Now there was an alien that Swain would gladly give to the NSA.

'It is not the Karanadon that comprises your greatest threat,' Selexin said.

'Then what does?' Swain asked as his wristband beeped again, announcing another message.

* OFFICIAL SIGNAL *
PLEASE RECORD THAT DUE TO EXTRINSIC

INTERFERENCE IT HAS BEEN DECIDED THAT THE
SEVENTH PRESIDIAN WILL BE ABORTED. GRATITUDE IS
EXTENDED TO ALL OFFICIALS IN ALL SYSTEMS FOR
THEIR ASSISTANCE THROUGHOUT THIS CONTEST. AN
INQUIRY HAS BEEN INITIATED INTO THE CAUSE OF THE
CONTAMINATION OF THE LABYRINTH.
* END OFFICIAL SIGNAL*
PRESIDIAN COMPLETE.
STANDBY FOR DE-ELECTRIFICATION.

Swain said, 'De-electrification? Is that what I think
it means?'

'Yes,' Selexin nodded. 'They will bring down the
electric field surrounding the labyrinth.'

'When?'

'As soon as possible, I suppose.'

'What about the Karanadon?'

'I presume that they will simply leave it here.'

'Leave it here?' Swain said, incredulous. 'Do you
have any idea what something like that would do in
this city? When they cut the electricity around this
building, that thing will be loose, and there will be no
way to stop it.'

'It is not my decision,' Selexin said sadly, vacantly.

Swain knew that the little man had other things on
his mind. Without the exit teleport, Selexin could not
leave. They had survived the Presidian and yet he was
stuck on Earth.

'Well,' Swain said, looking up at the dark elevator
shaft around him. 'It's not going to help us standing
around here doing nothing. If they're going to pull the
plug on the electricity, I suggest we find a place where
we can get out when they do.'

Holding Holly, Swain stepped from the roof of the

working lift onto the roof of the damaged one. Selexin didn't move. He just stood there sadly, deep in thought.

Swain and Holly climbed out through the crumpled outer doors into the Stack and looked back at Selexin.

'Selexin,' Swain said gently. 'We're not dead yet. Come on. Come with us.'

On top of the lift, in the darkness of the shaft, Selexin looked up at him, but said nothing.

'We have to get to an exit,' Swain said. 'So we can get out when the electricity is cut off.'

'Bellos.' Selexin said flatly, thinking.

'What?'

'Bellos knew of a way.'

'What are you talking about?' Swain said, checking the Stack behind him. 'Come on, we have to go.'

'He had to get the hoods out,' Selexin said. 'He said so himself.'

'Selexin, *what are you talking about?*'

Selexin explained. 'We were on another floor, I think it was number Two. Bellos was there, and he spoke to us briefly before the Rachnid arrived and they fought and we escaped. But at the time, I asked Bellos what he planned to do with the hoods if he won the Presidian, because I knew that if he left them here, they would certainly be discovered. What he told me was very strange. He said that the hoods would be long gone from the labyrinth by the time he went through the exit teleport.'

Swain watched Selexin intently, watched him thinking.

'But the only way he could do that,' Selexin said, almost to himself, 'was if he had a teleporter.'

'A teleporter?'

'A large chamber in which a teleportation field is created. And as you are no doubt aware, there are no teleporters on Earth.'

Swain thought for a moment, a hazy picture beginning to form in his mind. A picture of a puzzle that hadn't yet been solved.

'Just how big is one of these teleporters?' he asked Selexin.

'Usually very large, and very heavy,' Selexin said. 'And technologically, extremely complex.'

It was now Swain who was lost in thought. The hazy picture in his mind was slowly becoming clearer.

And then it hit him.

'Bellos brought a teleporter with him,' he said flatly.

'We don't know that,' Selexin said.

'Yes, we do,' Swain reached into his pocket, pulled out a sheet of paper—Harold Quaid's list of energy surges at the State Library that night.

'What's that, Daddy?'

'It's a list.'

'Where did you get it?'

Swain turned to Selexin. 'I found it in the pocket of another mystery guest who happened to find his way into your Presidian.'

'What is it a list of?' Selexin asked.

'Take a look.' Swain held out the sheet of paper.

Selexin stepped from one elevator roof to the other and then climbed out into the Stack. He took the sheet and examined it.

'Something from Earth,' Selexin scanned the list. 'Detecting energy surges of unknown origin. What are these numbers on the left?'

'Times,' Swain said.

Selexin was silent for a moment. 'So what is it?' he asked.

'It's a list of every teleportation that has happened in this building since I was teleported here from my home in Connecticut at 6:03 this evening.'

'What?'

'And now I've figured it out,' Swain said. 'Thirteen teleportations detected. Twelve in the library, one in Connecticut. Before, I could only account for eleven of the twelve surges that occurred in the library: namely, seven contestants with their guides, *plus* four hoods, equals eleven surges.'

'Uh-huh.'

'But I couldn't figure out the last surge,' Swain pointed to the bottom line of the sheet:

13. 18:46:00   N.Y.   Isolated energy surge/Source: **UNKNOWN**
                                             Type: **UNKNOWN** / Dur: **0.00:34**

'Look at it. It's thirty-four seconds long—three times longer than any other surge. And look at when it occurred: 6:46 p.m. That's nearly *twenty-three minutes* after the surge before it. All of the others occurred *within* twenty minutes.'

Swain looked at Selexin. 'The last surge was a separate surge. And it was big. Very big. Something that took a long time to teleport—thirty-four seconds to teleport.'

'What are you saying?'

'I think Bellos had someone *teleport* a *teleporter* into the library so he could get the hoods out of here before he left.'

Selexin took it all in silently. He examined the list again. Finally he looked up at Swain. 'Then that means . . .'

'It means,' Swain said to Selexin, 'that somewhere in this building is a teleporter. A teleporter that we can use to get you home.'

Selexin was momentarily silent as it all sunk in.

'So what are we waiting for?' Holly said.

'Nothing now,' Swain said, grabbing Selexin's shoulder, starting to run. 'Let's find it while we still have time.'

James Marshall stood at the base of the ramp leading to the parking lot. He was watching the grid of blue electricity stretched across the metal grille when his radio operator came up to him.

'Sir?'

'What is it?' Marshall didn't turn around.

Status Check: 0:01:00 to De-electrification.
Standby.

'Sir, we're not even getting a signal now. Commander Quaid's radio is completely off the air.'

Marshall bit his lip. The night that had begun with so much promise was not panning out well at all. They had already lost two men inside the library, destroyed one Radiation Storage Unit, lost track of a bum who had been seen by the southern wall of the library, and now had a building that was burning itself to the ground. And for what? Marshall thought.

Jack shit, that's what.

They had nothing to show for their night's work. Not a single fucking thing.

And Marshall would be responsible. Too much was

riding on this operation. Sigma Division had been given complete authority on this matter and they needed *something* to show for it.

Christ, not long before, the New York Fire Department had shown up in response to all the explosions and the NSA had held them back. The building was the source of a National Security Agency investigation, he'd said. Let it burn. But it's a National Register building. Let it burn. That wouldn't go down well with the bosses upstairs.

So now the situation was clear: if Marshall didn't get anything from this building, he would be the scapegoat. His career now depended on what they found inside that library.

They had to get *something*.

As it turned out, Swain, Holly and Selexin didn't have to run very far before they found the teleporter. In fact, they didn't even have to search beyond the Stack. But they almost missed it altogether. It was only Selexin's keen eye that had caught sight of a deviation in one of the long aisles of the Stack as they had been zigzagging their way toward the floor's central stairwell.

Status Check: 0:00:51 to De-electrification.

'It's so big,' Holly said in awe.

That was an understatement, Swain thought as he stood in the aisle and stared at the enormous machine.

It looked like a massive, high-tech, steel-sided telephone booth, with a glass door in its centre, and thick grey walls that almost reached to the ceiling. All of its edges had been rounded off to give it an elliptical shape and a big grey box sat on the floor beside it, connected to the teleporter by a thick black cord.

Surrounding the giant teleporter was a perfect sphere of emptiness that had been cut into the bookshelves and the ceiling around the big machine. The spherical hole in the air through which this machine had travelled had simply vaporised whatever had been standing here when it had arrived.

'That's a portable generator,' Selexin said, pointing to the grey box. 'Bellos had to bring one of those in order to operate the teleporter on Earth.'

Swain stared at the teleporter and at the bookshelves around it. They were right in the middle of the eastern section of the Stack, at least thirty yards from any entrance to the floor and surrounded by the towering floor-to-ceiling bookshelves. It was highly unlikely that anyone had been through here during the Presidian.

'Well hidden,' Swain observed.

'I do not think Bellos had much choice,' Selexin said.

'What do you mean?'

'Well, I have been thinking about this—about how Bellos teleported his hoods into the labyrinth. Do you remember that every time we saw him, Bellos always had his guide draped over his shoulder?'

'Yes.'

'Well, I kept wondering, *why did he need to immobilise his guide*? What I think happened was this,' Selexin said. 'On his home planet, Bellos steps inside the *official* teleporter with his guide. Once inside, the guide receives the co-ordinates of the labyrinth on the wristband, which he hasn't given to Bellos yet. Bellos then attacks the guide, beats him, steals the co-ordinates, and then reopens the teleporter and relays the co-ordinates to someone else.

'Then he and his guide are teleported to the labyrinth alone, while at the same time, at another tele-porter nearby, the hoods are sent.

'Much later, they teleport this teleporter, but they only have co-ordinates that are rather general. The teleporter could have arrived *anywhere* inside the library. It was impossible for them to teleport it inten-tionally into a dark corner. But then, when you're teleporting something into a *maze*, the odds are in your favour of teleporting it into a dark corner. A calculated risk, no doubt, but obviously one that Bellos was pre-pared to take.'

Status Check: 0:00:30 to De-electrification.

Next to Swain, Holly was staring up at the big grey machine. 'So what do we do now, Daddy?'

Swain frowned, looked back down the dark aisle behind him. In the distance he saw that some shelves were now on fire.

'We send Selexin home, honey,' he said. 'So he can tell the others what really happened, and so he can get away from here.'

'Oh,' Holly said, disappointed.

'That is right,' Selexin nodded slowly.

'Can't he stay, Daddy?' Holly said. 'He could live with us. Like in *E.T.*'

Selexin smiled sadly and reached up for the handle to the glass door of the teleporter. He said to Swain, 'When I came to the labyrinth, I thought about myself being assigned to guide the human contestant through the Presidian. And I was not happy at all. I thought you would not last a moment, and if you did not, I would not either. But having seen you, and the way you defended your life and the life of your daughter, I know now just how mistaken I was.'

Swain nodded.

Selexin turned to Holly. 'I cannot stay here. Your world is not ready for me, just as I am not ready for it. Why, even the Presidian was not ready for your world.'

'Thank you,' Holly said, crying. 'Thank you for taking care of me.'

Then she leapt forward and threw her arms around Selexin and hugged him tightly. Selexin was momentarily taken aback, unprepared for this sudden display of affection. Slowly, he raised his arms and hugged Holly back.

'Take care of yourself,' he said, closing his eyes. 'And look after your father, the same way he looks after you. Goodbye, Holly.'

She released him and Selexin turned to Swain and extended his hand.

'You are a little too tall for me to hug,' Selexin said, smiling.

Status Check: 0:00:15 to De-electrification.

Swain took the little man's hand and shook it. 'Thank you, again,' he said seriously.

Selexin bowed. 'I did nothing that you yourself would not have done for her. Or for me. I was only there in your absence. And besides, thank *you*, for making me change my mind about you.'

He reached for the door to the teleporter. It opened with a soft, pneumatic *hiss*.

Swain put an arm on Holly's shoulder. 'Goodbye, Selexin,' he said. 'You'll be a hard memory to forget.'

'That is just as well, Mr Swain. Considering you have forgotten just about everything else I have told you tonight.'

Swain smiled sadly as Selexin stepped inside the teleporter.

'Don't forget to teleport this thing back once you get there,' he said, pointing at the teleporter.

'Do not worry. I will not,' Selexin said, closing the glass door behind him.

Swain stepped away from the teleporter and looked down at his wristband.

STATUS CHECK: 0:00:04 TO DE-ELECTRIFICATION.

'Oh, damn . . .' Swain said, realising. 'Oh, *damn*!'

Inside the teleporter, Selexin punched some buttons on the wall and then stepped up to the glass door.

A brilliant white light glowed to life behind him and the little man pressed his finger up against the glass.

'Goodbye,' he mouthed silently.

The dazzling white light inside the teleporter consumed Selexin and then, abruptly, there was a bright, instantaneous flash, and the inside of the teleporter was dark again.

And Selexin was gone.

Holly was wiping tears from her eyes as Swain looked at the wristband again.

STATUS CHECK: 0:00:01 TO DE-ELECTRIFICATION.
STANDBY.
DE-ELECTRIFICATION INITIALISED—

Swain grabbed Holly by the hand and immediately began to run desperately down the narrow aisle, toward the central stairwell. Holly didn't know what was happening, just ran with him anyway.

A loud beeping filled the air.

Swain knew exactly what was going on now—it was what Selexin had been trying to tell him before. He didn't even need to look at his wristband to confirm it.

The damn thing was beeping insistently again and as he heard it ringing in his ears, he realised what aborting the Presidian really meant.

The electrified field was down.

His wristband was no longer surrounded by the field.

It had reset itself to self-destruct.

And nothing could stop it. There was no other electric field on Earth to surround it with.

Swain looked down at the wristband as he hit the stairs on the fly. It read:

PRESIDIAN ABORTED.
DETONATION SEQUENCE INITIALISED.
* 14:54 *
AND COUNTING.

Jesus.

SIXTH MOVEMENT

30 November, 10:47 p.m.

Outside the library, Marshall was barking orders.

'*Move! Move! Move!* Get in there!' he yelled, oblivious to the falling rain all around him.

Moments earlier, the grid of crackling blue electricity had vanished to nothing and Marshall had been faced with a gaping hole in the metal grille of the parking lot. Now he had Sigma's SWAT team racing past him, charging into the car park.

'Higgs!' he called.

'Yes, sir!'

'I want a total media blackout on this matter from now on. You go straight to Levine and you tell him to call the networks and pull some strings. Get those cameras out of here. And get me a No-Fly Zone over this whole area. I don't want any choppers within a five-mile radius of this building. Now go!'

Higgs ran off, up the ramp.

Marshall put his hands on his hips and smiled in the rain.

They were in.

Swain and Holly climbed the stairs two at a time, rounding the banisters, hauling themselves up, breathing hard.

They stopped at the Ground Floor. Swain peered out through the fire door.

The Ground Floor lay before him—wide and dark and bare.

Empty.

Swain could just make out the First Floor mezzanine above. It was still dark there, too. No fires here. Not yet.

There was no-one here.

Wristband.

14:23

14:22

14:21

There was a light over by the Information Desk. Swain stepped cautiously out among the bookshelves, heading toward it. Holly followed nervously.

When he was ten yards away from the Information Desk, he said to her, 'Stay here.'

Swain edged closer to the desk. He peered over the desktop and suddenly turned away, wincing.

'What is it?' Holly whispered.

'Nothing,' he said, then added quickly, 'Don't come over here.'

He glanced over the desktop again and saw the grisly sight again. It was the bloodied and mangled body of a policewoman.

Hawkins' partner.

She had *literally* been torn limb from limb—her arms were simply *gone*, each one ending at the bicep as a ragged bony stump. Her uniform was covered in blood. Swain could just make out the long jagged tear in her shirt where Bellos had ripped off her badge.

And then he saw her Glock pistol on the floor—lying inches away from her desperately outstretched hand.

Swain had a thought: *maybe he could shoot his wristband off.*

No, the bullet would pass through his wrist. *Not* a good idea.

He bent down and picked up the policewoman's gun anyway. Protection.

And then, completely without warning, there came a sudden, crashing *whump!* from somewhere behind him.

Holly screamed and Swain snapped around instantly and saw—

—the Karanadon, crouched on one knee, slowly rising to its full height.

Right behind Holly!

It must have been up on the First Floor! It must have leapt down!

Without even thinking, Swain levelled his newfound Glock at the beast and fired twice. Both shots missed by three yards. Hell, he'd never even fired a gun before.

Holly screamed through the gunfire, ran over to Swain.

Boom.

The Karanadon stepped forward.

Swain raised the pistol again. Fired. Missed. Two yards off this time. Getting closer.

Boom. Boom.

'Run!' Holly squealed. 'Run!'

'Not yet! I can hit it!' Swain called back, raising his voice above the beast's thunderous footsteps.

The Karanadon began to charge.

Boom. Boom. Boom.

'Okay, run!' he yelled.

Swain and Holly dashed for the bookshelves. The Karanadon was gaining. They rounded a corner and entered a narrow aisle, bookshelves on either side. Running hard, Swain looked over his shoulder.

And then, suddenly, his feet hit something—and he tripped—and went sprawling head-first to the ground. He hit the floor hard and the Glock went skittling off down the slick marble aisle.

Boom. Boom. Boom.

The floor all around him was shaking violently and Swain rolled onto his back to see what had tripped him.

It was a carcass. The ripped and torn carcass of the Konda—the grasshopper-like alien that the hoods had killed before, while Swain and the others had watched from the First Floor balcony.

Boom.

The floor rumbled a final time.

Silence. Save for the beeping of Swain's wristband.

Swain looked up and saw Holly standing on the other side of the carcass.

And behind her—right behind her—towering above the little girl, its massive frame silhouetting her body with total blackness, stood the dark shape of the Karanadon.

Holly didn't move a muscle.

The Karanadon was so close she could feel its hot breath on her neck.

'*Don't move,*' Swain whispered fiercely. 'Whatever you do, don't move.'

Holly didn't answer. She could feel her knees shaking. She knew that she wasn't going to move. Even if she'd wanted to, she couldn't. Beads of sweat began to appear on her forehead as she felt the Karanadon move slowly closer.

Its breath came in short, rapid spurts, as if it were breathing very, very quickly. As if it were—

Sniffing. It was sniffing her. *Smelling* her.

Slowly, the big beast's snout moved up her body.

Holly was terrified. She wanted to scream. She clenched her fists by her side and shut her eyes.

Suddenly, she felt a cold wetness touch her left ear. It was the Karanadon's nose, the tip of its dark, wrinkled snout. The nose was cold and wet, like a dog's.

She almost fainted.

Swain watched in horror as the Karanadon brushed the left side of his daughter's head.

It was taking its time. Moving slowly. Methodically. Intensifying their fear.

It had them.

Swain could hear the constant beeping of his wristband. How long to go? He didn't dare look—didn't dare take his eyes off the Karanadon. *Shit.*

He shifted his weight—and, oddly, felt a bulge in his pocket. It was the broken phone receiver. That wouldn't be much use here. Wait a second . . .

There was something else in his pocket . . .

The lighter.

Slowly, Swain reached into his pocket and pulled out Jim Wilson's Zippo lighter.

The Karanadon was sniffing Holly's ankles.

Holly just stood stock still, her eyes shut, her fists clenched.

Swain rolled the lighter over in his hand. If he could light something with it, the flames might momentarily distract the Karanadon.

But then, he recalled, the lighter hadn't worked in the stairwell before.

It had to work now.

Swain held the lighter up to the nearest bookshelf, up close to a dusty old hardcover.

Please work. Just once. Please work.

The Zippo flipped open with a loud metallic *calink!*

The Karanadon's head snapped up immediately and suddenly the beast was staring accusingly at Swain as if to say: 'And what do you think you're doing?'

Swain held the lighter closer to the dusty book but the Karanadon bounded quickly forward and in an instant Swain found himself slammed against the floor, face-down, the weight of an enormous black foot pressed hard against his back.

Holly screamed.

Swain was pushed down against the floor, his hands spread out in front of him, his face tilted sideways, one cheek flat against the cold marble floor. He struggled in vain against the weight of the Karanadon.

The beast roared loudly and Swain looked up to see that he was still holding the lighter in his left hand. On his left wrist, he saw his wristband, beeping insistently. In a distant corner of his mind, he wondered how long they had before it exploded.

The Karanadon saw the lighter.

And Swain watched in horror as an enormous black claw slowly descended upon—and clasped around—his entire left forearm. It gripped his arm tightly. Squeezing it. Cutting off the bloodflow. Swain saw his veins pop up everywhere. His arm was about to snap in two—

And then the big creature banged his wrist hard against the floor.

Hard against the floor.

Swain roared in agony as his wrist hit the marble floor. There was a loud clunking sound, followed by a sharp burning pain that shot right through his forearm.

With the impact, his hand holding the lighter reflexively opened wide and the Zippo dropped to the floor.

Swain never noticed it.

And he had instantly forgotten about the burning pain in his forearm.

Now he was staring. Staring at his left wrist in total disbelief.

The wristband had hit the floor, too.

And the force of the impact had unclasped it. Now it just rested loosely around Swain's wrist, still beeping incessantly.

Only now it was unclasped.

Now it was off.

Swain saw the countdown.

12:20

12:19

12:18

And then suddenly he felt a claw clutch the back of his head and push it roughly against the floor. The weight on his back increased.

Time for the kill.

Swain saw the Zippo. On the floor. Within reach.

The Karanadon lowered its head.

Swain quickly grabbed the lighter and held it to the

lowest shelf of the bookcase and then he shut his eyes and prayed to God that once, just once, Jim Wilson's stupid frigging lighter would work.

He flicked the cartwheel.

The lighter ignited for half a second, and that was all Swain needed.

A dust-covered book next to the Zippo burst instantly into flames, right in front of the Karanadon.

The big beast roared as the fire flared in front of its head, the bristled fur on its forehead catching alight. It pulled back instantly, releasing Swain, clutching desperately at its flaming brow.

Swain rolled immediately and in one swift movement, removed the wristband from his wrist, reached for the Karanadon's foot and clasped the band around one of the beast's enormous toe-claws.

The wristband clicked into place around the toe.

Clasped.

And then Swain was up. On his feet, running. He scooped up Holly, grabbed the Glock from the floor nearby and raced for the massive glass doors of the library's entrance. Behind him he could hear the wails and roars of the Karanadon.

He came to the doors, threw them open.

And saw about a dozen cars with revolving lights on their roofs parked out front. And men with rifles. Running toward him through the rain.

The National Security Agency.

'It's the police, Daddy. They're here to save us!'

Swain grabbed her hand and pulled her away from the doors, toward the stairwell.

'I don't think those policemen are here to help us, honey,' Swain said as they ran. 'Remember what happened to Eliot's house in *E.T.*? Remember how the bad guys put a big plastic bag around it?'

They were running hard. Almost at the stairwell now.

'Yeah.'

Swain said, 'Well, the people who did that are the same people who are outside the library now.'

'Oh.'

They came to the stairwell and started down the stairs.

Swain stopped.

He could hear voices . . . and shouts . . . and heavy footfalls coming from downstairs.

The NSA were already inside.

They must have come in through the parking lot.

'Quickly. Upstairs. Now.' Swain pulled Holly back up the stairwell.

They climbed the stairs.

And as they ran past the fire door leading to the Ground Floor, they heard the loud smashing sound of breaking glass, followed by more voices and shouts.

Swain shut the door behind him.

They were inside the photocopying room on the First Floor.

'Quickly,' he said to Holly, guiding her toward the Internet room, 'through there.'

They entered the Internet Facility of the New York State Library and Swain walked directly over to one of the windows on the far side.

It opened easily and he leaned out.

They were on the western side of the building. Beneath him, Swain could see the grassy park that surrounded the library. It was a fifteen-foot drop from the window to the grass down below.

He spun around and looked up at the wires hanging down from the ceiling.

'Daddy,' Holly said, 'what're we doing?'

'We're getting out,' Swain said, reaching up for the ceiling, yanking on some of the thick black wires.

'How?'

'Through the window.'

'Through *that* window?'

'Yep,' Swain yanked some more wires out from

various other outlets. He began to tie them together, end to end.

'Oh,' Holly said.

Swain walked over to the open window again and with the butt of his gun, broke the glass. Then he tied the end of the length of wire around the window's now-exposed horizontal pane and knotted it tight.

He looked back to Holly.

'Come on,' he said, jamming the gun back into his waistband.

Holly stepped forward tentatively.

'Jump on my back and hold tight. I'll climb us both down to the ground.'

Just then, they heard shouts from inside the First Floor. Swain listened for a second. They sounded like directions, orders. Someone telling someone else what to do. The NSA were still searching. He wondered what had happened to the Karanadon. They mustn't have found it yet.

'Okay, let's go,' he said, helping Holly onto his back, piggyback style. She gripped him firmly.

Then he threw the length of wire out the window and began to climb out onto the ledge.

'*Sir!*' a static-ridden voice said.

James Marshall picked up his radio. He was now standing outside the main entrance to the library. The majestic glass doors in front of him were now shattered and broken, totally destroyed by the NSA's bold entry only minutes earlier.

It was the radio operator in the van.

'What is it?' Marshall said.

'*Sir, we have visual confirmation, I repeat, visual*

confirmation, of contact on two floors. One in the lower parking structure and one on the Ground Floor.'

'Excellent,' Marshall said. 'Just tell everyone not to touch *anything* until I say so. Sterilisation procedures are in force. Anyone who comes within twenty feet of one of those organisms will be presumed to be contaminated and quarantined indefinitely.'

'Roger that, sir.'

'Keep me informed.'

Marshall switched the radio off.

He rubbed his hands together and looked up at the burning library above him. It was the building that would skyrocket his career.

'Excellent,' he said again.

Swain dropped to the grass and set Holly down beside him.

They were out.

At last.

It was raining more heavily now. Swain looked for an escape. They were near the south-west corner of the building. He remembered coming out of the subway before. Over on the *eastern* side of the library.

The subway.

Nobody would care if they saw him on the subway—his clothes ragged and torn, Holly's not much better. They would just be another bum and a kid living on the subway.

It was the way out, the way home.

If they could get past the NSA.

Swain pulled Holly eastward into the shelter of the southern wall of the library building, the rain pelting down around them. They passed the broken window at ground level that he had used to get inside before. Using the cover of the rain and the shadows of the oak trees in the night, Swain hoped they could get past the NSA undetected.

They came to the south-east corner.

Beyond the row of oaks, Swain could see the great white rotunda. And beyond the rotunda, the subway station.

Yellow police tape still stretched from tree to tree around the library, forming a wide perimeter. Swain saw a few NSA agents armed with M-16s stationed on that perimeter, their backs to the building, keeping the small crowd of helpless firefighters, local cops and late-night onlookers at bay. There weren't many NSA agents, just enough to secure the area. Swain guessed that most of the others were now inside the building itself.

'All right,' he said to Holly. 'You ready? It's time to go home.'

'Okay,' Holly said.

'Get ready to run.'

Swain waited for a second, peering around the corner of the building.

'All right, *now!*'

They dashed out from the building, across the open ground and into the treeline. They stopped beneath a big oak, catching their breath.

'Are we there yet?' Holly asked, breathless.

'Almost,' Swain said. He pointed to the rotunda. 'That's where we go next. Then on to the subway. You want me to carry you?'

'No, I'm okay.'

'Good. Ready?'

'Yes.'

'Then let's go.'

They ran again. Out from the treeline. Out into the open.

Boom.

Marshall felt the ground beneath him shudder.

He was still standing at the main entrance to the library. He looked inside, through the broken glass doors, to see what was causing the vibration.

Nothing. Darkness.

Boom.

Marshall frowned.

Boom. Boom. Boom.

Something was coming. Something big.

And then he saw it.

Motherfucker . . .

Marshall didn't wait for another look. He just turned and ran—down the steps, away from the entrance—a bare two seconds before the library's enormous doors were blasted from their hinges like a pair of matchsticks.

Swain and Holly were halfway to the rotunda when it happened.

A booming, thunderous roar echoed across the park behind them.

Swain stopped and spun. The pouring rain pelted down against his face. 'Oh no,' he said. 'Not again.'

The Karanadon was standing at the top of the steps of the main entrance. The huge glass doors of the library, now totally destroyed, lay in pieces in front of the enormous black beast. NSA agents were running in all directions to get away from it.

The Karanadon paid no attention to the people flee-ing from it. In fact, it didn't even acknowledge their presence at all. It just stopped at the top of the steps and stood there, its head turning in a slow, wide arc.

Scanning the area.

Searching.

Searching for them.

And then it saw them. Exposed between the tree-line and the big white rotunda, standing there in the pouring rain.

The huge beast roared loudly.

And then it leapt forward and with frightening speed, covered the distance between the library and the treeline in seconds. It bounded quickly forward, charging through the sleeting rain, its every step shak-ing the muddy earth beneath it.

Boom. Boom. Boom.

Swain and Holly ran for the rotunda. They reached it and climbed the steps, up onto the circular concrete stage.

The Karanadon hit the treeline and crashed through the branches of one of the giant oaks, charging toward the rotunda.

Then it stopped. Ten yards away. And watched them for several seconds.

They were trapped on the stage.

Marshall had his radio out.

'I'll give *you* fucking confirmation! The damn thing just charged out the front fucking doors! Get someone over here right now!'

The radio crackled back.

'I don't give a flying fuck what you're looking at!

Get someone over here *now* and tell them to bring the biggest gun we've got!'

Swain led Holly over to the far side of the stage. He picked her up as the Karanadon moved slowly closer. The rain drummed loudly on the roof of the rotunda.

'Stay down,' Swain said, as he lowered Holly over the railing at the edge of the stage. She dropped lightly to the ground, six feet below.

The Karanadon reached the base of the rotunda. The pouring rain had wet its fur, slicking it down like a dog's. A running trickle of rainwater ran down a crease in its long black snout, dripped ominously off one of its huge canine teeth.

The big beast took a slow step up the stairs.

Swain moved in an arc around the circumference of the stage, away from Holly.

The Karanadon stepped up onto the stage.

It stared at Swain.

There was an endless, tense silence.

Swain drew his Glock.

The Karanadon growled in response. A low, angry growl.

Neither of them moved.

And then suddenly Swain made a break for the railing and the Karanadon bounded forward after him.

Swain reached the railing and had just started to vault over it when a giant black claw snatched his collar and snapped him backwards, and he landed in the centre of the concrete stage with a loud smack.

The Karanadon stood astride Stephen Swain and lowered its snout until it was face-to-face with him. It had his gun hand pinned to the stage beneath one of its massive hairy claws.

Swain tried in vain to turn away from its hideous fangs, its foul hot breath, its dark wrinkled snout, set in a perpetual sneer.

The Karanadon cocked its head slightly, seemingly daring him to escape.

It was then that Swain turned his head and saw the beast's hind foot step forward.

A wave of terror flooded through his body as he saw the wristband that he had worn for the duration of the Presidian *right in front of his eyes.*

'Oh, *man . . .*' he said aloud.

The countdown was still ticking downward.

1:01

1:00

0:59

Only one minute to detonation.

Holy shit.

He began to wriggle and squirm, but the Karanadon held him down. It seemed totally unaware of the bomb attached to its foot.

Swain looked around the rotunda for an escape— at the white lattice handrail that circled the stage, at the six pillars supporting the dome-like roof. There was a small wooden box attached to the handrail, but its door was padlocked shut. In a detached corner of his mind, Swain wondered what the box was for.

There was nothing here. Absolutely nothing he could use.

He had finally run out of options.

Then suddenly, there came a voice.

'*Hello . . . ?*'

The Karanadon's head snapped up instantly, turned around.

Swain could still see the numbers counting down on the wristband inches away from his face.

0:48

0:47

0:46

'Hello? Yes. Over here.'

Swain recognised the voice.

It was Holly.

He looked up. She was standing over near the edge of the stage, the rain slanting down behind her like a curtain. The Karanadon swivelled to look at her—

—and abruptly something small smacked against the Karanadon's snout. It dropped to the ground next to Swain's head. It was a black school shoe. A girl's school shoe. Holly had thrown it at the Karanadon!

The big beast growled. A deep-chested rumble of pure, animal anger.

0:37

0:36

0:35

Then it slowly lifted its foot, moving toward Holly.

'Holly!' Swain yelled. 'Get out of here! It still has the wristband on and it'll blow in thirty seconds!'

Holly was momentarily startled. Then, in an instant, she understood and she began to run, leaping down the steps, vanishing from Swain's sight out into the park.

The Karanadon took one step forward in pursuit of her and then it stopped dead in its tracks.

And turned around.

0:30

0:29

0:28

It still hadn't released Swain's gun hand—still had it pinned down against the stage.

Swain struggled vainly against the giant creature's grip, but it was useless. The Karanadon was just too damn strong.

0:23

0:22

0:21

And then, just then, as he squirmed, something on the stage scraped against Swain's back.

Swain frowned—and saw that he had brushed up against a part of the stage that wasn't perfectly flush against the floor.

A small square of wood, sunken fractionally into the stage.

It was a trapdoor.

The same trapdoor that he had seen used in the summer pantomimes over previous years.

He was lying on top of it.

And then, realising, Swain's head snapped around—and his eyes fell on the small padlocked wooden box that he had seen attached to the lattice handrail before.

Now he knew what that box was for.

It housed the controls for the trapdoor.

0:18

0:17

The Karanadon stood over him, growling.

0:16

0:15

Even though his gun hand was still being held down by the beast, Swain's pistol was aimed roughly at the trapdoor's control box.

0:14

0:13

Swain fired. Hit the top corner of the box. The Karanadon roared.

0:12

0:11

He adjusted his aim. Fired again. This time the bullet hit the box closer to the padlock.

0:10

Third time's the charm . . . he thought, narrowing his eyes.

Blam!

Swain fired and . . . *shwack!* . . . the padlock snapped open, smashed by the bullet!

0:09

The control box's door swung open, revealing a large red lever inside. Simple operation: you pulled the lever down and the trapdoor on the stage dropped open.

0:08

Swain fired again, this time at the lever. Missed. He stole a glance up at the Karanadon—just in time to see one of its mighty black fists come rushing down at his face! Swain swung his head to the side, just as the gigantic black-clawed fist smashed into the stage *right next to his ear*, punching a hole clean through the trapdoor. The Karanadon raised its free claw again, for what would no doubt be the final blow.

0:07

Swain saw the big claw rise. He loosed several shots at the lever in rapid succession.

Blam! Blam! Blam! Blam!

Miss. Miss. Miss. Miss.

0:06

The Karanadon's claw reached the height of its backswing. Its knuckles cracked loudly as it tightened into a fist.

'Goddamn it!' Swain shouted at himself. '*Focus!*'

The Karanadon's fist came rushing down—

Swain looked down the barrel of his gun—

—and suddenly the lever came into crystal-clear focus. 'Gotcha,' he said.

Blam.

The gun discharged and the bullet whistled through the air and this time . . .

. . . *crack!* . . .

. . . it *slammed* into the lever, severing it at its hinge in an explosion of sparks, causing the whole lever mechanism to snap and fall and—

0:05

Whack!

Without warning, the trapdoor beneath Swain dropped away.

0:04

The Karanadon's fist hit nothing but air as it came rushing down, missing Swain's nose by centimetres as he dropped unexpectedly from beneath the massive beast, falling like a stone into the belly of the stage.

Swain landed with a dusty *thump* in darkness.

0:03

He saw the Karanadon on the stage above him, standing in a square of light, glaring down at him through the hole that only moments before had been the trapdoor.

Move!

He looked right and saw a vertical sliver of light in the darkness—a sliver of light that indicated the small wooden door that led out from underneath the stage.

0:02

Swain scrambled toward the little wooden door, firing his gun as he did so, pockmarking the door with holes, hoping to God he would hit the padlock on the other side.

0:01

And then he rammed into the door with his shoulder and it burst open before him and he flailed out into the pouring rain and landed clumsily on the wet grass that surrounded the stage.

0:00.

Cataclysm.

The explosion from the wristband—white-hot and blinding—blasted out horizontally, like a thousand-mile-an-hour ripple in a pond.

Swain scrambled on his hands and knees and pressed himself up against the concrete base of the stage as the white-hot wall of light expanded laterally—and spectacularly—above his head. He saw Holly on the ground over by the trees, her hands covering her ears.

The Karanadon simply disappeared as the brilliant white explosion shot outward from it, shattering all six of the pillars supporting the domed roof of the rotunda—reducing them to powder in an instant—and the massive white dome, without its supports, came crashing down onto the stage.

Behind Swain's back, the thick concrete base of the stage cracked under the weight of the explosion, but held.

White concrete dust and about a billion flakes of paint fluttered in the air before the pouring rain broken them up, dispersing them.

Swain stood up slowly and stared at the rotunda, its huge domed roof now crumpled flat on its stage, the rain beating mercilessly down upon it.

There would be nothing left of the Karanadon, the explosion had been too big, too hot. The Karanadon was gone.

Swain hurried over to Holly and picked her up.

He saw NSA agents running toward them through the rain, and was about to break for it, when it happened.

Suddenly.

Unexpectedly.

Concurrent explosions—six of them—white-hot balls of light, bursting spectacularly from different sections of the library.

The biggest explosion came from the Third Floor. It seemed to be a combination of two separate explosions, twice the size of the other white fireballs that boomed out from the Ground and Second Floors of the library.

Glass blasted outwards from nearly every window of the New York State Library. People all around the building were diving for cover when suddenly an *underground* explosion—strangely, right where the underground parking lot was situated—dispatched a large oak tree clear from its roots, sending a gout of soil and grass flying into the rainsoaked sky.

Shrouded by a veil of slanting rain, the whole library was ablaze with fire now. Flames poured out from every window and as Stephen Swain led his daughter inconspicuously away from the pandemonium, he saw the Third Floor cave in on itself and crumble downwards, crushing the Second and First Floors.

The building's roof was still intact when the sixth and last explosion rocked the library and the strangest sight of all appeared.

An empty elevator—rocketing upward through the shaft—burst through the roof of the building and shot up into the sky, reaching the height of its parabolic arc and then falling, flying, crashing, back down onto the roof.

It was then that the roof itself caved in and the New York State Library—amid the sound of girders creaking and explosions multiplying and fires burning—collapsed in a blaze of glory and, despite the pouring rain, began to burn itself into oblivion.

James Marshall stared in dumbstruck awe at the fiery demise of the building that had promised him so much.

There had been nearly thirty agents inside that building when the explosions had gone off. None could have survived.

Marshall just stood there, watching the building burn. They would get nothing from this building. Just as they would get nothing from the rotunda. Marshall himself had seen the big black creature crash through the main entrance. And he had seen it explode.

A white-hot—micro-nuclear?—explosion like that would not leave much behind. Christ, it wouldn't leave *anything* behind.

Marshall put his hands in his pockets and walked back to his car. Phone calls had to be made. Explanations had to be given.

This night had been the closest they had ever come to contact. Perhaps the closest they would ever come.

And now? Now what did they have?

Nothing.

Stephen Swain sat on the subway train with his daughter asleep in his lap.

At every jolt of the train, they would tilt and sway with the other four passengers in their carriage. It was late and the near-empty train would get them to the outskirts of New York City. From there they would catch a cab—an expensive cab—back to Connecticut.

Back home.

Holly slept peacefully in Swain's lap, occasionally rolling over to make herself more comfortable.

Swain smiled sadly.

He had forgotten about the wristbands that all the contestants in the Presidian had to wear. When the electrified walls had disappeared, their wristbands—like his—must have also been set to detonate. So when the Karanadon had exploded with Swain's wristband, the other wristbands had gone off, too, *wherever* they happened to be—Reese's in the underground parking lot, Balthazar's on the Third Floor, and even Bellos', at the bottom of the elevator shaft.

Swain looked at his clothes—greasy, black, and in some places, bloody. Nobody on the train seemed to care.

He laughed softly to himself. Then he closed his eyes and leaned back into his seat as the train rumbled off through the tunnel toward home.

EPILOGUE

New York City
1 December, 4:52 a.m.

Workers on the New York Subway called it the Mole, an ordinary electric engine from a subway train that had been converted into a street-sweeper on rails.

Late at night, when subway services were at a minimum, the Mole would amble through the tunnels, its rotating forward sweepers scooping up any debris that might have fallen onto the tracks during the previous day. At the end of its run, all that debris would be tipped from the Mole into a furnace and destroyed.

Later that night, the Mole made its usual trip through the subway tunnel adjoining the State Library. And as it passed the Con Edison Booster Valve, the driver began to doze.

He never noticed the open doorway, never noticed the crumpled interior—packed solid with collapsed bricks and fragmented concrete.

And he never noticed the soft *clink-clink* of metal on metal that rattled underneath the Mole as it went past the Booster Valve.

The Mole ambled off down the tunnel, and all that remained in its wake was a pair of handcuffs, clasped to the track.

AN INTERVIEW WITH MATTHEW REILLY

THE WRITING OF *CONTEST*

What inspired you to write Contest?

There were two key inspirations for me to actually sit down and write *Contest*. First, the works of Michael Crichton. I still believe that Dr Crichton is the best storyteller in the world today. Not only are his stories original, they are also told at a cracking pace. Back in 1993, the year after I finished high school, my brother, Stephen, gave me a book and said, 'I'm told Steven Spielberg is going to make this into a movie, it's about a theme park built around genetically engineered dinosaurs.' More than any other book I have read, *Jurassic Park* made me want to tell big action stories (especially stories with big scary 'animal' elements).

In terms of the *story*, the inspiration to write *Contest* came from my love of sports. I think there is drama in any kind of competition. All I did to turn that into a story was to make my contest the *ultimate* contest—if you win, you live; if you lose, you die.

Contest *originally appeared in late 1996 in self-published form. What are the differences—if any—between the self-published version and this one?*

In terms of the overall story, there are no differences. Structurally, it is exactly the same now as it was back in 1996. The differences come in the finer detail—in the *way* Swain does battle with the other contestants. The biggest alterations I made were in the 'final confrontation' scenes involving Swain and the three big villains of the book: Bellos, Reese and the Karanadon. In the original version of the book, these scenes were not as complex. Now they are bigger, badder and meaner.

The other big change was the addition of the Konda and the Rachnid. In the 1996 version, these two contestants weren't named or described. The reason for this was simple: when I originally wrote the book, I dreamed up six different alien species (Reese, Bellos, the Codex, Balthazar, the hoods and the Karanadon) and I just couldn't think up any more! But after a few years of thinking about *Contest*, I came up with these two extra species. So I put them in.

Apart from those, there are a lot of small changes, ranging from tightening the narrative in places to telling the reader how Swain's wife died, a piece of backstory that didn't appear in the self-published edition.

You mentioned that there are 'big scary animal elements' in your novels. Tell us about the various creatures in your books. Why are they there and why do you choose the ones you do?

I wish I could think of some loftier purpose, but the true reason for the big scary animal elements is very simple: they're there to eat people. I think there is nothing better in a book or movie than to see someone running from a big scary creature (think *Jurassic Park*, *Jaws*, or *Aliens*).

As for *why* I choose the creatures I choose, well, in *Ice Station*, for instance, I selected killer whales and elephant seals because I wanted the water to be a dangerous place—kind of like *Jaws*. The elephant seals were also the guardians, so to speak, of the underground cavern—making it a challenge to get there. In *Temple* I went one step further, and tried to make land *and* water dangerous places to be. There I used rapas (big, black, five-foot-tall cats which are the subject of myths in South America) and caimans (large crocodilians). I chose those animals because I wanted *Temple* to be darker and scarier then *Ice Station*.

As for *Contest*, well, as any Hollywood screenwriter will tell you, the best creatures of all are the ones you make up. For when you create an alien species, *there are absolutely no limits*. They can bleed acid (*Alien*), they can see via infra-red (*Predator*), or they can just be bigger, meaner and nastier than the biggest, meanest and nastiest Earth-based creatures.

Do you have the ending in your head when you start writing a new novel?

Ah, yes! This is Frequently Asked Question No. 1. Whenever I meet people and they discover I am an author, they always ask this question! The answer is: yes . . . usually.

The reason I say 'yes . . . *usually*' is because I feel that some flexibility is always required.

For example, the last line of *Temple* (which I won't give

away, for those who haven't read it) was something that occurred to me halfway through writing the book. I love that line, and it's a great reason to remain flexible.

As for *Contest*, one question that nagged me all the way through the writing process was: *how the hell am I going to kill the Karanadon?* The answer—using Swain's wristband—came to completely out of the blue. It just hit me. I started dancing around the house, pumping my fists in the air. It was so neat, so tidy, it saved Swain and yet it left no trace of the Karanadon. But neat as it appears in the book, it was not something I knew from the very start. Again, flexibility.

Pace and speed are key ingredients in all your novels. What drives you to make your books move so quickly?

For me, reading is all about being transported, being taken away from the real world. *Escaping.* Some people write to educate, inform, or explore character motivation in considerable depth. I write to entertain. Fast storytelling is part of that—if I can get readers to read fast, to literally *forget* that they are reading, then I think I have done my job.

A great inspiration for me in this department was Thomas Harris and his brilliant novel *The Silence of the Lambs.* That book was only 294 pages long (in hardback) and it packed a hell of a lot into those 294 pages.

One of the things I learned very quickly about writing books is this: *you do not have to waste words.* I know what it's like to start writing a book. You say to yourself,

'Gosh, this is a long piece of work, I'd better fatten it out a little.' Wrong. To my mind, readers quite simply don't have time for an author who wastes words. Now I know what you're thinking: how does a young guy like me, all of twenty-six, know this with such certainty? Simple: I am a reader. In fact, I am the most critical reader in the universe. If I find a book that I'm reading is getting too slow or wordy or ponderous, then I hurl it down and grab another. Life is too short. And besides, if not wasting words is good enough for a master like Thomas Harris (or for Michael Crichton, another great example), then I figure it's good enough for me.

Believe me, when I write my books, I re-read them over and over, with a red pen in my hand. Any wasted words get struck out fast.

So how has life changed for you in the past year? What are some of the strangest things you have experienced since the success of your books worldwide?

I once did a signing in the departure lounge at Singapore Airport between 10 and 11 p.m. During that signing, a very distinguished-looking fellow strode directly up to me, stood in front of my table—which, of course, was covered with piles of books and large posters of my smiling author photograph—and said, 'Excuse me, but can you tell me where I can buy stamps?' Ah, fame.

I appeared on *The Big Breakfast* television show in England, live, in front of 5 million people (no pressure). And I recently played in a celebrity cricket match with the members of INXS and, among others, the rugby player, Matthew Burke (who told me that many of the Wallabies have read my books—go, you Aussies!).

But the strangest thing: of late, I am getting more and more emails from *students*—both high-school and university—regarding assignments that they are doing on authors and writing. One high-school English student was doing a book report on *Ice Station* and he had to discuss what, at its core, the book was about, so he emailed me through my website and asked. I wrote back and told him (as any reviewer will tell you, the literary complexities of *Ice Station* necessitate quite a detailed analysis!). Another school student had to do a speech in his class about an author he admired, so he did it on me. (Digression: it is really strange to think that somewhere out there, without your knowledge, someone is speaking about you in their class).

So how does Matthew Reilly figure in the so-called 'literary' world?

Believe it or not, I was once asked, 'So, Matthew. What literary purpose do your books actually serve?' An interesting question (if a bit uppity). The answer, though, has only become apparent to me recently.

While I find that my books are read by both men and women (of all ages), I have discovered that the books, while maintaining this core market, are filtering into schools and the teenage ranks, in particular, teenage *boys* (a notoriously reading-resistant group). So, what literary purpose do my books serve? How about this: my books get people reading. Especially young people. I visit a lot of schools and you'd be amazed at how many students say they find reading to be a chore. My books may not win any awards, but if they get people reading, then they have a big literary function.

First and foremost, reading should be fun. Sure, some books will win awards. Mine probably won't. But I don't write them for award judges or book critics. I write them for people like me, people who just like a good yarn to take them away from the real world for a few days.

So what does the immediate future hold for Matthew Reilly?

My books have been sold to publishers in over a dozen countries now, in nine different languages, so I will continue to tour (in the last six months, I have been to South Africa, New Zealand, England, Singapore and Malaysia promoting the release of my books in those countries).

As far as writing goes, I have just finished the sequel to *Ice Station*, called *Area 7*. It'll be out later this year. It was an absolute blast to write! Not only was it very enjoyable to go on another adventure with some characters that I love (Schofield, Gant and Mother all return in the new book), but it was also fun to go totally ballistic trying to top *Ice Station*. My goals when writing *Area 7* were, first, to make it bigger, meaner and faster than *Ice Station*, and second, to make the reader absolutely *exhausted* by the end. I think I have succeeded, but ultimately only readers can decide that.

I have also written several original screenplays which are attracting attention—one is about terrorism at the Sydney Olympic Games (for which I have done some shooting myself), another is a supercharged action western (no genre ever dies, they just need to be re-energised from time to time). And since George Lucas hasn't asked me to write *Episode III* (yet), I've decided to create my own swashbuckling science fiction saga. As you do.

And, of course, there's another book in the pipeline but it's too early to talk about that!

Any final words?

As always, I just hope you all enjoyed the book, and I hope to see you next time.

MR
Sydney
March 2001

www.matthewreilly.com

Matthew Reilly
Ice Station

At a remote ice station in Antarctica, a team of US
scientists has made an amazing discovery. They have
found something buried deep within a 100-million-
year-old layer of ice. Something made of METAL.

Led by the enigmatic Lieutenant Shane Schofield, a
team of crack United States Marines is sent to the
station to secure this discovery for their country. They
are a tight unit, tough and fearless. They would follow
their leader into hell. They just did . . .

'The pace is frantic, the writing snappy, the research
thorough. Unputdownable . . .'
WEEKEND AUSTRALIAN

'It never slows down . . . it is unlike any other new
Australian novel'
DAILY TELEGRAPH

'There is enough technological wizardry, military know-
how, plot convolution and sheer non-stop mayhem to
place it in the premier league of international bestsellers'
THE WEST AUSTRALIAN

'His publisher compares him to Grisham and Crichton,
but I reckon the 23-year-old is a cut above'
RALPH

'This is Indiana Jones goes to Antarctica . . . backed
by good research about weaponry, science and
international jealousies'
NW

Matthew Reilly
Temple

Deep in the jungles of Peru, the hunt for a legendary
Incan idol is underway – an idol that in the present
day could be used as the basis for a terrifying new
weapon.

Guiding a US Army team is Professor William Race, a
young linguist who must translate an ancient
manuscript which contains the location of the idol.

What they find is an ominous stone temple, sealed
tight. They open it – and soon discover that some
doors are meant to remain unopened . . .

'There is no denying it. Matthew Reilly has really arrived'
DAILY TELEGRAPH

'Like *Ice Station*, *Temple* is well researched and
technically adept. Diehard action buffs will enjoy'
WHO WEEKLY

'Probably the most breathless read in the history of
airport fiction'
AUSTRALIAN BOOKSELLER & PUBLISHER

Cecilia Dart-Thornton
The Ill-Made Mute

The Stormriders land their splendid winged stallions on
the airy battlements of Isse Tower. Far below, the
superstitious servants who dwell in the fortress's
depths tell ghastly tales of evil creatures inhabiting the
world outside, a world they have only glimpsed. Yet it is
the least of the lowly – a mute, scarred, and utterly
despised foundling – who dares to scale the Tower,
sneak aboard a Windship, and then dive from the sky.

The fugitive is rescued by a kindhearted adventurer
who gives it a name, the gift of communicating by
handspeak, and an amazing truth it had never
guessed. Now Imrhien begins a journey to distant
Caermelor, to seek a wise woman whose skills may
change the foundling's life.

Along the way, Imrhien must survive a wilderness of
endless danger. And as the challenges grow more
deadly, Imrhien discovers something more terrifying
than all the evil eldritch wights combined: the
shunned outsider with an angel's soul and a
gargoyle's face is falling in love . . .

In a thrilling debut combining storytelling mastery with
a treasure trove of folklore, Cecilia Dart-Thornton
creates a lushly romantic epic adventure.

'Not since Tolkien's *The Fellowship of the Ring* . . . have
I been so impressed by a beautifully spun fantasy'
ANDRE NORTON, author of *Brother to Shadows*